ALL-AMERICAN *Muslim* GIRL

NADINE JOLIE COURTNEY

FARRAR STRAUS GIROUX
New York

Content Notes: Islamophobia, Anxiety, Heterosexism, Discussions of Homophobia, Discussions of Racism, Discussions of Misogyny, Death

Farrar Straus Giroux Books for Young Readers
An imprint of Macmillan Children's Publishing Group, LLC
120 Broadway, New York, NY 10271

Printed in the United States of America
Designed by Cassie Gonzales
First edition, 2019
10 9 8 7 6 5 4 3 2 1

mackids.com

Library of Congress Cataloging-in-Publication Data

Names: Courtney, Nadine Jolie, 1980- author.
Title: All-American Muslim girl / Nadine Jolie Courtney.
Description: First edition. | New York : Farrar, Straus and Giroux, 2019. | Summary: Sixteen-year-old Allie, aged seven when she knew her family was different and feared, struggles to claim her Muslim and Middle Eastern heritage while finding her place as an American teenager.
Identifiers: LCCN 2018056246 | ISBN 9780374309527 (hardcover)
Subjects: | CYAC: Muslims—Fiction. | Arab Americans—Fiction. | Family life—Fiction. | Prejudices—Fiction.
Classification: LCC PZ7.1.C682 All 2019 | DDC [Fic]—dc23
LC record available at https://lccn.loc.gov/2018056246

For those between two worlds,
defying easy classification.
Your story is valid.
You matter.

ALL-AMERICAN Muslim GIRL

We realize the importance of our voices only when we are silenced.

—*Malala Yousafzai*

PART ONE

CHAPTER ONE

We've passed through security and we're boarding the plane when the breaking news alert hits my cell phone: There's been a shooting.

Alerts like this trigger the same thought process, every single time. First: horror for the victims of the crime. But second: anxiety. Was a Muslim involved? *Please, God, don't let there have been a Muslim involved.*

The TV monitors in the boarding area are tuned to a show my father hates: Jack Henderson's nightly *The Jack Attack*, a cable news juggernaut. My heart tightens as images of the shooting flash next to Jack's face. I can't hear what he's saying, but I'm sure it's his usual bombast: immigrants, Muslims, borders, walls.

Next to the TVs, the beige walls are decorated with white lights and Christmas wreaths, a feeble attempt to bring seasonal cheer to the T gates.

Once safely on the plane, I poke my mother; my father is across the aisle from me, with a white man wearing khakis and a blazer in the adjacent window seat.

"Mom. Look," I say.

My mother puts down her iPad and takes the phone from me. "Oh no," she whispers. "That's devastating."

We lock eyes, and I know she's having the same thoughts: *Please not a Muslim. Please not a Muslim.*

Not that facts matter. Chances are good we'll bear the blame one way or another.

She turns on her seat-back TV, switching it to cable news. A red chyron blazes on the bottom of the screen: *Attacker still at large.* I hand the phone across the aisle to my dad. He stares at the screen for several seconds, sadness and frustration etched across his face. Silly Dad, the guy I've been teasing all morning, has disappeared. He's Serious Dad now.

As passengers continue boarding the plane, people around us frown at their phones. I study their faces carefully for the reactions. Dismay. Disbelief. Fear. Anger.

The man sitting next to Dad turns on his TV and lets out a sound of disgust. He glances sidelong at my father. Maybe it's my imagination, but I sense suspicion. My pulse quickens. He switches from cable news to sports.

"I bet it was a Muslim." A male voice behind us. Young.

"You think?" A female voice. Quiet.

"An attack like that? Most definitely. Screw those people."

"God, it's scary. You just never know."

"They're all the same. They shouldn't *be* here."

"Coulda been Syrian. Refugee, probably."

"I work with a Muslim. This chick Rabab. She doesn't pray and do all that crap. We went out for drinks last month."

"Yeah, for sure. There's plenty of good Muslims. I'm not talking about them."

Though their voices are low, muttering, they bore into my skull. I picture my grandmother in Dallas: my *teta* sitting in my aunt Bila's cheerful purple room, watching Amr Diab music videos and reading gossip magazines spilling dirt on *Arab Idol* judges. I wish I could show the passengers behind me what a Syrian Muslim in America looks like. Ask them if *she* is something to fear.

Of course I can't, and even if I could, I'd chicken out. Dad's said it forever: Harsh words equal short-term satisfaction. They always backfire. Best to take the high road.

My dad's phone rings, and he pulls it out of his pocket. "*Kefic, ya Mama? . . . Mabsoot, mabsoot . . . Hamdullah . . . Enha a'al tayaara . . . Inshallah, inshallah,*" he says quietly. "*Ya habibti . . . yalla, ma'asalaama.*" He's going through the motions with *Teta*, a routine ten-second phone call: How are you? I'm good. We made it on the plane safely, thank God. I'll let you know when we've landed, God willing. Love you. Okay, gotta go.

But the man next to him is now glaring at my father. My dad keeps his head down, his gaze neutral.

Things have become so charged, so ugly. He shouldn't have taken the call.

The man stands up abruptly. "Excuse me." He steps over Dad.

I lean forward in my cramped seat, watching him walk up the aisle to the galley. He talks to the flight attendant, who looks our way. He seems agitated, his arms gesticulating.

Her face hardens.

"Dad," I say.

Before I can say more, the flight attendant is standing in front of my father. "Sir. Is there a problem?"

My father looks up at her, blinking several times. "No, ma'am. No problem."

"We've had complaints about you," she says.

"Complaints?" I say. The venom in my voice surprises me. "Or just one, from *that* guy?" I nod toward the man still standing in the galley.

"Allie," my father says, voice low. He shakes his head, almost imperceptibly.

The flight attendant appraises me, her brow knitted. I can't tell if she's irritated or confused. She turns back to my father. "Passengers have expressed concern. They said you were speaking Arabic and they heard the word '*Allah*' repeatedly."

"'*Allah*' is a really common word in Arabic, ma'am," I say. "It's in, like, every other phrase."

"Allie, please," my father says.

Normally I would shut up. I'd be obedient and just listen to my dad, like always.

Today is not that day.

"He was talking to my grandmother, ma'am. She doesn't speak English. We're flying to Dallas for a family reunion. We live here, in Atlanta. Actually, just north of Atlanta—in Providence.

You know Providence, right?" A gentle Southern twang creeps into my voice, even though I've lived in Georgia for barely six months.

She looks back and forth between the two of us.

My dad opens his mouth again. "Ma'am, there must have been a misunderst—"

"I'm his daughter," I say, putting on my best For the Adults voice. Dad doesn't *get* these people like I do. Thank God I dressed nicely and wore makeup for the flight. "I'm a student at Providence High School outside Atlanta. So we've just celebrated Christmas, and now we're spending New Year's Eve with the rest of our family. For a reunion." I repeat, my tone upbeat and friendly. I pull out my phone, Googling my father's name. "See? Here's my dad on the Emory website. He's an American history professor there. He has a PhD from the University of North Texas." I click around on my phone, pulling up another entry. "Oh, so this is an article about my dad in the *LA Times* a few years ago. He wrote a book when he was an assistant professor at UCLA, and it got great reviews. Here's another one, when he was an associate professor at Northwestern." I put my hand gently on my mother's arm. She tucks her blond hair behind an ear, looking concerned. "This is my mom, Elizabeth. She's a psychologist affiliated with Grady Memorial. We're American. We're *all* American."

This is so not me, speaking up, but I *have* to. It's my dad.

Listing my parents' résumés seems to mollify the flight attendant, but Dad's seatmate is still in the galley. His arms are crossed against his chest, his eyes sweeping over my father accusingly. I can practically hear his inner monologue: *The daughter and the wife don't look Muslim. But the dad . . .*

I stand up slowly. No sudden motions.

"Here, Daddy," I say, pulling gently on his arm. "Why don't we switch seats? You can sit next to Mommy." I never call her Mommy.

Wordlessly, he stands up and slides into my seat.

"Please, sir," I call to the man who has accused my father, gesturing palm up toward his empty seat. "After you."

He walks back down the aisle, frowning and avoiding eye contact.

"So sorry for the confusion, sir. My grandma is so silly," I say, smiling as I sit next to him. Smiling is key. It confuses them. Anger . . . indignation . . . that's a luxury we don't have. "I've been trying to get her to learn English for *years*. She should learn! But you know how it is, right? Can't teach an old dog new tricks."

He blinks, looking back at me. His dubious expression softens.

"I'm so sorry you felt uncomfortable." I'm still using the Voice. "Thank you so much for being so understanding, sir. It's very kind of you."

Finally, he nods at the flight attendant. "It's okay."

She scurries away, obviously relieved.

I want to slap him across the face. I want to say: *How dare you judge my father? What gives* you *that right?* Instead, I draw from years of lessons and hold out my hand, smiling. "I'm Allie, by the way."

"Larry," he says, shaking my hand in return. He gestures toward my dad, though still not looking at him. "You're obviously a very well-brought-up young lady. I didn't realize you were together." He clears his throat, seeming embarrassed. "Sorry for the misunderstanding. But you know what they say: If you see something, gotta say something. Never can be too careful."

Now he's smiling, too. I've convinced him we're safe.

Human, like him.

"Good" Muslims.

I spend five minutes forcing myself to chat with him until I'm sure we're out of harm's way. He's an insurance analyst based in Dallas, returning from a business trip. I remind him of his daughter. She's a redhead like me. Twenty-three. Graduated from SMU last year.

I smile, working to look interested and make him feel comfortable.

Once the flight takes off, I politely make excuses and pull out my iPhone, finally feeling safe enough to relax and read a new novel I've downloaded. The guy nods off somewhere over Alabama, and it's only once he's asleep that my father gets up to use the bathroom, kissing me on top of my head before walking into the back.

My mom leans across the aisle. "I'm sorry, honey," she whispers.

"It's okay."

The rest of the flight passes without incident. When we land, the guy takes a phone call as soon as we're on the ground, loudly talking as we deplane. He doesn't make eye contact with my father, disappearing into the crowd at DFW.

Look, I did what I had to. If you break open your moral piggy bank and spend a little, you'll buy a lot of goodwill in return.

I've paid frequently over the years—turning the other cheek, smiling at offenders, pretending I don't mind, laughing.

Do you feel comfortable? How can I help? Here, that ignorance must be superheavy—let me carry that burden for you.

Thing is, my emotional piggy bank is running out of change. Soon, I might not have anything left.

In Aunt Bila's sedan, as my family gossips about the usual drama, my parents don't mention a thing. I sit in the back next to my mom, staring out the window.

What would have happened to my dad if I hadn't been there?

Would it have escalated? Would the police have been called? Would they have kicked him off the plane?

Or worse: Could he have been arrested? Just for being Muslim?

Nobody's getting arrested just for *being* Muslim.

I don't think.

Maybe I'm being way too dramatic. Dad's always told me to keep the Muslim thing on the DL, because people get *weird* when they hear the M-word. It's a safety issue.

Honestly? It's a convenience issue, too.

Sometimes it's better if people don't know.

For me, hiding is easy: reddish-blond hair, pale skin, hazel eyes. It doesn't matter that I look textbook Circassian, like a lot of light-skinned Muslims from the Caucasus region. (Hey, they don't call it Caucasian for nothing.) I don't trigger people's radar. People have an image in their head when they hear the word *Muslim*, and I just don't fit.

But Dad doesn't have that luxury. When people meet him, they take one look and decide he's clearly From Somewhere Else—no matter how much he tries to blend in and deflects by saying "From Texas" when people ask that annoying "Where are you from?" question. Assimilate, try to shed the accent, it doesn't matter. Once people mark him as different, they treat him that way, too.

I try to drown it but the million-dollar question bubbles up once again—the one that haunts the edges of my brain every time there's an incident, every time people float casual bigotry, every time I move to a new school.

Will people still like me if I show them the real me? Maybe I'm betraying my fellow Muslims by stuffing half of my identity away. Maybe I'm just a cowardly traitor dripping in white privilege.

We barrel down President George Bush Turnpike, the exits a blur of strip malls and steakhouses, the horizon visible for miles. It reminds me of childhood, a fuzzy collection of afternoons spent daydreaming in the back seats of cars. Everything is bigger in Texas.

My family was still living in Richardson when I started to realize my dad wasn't treated like my friends' dads. The incidents were piling up—little comments, little looks.

We were at Albertson's, the bag boy playing *Tetris* with my dad's groceries as the cashier looked at my dad's ID suspiciously. "Muhammad Abraham?" the guy said. He turned the ID over a few times, as if a new name and country of origin would suddenly materialize.

"That's me," my dad said, wallet in hand. "But I've gone by Mo since I was eighteen." Not coincidentally, that's the year Dad moved to the US, to study history at Columbia. My *teta* loathed the new nickname and refused to use it, considering any shortening of the beloved Prophet's name unforgivable blasphemy.

"Uh-huh," the cashier said, looking unconvinced.

"Is there an issue, sir?" my father asked politely. I looked back and forth between the two of them, not sure what was going on but knowing it wasn't good. He was just trying to buy groceries. With Dad finishing his PhD, Mom was the breadwinner—household responsibilities were his domain.

The cashier peered at the driver's license again before staring at the contents of the grocery bag. "Sure you're allowed to drink with a name like that?"

"I won't tell my parents if you don't," Dad said.

The cashier laughed, disarmed, handing the ID back to my dad as he ran the credit card. "I get it. You're not one of *those* Muslims." He gestured to me. "This your daughter?"

At seven, I still had strawberry-blond hair, not yet deepened into dishwater brown, begging to be dyed. My eyes were less hazel, more green, and my face was covered in freckles. If you saw photos of my dad when he was a kid or were familiar with Circassians, you'd know I strongly resembled him—but to a stranger, I couldn't have looked less like him if I'd been adopted from Sweden.

My dad was as patient as ever. "She is."

"Okay, Mo. Enjoy. Good luck to you both," the cashier said, pushing our groceries toward us and turning to the next customer.

"What did he mean, Daddy?" I asked. "By 'those Muslims'?"

My father waited until we exited the store. He held the door open for a series of shoppers, going out of his way to smile and be polite and nonthreatening,

"He was being silly," Dad said, opening the car door for me.

"He seemed mean, not silly. Does he think Muslims are bad?"

"I don't think he was mean," Dad said, with that familiar look reassuring me that everything would be all right. He checked to make sure my belt was secured in the booster seat. "I think he was scared."

"Why?"

"People are scared of what they don't understand. Right now, a lot of people don't understand Muslims, and fear brings out the worst in them. It doesn't make them bad. It just makes them . . . confused. Do you understand?"

"I think so," I said.

He got in the front seat, turning around. "Sometimes it's best not to tell people you're Muslim, though. It's . . . safer if people don't know."

"Oh."

And now, nine years later, I'm still trying to work it all out.

After all, no matter how much their words sting, no matter

how much their actions wound, nobody sees themselves as the bad guy.

So here we are. I've spent the past several years trying on masks—taking my dad's lessons about hiding to heart, amplifying the American part of me, being whatever people need me to be. Learning how to pass as the perfect surfer girl in California, as a Tory Burch– and Vineyard Vines–wearing prep in New Jersey, as a laid-back athleisure kid in Chicago. Now that we live in the South, the land of pearls and sorority legacies and Instagram makeup, I went for a classy Old Hollywood vibe. My 1950s thrift-store dresses have become my *thing* in Providence, Georgia, these past several months, as much as my self-deprecating snark and my love of movie musicals. My friend Wells commented recently on an old Instagram photo of me wearing an oversized sweatshirt, my hair scraped up in a topknot—"Whoa! You look so different!"—and I was both embarrassed and thrilled. He'd had to scroll *way* back to find that picture. You'd never know it was me.

New town. New school. New look. New life.

"You okay, Alia?" Aunt Bila glances in the rearview mirror as she exits onto Jupiter Road. "You're quiet, *ya rouhi*." Mom puts her hand on mine. She's been quiet during the ride, too.

"I'm fine, *Amto*!" I stuff my voice with cheer. "Excited to get to your house and see everybody!" Aunt Bila doesn't know what happened. And ultimately, it was nothing. Less than nothing.

Just like all the other times.

CHAPTER TWO

On New Year's Eve, Aunt Bila's large ranch-style house in Richardson is family HQ, as always. Strains of Nancy Ajram music and laughter fill the rooms, packed with a raft of extended family still jet-lagged from Saudi, Jordan, London, and New Jersey, here in Dallas to celebrate New Year's Eve together. Everybody is a cousin, or a friend of a cousin, or the cousin of a friend—and they all go back decades, most to the old days in Jordan.

In the living room, my head ping-pongs back and forth as I work to decipher the Arabic conversation between my favorite cousin Houri, her older sister Fairouza, and three elderly Jordanian women who are related to me. (I think. Like, 75 percent sure.) Events like these are equal parts exhilarating and exhausting—I love seeing my billions of cousins, but it's overwhelming going from our quiet, boring routine of spaghetti, Scrabble, and Netflix to Aunt Bila's lively universe, where everything is sparkly purple, the Arabic music is blasting at volume nine thousand, and I'm constantly playing a game of Telephone to understand my own family members.

Houri catches my confused look. She gets it, as usual. "Speak English so Allie can understand."

One of the women asks a question in Arabic and Houri shakes her head no, responding, "*Laa.*"

"You are a member of the family?" one of the women asks me kindly in heavily accented English.

I nod. "I'm Mo's daughter—um, Muhammad's daughter. Alia. Allie."

Her eyebrows zoom toward the ceiling. "*You're* Muhammad's daughter? Why don't you speak Arabic?"

I look into the next room, where my dad is sitting in the formal living room drinking a cup of tea, surrounded by my uncles, his younger brothers. Uncle Sammy cracks a joke and everybody laughs, looking at Dad. He stiffens, smiling politely. Ever since my grandfather *Jido* died, my dad might technically be head of the family, but there's always something invisible, indefinable setting him apart.

I know a little something about that. Every family reunion, we take a group photo of all the cousins. It's a sea of dark brunettes, chattering and laughing in English and Arabic—and then me, on the fringes. One of these things is not like the others.

"He never taught me," I say quietly.

The woman makes a disapproving noise—whether for him or for me, I'm not sure. "But you pray, right?"

Houri stands up before I can disappoint further, pulling on

my elbow. "C'mon. Let's get some tea." She drags me away from the living room and down the hallway. I feel the women's curious eyes on my back. "I don't really want tea," she says in a low voice. "But I *can't* with the judgment. Besides, I don't pray, either."

"Hi," I say, adopting a jokey tone to hide confusing pangs of emptiness. "Welcome to my world."

The thing is, I'm not religious—I barely know what being religious *means*. Growing up in America, I probably know more about Jesus than the Prophet Muhammad (peace onto him . . . peace be upon him?). I know you're supposed to say *something* after his name out of respect, I just don't know what.

And after so many moves, so much change, so little stability, it's started to feel like something's . . . missing.

"Remember when I took those cheesy Arabic lessons? That book was the worst."

Houri's got two laughs: the polite one and the belly one. She busts out the belly one. "Right! Seriously, who still teaches Modern Standard Arabic? It's like Shakespearean English. Besides, your accent was all wrong."

"Points for trying, though, right?" I ask hopefully.

"Sure. But who cares?" Houri waves a hand dismissively. "Your dad's right—you don't need Arabic. You're fine."

Easy for Houri to say: Like all thirty-seven of my first cousins, she grew up speaking it fluently, zipping between English and Arabic with zero effort.

At least I know a little: You can't grow up in a family like mine without soaking up something through osmosis.

Inshallah is probably the most important word. It means

"God willing," and you'll hear it constantly. You say it before something happens, or if you want something to happen—like, "*Inshallah*, Allie will get into a good university."

Hamdulilah means "thanks to God." It's one of those anytime phrases: partially sincere but also filler. You say it after something happens, if you're grateful for something happening, or if you don't know what else to say. My family swallows the word—it sounds like *ham-du-lah*—and I always wonder: Is that a Circassian thing? A Jordanian thing? A people-from-Amman thing? Or is it just my family being lazy?

The mystery persists.

There's *mashallah*, which I guess means "God willed it," but is really like a talisman against the evil eye. It's an absolute *must* when complimenting somebody, unless you are a horrible person who wishes to curse their family. If you're saying how beautiful a baby or bride is, you'd better be *mashallah*-ing all over the place.

Wallahi means "I swear to God." Used a *lot*.

And then there's the word you'll hear every eight seconds in a house with kids: *yalla*, which means "hurry up," not to be confused with *ya Allah*, meaning "oh God." Like, "*Ya Allah*, my son is dating an actress!"

Dad has always promised to teach me more. Mom wants to learn, too. We've tried over the years, listening to phone conversations and asking what this or that means.

The lessons never materialized. I took things into my own hands the summer before seventh grade, buying books and downloading lessons and practicing on my cousins. But my accent sounded Egyptian, they would say, giggling, instead of Jordanian like theirs.

Within a few weeks, I'd stopped trying.

If I'm being honest with myself? My dad probably never wanted to teach me Arabic. He married the most American woman in all of America. (Okay, they're soul mates, too, but details: She's a tall blond psychologist who was class president of a private high school in Key Biscayne and grew up taking ski vacations in Gstaad, Switzerland, for God's sake.) He never calls me Alia, only Allie. He's never taken me to a mosque—the few times I've been were with my *teta* when I was little, her patiently washing my feet and slowly enunciating the prayers. He goes by Professor Abraham or (*haram!*) Mo, rather than Muhammad, and we don't have a Qur'an in the house.

Aunt Bila's house is covered in beautiful, elaborately calligraphed Islamic texts; Rashid's even talked Houri into putting a few up.

Ours has none. No reminders of Dad's heritage. No reminders of his religion.

For somebody who's devoted his life to history, he seems pretty eager to forget his own.

We find an empty sitting room and collapse on a purple overstuffed couch underneath a gold mirrored decoration of the *Ka'baa* in Mecca, pulling a blanket over the two of us like we've done since we were kids. Aunt Bila's lived in this house for decades and we didn't leave Dallas until I was nine, so gossip sessions with Houri on this couch have been a rare constant in my life.

In the center of the fireplace, an extravagant, gold-framed photo of my beloved grandfather *Jido* in military uniform sits in the place of honor, surrounded by oversized candles. The walls are covered in sumptuous, brightly colored orange, purple, and gold tapestries that I'm pretty sure Aunt Bila picked up in Amman for a shocking amount of money, with shiny purple curtains threaded with gold draped over the windows. Mirrors cover every inch of available surface. It's a bit over the top—okay, it looks like the sitting room of a narcissistic genie—but I love it.

"We haven't had a moment alone, just us. I've missed you, Aloosh," she says, pulling out an ancient nickname.

"Aloosh. Wow. I haven't heard that one in a trillion years." My phone buzzes and I pull it out of my pocket, hoping it might be Wells.

Nope.

"How's mom life?"

"The best. The worst. Incredible. Exhausting."

"Where's Lulu?"

"Rashid's on it. *Baba* thinks splitting baby duty is weird. He barely lifted a finger until I was in middle school."

I love Houri and Rashid's equal partnership. Just like my own parents.

My phone buzzes again.

"Got someplace you'd rather be? Am I boring you?"

"Sorry." I laugh. "It's just Snapchat." I swipe through my phone, turning it to show her a photo of Emilia and Sarah blowing noisemakers. "All my 'friends' are at this party."

"Why the tone?"

“What tone?”

“You said ‘friends’ in air quotes.”

“I don’t know.” Emilia and Sarah. They’re as interchangeable as Madison, Hannah, and Ashley were in Wayne, or Chloe and Jess in El Segundo, or Rachel and Olivia in Evanston. “We don’t talk.”

“You use sign language? Morse code?”

“I mean we don’t *talk* talk. Not about stuff that matters.”

The upside of moving every couple years? I’m a chameleon and have learned from necessity how to slot into a new social scene easily. I joined the JV cheerleading squad at Providence this year: an easy-though-temporary path to an instant group. The downside? I’ve spent half my life being friendly with everybody, and friends with nobody. Worse: I can’t remember the last time I said what I truly think at school. And I haven’t had a *real* best friend since Sophia Weinstein in third and fourth grade, before Dad finished his PhD and we hopped on the academia hamster wheel.

But now Dad finally has a tenure-track job, so we’re in Providence to stay. We’re putting down roots, they say. We’ve bought our first house, so we *can’t* move.

We’ll see.

“Any guys?” Houri asks.

I pause. She picks up on it.

“There *is* a guy! Not surprised—you’re a hottie with that red hair. It’s better than the boring brown.”

“Gee, thanks.” Despite myself, I blush.

“This boy.” She rubs her hands together, grinning. “Tell me all the things.”

"Shh. They'll hear you."

She nods knowingly. "Sneaking around?"

"There's nothing to tell. He's just a friend."

"Friends to lovers."

I snort. "We don't call it 'lovers,' Grandma." Even though Houri is five years older and already a mom—I can't—she's the closest thing I have to a sister.

"Didn't your parents always say you could date once you hit sixteen?" She tugs at her brown curls, pulling them into a loose bun on top of her head. Uncle Ramy, her dad, is Egyptian, so Houri looks more like that side of the family than the pale Circassian Ibrahimis.

"Supposedly," I say, "but it's not an issue—because *I'm not dating.*"

"Dads and dating. The worst combo ever."

Houri had to sneak around with her early high school boyfriends. It wasn't until she started dating Rashid that she decided to test the waters with her dad.

None of the cousins had ever had a Black boyfriend, and Uncle Ramy was clearly prejudiced despite all his protesting—but Rashid was Muslim, which was ultimately what mattered to my uncle. He was one of us. Unlike cousin Amal's longtime boyfriend, Bret, who was captain of the golf team and talked a lot about wakeboarding on Lake Texoma.

Rashid magnanimously forgave my uncle, although I'm not sure he ever forgot. How could you?

"Is he hot?" Houri asks. "Tall, dark, and handsome?"

"He's *really* tall, he has the cutest curly dark hair, and he's beyond gorgeous," I say, pulling up Wells's photo on my phone. "See?"

She laughs. "You *do* have it bad."

My phone pings.

Stop the presses: Wells has texted.

"Oh my God," I say. "He texted."

"What's it say?"

"It says 'Happy New Year!'"

She leans over, grabbing my phone. "What are you going to write?"

"Um . . . 'Happy New Year'?"

She laughs. "No game at all."

"Houri, stop. He's just a friend."

"So you said."

I look down at my phone. "Should I add an emoji? I'm not sure if he's an emoji guy. He might think it's uncool."

She leans back on the couch, putting an arm behind her head and smiling. "Why do you care? You know: if he's just a friend."

I blush. "Maybe one emoji," I say, adding a party hat before pressing SEND.

Shakespeare's got nothing on you, Allie.

"What are you doing in here, girls?" Aunt Bila asks, entering the room carrying a tray of sticky dessert covered in crushed pistachios. "Houriya, Alia, *yalla*. I made *kanafeh*. *Ta'alou*."

"Coming, *Amto*," I say, standing up and following her into the formal living room, where my parents have each ensconced themselves in one of the scores of chairs Aunt Bila has procured, my grandmother holding court in the center. Aunt Bila's house has an open-door policy, and most of her six kids are always popping in to say hi, ask for advice, borrow things, eat dinner, or drop off their babies while they go to the store. Today is no exception, but instead of six guests, there are probably sixty.

Some of the women are dressed casually, like Houri's oldest sister, Amal, who favors flouncy dresses, tank tops, and everything Who What Wear recommends. Others, like Houri's other sister, Fairouza, are wearing silk or cotton headscarves. Aunt Bila and Uncle Ramy aren't thrilled by Fairouza wearing a hijab, but they long ago learned to pick their battles. My family runs the gamut: religious, liberal, devout, devoid, and everything in between.

Aunt Bila places the *kanafeh* on the table, next to a stack of china plates. "*Yalla*, please. *Sahtain*," she says to the family and friends spread out around the room. She serves a plate to my grandmother before leaving the room. Houri sits next to Rashid and pulls their toddler Lulu onto her lap, covering her sticky face with kisses. Lulu giggles before reaching out to play with her father's long, meticulously groomed beard.

"Alia," *Teta* says. "*Ta'ali hone*." My grandmother puts down her dessert and pats her lap. I do what's expected of me, walking across the room and sitting on her lap. She pulls me down to her chest, smothering me against her bosom as she dots my head with kisses. Kids run in and out of the room, screaming, while Aunt Bila deftly navigates around them with a tea tray, pouring steaming cups. In the adjacent den, several of my cousins pray together.

"Um, *kefic*?" I say, asking how she is.

"*Mabsoota, ya omri, ya Alia. Wa enti*?" I'm happy, my life, Alia. How are you?

"*Mabsoota, ya Teta.*" I'm happy, too, Grandma.

"I kiss you, my eye," she says in her thick accent, pulling out a lost-in-translation phrase I'm 75 percent sure is an expression of deep love. Her English is about as good as my Arabic.

"*Ya habibti, Teta.*" You're my beloved, Grandma.

We stare at each other awkwardly, our conversational limits reached. I pat her on the shoulder and lean down to give her a kiss on the head before scooting off her lap and grabbing a plate of *kanafeh*.

As the clock ticks down to midnight, my father commandeers the remote and switches it from an Arabic satellite music channel to a replay of the ball drop in Times Square, bringing to an abrupt stop Assala Nasri warbling "Ad El Horouf" to the haunting strains of oud and violin.

"We were listening!" my cousin Salma says, protesting more to her sisters dancing around her in a circle than to my dad. Although my dad is off in his own world, he's still the eldest son and, since *Jido* died, the de facto head of the family. The few times a year he's back in Dallas, whatever he says goes.

Muna, Salma's beautiful older sister, pulls up an Arabic playlist and blares it on her cell phone's tinny speakers, and the girls relocate to the kitchen to resume their hypnotic forearm swaying and finger snapping.

Near midnight, Wells responds to my text.

Hang when you get back?

I stare at my phone.

What do I say?

Should I be noncommittal? Breezy? I could do sarcastic and poke fun at him.

Maybe sarcastic is a cop-out. Maybe it's better to be earnest.

Oh God. What do I say?

You're overthinking this, Allie.

After typing out and erasing several responses, I reply with one bulletproof word:

Cool

I stuff the phone back into my pocket, feeling like I have the world's most wonderful secret as my gigantic family crowds into the living room to watch the ball drop, popping Martinelli's sparkling cider and blowing on noisemakers.

He only said he wants to hang. That's it. We've hung out before. Actually, we've been hanging out a lot recently.

It's not a declaration of like. It's not a declaration of anything other than *Your company isn't horrible, and I want more of it, please.*

But as the clock strikes midnight, I can't contain my jubilation, hugging my family members extra hard and giggling with my cousins as we launch into a rendition of "Auld Lang Syne."

New year. New life.

CHAPTER THREE

Sunday. Back in Providence. Exhausted.

One of these nights, I'm going to sleep longer than five hours.

"Allie? Breakfast!" my mom calls.

I shower quickly, trying to wash my anxiety down the drain. I woke at three in the morning, yanking myself out of a nightmare. Faceless police officers were dragging Dad away in handcuffs, Mom and me running down the plane aisle screaming, failing to save him as strangers held us back.

"You're one of us now. Isn't that what you wanted?" a Southern voice was cooing in my ear as hands gripped my arms.

Yeah, that wasn't creepy or anything. It took me a while to fall back asleep.

After blow-drying my red curls sleek and using an iron to

create fat waves, I give my hair several aggressive spritzes of finishing spray. I use a hand mirror to painstakingly examine my hair from the back, fluffing and spritzing it again and again until it's perfect.

In the kitchen, Mom and Dad are at the table, Mom reading news on her iPad and mainlining coffee. Dad is, as always, plowing through work.

"An outfit on a Sunday?" Mom asks, looking at my pleated skirt and pussy-bow blouse. She says the word *outfit* like the name of a distant cousin or a weird uncle. She still finds it amusing that I ditched my leggings and messy buns in favor of tailored dresses and sleek waves once we moved to Providence. "I thought those were for school."

A buffet-style spread of Middle Eastern foods spans the table: homemade hummus; tabouleh; *foul mudammas*, a fava-bean dish; chopped tomatoes drizzled with olive oil and artfully arranged on a plate with parsley leaves; a selection of cheeses; pita bread; black olives; and Arab sweets. My dad goes ten miles out of his way to an Arabic grocery store in Midtown Atlanta once a week on the way home from Emory. The weekend is the only time we eat Middle Eastern food. Otherwise, it's easy-to-prep meals: spaghetti, burgers, grilled chicken. Boring.

"I have plans. Remember, I asked for a ride . . . ?" My eyes dart to my father, who is drinking probably his fifth cup of coffee for the day, though it's only eleven.

My mouth waters at the sight of the *foul*, but *no way* am I going over to Wells's house for the first time reeking of garlic.

My phone buzzes. A text from Wells with his address.

I still can't believe I'm going to his house.

I met Wells in Algebra II class on the first day of sophomore year. He walked in, sat down next to me, and smiled. First impression: kind eyes, easy smile, messy curls, mouth slightly too big—like Harry Styles. I immediately wondered what it would be like to kiss his lips.

He spoke first.

"Hey, I'm Wells."

"I'm Allie."

"You're in chorus, right? Second period?"

I nodded.

"Thought I recognized you. Are you new?"

"Yeah. Today's my first day."

"Technically, today's everybody's first day," he said, smiling to let me know he was teasing.

I smiled back. "I just meant I'm new here."

"Happy first day, Allie. Where are you from?"

I paused. An opportunity. Clean slate. I could be whoever I wanted here. Not shy and dorky. Cool and confident. The kind of girl worth paying attention to. I took a deep breath and then tossed my head a little, the way the girls who never doubted themselves did it.

"Heaven."

His laughter burst out of him like rocket fuel. "The new kid is a comedian, folks."

Bantering was *so* not me. Talking to most boys usually made me tongue-tied. But Wells's gentle eyes and encouraging smile made me feel bold.

It was a good feeling.

"I've moved a lot," I said, still smiling. "Chicago via New Jersey via LA via Dallas . . ."

"Whoa. Military?"

"My dad's a professor. Forever in search of the perfect job that doesn't exist. Yay, academia."

"My dad's family's from New York," he said. "Never been to New Jersey, though."

I didn't know how to respond. Students started filing into the classroom.

"Wanna hear something?" he said after a pause.

"What?"

"Today's my birthday."

"Your birthday is the first day of school? That *really* sucks."

He shrugged. "August birthday, price you pay."

"And I thought I had it bad with a February birthday."

"Why? Valentine's Day?"

"Basically."

"C'mon, what are you complaining about? You get valentines and birthday presents. Double trouble."

I wanted to reach over and poke him gently. I was looking for an excuse to touch him. But there was none. Instead, I said, "Hey, so I have a present for you."

"How? You didn't even know me five seconds ago. Quick, what's my name?"

"Walter? Warren? Wallace?" OMG, I was still bantering.

"I look like your grandfather?"

"It's Wells," I said.

"Good memory, Artemis."

I made a big show of rolling my eyes, but secretly I was d-y-i-n-g.

"Okay, birthday boy," I said. "Meet me after school by the picnic benches near the log cabin. That's where you shall receive your reward."

Look at me, being all breezy.

He squinted at me. "Sounds like the prelude to a horror movie. Should I holler, 'Be right back!' before I walk outside?"

"Only if you say it immediately after losing your virginity," I said, trying to act cool by referencing the famous movie cliché but instead promptly blushing.

Some people blush nicely, all cute and delicate and dainty. Not me. My blushes are splotchy and mottled and impossible to ignore. My face and neck are always looking for new and interesting ways to betray my perennial embarrassment.

He laughed.

"I still can't believe I'm at a school with a log cabin," I said.

"Welcome to Georgia. We fancy."

Mrs. Martinez entered the room as the bell rang. She launched into the Algebra II syllabus, but I spent all class sneaking glances at Wells and noticing the way his Chuck Taylors tapped against the desk to an invisible rhythm. I felt giddy, like I had a new secret.

After school, I grabbed stuff from my locker and walked to the log cabin, excited to see Wells again. Anxiety and curiosity jockeyed for dominance, which sums up my life pretty well:

The Allie Abraham Story: Anxious but Curious

Wherever paperbacks are sold.

He was waiting for me.

"Hey!" He stuffed his cell phone in his pocket.

"It really is your birthday, right?" I asked, suddenly consumed by doubt. Maybe this was a bad idea. What was I thinking? I couldn't pull this off.

"Yeah. Wanna see my permit? Once I take driver's ed, it'll be a license."

I reached into my backpack, pulling out a cupcake from a brown bag. "Happy birthday," I said, offering it to him with a little smile.

He looked at me doubtfully. "Got a cupcake vending machine in your locker?"

"My mom stress-bakes. She put it in my bag this morning."

"You're giving me your leftovers and calling it a present. Smooth." He smiled at me to show he was kidding.

"Okay, well, if you don't want it . . ." I pulled the cupcake back, and he put his hand on my wrist. It was soft. My heart leaped at the feeling of his skin on mine.

"I didn't say that," he said, and grinned.

I held the cupcake out again, and he stepped closer, looking down at me. Our eyes met—we didn't just look at each other, but for a second it was like we were looking *into* each other—and I nearly passed out. Instead, I said, "Imaginary candle."

"Imaginary wish," he replied, leaning over and blowing out in a short puff as my heart beat a staccato *ohmigod ohmigod ohmigod.*

And that was that. New friends.

Maybe more.

"What's that smile?" Mom now asks.

"Nothing," I say, jamming my phone into my bag.

"Is it time for the sex talk again?"

My face burns red. I glance at Dad. "Mom. C'mon."

Dad frowns, pausing from grading papers. "Be careful."

"Would you say that to our son?" Mom asks him.

"We have a son?"

"If we had a son."

"If we had a son, I would be exhausted. I would be forty years old, raising a baby. Is there something you're trying to tell me? Can my boys swim again?"

"There's no son," my mom says. "It's a metaphor. And plenty of forty-year-olds have babies."

"Okay . . ." Dad smiles impishly at me. "This fictional son—I hope he likes the LA Galaxy, by the way—yes, I would also tell him to be careful."

"Mm-hmm," Mom says. "Sure you wouldn't take him out back for cigars?"

"I abhor cigars. Smoking is terrible for you. I would never."

"Do I need to separate you two?" I tease.

Mom laughs, nodding meaningfully toward the phone in my hand. "Can't wait to hear more."

I blush.

No surprise, Dad's a little weird about guys. On the other hand, Mom has always been supportive of my secret crushes—even when they were on unworthy-but-cute boys. (RIP the Dusty Diggerson obsession of seventh grade.)

But here's the thing with Wells: He's cute, but his personality makes him even cuter.

That's the kind of thing my mom used to say when she'd catch me swooning over a hot guy and would take my half-baked attraction as an opportunity to launch into yet another one of her patented I Know You're Eventually Going to Have Sex, So Please Be Safe talks. (Way more awkward than the Drugs Ruin Lives, So Please Don't Do Them, Except for Maybe Occasionally Cannabis, but Just as a Casual Experiment and Never While Driving in a Car, Okay? talks.)

Mom: "It's what's on the inside that counts."

Me: "That sounds like something you'd get from a fortune cookie."

Mom: "When you're older—"

Me: "Mom. You are not seriously playing the 'When you're older, you'll understand' card."

Mom: "When you are older, *you'll understand that good looks are nice, but attraction can fade. It's important to find somebody quality. Somebody who shares your values."*

Me: "I value extremely ridiculously good-looking boys."

Mom: "Hilarious. I give it a five out of ten. Your routine needs work."

Me: "I especially value—"

Mom: "No, no. We're done here."

I would always joke with my mom about the It's What's on the Inside thing. Then I met Wells. Now, I get it.

He has a great sense of humor—teasing and generous. Last month's newly learned fact: He volunteers at the animal shelter near his house. He's incredible at soccer, and used to do Quiz Bowl, just like me, and can match me point for point on everything from the best Star Wars episode (he votes *The Empire Strikes Back,* but *The Force Awakens* is way better) to the greatest band of all time (Wells says it's a tie between Pearl Jam and Foo Fighters, but I've been in love with the Beatles since I was a kid, because my dad used to sing me to sleep with their songs).

Even better, he's not arrogant. He must know how girls look at him—but he also has that obliviousness you see when people didn't grow into their looks as fast as everybody else. He's humble and he's kind and he likes cats, and I just died because he's perfect.

And he actually . . . maybe . . . likes me back.

"So, what's his name?" Mom asks.

Busted.

Dad looks up from his stack. He refuses to switch to an iPad, insisting on grading papers by hand. "Whose name?"

"Wells," I mumble.

"Wells?" Dad says, his brow furrowing as he looks between us.

"He's a boy, honey," Mom says.

Dad's frown deepens. "A *boy*?" he repeats, his entire being one giant italicized expression of incredulity.

Fear grips my stomach. Has my dad been pretending to be cool this entire time? Is now when Scary Dad unmasks himself and reveals he's actually *not* cool with me dating?

"A friend," I say, clarifying.

Who I want to make out with.

Dad doesn't say anything.

"We're going to study," I say.

Mom cocks her head. "Oh? You don't have any homework yet."

"For Quiz Bowl."

The corners of my mother's mouth turn up. "Looks like a perfect Quiz Bowl studying outfit. Besides, I thought you were dropping Quiz Bowl this semester so you could focus on your course load."

I shoot her a look.

"Odd given name," Dad says. "Wells. Maybe it's a family surname. British, no doubt. Or perhaps Irish." His dark eyes narrow as he ponders.

The joke of it is, people are constantly trying to guess my father's background—dark hair and bushy eyebrows contrasting with paler-than-you'd-expect skin and an accent he's never managed to shake. Northern Italian? Serbian? Croatian? Nobody ever guesses Circassian via Jordan—nobody's even *heard* of Circassians.

I'm relieved he's focusing on the name of the guy rather than the fact that there's a guy, period.

After all, though my dad is progressive compared to a lot of Muslim dads, most Muslims don't really date.

Then again, I'm barely Muslim.

"He's the same guy you hung out with before Christmas, right?" Mom's face is serious, but her eyes are laughing. She takes way more pleasure out of embarrassing me than is appropriate for a parent.

"Yeah. I can go later, if you want," I say, praying she won't take me up on it.

"Go! I'll drive you." Mom pushes back from the table, taking one last sip of coffee. "I'm going to have a rage aneurysm if I keep reading the news."

"It might be a diminutive for Wellington," Dad says, stuck on the name. "In which case, still British."

"You sure it's okay?" I ask hopefully. "I feel bad missing breakfast." We haven't spoken about it, but what happened on the airplane has felt like the elephant in the room ever since.

It's not like Dad hasn't been discriminated against before. But with the way things are going nowadays . . . it feels different.

It's hard to explain.

"My sweet girl." Dad raises his cup of coffee in my direction. "Have fun studying, pumpkin."

"Studying. Riiiight," my mom teases, grabbing the car keys from the bowl and walking toward the door.

I shoot her a look—*OMG, will you stop?!*—before giving Dad a kiss on the cheek.

"Love you both—even when you're the worst."

"This can't be right."

I double-check the address Wells texted me. His house is fifteen minutes away from mine, on the other side of the border between Providence and Milton.

It's a three-story brick Colonial with a cross-gabled roof, white columns, and a sloping green lawn wide enough to land a fleet of jumbo jets. In the distance, I see stables.

You have got to be kidding me.

This isn't a house. It's a freaking mansion. Mom looks impressed. "You didn't tell me the new boy's a Rockefeller."

"I would have," I say, "if I'd known."

I fire off a couple of texts.

ME: I'm outside.

ME: Also, um, your place is bigger than the White House.

WELLS: Coming out now

WELLS: PS Don't judge

"Park behind that, I guess," I tell Mom, pointing to a black Mercedes G-Wagen in the circular driveway.

A minute later, Wells comes out from the side of the house. When I see him, I feel like I'm free-falling.

Every single time.

He smiles as I get out of the car, gently closing the door. "Hi," he says. His voice is low and scratchy.

"Hi back."

I turn toward Mom, waving her off. Instead, she rolls down the window, grinning at Wells. "Hi! You must be Wells. I'm Allie's mom."

Wells walks over to the window and reaches through, offering Mom his hand to shake. "It's nice to meet you, Mrs. Abraham. I've heard a lot about you."

"Likewise." Mom is still grinning, and now fully checking him out.

Seriously, this is mortifying.

I look him up and down, seeing him through her eyes. Messy

brown curls. Straight-cut dark-denim jeans. Chuck Taylors. One hand jammed into the pocket of the same faded navy zip hoodie he always wears. It's unzipped, with a white T-shirt underneath. It says THIS IS WHAT A FEMINIST LOOKS LIKE.

"Have fun, you two!" Mom says. "Call me to pick you up, Al. Give me half an hour heads-up, okay? Love you!"

With a wave out the window, she's finally gone. "I like your dress," Wells says to me shyly. It's a skirt, but I don't bother correcting him.

"Thanks," I say, trying and failing to hide my dorky smile.

Wells and I take a step closer to each other and hug awkwardly. He smells fresh, like soap and cinnamon gum.

As we break apart, he lightly taps me on the hand. "Joey and Zadie'll be here any minute. Mikey and Sarah are running late, and Emilia's at a horse show. My mom ordered pizza. Hope you like pepperoni."

I don't eat pepperoni. My lapsed dad might drink alcohol, but pork? That's a deal breaker. I don't want to seem high-maintenance, though—and I definitely don't want to get into it. "Sounds great!" I say.

I'll pick it off when he's not looking.

I follow him into the house. We walk through a large vestibule filled with muddy boots, dog food, and umbrellas, into a windowless back hallway covered in pastoral horse drawings and inspirational plaques. I read one: FAITH IS BEING SURE OF WHAT WE HOPE FOR AND CERTAIN OF WHAT WE DO NOT SEE. He leads me down a set of stairs to a finished basement.

"And this is where the magic happens," he says, raising his hands to the ceiling, palms up, as if a shepherd welcoming his flock.

I giggle. "Magic? Is that what you call it?"

His face goes pink.

Mine does, too. Couldn't pull it off.

I reach into my bag, clearing my throat. "Hey, I brought you something." I hold out the latest Black Series Star Wars figurine.

"Whoa! Where you'd get this?"

"I went to a couple stores." Five over the holidays, to be exact, spending my entire allowance for the week. "You like it?"

"It's awesome." He grins, looking back and forth between me and the limited-edition collectible. "*You're* awesome for remembering."

"It's not a big deal." I wander around the massive basement room so he can't see my blushing cheeks. There's a big-screen TV opposite an L-shaped leather couch, with an old-school *Ms. Pac Man* arcade machine in the far corner. The TV console shelves display soccer trophies, a lone Quiz Bowl trophy, and Manchester United gear: framed and signed pictures, a Man U flag, bobbleheads. Framed concert posters cover the walls, mostly bands I've never heard of.

"Metallica? Are we in 1990?"

"Yeah. What? They're rad," he says, sitting down at the massive drum kit in the corner. He picks up a drumstick and twirls it between his fingers. I debate making fun of him—he's clearly trying to impress me—and yet I *am* impressed, so the joke's on me.

"*Rad*? Okay, now I know you're trolling me. You don't seem like a heavy-metal fan." He's such a cheerful teddy bear.

He laughs. "Mental note not to expose you to my full music collection. I'll stick to socially acceptable stuff that won't freak you out."

"I might surprise you."

"What's your thing? Music, I mean."

"I like everything."

"Heard that before. You mean everything *but* country and rap, right?" he says, looking doubtful. "And opera, and musical theater, and classical, and blues . . ."

"No, really. Everything." I shrug. "Good music's about storytelling. If you're open to someone else's story, you can appreciate anything."

He stares at me. The searching look makes me feel exposed, as if I'm under a microscope.

I break away from the heat of his gaze, making a beeline for the bookshelf on the opposite wall. Books. Distraction. Conversation. "Nice, you've read *Under the Rainbow*? One of my faves." I pull it off the shelf—an old, tattered copy with a weather-beaten cover and dog-eared corners. Well loved. My favorite kind of book.

"I know—you mentioned it after Star Wars."

"And you bought it?"

"You have good taste. I knew it'd be all right," he says, shrugging.

I run my finger lightly over the tops of his books, continuing to scan. "Okay, you have *not* read *Ulysses*."

"I skimmed the last chapter," he says, grinning.

"Fail."

"Ooh! *Harry Potter*!"

"Favorite one?" he asks, putting the drumsticks down and coming over to stand next to me. He brushes the back of his hand against mine casually as we face the bookshelf. The unexpected touch startles me, but I keep my hand still, trying to play it cool.

"Tie between *Goblet of Fire* and the *Deathly Hallows*. You?"

"*Deathly Hallows*," he says. "Gotta love the Horcruxes. And Mrs. Weasley screaming at Bellatrix. Epic."

"Best house?" I ask.

"Ravenclaw. No question."

I exhale. "You have passed the test, young Jedi," I say, knowing picking the same house doesn't mean anything and yet secretly feeling it really, really does.

"We're probably the coolest people in school," he says.

I want to grab him and kiss him in response, but I don't. Of course I don't.

The truth is, I've never kissed a boy.

It has nothing to do with being Muslim—okay, maybe a teeny bit. It's hard not to internalize the message against dating, even with liberal parents like mine. But it's also only been a year since I've realized boys sometimes flirt with me. Not all the time. But sometimes.

And it's weird and it's cool and it's scary and I don't know what to say when a guy smiles at me in a way that's less like

Thanks for lending me your phone charger, and more like *Hey, let's make out.*

If you had asked me last year, I would have said it was impossible: No boy would like me, ever. I would make it through my entire high school life without experiencing the miracle of liking a guy *at the exact same time* he liked me back. Without somebody holding my hand. Without a first kiss.

But now here I am. And he keeps inviting me to hang out with his friends at the mall after school. And he laughs at my silly jokes. And now we're alone in his basement. And he's looking at me with *that* look—the look I've wanted but have barely allowed myself to dream about, for fear of being disappointed.

The look that makes me feel dizzy and panicky and alive.

Like I make him happy, too.

"Hi!" It's Zadie Rodriguez, walking down the stairs carrying pizza boxes, followed by Joey Bishop. Wells and Joey high-five.

"Hi!" I say, standing up and giving them suitably breezy air-kisses. Of all Wells's friends, I feel the most comfortable around these two: Zadie and Joey are awesome.

Zadie wears her coolness like a badge: the purple streaks in her hair, the way she carries herself with pride and holds people's gaze and never mumbles. She is who she is, and she's confident but not rude, and if you don't like what she says, that's your problem, not hers.

I wonder what that feels like.

Then there's Joey, who's brilliant—he had the second most points in north Fulton County on last year's Quiz Bowl team—but doesn't show it off. Not to mention he's an incredible soccer player—even better than Wells. He's tall and lean, and his skin is a warm sepia brown. He always looks as if he just finished doing something wholesome, like fishing or sailing or playing touch football on the beach. He's basically a Hollister ad come to life.

Like me, they're stealth dorks, though. At least there's that.

"Your mom gave me this," Zadie says to Wells, holding up the pizza boxes before setting them on the coffee table. She grabs a slice and sprawls out on the couch.

"Pizza?" Wells asks me, leaning down to give me a slice.

I take it, discreetly rearranging the pepperoni and taking strategic bites.

Except Zadie notices. She does that: pays attention. "You don't eat pepperoni?" she says.

Busted. "I mean . . . not really," I say. "It's okay. No worries."

Wells frowns. "You should have told me. I would have ordered one without."

"It's not a big deal, really. I can pick it off. See?"

"Vegetarian?" Zadie asks. "Or full vegan? My sister Tali is vegan, and it drives our *abuela* up the wall."

"Nah. Just not my thing," I say. I don't know them well enough to get into it.

See, here's the deal.

I haven't always felt comfortable telling people my . . .

I hate using the word *secret*. It implies that being a Muslim is something to be ashamed of, when it's not.

But the older I got, as the incidents piled up (even for my blond-haired, blue-eyed, Catholic-born mother) and *especially* after we moved to Georgia, it became abundantly clear that there were people you told, and people you accidentally forgot to tell.

Unless I tell them, nobody realizes I'm a Muslim. I'm cloaked in white privilege. I look like them.

Which makes me safe for bigots.

It's happened my whole life: In the back of an Uber, with the white driver conspiratorially telling Mom and me about the smelly foreigner he just drove. At school, with nice kids you wouldn't expect making random jihad jokes.

Once I tell people, things change a little.

Even with liberals.

Most of the time, I don't think about it: Self-preservation is easier. Of course, you know how it goes when you try to keep yourself from thinking about elephants.

Providence High School has a Muslim Student Association, but I don't really know any of the kids. And when I see them in the hallways or sitting at their usual table in the cafeteria, I feel guilty, like I should say something in solidarity. Like I'm siding with the wrong half of my heritage. Like I should do a better job of announcing myself, instead of trying to pass.

It takes a *lot* for me to publicly claim my Muslimness. But every once in a while, something snaps.

The few people I've pushed back on—sometimes even pulling out my crappy Arabic—always respond with the same textbook progression.

First: flustered. ("Oh! Oh my goodness!")

Next: confused. ("I mean . . . how? You don't look . . .")

Finally: three potential scenarios.

Scenario A: "Whoa, I never would have known! That's cool. So, do you pray five times a day, or . . . ?" (Translation: Are you a "scary" Muslim, or a "just like us, so I-can-pretend-you're-not" Muslim?)

Scenario B: annoyed. (Translation: Look, I'm not talking about people like *you* . . .)

Bigotry is always horrible, but it's especially awkward when somebody realizes you're not a safe receptacle for their garbage.

I've never had to deal with Scenario C, but I know it exists: danger.

"Dude, why'd you drop Quiz Bowl?" Joey asks Wells now.

Wells shrugs. "I don't have enough time. I'm doing the music thing hard this year. Soccer, plus volunteering, plus SAT prep classes starting . . . it's a lot." I like this about Wells. He's not one of those people who think trying or caring is uncool.

"So you were insecure about getting fewer points than me," Joey says. "I get it."

"Dream on, man," Wells says.

He rolls up a straw wrapper and blows it at Joey's face. It bounces off his forehead, and they both laugh. Joey crumples up a napkin and lobs it at Wells in return, and they spend a good minute lobbing it back and forth like a tiny volleyball until Wells drops it.

"No!" Wells cringes.

"Victory!" Joey raises his hands above his head in mock celebration.

Zadie shakes her head. "Y'all are dorks."

"And that's why you love us," Wells says.

Eventually, the conversation turns to somebody named Tessa.

"Who's Tessa?" I ask.

"My girlfriend," Zadie says.

"Wait, you have a girlfriend?" I say.

The three of them laugh, and I feel embarrassed, like I've somehow gotten it wrong.

"I mean, of course I knew you dated girls," I hasten to say. "I just didn't know there was *a* girl."

"I wish Tessa would move back," Wells says.

"Me too," Zadie sighs, looking wistful. She looks at me. "Her dad flies for Delta. They bought a new place in Peachtree City last year, and she goes to school there now. You know Atlanta—she might as well live in Florida, it's so far away."

"Do they *really* drive golf carts around Peachtree City," Wells asks, "or is that just a myth?"

Zadie nods. "It's real. And it's *so* weird. There's a golf-cart parking lot at Tessa's high school." When she mentions her girlfriend's name, she looks sad again.

"I'm sorry she moved," I say. "That sucks."

"It's all good. We're 'long-distance'"—she uses air quotes—"until college, and then we're both applying to Georgia. Fingers crossed."

"College." Joey picks up a Manchester United coaster from

Wells's coffee table and twirls it like a top. "I don't want to think about it."

Wells leans forward and snatches it up. "We've got at least a year before we need to panic."

"What are you worried about?" Zadie scoffs. "You're a shoo-in."

"A shoo-in?" I say. "For where?"

"Didn't you know?" Zadie says. "Wells is going to Yale."

He scowls. "I'm not. I'm not even applying."

"Um, sorry," I say. "Why *wouldn't* you go to Yale?"

He pulls a face.

"He's a legacy there," Joey explains. "And his dad, and his grandfather, and his great-grandfather . . ."

"Can we not?" Wells snaps.

"Easy, boy," Zadie says, holding up her hands. She mock-whispers to me, "Touchy subject."

"Sorry," Wells says, sinking into the couch cushions and resting his head on my shoulder for a second. The unexpected touch sends a jolt up my spine. "College means something. I don't want to be bullied into reliving my dad's glory days."

I want to slap some sense into him, thinking: *What a luxury, to have a dad who could get you into an Ivy League university with a single phone call. Why would you scoff at that chance?*

I mean, my dad went to an Ivy League university, too . . . but through the back door, after transferring in from a military college in Jordan. No freaking way could he call up the president of Columbia University and piggyback me in. Legacies are only for rich people.

I banish the frustration. "What is this integrity you demonstrate?" I say.

We lock eyes, and a grin slowly spreads across both of our faces. Looking at him makes my eyes happy.

And now it's just the two of us—like we're in a staring contest and I can't look away.

"Okay, people, get a room," Zadie says.

I snap out of it, certain I'm beet red.

He shifts on the couch again, and now our hands are lightly touching.

"Hey, losers!" Mikey Murphy says, bounding down the stairs like a Labrador retriever. He's carrying a six-pack of Coke. Kids he's never spoken to know details about his personal life. He's been on homecoming court two years running. It's like his entire life has been a practice run for high school.

"Zademeister," he says. "Broseph." He slings the Cokes on the table, pulls out his vape pen, and takes a puff.

Joey and I smile, because that's what you're expected to do when Mikey shows up. But Zadie—she can barely hide her disdain. Apparently, Mikey's known Wells since they were in preschool. It's one of those hard-to-shake friendships that only makes the cut because of personal history.

I try to focus on the rest of the conversation: on how hard Joey's mom's fibromyalgia has been recently; on Zadie's *abuela* finally taking English lessons; on Wells's expensive car conking out, though his mom bought it only a few years ago for herself.

But all I can focus on is Wells's hand, brushing against mine. On the deliciously clean scent he wears, which wafts my way every time he shifts on the couch. And on the fact that I wish I were brave enough to take him by the hand, pull him into the back room, and press my lips against his for the first time.

CHAPTER FOUR

Dad offers to drive me to school the first day back, a rare occurrence. Mom's office is much closer than the university, which means Dad must want QT.

Sure enough, as we're stuck in traffic on Old Milton Parkway, he ventures down the path of Serious Conversation.

"How are you feeling, pumpkin?" My aunts and uncles use Arabic terms of endearment—*hayati, ahsal, habib albee*—but I've been "pumpkin" to my dad since before I can remember. He lowers the volume as "Ob-La-Di, Ob-La-Da" comes on.

"Fine," I say. "Good."

"I worry."

"Why?"

"We've had lots of change this year. And of course there was that . . . incident . . . on the airplane. Do you need to talk?"

"Dad. You know I don't have problems fitting in. I make

it work. And, besides, the airplane thing was like forever ago. I don't even think about it anymore," I lie. "I'm fine."

He fixes me with one of his looks. It's the I See Through You look.

Except, for once, I'm not sure he does. Because even *I* don't understand why I suddenly can't stop thinking about this thing I've spent so long avoiding.

Religion? We don't talk about it.

Not in a positive way, at least.

While my Ibrahimi cousins were going to Sunday school, learning how to pray, and practicing their Arabic, my family was going to museums on the weekend, making our way through the AFI 100 Greatest American Movies list, and practicing our world capitals.

When talking about other people, religious people, my dad would frown and shake his head. There'd be a negative comment: "I don't understand how anybody believes in that nonsense," or "You know what Karl Marx said about religion," or "Unfortunately, the majority of the world's abuses have been committed in the name of God."

Mom would gently assent before coming up with a counterargument—"C'mon, Mo. Religion can be comforting. Besides, they're parables and stories to help people. You don't have to take the stories as fact"—and Dad would go off on a tangent about how people *did* take them as fact, and how science was the only God he believed in.

Maybe right now would be the perfect time to talk to my father, as his guard is down and we're listening to the Beatles, but though my father is perfect in almost every other area of life, he doesn't exactly have a good track record when it comes to religion.

"I'm *fine*," I repeat, struggling to contain my irritation. I switch to my cheery voice. "Don't worry about me. Honestly!"

"It's okay if you're not." He looks at me. "Fine, that is."

I pause. I didn't expect to be talking about this so long after the fact. I'd buried it deep away.

"It was a little upsetting," I admit. "But, I mean, it could have been way worse, right?"

"Mmm. It could have."

When we arrive at drop-off, he turns to me. He clears his throat, as if he wants to say something but is gathering the courage. Finally, he simply says, "I'm proud of you."

I lean over, giving him a kiss on the cheek. "Love you, Dad."

I will *fight* anybody who comes for him.

Inside, Providence High School looks like every other school I've attended: trophies next to the administration office, linoleum floors, brick walls, hallways lined with lockers and hormones.

I can't count the number of schools I've been to.

Actually, that's not true.

Seven.

There was kindergarten in Dallas, and a second kindergarten when I got into a prestigious charter program in a fancy area of town after the school year started. I had to bus half an hour to and from school each day, but Dad talked Mom into it, saying education was the most important thing and it would be worth it.

We moved to Wayne, New Jersey, in fourth grade, when Dad

finally graduated and got a position as an assistant professor not far from where Uncle Sammy lived, and then to El Segundo in fifth grade, when Dad got a position at UCLA. Then I started middle school. Next, it was off to Evanston, Illinois, in seventh grade, where he got a job at Northwestern, which is pretty much my dream school.

Evanston was a game changer.

It was like a movie set: charming Victorian houses, sandy summertime beaches, and shady streets lined with twisting oaks and leafy maple trees. It was cozy and contained—I felt safe. I thought we'd be there forever, and I loved the idea that I could go to college and still come back to our cute rental town house for dinner. But then Dad got yet another professorship, and he swore *this* job was *the* job—the culmination of the climbing and striving and endless hours applying for tenure-track positions. We lived at an extended-stay for the summer while my parents began an exhaustive search. That's how long it took to find a small house my parents could afford, not to mention one with all Dad's requirements. The winner: a slightly old two-story brick house in the farthest reaches of Providence—less than half a mile from Forsyth County, but on the Fulton side of the border—with a third bedroom for a study and a decently sized backyard, and *of course* in the right school district. Best of all: cheap enough that they could finally afford a down payment after years of scraping and saving. Our very first home.

So here I am.

People smile at me as I walk through the hallways, lobbing

"Hi, Allie!" and "Hey, girl!" my way. It's funny, but even though I feel like an imposter, most people here seem to like me.

Then again, everybody likes the new girl until they get to know her.

The house—*our* house—should make me feel safe: It's supposed to mean permanence. But we've been here for around half a year—about a quarter of the time I spent everywhere else. Which means we should start slackening the cords and pulling up the stakes in another year, if trends keep up—despite what Mom and Dad say.

Which means, no matter how much I try, it's impossible for me to stop holding my breath.

Recently, I read about something called duck syndrome. It's where you look as calm and placid as a duck gliding across the water, but underneath, the feet are paddling furiously, desperately trying to keep up, struggling to maintain the illusion.

Everything looks perfect on the surface, but in reality you're simply trying not to drown.

I float through the morning until I get to my elective: chorus.

Chorus is the best—a place where I can forget all my stress and simply focus on the music. I love to sing, and I don't completely suck at it.

Oh. And Wells is in chorus, too.

No surprise he's not here yet. He's always late to everything.

Half the class is already scattered around the room, and Emilia is surrounded by people, of course. You know how life just comes easy to some people? That's Emilia Graham: pretty, good grades, sympathetic, great at small talk. You can't even hate her: She's too nice.

She sees me and smiles brightly. "Hi, Allie!" She's sitting straight up in the plastic chorus chair, like she always does. That's her thing: perfect posture. I wonder if she secretly slouches like the rest of us when she's at home, or if her every waking hour is truly spent with her back ramrod straight.

I banish the thought. "Hi, Emilia!"

We met doing JV cheerleading last semester, and now we're part of the same loose social orbit. I'm just one of the satellites, though. Emilia's the sun.

"Sorry I missed y'all this weekend," she says. "I had a horse show down in Conyers." She does dressage, which is this sport that makes zero sense to me and costs shocking amounts of money to compete in.

"Wells mentioned it," I say. "How'd you do?"

"First place," she says.

"That's incredible, Emilia. Congratulations!"

"Dancing horses," Mikey says. "So weird."

For once, we're in agreement.

"It was all my horse, Pepita," she says humbly, tucking her dark hair behind her ears. "It's a pleasure riding her. But the day started off *beyond* stressful because of all these extra security measures."

"Security?" I ask. "Why?"

"You know. Because of that attack." She sighs.

My stomach clenches. "Horrible." Her recent Instagram post displayed a photo of the Earth with hands wrapped around it, the words PRAY FOR THE WORLD emblazoned across the image. I liked it and posted a triple blue heart in the comments.

"Why would they need security at a horse show?" Mikey asks. "Not exactly a high-profile target."

"Maybe because the manhunt's still going on? Who knows?" Emilia says. "But Pepita was a rock star, as usual."

Mikey turns his chair around, straddling it casually and leaning in. "They suck." He flexes his arms, his biceps taking part in the conversation. They ripple underneath his rugby shirt.

I look at him warily. "They?"

"Those Muslim pieces of trash. Round 'em up. One-way ticket back where they came from," Mikey says. "You wanna attack people, do it on your own turf. Leave America out of it."

A few of the chorus kids casually listening—Alyssa, Morgan, Brianna—nod in agreement. I look around, alarmed. Is today National Scared of Muslims Day?

Oh, wait. That's every day.

"We don't know it was a Muslim," I say quietly. "They're still trying to find the guy. Or girl, I guess. It could be anybody."

"It's always a dude, and it's always a Muslim," Mikey says firmly. He strokes his face, where the faintest hint of a baby goatee is desperately trying to make itself known.

Sarah frowns. "Not *always*. Sometimes it's a white guy."

"I don't mean *all* Muslims," Mikey says, backpedaling as if he suddenly realizes how it sounded. "Hassan's one of the best tight ends on our team. I'm just talking about, you know, the bad ones. Terrorists."

Emilia sighs. "I know they're a product of their culture, but"—she bites her lip—"it's like, why don't you just blow *yourself* up, instead of taking other people with you?"

"Totally," Brianna says.

"Because they're subhuman," Mikey says. "They don't care. They're evil."

"Not all Muslims," Emilia says, her face sad. "Obviously. But there's a problem with radical Islamic terrorism. And Muslims always say, 'Oh, it's the religion of peace,' but then why is it always *them* causing problems?"

I should say something. I have to. But what?

I hate conflict. It makes my palms sweaty, my heart race. The whole world comes to a halt and literally the only thing I want to do is run and hide until everybody's happy again. I'll say anything, be anybody, just to make that awful, panicky feeling go away. And I don't know why I'm like this. Desperate to make people like me, at all costs.

Maybe in a parallel universe, there's an Allie who doesn't care if people like her or not. Who doesn't apologize even when she's right. Who says what she's actually thinking.

Who calls her friends out on their toxic BS.

"Um . . . I hate to say it . . . but it's sort of . . ." My voice falters.

Everybody looks at me.

"What?" Emilia asks.

"It's just . . ."

"Spit it out!" she says.

"It's kind of offensive to say 'radical Islamic terrorist,'" I say, hating how tiny and tentative my voice sounds. "The phrase, I mean. 'Radical Islam.'" I pick something small and concrete to focus on. Easier to defend.

They exchange looks. Mikey starts laughing. "Whatever, Lincoln." He's always doing that: laughing at serious things, not to mention making up names for people. I'm Lincoln, because apparently simply calling me by my last name isn't creative enough.

"Yeah, but you have to name the problem," Emilia says. "Refusing to face it head-on doesn't do anybody favors."

I want to explain that some Muslims think the phrase is offensive and problematic—that it demonizes the religion as a whole. I want to take them to task for their comments—all of them.

But I don't.

Instead, I just say, "Yeah, I guess so," as Emilia smiles warmly at me.

And I hate myself for it.

Mr. Tucker walks into the room. "Good morning, children!" he says in his singsong voice. It always feels like he's trying too hard, as if he's playing the part of a chorus teacher.

Once the bell rings, Mr. Tucker passes out music. A minute later, Wells enters. He's wearing a retro knitted sweater and a beanie cap over his shaggy hair.

"What's the excuse this time?" Mr. Tucker asks, a sigh emanating from every fiber of his being. It's funny that Mr. Tucker doesn't seem to like Wells, because he's one of those upbeat kids teachers normally have a soft spot for.

"I have a note!" Wells says, holding aloft a yellow sheet of paper from the guidance counselor's office. He sounds as surprised as Mr. Tucker looks.

Mr. Tucker accepts the note, tossing it onto his music stand without looking at it. "Now that we're back from break, it's time to plan the spring musical. We have three contenders to choose from, so my classes will be voting on them. Once we pick a winner, I'll begin holding auditions later in the month."

"Hey," Wells says quietly as he takes an empty seat behind me. "Had to deal with a thing." His breath tickles my neck as he leans forward to whisper in my ear, and it's all I can do to keep from closing my eyes and swooning to the side, like a damsel presenting her neck to a sexy vampire.

"No talking," Mr. Tucker snaps, glaring at Wells. A few kids in class giggle.

Emilia raises her hand.

"Yes, Emilia?" he says, the scowl softening into a smile.

"What are the options, Mr. Tucker?"

"Good question, Emilia. We'll be choosing between *Beauty and the Beast*, *The Addams Family*, and my personal favorite, *Grease*. As always, you're not required to audition for an onstage role, but participation in some form or another is mandatory, whether through backstage work or front of house."

Wells leans forward again. "Ten thousand bucks says we do *Grease*, even if it gets no votes," he whispers into my ear. "No way Dictator Tuck loosens the reins."

"Mr. Henderson! Do I need to send you right back to the front office?"

"No, sir. Sorry, sir. Silence, sir." Wells salutes Mr. Tucker, and the whole class laughs.

When the bell rings, Wells and I walk out of class, my silver flats making *clap-clap-clap* sounds on the linoleum floor as we do the long trek to Algebra II together. Providence is so spread out it might as well be a college campus.

There's a hint of tension in the air between us, after we were overtly flirty at his house. Or maybe it's just my imagination.

But we keep walking, and neither of us says anything.

"I like your skirt," he finally says, pointing at the flippy black wool piece I picked up at Providence's only secondhand shop. "It's cool you don't wear jeans and sneakers like everybody."

My classic Hollywood outfits feel like armor—today's black-and-white ensemble was inspired by Grace Kelly in *Rear Window*. "Oh, I, uh . . . my dad always says clothing influences how people see you, so it's important to put your best foot forward."

Wells hooks a thumb through the strap of his messenger bag. "He sounds smart. Mine says there's a sucker born every minute."

I laugh. "Dark. I like it."

"Hey, so did you say your birthday's coming up soon?" he asks as we walk up the stairs toward math class.

"Yeah, it's a few days before Valentine's Day."

I hope that didn't come out like I'm fishing for a Valentine.

We walk into Mrs. Martinez's class and sit down next to each other in our normal seats by the window.

As Mrs. Martinez talks about logarithmic equations, a message pops up on my computer screen. The school blocks messaging on our Chromebooks, but—please—everybody knows how to get around it.

The message is from Wells. Who is sitting approximately sixteen inches to my right.

WELLS: Did she just say this won't be on the quiz? So why are we learning it?

ME: I don't know, I missed it

WELLS: Distracted by me. I get it.

ME: Haha, you're hilarious

ME: By the way, want to see another movie this weekend?

WELLS: Yeah, but I think Mikey might have people over. I'll find out

ME: Cool

WELLS: Btw, birthday girl, what are you doing for the big day?

ME: No plans

WELLS: Okay, you've got plans now

ME: What do you have in mind?

WELLS: It's a surprise

ME: Ooh, I love surprises!

WELLS: I know 😀😈

ME: Is everybody coming?

WELLS: Thought we could hang just us. Is that okay?

I die and come back to life, only to die again.

ME: Cool

"Wells," Mrs. Martinez says, startling me. She's looking at

him with an exasperated look on your face. "Can you please pay attention? It's the third time I've had to tell you."

"Sorry, Mrs. Martinez," he says, looking sheepish.

Once her back is turned, he looks over at me and grins. He's so cute. Ugh.

I wonder what he has in store for my birthday? I squirm in my seat excitedly.

For once, Dad's corny New Year's toast might be right. This year is definitely looking up.

CHAPTER FIVE

One day, I wake up and realize it's already three weeks into the new year. So far, it's been mostly consumed by homework, and hangouts with Wells and his friends, and binge-watching Netflix with my parents.

What else is there, really?

Sometimes it smells like dinner when I get home from school, but tonight it's a silent, odorless house. Mom and Dad take turns cooking, depending on who gets home from work first (although Dad's cooking is highly superior), and there's often something sizzling on the stove or smoking in Dad's beloved Big Green Egg out back. Tonight, nothing.

I walk into the kitchen, and nobody's there. There's no chopping board, no medley of colorful vegetables, no chicken marinating in cumin and olive oil. I peek out the window to see if Dad's lovingly tending to meat on the Egg. Nope.

"Hello?" I call.

"Upstairs, Al!" Mom replies.

I find Mom and Dad in the small office, the two of them frowning at something on her laptop. Dad has a stack of papers from one of his classes tucked under his arm.

"What's up?" I ask.

"Syria," Mom says, shaking her head in horror. "It never ends. Thank God *Teta* got out when she did."

I look at the picture on the screen—a young boy covered in burns—and turn away, tears in my eyes.

When *Teta* married *Jido*, set up by their families, she moved from Damascus to Amman—jumping into the unknown at only seventeen. They spent decades in Jordan. It wasn't until after my dad moved to America that *Teta* and *Jido* followed, just before 9/11.

Either the world's best timing, or the worst.

"Stop watching this," I say, snapping my mother's laptop shut. "This isn't helping anybody. Let's watch a movie."

I corral my parents downstairs. "Sit down," I command. "I'll bring you tea."

The two of them sit on the couch. Dad reaches for the remote and clicks on the TV, turning the volume up. Jack Henderson, the political commentator, sits behind a shiny desk with a stack of papers in front of him. The word IMMIGRATION is emblazoned across the screen in a big red font.

"No cable news!" I shriek. "Netflix!"

Jack's voice goes silent.

I unwrap the tea bags and pour the water, letting the tea

steep for a few minutes. When I walk back into the room, a steaming mug of tea in each hand, I find my parents curled up on the couch together underneath a shaggy blanket. They're clutching hands, my mom's head resting on my dad's shoulder as they stare at the TV.

Dad looks up and sees me standing in the doorway. He smiles, holding out an arm.

"Come here, pumpkin. Watch with us."

I put the mugs on the coffee table and snuggle under the blanket with them, crawling under my dad's outstretched arm and feeling about five years old. He presses PLAY.

I'd never admit it to my friends—I'm not about social disaster, thank you very much—but at this moment, safe with my parents, there's almost nowhere else in the world I'd rather be.

After takeout dinner and a couple episodes of a British comedy, we've moved on to *An American in Paris.* The coffee table is covered with half-eaten containers of guacamole and salsa, plus various books and paper stacks and open laptops.

Dad's phone rings. It's *Teta*, FaceTiming.

"*Marhaba, Mama. Kefic?*" Dad says, launching into a conversation. I catch the words *Suria* and *haram* and *tayaara,* and understand they're talking about an air attack. It must be especially scary for *Teta*. Her sister, brother-in-law, and several nieces and nephews still live outside Damascus.

I pause the TV as Mom walks into the living room with a tray covered in ice-cream toppings.

Our nightly tradition has been the same ever since I was a kid: We gather in front of the TV and make an ice-cream sundae while Mom and Dad catch up on work and I do homework. As I've gotten older and my homework routine has become more intense, I don't always stay downstairs—too many distractions—but I *do* always make time for dessert.

My dad has favorites he returns to over and over. He's not big into foreign films with subtitles and doesn't have much patience for noir, gangster, or shoot-'em-ups. (Except *The Godfather*. Always *The Godfather*.) His favorites are the big Technicolor cotton-candy musicals from the golden era: *Meet Me in St. Louis*, *The Sound of Music*, *West Side Story*, and his beloved, the one he goes to when life has him down, *Singin' in the Rain*.

It's no wonder I like chorus. I grew up with musicals as second nature. It's a magical world where everything is beautifully decorated, there's nothing that can't be cured by singing about it, and everybody gets a happy ending.

While Dad talks, I pick up my phone and zone out, scrolling through Instagram and peeping on people from school.

"Allie?" he says.

"Sorry?"

"*Teta* wants to say hi," he says, holding out the phone.

My stomach clenches. Time for another round of awkward We Don't Understand Each Other pantomiming.

"*Marhaba, Teta!*" I say cheerfully. "*Kefic?*"

"Mabsoota, ya Alia! Wa anti kefic?"

"Mabsoota, ya Teta."

Aaaand, we've reached our limit.

"Um, love you, *bahebak, ya habibti,*" I say, smiling at her brightly, as if that will make up for my conversational deficiencies.

Mom goes through the same painful routine over FaceTime before hanging up. It's fresh torture every time. I love my grandmother, but the conversations just remind me I'm not one of them.

"Okay, you ready?" Dad says, picking up the remote. "We've got a date with Gene Kelly and Leslie Caron." He sees the scowl on my face. "What's wrong?"

"I hate not being able to speak with *Teta,*" I say sullenly. "I wish you had taught me Arabic like I asked."

He looks taken aback.

"I asked you over and over," I say. "And you never taught me. And now I can barely communicate with her. I hate it."

"Those are valid feelings," Mom says, making me feel like a jerk.

Dad looks stricken.

"Sorry, Dad," I say. "I'm in a mood. It's not your fault."

He nods. "It's the Zeitgeist. I think the whole world is on edge these days."

I'm grateful to him for letting me off the hook. I feel like a petulant brat. I need to make up for it.

"Sorry," I repeat. "Hey, you want more ice cream? Extra chocolate syrup?"

He smiles. "Sure, pumpkin." But the smile doesn't fully reach his eyes.

CHAPTER SIX

Wells shows up outside my house at 7:45 a.m. sharp. I tighten the bow in my ponytail and smooth down my checkered trousers—today's an Audrey Hepburn moment, complete with sleek black turtleneck—before racing outside, where Wells is waiting in a new car: a shiny black tricked-out pickup truck.

"Whoo-whee! Are we country or are we country?" I say as I step up and climb in.

He grins, patting the car. "This ol' baby? She's new."

"Yeah, I can tell." I sniff the air. New-car smell. "Nice, but not quite as swish as mine."

"What do you drive?"

"Uh, I don't. My mom keeps begging me to get my driver's license, but what's the point when you can have people drive you everywhere?" I make a silly face to show him I'm kidding. Mostly.

"Not me." He slides his hand protectively over the steering

wheel. "Wheels mean freedom. You can take your driver's test next week, right?"

"Yeah. Then my ride will be my dad's Cadillac. Don't be jelly."

He laughs, but I suddenly feel disloyal making fun of the car. My dad upgraded from an ancient Ford last year, and it was kind of a huge deal. He'd always dreamed of owning a Cadillac.

With each week, my relationship with Wells is deepening. We text each other every night after Wells gets home from soccer practice, and we've started hanging out alone, too—without his friends as a buffer.

Still, I don't say anything to him.

You know. The Muslim thing.

I can't.

Besides, what would I say?

Hey, you were totally right about Mr. Tucker picking Grease *for the school musical despite the fact that everybody voted for* Beauty and the Beast, *and I can't wait for my birthday surprise next week, and, oh, by the way, I'm a member of a marginalized and misunderstood religious group, and because I am invisible and everybody sees me as a Generic White Girl, I am a receptacle for unguarded Just Between Us White People ignorance.*

I mean, it just *flows.*

I'm well versed in pushing uncomfortable and inconvenient thoughts out of my head, though. It's one of my superpowers.

"I brought coffee," he says, handing me a paper cup. "Venti latte, extra foam."

"I'm impressed."

"That's what it takes to impress you? Basic listening skills?"

I buckle my seat belt as he reverses out of the driveway.

"Here I was planning a big birthday surprise," he says. "Note to self: Just remember a Starbucks order."

I giggle.

He puts on some music as we drive through the back roads of Providence, the road winding under a canopy of dogwood trees.

"Wait a second," I say, my attention snapping back to the music. "Is this you?"

He grips the steering wheel tightly, not looking at me. "Yeah. What do you think?"

"Holy guacamole. You're amazing!"

Now he glances my way, a hopeful smile lighting up his face.

"I had no idea you could sing," I say.

"We *did* meet in chorus."

"We met in algebra, so nice try—and I mean, *really* sing. Is this you on guitars, too?"

"Yup," he says softly. "Guitar, drums, vocals. Dave Grohl recorded the entire first Foo Fighters album himself, you know."

"Dude, you have serious talent."

"Dude?" he asks, smiling.

"I used to live in California. Let it go. You need to start a YouTube channel or something."

"I have one," he mumbles.

"I can't believe you didn't tell me." Translation: I can't believe my social media stalking didn't bring anything up. "Do you perform?"

"Once. This tiny club in Midtown. I'm hoping to talk my

dad into paying for studio time, too. Working on it." His face tightens. "My dad is weird with money."

He tells me the name of his YouTube channel, and I find a video. I watch him alone in his room, strumming on a guitar and singing an original composition. His eyes close a few times, as if he's lost in the music—a quiet, lovely song about shaking off expectations.

He's too gorgeous. I can't.

I look back at the real Wells, zeroing in on his hands on the gearshift. Something about him driving a stick shift seems manly.

Eyes up here, Allie.

I feel like I need to crack a window to keep from passing out. I want to kiss him so badly I can barely breathe.

He misreads my silent lust for dislike. "You hate it," he says.

"I don't! I love it!" I'm surprised he's being needy. I've never seen this side of him.

"Anyhow, it's something I do for fun. My dad says music is a hobby." A shadow passes over his face, then it's gone.

"Are you going to try out for the musical?"

"I dunno." He shrugs. "Maybe. You?"

"I thought I might. Why don't we do it together?"

He turns onto the road leading to school, drumming on the steering wheel. "Cool, cool. Let's do it."

After Wells and I part ways, I see a large attention-grabbing table outside the library on the way to French. There's a sign in front saying MUSLIM STUDENT ASSOCIATION and, beneath it, SUPPORT SYRIAN REFUGEES.

The girl behind the table has delicate features, copper-brown eyes, and bouncy waves coiling midway down her back.

I recognize her.

She's one of them: the other Muslim kids at school.

The ones I pretend not to notice.

It's not as if Providence is a *completely* homogenous place: There are a handful of Muslim kids, including a senior girl who wears a headscarf and mostly keeps to herself, and this girl, who I'm pretty sure is in my grade.

I decide to say something to her.

"Hi!"

She looks up at me, smiling. "Hi there!"

"I'm Allie."

"I'm Dua."

"So . . . uh . . . what are you doing here?"

"We're raising money for the International Rescue Committee, supporting Syrian refugees. We're trying to hit five thousand dollars. And, as you can see, we're rocking it." She points at a poster board with their goal. They've raised seventy-three dollars. "Wanna donate?"

"Definitely." I rummage in my purse for my wallet. "You take cash?" I fish out all the money I have in my wallet: twelve dollars. "I'm sorry it's not more. I don't get a huge allowance."

"Thanks! Every bit helps." She takes the money and puts it in a lockbox.

"Will you be here next week, too?" I ask.

"We only got permission through the end of the week, but we'll keep raising money online. Facebook. Instagram. Carrier pigeon. Whatever it takes."

I laugh at her joke. "Okay, cool. I'll bring more next week."

She smiles. "Incredible. Thanks!"

And I walk off down the hallway—wanting to say much more but not sure where to begin.

Wells, Zadie, and Joey have second lunch, which means I sit with Emilia, Sarah, and Mikey. Every once in a while, I'll take my lunch and eat by myself by the log cabin.

Sometimes I just need to be alone, and I don't know this group well enough yet to explain why.

They're talking about the same stuff they always talk about: who's hooking up with who, whether or not the football coach is gay, how they did on the latest quiz, whose parents are going to be out of town, PSAT prep.

Somehow the conversation turns to the Muslim Student Association's fund-raising table, and my Spidey sense tingles.

Danger, danger.

"I think it's nice. I gave five dollars," Emilia says. "Those poor people, they need the money."

"Bleeding heart alert," Mikey cracks, popping a potato chip in his mouth. During football season, he's on a strict diet, but it looks like that's out the window second semester.

"Come on," Emilia says, "at least I have a heart. Besides it's not their fault. Not all Muslim refugees are bad. You don't pick where you're born. Right?"

Something in her tone rubs me the wrong way. Even while she's defending Muslims, she's othering us.

"Look, I'm not a monster. I feel sorry for them, but there's no room for a bunch of refugees right now," Mikey says. "We're a little maxed out. America isn't a free buffet. It's not personal." It's as if he's parroting talking points—whether from his parents or TV, I'm not sure.

"Are you going back to Europe, Mikey?"

I say it before I can stop myself.

"Huh?" He looks at me, surprised.

I'm surprised, too.

I press forward. "I mean, your family immigrated here. You're saying everybody who's not Native American should go back where they came from? Unless you're Indigenous, you're an immigrant. That means you, too."

He snorts. "C'mon. That was five hundred years ago."

"And?"

"America isn't full of Cherokee anymore. We're for white people now."

If looks could kill.

He hastens to add, "Dude, Lincoln, you know what I mean: I don't mean *only* white people. I meant it as shorthand. European ancestry."

Now it's not just me looking at him incredulously. Emilia

and Sarah shift uncomfortably in their chairs, suddenly very interested in their food. If Zadie were here, she'd tear him a new one.

I gather courage, calling him out. "That's racist. On multiple fronts." My voice wavers but I hold his gaze.

"For real?" he says, his face stunned. "You're calling me racist?"

My heart pounds. Maybe I've gone too far.

"That's hella offensive. Just because I'm saying a bunch of foreign freeloaders shouldn't get an automatic one-way pass? Use your brain. They could be *dangerous*." He grabs his bottle of water, unscrews the cap furiously, and starts chugging it. "I am one hundred percent not racist. Joey and Hassan are my legit bros. I love those guys."

Sarah clears her throat. "Hey, did y'all hear about Mrs. Russell? Rumor is she won the lottery. She just upgraded from a beater to a Tesla."

"Look, Mikey," I say, ignoring Sarah, "just tell me this. You do get that those people—the 'dangerous' ones—aren't real Muslims, right? Like, they're killing their own kind. They're bombing mosques. They *literally* keep trying to blow up Mecca. That's not Muslim. Syrian refugees have nothing to do with them."

"BS. Of course they're Muslims."

"They're not."

Normally, I'd let it go to keep the peace, but suddenly, I feel like I'm part of the problem.

Holding up the status quo.

Keeping my mouth shut to avoid making people uncomfortable.

I continue. "The attacker from winter break: Now we know he wasn't Muslim, but everybody just *assumed* he was before they found him."

"I don't know. That whole thing was shady."

"Mikey, he's a white guy."

"Maybe. Maybe not. My dad says they're hiding the facts."

"Okay, conspiracy theorist," I say, rolling my eyes. "What about all the guys who keep terrorizing churches and synagogues and schools? Why don't you call them terrorists? Because they're white?"

He frowns. "You're being naive. It's not my fault some people hate America."

"How come if somebody named Ahmed kills people, that's terrorism," I say, "but if it's some white boy, it suddenly becomes just a regular crime? A lone wolf, right? As if Muslims can't be terrorized? As if murderous white people get a pass?"

"Allie," Emilia whispers. "I totally agree with you, but keep your voice down, okay?"

"I'm sick of people automatically blaming Muslims," I say. "It's bigoted and it's wrong, and we're better than this. Or we should be."

"I'm feeling you," she says quietly, "but maybe let's take it down a few notches. Cool?"

I don't know if Emilia is taking offense to *what* I'm saying or simply how I'm saying it.

Keep it calm, Allie. Nobody likes an angry girl. "Mikey, you get that demonizing billions of people because of a few isn't cool, right?" A pleading tone has crawled into my voice to replace my aggressive one.

"Love ya, Lincoln, but you're delusional." Mikey snorts. "It's more than a few."

"So every Muslim needs to wear the scarlet letter?"

"You shouldn't be this sensitive."

"You need to learn words matter."

Mikey makes a *blech* noise. "Can we stop talking politics?" he says. "It's *boring*. I wish everybody would shut up about it."

"But *you* brought it up," I say. "We were talking about SAT prep before you went off on the MSA fund-raising table."

I can't believe I'm not letting this go.

I *always* let it go.

I break my gaze away. I feel hot and dizzy, with a pounding headache. Confrontation takes it out of me.

"I'm sorry, okay?" I say, not entirely sure what I'm apologizing for or who I'm apologizing to. "I'm passionate about it, that's all."

"You should write an op-ed for the school paper or something," Sarah says. "Ooh! Or run for student council!"

Emilia looks relieved. "I'm sorry, too. I know you meant well. And I love your passion."

Thank goodness they're letting me off the hook. I've spent the entire year trying to coast below the radar, and here I am, ruining it in five seconds.

"I don't," Mikey mutters, riling me right back up.

"While you're at it," I snap at him, "don't talk about Coach's sexuality. That's none of your business."

"Jesus, Allie," Mikey says. "What's got your panties in a twist?"

I stand up, taking my tray over to the trash and dumping it out to the sound of giggles behind me. Across the room, I see Dua eating lunch with a few girls.

By the time I storm through the lunchroom doors, I can hear Mikey's voice carrying: He's already talking about Claire Sanchez and some epic party she's planning.

Five seconds, and forgotten—just like that.

As soon as I get home, I collapse on the couch. I put my phone in do-not-disturb mode, leaving it facedown on the coffee table, next to my dad's history books and out of arm's reach. I can't with social media right now. I need a break from the world.

Mom gets home later than usual, wearing her personal uniform: black jeggings, white button-down shirt, and black flats. On the weekends, it's her other uniform: Lululemon leggings, V-neck tees, and old-school Adidas, which makes her look like she's always one protein shake away from hitting the gym.

"Hi, honey," she says, her voice exhausted.

"Long day?" I ask.

She nods, rubbing her hand across her eyes and looking vulnerable. "Yeah."

Considering how warm my mother is with me, she's surprisingly tight-lipped about work. Maybe it's too tough to bring home with her. It must be difficult, hearing people complain, talking through their issues nonstop, being a repository for so much suffering. She's like a crab—tough on the outside but a big, gooey softy on the inside.

"Nobody went off the deep end, though, right?" I say.

She laughs. "Not quite, Allie. Thank you for your confidence in my skills."

"Okay, good."

She sits down next to me, and I put my head on her lap, like I used to do when I was young. She strokes my hair, and suddenly I'm six years old again.

"How was your day, love?" she says.

"It was okay." I think about Mikey, and how much it hurts when people bash Muslims in front of me, not realizing they're insulting my family. Insulting me. I think about meeting Dua, and about how I'm a horrible Muslim . . . because I'm barely a Muslim at all.

Her hand is soft on my head.

"The thing with Dad on the plane last month," I say, looking up at her. "Has something like that happened before?"

There's so much unsaid in Mom's look: surprise, concern, pity, fear. She's quiet for a long time, as if weighing her words.

"Once or twice," she says.

She's downplaying.

I sit up, grabbing the remote and hitting MUTE. In the background, the TV flickers.

"Why aren't we religious?" I say.

Mom sits up straighter on the couch.

"I wouldn't say I'm *not* religious. I consider myself spiritual," she says. "Maybe 'curious' is a better word. I find religion comforting, even if I don't buy into every last detail. I like the ritual of it."

"So why aren't you and Dad like the rest of the family?" I say. "We never do the stuff they do. We don't fast. We don't go to mosque. You both drink. It's like the worst of both worlds: the stress of being Muslim and none of the benefits."

"I suppose . . ." She scratches her head. "Islam isn't like other religions. It requires absolute belief. It's easy to feel if you're not doing it all the way, you shouldn't do it, period."

"But . . . why did you convert when you married Dad?"

Mom leans forward, rubbing the scar running down the length of her arm. It's an old injury, back from her days as head cheerleader of Key Biscayne Prep in the nineties—a car accident following a football game. I grew up poring over her photo albums, marveling over how young and preppy my mother looked, with her blond hair tied back in ribbons and her fists clenched at her hips, elbows out, like Wonder Woman. She displays the scar proudly, defiantly, wearing sleeveless dresses and short-sleeved blouses. Whenever she's nervous, she rubs it absentmindedly.

"You remember how we met, right?"

She's stalling for time.

"Your suitemate Susie was going on a first date," I say. "A *real* date—with this guy from your James Joyce seminar. And he was friends with Dad, and Susie decided it would be more fun to double-date—"

"I don't know if she thought it would be more *fun*, but Susie was quirky like that."

"And so the guy invited Dad, who was his Pike brother from Columbia. And Susie invited you, and you all went to the West End for beers, and you ended up at the Heights for three-dollar margaritas at like two a.m."

"On second thought," Mom says, "I'm not sure if I like this story coming out of your mouth."

"And you were immediately swept off your feet by Dad, and you thought he was, like, the most handsome guy you'd ever seen, but you also had this rule against dating frat guys—"

"Not a rule . . . a guideline."

"A rule. And Dad walked you home, and you were living in a Columbia dorm that year instead of Barnard, and the two of you kissed outside Struggles."

My mom bursts out laughing. "The dorm wasn't called Struggles, Allie. That was just the nickname. Ruggles."

"Whatever. And you woke up the next morning, and Dad had left you a message on the Columbia phone system—because this was the 1800s, and cell phones hadn't been invented yet—and you saw him again that night at AmCaf, and you fell in love and got married after graduation, and have been together ever since."

My mom smiles, looking pleased. "Memories."

"But that doesn't answer my question."

She rubs her scar again.

"My family was shocked when I brought him home over Christmas," she says. "My mom kept asking me if I was sure he was Muslim, since he drank, and he didn't have a beard, and he was progressive—all these ridiculous bordering-on-offensive questions."

I'm not close to my mom's side of the family. Even though she also comes from a large family—I have five uncles on that side, Mom's younger brothers—none of them keep in close touch. No family reunions. No phone calls. They barely send cards on birthdays. I'm friends with two of them on Facebook, where they post photos of their boats and the fish they've caught. My grandfather died before I was born, so the only person from my mom's family who I'm even *slightly* close to is my grandmother—possibly the WASP-iest woman on planet Earth, though she's Catholic.

"It's hard to explain," Mom says. "When I met your father, I just knew."

"You knew what?"

"I knew he was the one. I knew we were meant to be together. I knew he would be kind, and would take care of me if I got sick, and would be my partner through the good and the bad. An equal."

I'm not used to hearing Mom talk like this. She doesn't typically get emotional. She clears her throat, shifting on the couch. "It obviously would have been *easier* if he were Catholic. Or if I were a Muslim. Your dad never asked me to convert, by the way. He would have married me regardless—we were impatient to start our lives together. For him, the conversion was a plus, though an unnecessary one. We both recognized the relationship the other had with religion."

"Which was?"

"Hopeful but bruised. Weary. Open to another path."

"What happened?"

Her fingers keep kneading the scar. "*Teta* asked me to consider it, when we visited them in Dallas for the first time."

I frown. "So Grandmother was right. I always thought she was making it up."

We were visiting my grandmother in Florida the first time I realized she wasn't happy my mother had married a Muslim.

She didn't dislike *all* Muslims, of course. There were plenty she liked: my father, and Dr. Oz, and "that lovely older actress—you know the one, with the black hair, what's her name."

"Maybe you'll reconsider this Moslem thing," my grandmother said to my mom the morning after we'd flown in from California. Dad was at the store, stocking up on groceries. She loved his cooking. Exotic, she called it. We sat by the pool of her home in Key Biscayne, the air salty and sticky.

"This *Muslim* thing?" Mom said, trying to correct her.

"Yes, dear. I told you becoming a Moslem was a terrible idea. Can't you simply . . . take it back?" She looked over at me and smiled. "More guava juice, darling?"

I pretended to look up from my book as if I had been actually reading instead of listening intently. "No, thank you, Grandmother."

"I converted my religion, Mother," Mom said, scowling at her. "I didn't buy a handbag at Neiman Marcus."

"You did it to impress his mother. She'll get over it."

"That's not why I did it."

"I gather you're saying—"

"No, I can't just take it back. More importantly, I don't want to. Islam is a beautiful religion."

Grandmother sighed. "You refuse to take my advice."

"Maybe I would, if it were good advice," Mom said.

The memory is fuzzy, and it's tempting to insert details. When I think back on that moment, though, one thing stands out clearly:

It's the first time I realized somebody could like me—even love me—and yet not accept me.

I was ten.

Mom makes a face. "My mother has her own baggage. It doesn't mean she's right."

"It sounds like she *is* right. You converted to make *Teta* happy."

When Mom is trying to be diplomatic, she pauses, puts her fingers together, and purses her lips. She's doing it now.

"*Teta* never pressured me. Your dad never pressured me. If I hadn't converted, you would still be a Muslim: If the father is a Muslim, the child is a Muslim."

"So it was all about me? *Teta* was worried I wouldn't be Muslim enough?"

Mom's sigh comes from deep within. "It was ultimately my decision. I thought it might make our family complete. I was trying to make things easier on your dad with his family. Muslims marry Muslims. It wasn't a big deal."

"Changing your religion wasn't a big deal?" I ask incredulously.

"Allie, you know neither your father nor I is religious. Muslim, Jewish, Christian, Buddhist, Mormon—what's the difference? It's all man-made."

I frown. "I disagree."

"And that's your prerogative. Dad and I wanted you to choose your own path. It's the biggest mystery in life, the biggest question out there: Isn't it important to allow your children to choose what they believe?"

"Maybe," I say tentatively, "it's important to raise your kids with *something*, so they don't feel . . . lost?"

My mother looks stricken.

"You feel lost?"

Now it's my turn to choose my words carefully.

"Not lost. But not found, either."

She's quiet again. I hear the *tick-tick-tick* of the clock on the fireplace mantel.

"We thought we were doing right by you," she says.

I look down at my hands. "I know."

"I went through a period where I doubted God existed."

"You were an atheist?"

Her smile is small, quiet. "Briefly. When I was your age."

My heart thuds against my chest. "You're not now, right?" Her response feels like the most important thing in the world.

"Not now. Don't get me wrong: The idea of a superhero in the sky . . . it's a bit convenient."

We stare at each other. She puts her hand on mine.

"But I remember how it felt when you were born and I cradled you in my arms for the first time," she says. Her tone is an offering. "I remember the energy in the room when my father died. I remember the devastation of losing the babies after you, of holding Rania's tiny body in our hands at the hospital.

I believe there's something out there, and I don't care what you call it. It's all the same to me."

I feel like I'm going to cry.

"It's a lonely thing, being a convert. People *born* into a religion take it for granted. But when you adopt it as your own, it's hard to find the right path. Some people go overboard and hold themselves to an exacting standard. Others become wayward. I suppose that's what happened to me. I converted as a technicality, but the longer we were married—the longer I spent around your *teta* and *jido*, and saw how much comfort and peace Islam brought the family—the more I wanted to know about it. I didn't have much support from your father, though, and . . ." She shrugs. "I have nobody to blame but myself. I could have learned more on my own. I didn't."

"Dad didn't support you?"

She puts up her hands. "Your father is the most supportive man I've ever met. I was too passive. I could have gone to the mosque by myself, I could have taken Arabic lessons."

"But you didn't?"

"But I didn't. People judge your father, and that's unfair," she says. "They don't know his path. He doesn't have the comfort of religion to fall back on. Strangers who know nothing about him place him in a box, judge him off unfair stereotypes. And, conversely, the family isn't thrilled with his views."

"Is Dad an atheist?" I whisper.

"No. Despite his scientific bluster and bravado." She puts her hand on mine again. "If God takes root in your heart, it's hard to stop fully believing."

"But he's not religious."

"You don't have to be religious to have a relationship with God."

I'm quiet for a long time.

"Are you interested in exploring Islam?" Mom says. "Or . . . another religion? I don't want to assume."

"Yes," I say quietly. I clear my throat, gathering the courage. "Islam."

I didn't know I wanted it until I say it.

"That's wonderful," she says softly. "Islam is a beautiful religion, if you open yourself up to it." She looks like she wants to say something else.

"Will Dad understand?"

"Your father is the best man I know." She sighs. "Everybody has a weak spot."

We fall into silence.

"My turn," she says, sitting upright.

"What do you mean?"

"Since we're being honest . . . can I ask you something?"

"Okay . . ."

"This kid Wells. You two are hanging out a lot recently. Is he your boyfriend?"

I squirm. "I don't know. People don't really do the boyfriend-girlfriend thing anymore."

She laughs, burying her face in her hands. "When did I get so old? Okay, fine, are you two 'hanging out'?" She says it exaggeratedly, using air quotes.

"Mom! I don't know!" I'm so not into this conversation.

"I'll take that as a yes. Does he know we're Muslim?" she asks.

That's why.

"No."

"Are you going to tell him?"

"I don't know."

She nods.

"Do you think I should?"

I rarely ask my mom to straight-up *tell* me what to do. Desperate times.

She purses her lips. "I met him for five seconds. He seemed kind. But if he doesn't accept you for who you are, he doesn't deserve your company in the first place."

"Okay, Hallmark card," I say.

She laughs, kissing me on the head. "Hey, kiddo. You're awesome. And don't you forget it."

Later, Dad knocks on my door, startling me while I'm working on homework.

"Everything okay? You were quiet at dinner."

I lower my laptop screen, a nervous feeling in the pit of my stomach.

"Yeah, all good."

My dad swings the door open wider. "I stopped by the store to pick up extra toppings—got chocolate sauce, pistachios, and raspberries. Thought we could tuck into *The Sound of Music* again tonight. I'm in the mood for some singing nuns. If you want to watch while doing homework."

"For you, Dad, I always have time."

I stand up, unplug my laptop, and follow him down the stairs as he chatters happily, telling a dad joke, wondering how *do* you solve a problem like Maria?

My anxiety levels about what Dad will think when he finds out I want to explore the religion are sky-high. He places his confidence in science. In facts. Religion is for suckers, he says.

What does that make me?

CHAPTER EIGHT

"Who's meeting us there?" I ask Wells as he drives us to the movie theater that Saturday afternoon, his fingers drumming on the steering wheel.

"Oh, uh . . . everybody was busy."

Something about the way he says it makes me suspect they weren't invited.

"That's too bad."

"Is it, though?" he cracks. The levity in his voice reminds me of that jokey thing I've mastered over the years—when I'm trying to protect my true feelings. He pulls into the parking lot. "So fair warning: The reviews are god-awful."

"You mean the popcorn movie about a giant robot attacking a major city *isn't* a best-picture contender?"

"Laugh it up. Didn't want you to think I had horrible taste, that's all."

"Oh, you definitely have horrible taste. I still like ya."

We grin at each other before he maneuvers his giant truck into a spot.

"I have to ask. This truck. What's the deal?" I say as I drop down from the cab, closing the door with a satisfying *thud*. We got here early so we could go to the bookstore next door before the movie.

"What do you mean?" His voice is suddenly defensive.

"I mean . . . are you auditioning for another *Transformers*? Preparing for a monster-truck rally?"

His cheeks turn a little pink. "It's my dad."

"Huh?"

"He picked it out. A gift. It wasn't a discussion."

"There are worse gifts than a brand-new truck," I say.

He shrugs.

He looks at his watch. "The movie starts in forty-five. Plenty of time for the bookstore." As we approach the door, he scurries ahead of me to hold it open. "My lady."

"You dork," I tease.

We make our way to a fiction aisle, where we scan the shelves, picking up bestsellers and reading staff recommendations.

I love being inside a bookstore. There are endless possibilities. Infinite stories. Places to lose myself. It's heaven.

I wait until he wanders over to the graphic novels to make a break for the religious section.

I'm looking for a Qur'an.

I find the one I'm looking for: a simple blue Oxford World's Classics copy I've seen at Aunt Bila's house. I flip to a random page, playing an old game I enjoy with books: I'll look at a random page and see if it has meaning.

The Qur'an passage reads: "*Whoever accepts guidance does so for his own good; whoever strays does so at his own peril.*"

"Whatcha got there?" Wells asks.

I startle. I instinctively turn the Qur'an over and shield it with my hands as I turn toward him.

"Nothing."

"Is that . . . Wait, is that a Qur'an?"

I freeze.

He looks at me, amusement in his eyes. "A little light reading?"

"Ha," I say, putting the Qur'an back down on a random bookshelf. "Yeah."

It's the perfect opportunity.

What are you waiting for, Allie?

I can't. I'm not ready.

Wells and I wander over to the young adult section to browse. A few minutes later, he says he wants to check out a music biography of Keith Richards. I have three minutes, tops.

I race back to the Qur'an, take it with me to the front, and quickly pay in cash with my allowance money for the week. I'm back in the young adult aisle with the Qur'an and a receipt stuffed into my bag before he returns.

"Are you getting it?" I ask. "The Keith Richards book?"

"Nah. I'll borrow it from the library," he says. "Ready to go? Movie in ten."

"Robots activate!"

Incredibly, he laughs at my silly joke.

The Qur'an is burning a hole in my bag. I feel a confusing rush of emotions: excitement, anxiety, embarrassment, and also, weirdly, shame.

Once inside the theater, I barely pay attention to the movie. Number one: because it's the worst. Number two: because Wells is sitting next to me in a dark room.

Is this a date?

We're seeing a movie alone together.

He picked me up.

We're sharing popcorn.

This *might* be a date.

Except, he doesn't put his arm around me. And there's no moment when we brush fingers reaching for popcorn, looking at each other shyly before breaking into giggles. In fact, when I accidentally let out a tiny burp after taking a too-large sip of Coke, he cracks up laughing, instead of looking horrified or embarrassed for me.

So I don't know.

Maybe I've been reading into this whole thing.

Maybe he *doesn't* like me back.

Maybe he sees me as his awesome gal pal Allie—she of mouthy quips and neurotic tendencies—and the idea of kissing me (*which has never crossed his mind*) would make him cringe.

On the drive home, I keep retreating into myself, doing that thing where I shrink into a protective emotional shell, getting into my own head—until I'm giving monosyllabic answers to his questions and pretending to ignore him.

"You okay?" he asks. On the radio, Tom Petty sings about girls raised on promises.

"Hmm? Yeah. Fine."

"You seem . . . off."

"Nope. All good," I say in what I hope is a breezy I Couldn't Care Less tone.

Except, I couldn't care more.

When he drops me off at my house before dinner, the February sky a dusky purple, I can't bounce from the car fast enough. I lean over the seat stiffly, patting him twice on the back and mumbling, "Catch you later," before bolting into my house.

Mom and Dad are on the couch doing work when I get home, cable news on in the background and dinner simmering on the stove.

"Have fun?" Mom asks, looking up from her laptop.

"Uh-huh." I plop down on an armchair, feeling dazed. I might have screwed things up with Wells for no reason.

"Where'd you go?" Dad asks, looking up from a World War I book. Research. He's writing his next book, a take on "the Great War" (as he calls it), focusing on how the closing years and the aftermath transformed American society, heightened consumerism, and led to greater isolationism and an increased sense of American exceptionalism.

I've heard the summary a time or two thousand.

"To the movies," I say.

"With that horse girl? Emilia?" His brow furrows. He doesn't seem to like her, and I'm not sure why. She's the kind of straight-laced student any normal parent would *love* their kid to hang out with. No wild keggers on Emilia Graham's watch.

"No, uh, with Wells."

He sets his book down on the couch. "Ah. Right. The boy." The word—*boy*—is heavy in his mouth, laden with meaning.

"Oh, Mo, lighten up," Mom says. "She's sixteen next week."

He looks back and forth between the two of us, eyebrows raised. "Am I being ambushed? Is this some sort of mother-daughter plot to pull one over on your doddering old dad?"

I think he's kidding. Like, 95 percent sure.

"Please," I say. "You're not old. You're nearly a millennial."

"How *dare* you," he says, chuckling. "And, might I say, your attempts to distract me are weak. More details on this boy you're suddenly spending time with, please."

I fight to keep my voice even.

Yeah, he's mostly chill, but he's still my dad. If I get defensive, he might change his mind about the dating thing, and then I'll be screwed. "It's not sudden, Dad. We've been hanging out all year. He's in chorus. And algebra, too. He's smart—he used to do Quiz Bowl. He loves soccer, like you. And he's just a friend, by the way."

"Hmm." Dad frowns, not looking convinced.

"I'm pretty sure he's a Galaxy fan," Mom says in a teasing voice.

"At least he has good taste," Dad says.

I don't bother to correct them.

He looks back down at his book, rapping on it with his fingers. He sighs. "Is this happening?"

"Is what happening?" I ask.

"You're almost sixteen," he says, sounding resigned. "I gave my word you could start dating. I guess I didn't expect—"

"News flash: Just because a guy and girl hang out doesn't always mean it's a date."

He shoots me another patented Mo Abraham look. The one that's always been way more effective than getting angry or arguing his case. The look that says: *You can't get anything past me.*

Dating was something I never thought about until I turned twelve. When I asked my mother if I'd someday be allowed, she demurred, saying, "I'll talk to your father." That surprised me, because my mother grew up American and so I automatically assumed she'd be on my side. Wrong. The two of them were big on Team Abraham. She'd need to talk to my dad and formulate a plan.

The funny thing is, my dad is the cool one in the family. He's even-keeled when it comes to dealing with obnoxious strangers, and he's great about giving advice to other family members when they get too hardhanded with their children. ("You don't own them. You're only there to steward them," he'd said to his brother-in-law when he threatened to boycott my cousin Danna's wedding for choosing a Christian husband.)

But apparently my dad's levelheadedness goes out the window when it comes to dating and me. He got weird in seventh grade when Mom told him I had a massive crush on Dusty in my chorus class.

One evening, he said out of nowhere, "You're not allowed to date until you're sixteen, you know."

"Huh? I'm not dating."

Dad looked at me, unblinking. Suddenly, it felt like a game of chicken. Finally, he said, "Okay. But just . . . remember . . . no dating."

"Until I'm sixteen. I know, I know," I said, laughing.

He didn't laugh back.

Later, I yelled at my mother, threatening not to confide in her ever again. But, of course, I did tell her when Dusty said hi to me unprovoked during gym class, and I told her about another time when he passed by me in the hallway during Colors Week and said "Heyyy, Allie," smiling.

I didn't tell her about the time Chloe Stern dared me to ask him to play Spin the Bottle with us downstairs at her house after her bat mitzvah.

How he turned me down.

How I cried for a week.

Then we moved again, and it was a nonissue.

I understood Dad was disappointed in himself, because he wanted to be better than his parents. Although a lot of Muslim parents were becoming more progressive, the old generation was still conservative.

To be fair, this was something my Catholic cousins had to deal with, too. My older cousin Julie told me at an aunt's funeral that Uncle Robert once made a sexist joke about a shotgun and an alibi.

So maybe it's not a religious thing. Maybe it's generational.

Or maybe it's just my family.

Lucky me.

Mom ignores me, turning on her soothing psychologist voice for Dad. "Your child turning sixteen, starting to date, perhaps displacing you in your mind, making you feel older than you see yourself . . . these are milestones. It's only natural to have big feelings."

Big feelings. OMG. She's using toddlerspeak to pacify my dad.

He frowns again. His face is one permanent, never-ending frown.

"I swore I wouldn't be like *Jido* was with my sisters. And here we are." He clears his throat a couple times. "I gave you my word, and I intend to keep it. Why don't you invite Wells over to the house? Give us a chance to meet him."

Abort! Danger!

"I mean, he really is just a friend . . . but sure," I say, knowing there's no way out of it. "He mentioned doing something for my birthday. Maybe he can come inside for a few minutes beforehand."

Dad looks wounded. "You're not spending your birthday with us? I thought we could pick up a cake, pop some Martinelli's, watch whatever movie you like . . ."

His face breaks my heart.

"Sounds incredible, Dad. Could we do it the night before, instead?"

He sighs. "It begins."

I give my parents kisses on the head and race up the stairs

two at a time, feeling as if I've won some battle I didn't know I was fighting.

After closing my door and double-checking to make sure it's locked, I scoot against the headboard, reach into my purse, and take the Qur'an out of the bookstore bag. I run my fingers over the cool, smooth cover and flip through the book, turning the pages. Contraband.

I remember once hearing there were special rules for handling the Qur'an, but I feel embarrassed that I don't know if this is true. I grab my phone, turning to Professor Google, which says:

> The central religious text of Islam, the holy Qur'an is a divine revelation directly from God through the archangel Gabriel to the final Prophet Muhammad (PBUH). Due to the Qur'an's sacred nature, there exist special rules that Muslims must follow when touching, handling, or reading from it. It is *haram* to touch the Qur'an before performing ritualistic *wudu* cleansing, and it is *haram* to touch the Qur'an while unclean. When not in use, the Qur'an must be stored in a clean, respectable place, with nothing on top of it, and should never be placed on the floor or brought into a bathroom. Above all, it is always essential to show respect for the Qur'an's sacred nature.

I cringe, thinking of the Qur'an jammed at the bottom of my bag all day. After putting my phone in do-not-disturb mode,

I open the Qur'an and start from the beginning. The first chapter is Surah al-Fatihah—literally, "The Opening:"

In the name of God, the Lord of Mercy, the Giver of Mercy!

I lose myself in the pages, reading passages and pausing to cross-reference them online.

"Allie! Dinner!"

I startle at my father's voice and shove the Qur'an into my nightstand, between my Bullet Journal and some old copies of *Entertainment Weekly*. I'm at the door before I guiltily realize what I've done. I remove the Qur'an from the drawer carefully with both hands, as if my sudden reverence will make up for everything.

We try to have a proper family dinner together every night. My dad says it was chaos when he was a kid, and Grandfather was always at the hospital during my mom's childhood. Each of them vowed they'd do sit-down dinners when they had their own kids.

It's wine for Mom and Dad, cran-raspberry LaCroix for me. We clink glasses and cheer.

Mom passes the meatballs, launching into a story about how she accidentally double-booked clients when her assistant was on vacation. The clients showed up within two minutes of each other and each tried to convince her their needs were more urgent.

As Dad talks about the stresses of grant applications, I smile and nod politely. I want to get back upstairs so I can read more of the Qur'an.

A thought I *never* thought would run through my mind.

When Mom brings up Wells again, I look at her like, *What are you* doing, *woman?*

"Do you know what you two are doing for your birthday?" she says.

"No," I say.

"What's he like?" Dad asks.

"Uh . . . I don't know. Nice. Funny. Cheerful."

"A rousing endorsement," Mom says. She doesn't mention she's already met him. "What's he into?"

I shrug. "Soccer. Classic rock. Conservation stuff. Star Wars."

Dad puts his napkin on the table.

"What kind of things do you do together?" Mom says.

Seriously. She's trying to kill me.

"I dunno. Do homework. Listen to music. Watch movies."

She nods knowingly. "Netflix and chill."

Dad and I exchange a look. I can't help laughing, even though I'm mortified.

"Elizabeth," Dad says, "that doesn't mean what you think it means."

"What?" Mom says innocently.

At the end of the meal, Mom brings out a plate of cupcakes.

"Stress-baking?" Dad asks.

Mom exhales in a puff. "Last week took it out of me."

When Mom gets overwhelmed by the emotional demands of her job, she finds solace in flour and sugar. She once explained it to me: "There's no concrete answer with people. Baking is different. It's precise, like math. There's an equation. You do it properly, you get it right."

If only life were that simple.

After Mom heads upstairs to read, Dad turns to me. "I'm playing hooky from doing dishes. Should we do Quizzes before I grade papers?"

Quizzes is my dad's shorthand for practicing a wide variety of Quiz Bowl topics: everything from world capitals to famous works of art to notable dates in history. It's another way Dad and I have bonded: him shooting rapid-fire questions, me lobbing the answers back. We've been doing it since I was a kid, and it's why I'm so good at *Jeopardy!* and Trivial Pursuit, and anything involving the parroting of useless, easy-to-memorize facts.

If I'm being honest? Quizzes is the *last* thing I want to do tonight. I want to read more Qur'an. I've got homework to do. I have to warn Wells about meeting my parents. Plus, after today's awkwardness, I need to digest what the heck is going on with Wells in the first place.

I'm busy.

I can't say that to my dad, though. After our conversation earlier, it would crush him.

"Sure, Dad." I muster up every last bit of energy to make my smile look enthused.

"Should we do American history?" His favorite, of course.

"Perfect."

"What year was Jamestown settled?"

"In 1607. Although obviously the Indigenous people were there long before Captain John Smith arrived."

He nods. "Points for background. When did the Boston Massacre happen?"

"March 5, 1770."

"Boston Tea Party?"

"Dad. Come on. December 16, 1773. This is middle school stuff. Give me a hard one. More than just dates." Despite myself, I'm getting into it.

He looks down at the floor as he strokes his face, pensive. "Which group of leaders was established by the National Security Act of 1947?"

"Ooh. Hmm. The Joint Chiefs?"

"Right. Which president's farewell address warned against the unwarranted influence of the military-industrial complex?"

"Dwight D. Eisenhower?"

"Well done!" He beams. "My smart girl."

I grin. "I'm getting good, right?"

"Proud of you. Should we try literature? I've got a few Shakespearean quotes up my sleeve," he says. "Which character fears her husband is 'too full o' th' milk of human kindness'?"

My phone buzzes in my pocket. I pull it out. It's Wells.

Hey. Did I say something to make you angry?

"Dad, I hate to stop, but I have a ton of homework," I say. "It's Lady Macbeth, by the way. Can we do more tomorrow?"

To his credit, if he's disappointed, he doesn't show it. "Sure, pumpkin."

He stands up, giving me a kiss on the head and wincing a bit as he walks into the kitchen to fulfill his dishes duty. He was in the Jordanian army when he was young, and hurt his back during a military exercise. It's been more than twenty years, and he says he can still clock the weather by his bad back.

I feel guilty as I watch Dad walk away. Being an only means there's no buffer between my parents and me. It's just us against the world. You have to be cool with your parents; otherwise, it wouldn't work.

And anyway, my parents are cool people.

Most of the time.

My phone buzzes again, and I jump up, run up the stairs to my room, and close the door.

Privacy at last.

I pull out my phone, staring at Wells's text.

The realization that I have any sort of power over Wells is a heady one. The simple act of me pulling away from him seems to have thrown him off-kilter, so he's now reaching out to make sure it's all good.

It's a fascinating realization: Even the cutest guys get nervous, too. Wells is a person with insecurities, the same as me.

And suddenly, knowledge dawns with absolute certainty:

This guy really likes me.

CHAPTER NINE

"You look wonderful, Allie," Mom says, beaming.

"You look very nice," Dad says, looking like he's smelled something slightly unpleasant.

The three of us sit in the living room, waiting for Wells to arrive. I'm wearing a blue dress that flatters my skin and sets off my red hair.

"When we said you could date at sixteen, who knew you'd take us up on it the day of your birthday." Mom laughs. "Eager beaver."

Dad purses his lips as the doorbell rings.

Let's do this thing.

I open the door, and Wells enters, looking edible. He's wearing a pair of dress loafers and has on a nice button-down shirt tucked into a pair of khaki pants. His hair is slightly wet, and his curls are raked back.

It feels like we're playing at being adults.

"Wells," Mom says, stepping forward and hugging him. "It's good to see you."

Dad's head swivels toward Mom. I read his thoughts: *See? Not meet?*

Wells clears his throat, looking at Dad warily. They reach out and shake hands, engaging in a rousing pumping: up-down-up-down-up-down-up-down.

"Allie says you're a professor at Emory, sir," Wells says.

"That's right." My dad takes a step back, fidgeting and scratching his nose.

"History?"

"That's right."

"Dad, Wells has family in New York," I say, hoping to steer the conversation along.

"Is that so?" Dad asks. "Where in New York?"

"About an hour outside the city. In Purchase?"

Dad nods. "College town."

"Yup." Wells is nervous, too. "We spend holidays there every other year."

"Nice place."

"You've been there"—he clears his throat—"sir?"

"No, but I know of it."

I've never heard of Purchase, but judging by Wells's current fortress and the fact that Dad is now looking semi-impressed, it must be nice enough to warrant a drive-through and house-gawk.

"Oh, Dad. Wells loves soccer, too. He's on the JV team."

"You mentioned," Dad says, looking interested. "Galaxy fan, right?"

"Man United, actually. What about you?"

"Galaxy," Dad says, looking mildly disappointed.

Strike one, Wells.

"Photo time!" Mom walks back into the foyer, brandishing the camera.

"Mom," I hiss. "Come on, you have a billion photos of me."

"It's your first date! *And* it's your birthday."

"But, for the love of kittens, it's not prom."

I don't say, *It's not a date*, because . . . I think it's a date.

"Cut your poor mother a break," Dad says. "Okay, stand over here. Wells . . . you go right there . . . On her left, yep, there . . . Perfect, that's good."

I stiffen as Wells comes and stands next to me, praying he won't do anything embarrassing, like put his arm around me or, *God forbid*, hold my hand. Luckily, he reads my mind, standing shoulder to shoulder with me and facing the camera, with his hands clasped in front of him. I clutch my purse in front of my stomach, a protective shield against the painful awkwardness.

This would be a zillion times less weird if Dad weren't here. It doesn't help that the look on Dad's face is somewhere in between perturbed and constipated: I think he's enjoying this about as much as I am.

Still, at least he's trying.

Mom snaps the picture. "Happy birthday, sweetheart!"

The two of them give me a hug, and Wells shakes Dad's hand goodbye.

"Happy freaking birthday," he whispers to me as we walk out the door.

"Shh. Let's get out of here."

We giggle quietly as we rush toward the truck, my parents' silhouettes framed in the doorway behind us.

Wells drives through Milton, the radio turned to the alternative channel playing a jaunty old Foo Fighters song.

"So you've never been on a date, huh?" Wells says.

"I turned sixteen like five seconds ago. Has *anybody* we know been on a date?"

He laughs. I love his laugh. It makes me think of a country song, full of honey and heartache. I wonder what else makes him laugh.

"*Is* this a date?" he says, amusement in his voice.

I blush. I look down at my sleek dress. Tonight I went for a Carolyn Bessette-Kennedy vibe. "I don't know. No. Maybe. I told them we're just friends."

He glances over at me at a red light. I want to crawl across the steering wheel and plant one on him. "Too bad," he says.

I giggle nervously, a Jackson Pollock patchwork of embarrassment no doubt renting advertising space on my chest.

"Your parents seem cool," he says.

"Yeah. They're both total dorks, but it's only the three of us, so . . ." I shrug. "You? Siblings?"

"A younger brother. Sawyer. He's annoying."

"Like all little brothers."

"My parents aren't as cool as yours."

"No?"

"Okay, it's mostly my dad. My mom's the best."

"What's his deal?"

He grips the steering wheel, shrugging. "You know dads."

A tight-lipped nonresponse. I don't press the issue.

We park at Avalon, Alpharetta's fancy outdoor mall, and walk to a steak house at the far end, passing ice-cream shops, wine bars, and clothing boutiques.

"Holy kittens, we're eating here?" I ask.

Wells grins. "Come on, birthday girl."

"Wells Henderson, two for six thirty," he says to the hostess. I swear, his voice sounds like it's dropped an octave. She escorts us through the dimly lit room to a corner booth.

I check out the room. It feels like a country club: low lighting, leather banquettes, wood paneling. "Wells, this place is *legit*."

He unfurls his napkin with gusto, looking proud. "Do you like it?"

"Obviously."

But my stomach clenches when I read the menu. What is all this foie gras and beef tartare and duck confit crap? Can't a girl get a regular cheeseburger—one *without* feta?

The two of us peruse the menu in silence. At one point, I glance up, and Wells is frowning, looking as dismayed as I feel.

"Uh, what are you getting?" he asks.

I review the menu for the fifth time, as if a nonfancy option will suddenly present itself. "Um."

He peers at the menu. "What's caponata?"

I pull out my phone. "Looks like it's Sicilian eggplant."

"Oh. I'm probably just going to get the burger. Plain."

"Me too."

We both start giggling.

"Zadie would be *so* disappointed in us," I say. She's the adventurous eater of the group.

"I'm sorry," he says.

"Don't be sorry!"

"You hate it."

"I might not love the menu, but I love the gesture."

He looks dejected. "I wanted to make it special."

"Wells, it *is* special. This is awesome. I've never been to a place like this without my parents. It's like we're in college. Perfect for my sixteenth birthday. Thank you."

I reach across the table and put my hand on top of his. The touch makes his frown melt away.

"You deserve better," he says. "I have an idea."

Ten minutes later, after apologies to the waitstaff and the hostess, we're sitting in a pizzeria farther down the promenade, tucking into a large formaggio.

"Now *this* is perfect." I smile at him, taking a sip of Coke. "God, this pizza is soooo good."

"You sure?" he asks, looking anxious.

"It's perfect. I mean it."

After we demolish the cheese pizza together, we walk to a nearby ice-cream parlor, talking until our throats are scratchy and it feels like we've covered absolutely everything.

I tell him about my comp sci project and my mega course load, and how I'm dying to go to Northwestern, and how I kind of want to be an actress even though I'm shy, and how sometimes I suspect maybe the secret of life is to become a rich lawyer and eat your feelings.

He tells me about his YouTube channel and the recording studio sessions he's saving up for, and his insomnia and his worries about the environment, and how, when he's in front of a crowd, his nerves magically disappear and for a few moments, he feels free.

We talk and talk—except there are still worlds left unsaid.

I don't tell him about my heritage. I don't tell him the horrible things people have said to me about Muslims. Not just in Georgia. In Chicago, New Jersey, LA, Dallas. Everywhere.

I don't tell him I have a hard time saying no because I don't want people to dislike me.

I don't tell him that, sometimes, after I go to sleep, I curl up with a blanket *Teta* gave me when I was two years old, and I smell it and I remember being little, and I feel safe.

I wonder what he's not telling me.

Back in front of my house, the two of us sit in his truck, the radio turned low as Wells puts the engine in park.

"Hi." I laugh nervously as he turns to me.

"Hi back." His brown eyes dilate, his pupils large like a thousand black holes, dragging me into the depths of Wells.

"Tonight was incredible," I say.

"Really?"

"Are you for serious, Henderson?"

We grin at each other, but then the mood shifts.

I look down at my hands, because I'm not sure where to look, and then I decide to take a chance and look back up. The emotions flicker across his face in rapid fire: tenderness and anxiety, mixed with a heavy dose of lust.

"Wells," I say, half question, half invitation, looking into his eyes and thinking about how there is nothing more I want in the entire world than to finally kiss him.

So I do.

I lean over the armrest, putting my hand on his hair and pulling his face toward me. His lips are soft and warm, and as they part, gently pressing down onto mine, a strange feeling takes over my body. I know I'm not supposed to be doing this, I know this goes against my religion, I know my parents would not be thrilled if they peeked through the curtains and saw me sucking face with Wells Henderson in his monster truck, but I don't care. Because right now the only thing that matters is Wells, and his lips, and his arms wrapping themselves tightly around my back—pulling me closer until it feels as if we're one.

It's the perfect first kiss.

And the best birthday ever.

CHAPTER TEN

I wake up fretting.

What happens after the first kiss?

Are we boyfriend-girlfriend?

What if he pretends it never happened?

What if he changes his mind?

What if he decides I was a horrible kisser, and ghosts me forever?

I roll over, picking up my phone: 9:17 a.m.

There's a text waiting from Wells:

Wanna come over today?

Ahhh. Praise kittens.

Any lingering anxiety is dispelled once my mom's car disappears from sight after dropping me off at Wells's house.

"Hey," he says in that cute voice, looking kind of nervous. He takes a step forward, picking up my hand and pulling me toward him.

"Hi," I manage to squeak.

He wraps his arms around me, and I melt into him for a long, delicious kiss. He puts his hand on the side of my face.

Okay, I'm pretty sure he likes me back.

Later that afternoon, after takeout Mexican and a make-out session, followed by a viewing of *Rogue One* on Wells's basement big-screen, somebody calls to us from upstairs.

"Wells?" It's a woman's voice.

"Coming!" He turns to me. "My mom. Wanna meet her?"

"Sure," I say casually, as if this isn't a gigantic deal.

We enter a gleaming white kitchen. My eyes dart around the massive room: matching dish towels, artfully propped-up cookbooks opened to recipe pages and probably *not* covered in sticky leftover goo, decorative porcelain plates. It's like being inside a Williams Sonoma.

His mother stands at the white marble island. "Thought you and your friend might like some, Wellsie," she says, proffering a tray of freshly baked cookies.

My mom occasionally bakes cookies, too, but she doesn't look like Martha flipping Stewart while she's doing it. Meanwhile, Wells's mom is straight from perfect-Providence-mom central casting: white-blond hair, pale-blue eyes, pearls in her ears, a gigantic gleaming diamond on her ring finger.

"Mom," Wells says, "this is Allie."

"Allie," she says. "It's lovely to meet you. I'm Serena." She gives me a hug, smelling of vanilla. "Are you in a rush?" She directs us to the kitchen table. "Go sit. I'll bring you a tray."

"It's okay, Mom," Wells says.

"You'll love them!" she insists.

When somebody makes you homemade cookies, you don't say no.

Around five thirty, stuffed with cookies and drunk on Wells, it's time for me to go home for dinner.

Wells and I walk outside, waiting for my mom.

He brushes his fingers through my hair.

"Killing a bug?" I say. That's what I do when I feel awkward. I make bad jokes.

In response, he leans down and kisses me. The two of us lean into each other, swaying back and forth. Wells's touch is magic—when his arms are around me, my anxiety disappears.

A black Cadillac Escalade pulls into the long circular driveway, letting out three staccato beeps. Wells's face tightens.

"My dad's never home this early."

The driver's-side door opens, and an imposing man steps out. He's surprisingly handsome, with sharp brown eyes and a square jaw. His white shirt is crisp, his black suit is subtly shiny, and the red bow tie around his neck perfectly matches the square tucked into his lapel pocket.

It takes me two seconds to realize who it is, and in those two seconds my heart falls into my feet, smashing into a million little pieces.

Wells's father is Jack Henderson.

TV pundit Jack Henderson.

Blowhard Jack Henderson.

Muslim-hating Jack Henderson.

He's always on TV, barking about immigration and "radical Islamic terrorism" and the "tyranny of safe spaces." And, of course, he famously lives in Atlanta—cable news central.

"Dad, this is Allie." Wells sounds nervous. "Allie . . . this is my father."

Jack Henderson shakes my hand. "Hi, Allie," he says, his voice deep. "Nice to meet you, darlin'. You're at Providence with Wells?"

I nod.

"Looks like you already know my son pretty well."

He pats Wells on the back with a wink and gives me a big smile—so that's where Wells gets his perfect teeth from. He heads inside before we have a chance to say anything else. I'm literally trembling as he walks away.

"You okay?" Wells asks.

"Yeah."

"I should have told you. I worried—"

"It's fine."

"Everybody has that reaction at first. Not *everybody*, but . . . you know . . . people who aren't . . . fans." He clears his throat.

He doesn't even know.

"It's fine," I repeat.

"You sure?"

Just then, my mom pulls her car into the driveway behind Wells's dad's. She waves, looking happy for me.

"I gotta go," I say. I stand on my tiptoes to give Wells a peck on the lips. I'm tall, and he still towers over me. "Text you later."

As mom drives away, humming along to the Dave Matthews Band, I watch Wells receding in the rearview mirror. My heart pounds as I try to make sense of what happened—and of what's about to happen.

"A kiss, huh? Not just a friend anymore?" Mom smiles at me, oblivious.

"Mmm."

Wells's nervousness had nothing to do with me, and everything to do with him. God knows, I don't want to be cynical. I want to have faith.

But I don't need a crystal ball to predict that once he finds out the truth, things will change—and probably not for the better.

After all, I'm sure America's most famous conservative pundit—the author of bestsellers like *This Land Is My Land . . . So Get Out!* and *Not Safe in Our Own Country: Radical Islam's War from Within on the American Way*, the man who's made yelling a national sport—will blow a gasket when he finds out his son's new girlfriend is Muslim.

PART TWO

CHAPTER ELEVEN

I knock gently on the door, where several kids are in the first-floor biology classroom across from the library. It's half an hour before first bell.

Heads swivel, a handful of welcoming faces.

"Hi," I say shyly. "Is this the Muslim Student Association meeting?"

"Allie! Hi. *Salaam.* Come in." Dua, previously hidden, stands to greet me. "Everybody, this is Allie Abraham."

They say hi, an intermingled chorus of "*Salaam*" and "Hey" and "Hi."

I take a seat in the back, underneath a double-helix poster.

The last twenty-four hours have been surreal.

Wells is now my boyfriend. *Are we using that word? Let's use that word.* Dad hasn't had a coronary about me dating. And I'm finally sixteen. So I'm basically all grown up.

But.

Apparently, my new boyfriend's father is the biggest racist in America.

Jack. Freaking. Henderson.

Of all the parents in the world.

People are on edge again. At the mosque near Aunt Bila's house in Dallas, there was a bomb threat. Aunt Bila told Dad she and *Teta* were hissed at yesterday while shopping for groceries, some woman telling them to "take those things off" their heads.

And worse. In Virginia, a mosque was set on fire.

It's not a talking point. It's not theoretical. It's real.

I feel guilty it's taken me this long to stop hiding.

I hope other Muslims can forgive me.

Wells and I haven't talked about his dad. Last night was the first one in a long time where we didn't text before bed. It took me all night to process, but while showering this morning, I thought: *What am I scared of? Why am I holding back? Talk to him.*

Yeah, I'm white-looking. Sure, my mom is a convert.

I'm still Muslim. I'm allowed to claim it.

So here I am.

"It's a mistake," a boy says, clearly picking up a conversation from before I entered. His voice is full of confidence, but he's small and scrawny—obviously in ninth grade. I wonder if I ever looked that tiny to older kids. "They should use the money for a new STEM center. Why do we need a bigger football stadium? Who cares?"

"Um, everybody," a tall girl with olive-brown skin and a

shoulder-skimming haircut replies. "This is Georgia, Hamid. Not San Francisco."

"More robots, fewer running backs. Got it. Good luck with that," Dua says, glancing at her phone to check the time. "Okay, everybody here?" She takes roll.

There are two boys and six girls in the group, some faces new to me, others I vaguely recognize from around campus: this guy Pratam from the baseball team, this girl Maya who I think might be in marching band. Dua moves from topic to topic with self-assuredness, clearly the group leader.

I sit, listening quietly and not saying much. I expected it to be a Qur'an study group, but instead they discuss issues such as graffiti at a local mosque and prominent Muslims to follow on Twitter. I make a mental note to create an account.

When Dua starts talking about the International Rescue Committee fund-raiser, I realize they haven't met their goal yet.

"A hundred and ten bucks, people. Not great."

"Our goal is five thousand," Hamid says.

"Aaaand that's why I'm bringing it up," Dua says in a gentle tone. "Any suggestions?"

A few people throw out ideas.

"Bake sale?"

"Car wash?"

"We should totally do a GoFundMe."

I wait until everybody else has gone before raising my hand.

"Allie," Dua says, pointing to me as if she's a teacher.

"I have a little more to contribute," I say, reaching into my purse and pulling out twenty dollars, my allowance for the week.

It'll mean forgoing the movies this weekend, but after I talk to Wells about his dad, chances are my schedule will be cleared indefinitely.

At the end of the meeting, everybody prays together before saying goodbye and making plans to meet in a month.

"Should we do Waffle House next time?" Hamid asks.

Dua pulls a face. "Seriously?"

"There are no bad suggestions," he huffs.

As I'm heading out the door, Dua calls after me.

"Hey, Allie."

I turn back. "Yeah?"

"I'm happy you came."

I give her a dorky little wave as I turn back out the door, feeling grateful to be included.

Wells and I don't talk about his dad during chorus or algebra. We don't talk much period, actually. It's a simple equation: awkwardness + avoidance = silence.

It's not until after school, when we're sitting next to each other in the auditorium for musical tryouts, that I work up the courage to bring it up.

"Your dad."

My heart pounds in that jackhammer way it always does when confrontation is imminent. Normally, I'm all about that avoidance life. This is different.

He leans back in his seat, not looking at me. "Yeah."

"Does everybody at school know?"

He shrugs. "Yeah. I guess. But it's not like I go around broadcasting it." His word choice feels ironic, considering his father's job. "People know I don't really talk about it."

"Is he different?" I say. "Than on TV? Is that just a character?"

Wells scratches his head. "I dunno."

I try a different tack.

"Do you share his views?"

This yanks Wells out of his stupor. He glances my way. "No."

"I mean . . . you can see why I'd be concerned, right?" My voice is so icy it could freeze Lake Lanier. "With him spouting that divisive BS?"

Wells frowns. He looks conflicted. "I get it."

"Do you?" I ask, cocking my head.

He knits his brow. "Are you okay?"

"I was surprised, that's all."

We sit in silence, watching the kids file into the auditorium. Emilia enters, smiling and waving at people like she's on the red carpet at the Oscars. Mr. Tucker waits onstage, bathed in the glow of the theater lights.

"Does your dad know Zadie is half-Mexican?" I ask Wells.

Wells looks startled. "I don't know. Probably."

"What about Joey? Does he have an issue with the fact he's Black?"

"Allie, where are you going with this?" Wells sounds irritated.

I blow out my frustration in a puff. "Your dad is kind of toxic, Wells. Can't you see that?"

"Allie. Come on."

Something inside me snaps.

"Are you collecting people?" I say.

"What?"

"I mean, all your friends are from groups your dad actively hates. How do you think that makes them feel?"

Wells looks pissed. "Stop it. He's still my dad."

He stands up and walks across the aisle, sitting in a chair a few feet away from me.

"Good afternoon, students!" Mr. Tucker says. "We'll go in order of last names, alphabetically. When I call your name, please come up here and tell us which character you intend to audition for, and what song you'll be performing."

I'm first—the burden of having a last name beginning with *A*. I go through the motions, performing a middling version of "Hopelessly Devoted to You," then sit through several more auditions waiting for Wells's turn.

Once he's finished singing "Sandy," he walks up the aisle and out of the auditorium, the door shutting behind him without him giving me a backward glance.

CHAPTER TWELVE

Bell rings. Twelve noon. Lunchtime.

After grabbing my lunch cooler from my locker, I walk outside, forgoing the cafeteria. I can't deal with Mikey, Emilia, and the crew.

Wells and I haven't talked or texted since our fight yesterday. This morning, I didn't walk into chorus until after the bell rang, and I sat as far away from him as possible. We made eye contact in algebra once, but that was it. Otherwise, nada.

There's a row of park benches in the front of the school, to the right of the parking lot and by the old log cabin near the cemetery.

Dua sits alone at one of the wooden tables, drawing in a notebook. Her hands look like they're used to sketching—her thumb and forefinger have deep inky smudges on them.

I cough. "Um, hi."

She looks up, startled. When she sees it's me, her face relaxes. "Oh, hi, Allie! What's up?"

"Do you mind if I sit?" I feel nervous.

"Knock yourself out."

I sit down at the table next to her, pulling out my sandwich and eating in silence. Dua seems content to draw, and I don't want to bother her more than I already have.

It's not until I'm halfway through the sandwich that it occurs to me Dua's not eating. I look her clothes up and down—she's not wearing the unofficial Providence High School uniform of Hollister, Michael Kors, and Tory Burch, but I don't think she's low-income, either. She probably can afford lunch, but I don't want to assume—Providence has its fair share of underprivileged people. After all, it used to be a rural suburb—a literal one-stoplight town. Not that you'd know it from the student parking lot full of brand-new luxury cars.

"Um, I'm not eating this other half," I say. "Do you like turkey? Want it?"

"Nah, I'm good," she says. "Thanks."

"You probably already ate," I say, feeling silly.

She pauses, as if weighing her words. Finally she smiles and says, "No food for me today. I'm fasting."

I put my sandwich down, fascinated. "You're fasting? Why?"

She pauses again.

"I'm sorry. I'm so rude. You don't have to answer—obviously."

"No worries. I'm making up Ramadan days I missed last year."

I nod, saying, "Ah, right," in a tone implying I know what

she's talking about. The fact is, I didn't know you could make up days for Ramadan. I've never fasted before.

To be fair, my parents never asked me to fast. Most of my cousins do, but they grew up in households where Ramadan was a *thing*.

As opposed to mine, where Ramadan was a thing to be avoided.

Her eyes run over me as if my innermost thoughts are a barcode and she's the LED light scanning my secrets. She says, "Your dad is Mo Abraham, right?"

"Yeah. How'd you know?"

She nods triumphantly, as though a crucial fact has been gleaned. "My mom has his books. Plus, it's not like Providence is crawling with Muslims. You know who's who."

"That makes sense," I say, feeling guilty, like I should make an excuse for why I'm not more open about my family. I look down at my sandwich. "Do you want me to put this away? I shouldn't be eating in front of you. Sorry."

"It's fine! I'm used to it," she says. "It's not your fault I'm fasting—my choice."

I nod, desperately wanting to ask her a million questions but not wanting to be rude.

She must see it in my eyes, because she laughs. "What do you want to ask me?"

"It's just"—I say gratefully—"why do you have to make up the fast?"

"If you miss days, you need to make them up later. Otherwise, your fasts don't count."

"Right. Totally." I don't ask her why somebody might miss a fast. I'll look it up online later.

"My turn," she says. "Can I ask you a question?"

"Of course."

"Your mom is Christian, right?"

"No, she's Muslim. She converted when she married my dad."

Dua looks surprised. "Really? Huh. Okay."

"Why?"

"I shouldn't have assumed. Do you practice?"

"No," I say, my cheeks feeling hot. "My dad's kind of weird about religion. I call his family on *Eid*, and if we're in town, my mom's family makes me go to church on Easter. That's about it."

She smiles. "I love those ornate Gothic cathedrals—the kind where it smells like incense and dead guys are buried in the alcoves, you know? The bigger the better. Don't tell my mom." She stands up, looking at her phone. "I gotta go. See you around? Next MSA meeting?"

"Definitely."

"Don't worry, we're *not* doing Waffle House." She walks away, giving me a tiny wave.

As she's halfway across the driveway, she turns around. "Hey, Allie?"

"Yeah?"

"No pressure, but if you're into it, I'm part of a Qur'an study group. No guys, no regressive gender politics, total safe space. We meet once a week, on Sundays."

"Oh!" I say. "I'd love to." I hope she can't sense my anxiety.

The idea of hanging out with Muslim girls who aren't my family makes me nervous. I'm not one of them.

"Cool!" she says, coming back to the table. "I'll text you the info."

"Can't wait," I say, handing her my phone and trying to put on a confident, breezy face masking my terror.

After I finish my sandwich, I look at my watch. There's still time left in lunch period. Nothing to do but walk back inside to my usual table.

"There you are!" Emilia scoots over to make room.

"Did you get in trouble or something?" Sarah says. She and Emilia are both wearing red polo shirts with red ribbons in their hair; they must have a softball game today.

"I ate outside today."

"Why?" Emilia takes a dainty bite of her farfalle pasta. "It's gross outside."

"I needed to get some homework done."

They turn back to their conversations, seeming satisfied by my lie.

"And then my dad goes, 'I promise, it's not what it looks like!'" Mikey says, continuing some story, oblivious to me. "But it was nasty, dude. You do *not* want to catch your parents like that."

As my friends surround me, talking and laughing—friends I've worked so hard to make over the past few months—I've never felt lonelier.

CHAPTER THIRTEEN

That's how I find myself in a car with Mom two days later, on the way to Dua's house for study group.

"Since you're sixteen, we should think about finally going for your driver's license," she says, for the fiftieth time.

"Maybe next month," I reply, for the fiftieth time.

She grumbles as we barrel down State Bridge Road, passing yet another Waffle House—Atlanta mandates one on every street corner in the burbs. "When I was your age, a car was freedom," she says. "It's *beyond* me why you're not begging me for your real license. I harassed my mother every day until she let me get a car."

I grin at her as we turn onto Medlock Bridge, toward Dua's house. "Why get a car when it's easier for you to drive me?"

"Easier for whom?" she says, rolling her eyes.

"But we get to spend quality time together!"

She bursts out laughing. "You're good, kid. You're very good."

I peek at my phone as we turn into the subdivision. Still nothing from Wells. It's been radio silence since our fight.

Normally, I'd reflexively apologize for going off about his dad, but something inside me has shifted. After finding out he's Jack Henderson's son, I see him differently. I know that's not fair, but I can't help it—and if we're going to work, I need him to meet me halfway.

But now it's been *three* whole days since we've spoken—an actual, literal I-can't-even-deal-with-it eternity.

What sucks is we were finally starting to get close to each other.

Although I guess not *that* close.

The group is at a different person's house each week. This week is Dua's turn.

Once she sees Dua answer the door, my mother waves cheerfully and drives away, pantomiming using a telephone for picking me up later.

"Hi! I'm happy you made it," Dua says, hugging me.

I hug her back, grinning. "Me too."

Inside the foyer, the Mahmoud house initially reminds me of my aunt Bila's: elaborate gold-plated Qur'an calligraphy art framed on the walls, potted plants almost as tall as the ceiling, intricate Persian rugs. But where Aunt Bila's house is colorful and chaotic, Dua's is soothing and elegant: shades of beige, cream, and taupe; cashmere throws; soft lighting.

The great room is massive, with an open-plan two-story layout, but it somehow manages to feel cozy instead of cavernous.

In the center, there's a wooden coffee table covered in sweets and displaying an expensive gold tea set, with the other girls in the group perched on a long L-shaped wraparound couch, shoeless feet tucked underneath them. They look at me expectantly as I trail Dua into the room. I want to hide—instead, I picture "I Have Confidence" from *The Sound of Music*, an imaginary nun running around the corners of my brain and belting out inspiration.

Why, yes I *do* bring imaginary singing nuns with me to Qur'an study group. No wonder I'm so mixed up.

"Everybody, this is Allie, from my school. Allie, this is Fatima Thompson, Leila Elmahdy, and Shamsah Amin. And, of course, our fearless leader Samira Wahab." Everybody laughs.

Samira is older than the other girls—maybe midtwenties. She has a pleasant smile and wears a peach-colored headscarf with blue flowers on it. I wonder how she manages to look so pretty in the scarf with her round face. Over the years, whenever I've tried playing with a headscarf—in the privacy of my room, obviously—I look ridiculous.

"*Salaam*, Allie. Thanks for coming!" Samira's voice is soothing, with a slight Southern lilt.

"*Salaam*," I say shyly, putting my hand up in a wave. I gingerly take a seat in a sectional chair opposite them, which has the effect of making me feel like I'm either interviewing or on trial. "Thank you for having me."

"Hi, Allie," the girls say back in unison, their faces happy and smiling. I bet they come from homes where they say "*bismillah*" before driving, and where there's a Qur'an by the bed, and where none of them have ever felt they weren't Muslim enough.

Or maybe I'm projecting.

"Shall we introduce ourselves and tell Allie how we came together?" Samira says. "I'll start. I'm Samira, just graduated from Emory with a degree in Islamic civilizations. I was born and raised in Atlanta. I'm active in the North Fulton Muslim community, where I met Dua and Shamsah's mothers. I love running and have a weakness for spicy food." She grins. "It's the Malaysian in me."

A girl in an electric-blue hijab smiles at me next, her white teeth highlighted by candy-apple-red lipstick. "Hey, Allie, I'm Leila. Um, I'm originally from Florida, outside Fort Lauderdale. My mom and Shamsah's mom are like BFFs, so. I'm a junior at Northview, and I'm still not over y'all crushing us at homecoming, so you're gonna have to make it up to me," she says, and laughs. "Um, let's see. I'm also obsessed with SoulCycle."

"Shamsah," another girl says next, raising her hand in greeting. She has a sandy complexion, curly black hair, and wide-set eyes, heavily rimmed with makeup. There's a coiled, confident way about her. "Senior at Westminster." The Harvard of Atlanta prep schools. "If we're doing the dating profile thing, I like weekends at the lake and Zendaya movies."

"Hi! I'm Fatima." A younger-looking girl with dark-brown skin smiles at me. "My family converted when I was six, but that was a long time ago. I'm in ninth grade at Johns Creek, and Dua and I met last year—our brothers are friends. I love to cook, and I'm gonna go to culinary school so I can open up my own restaurant in VaHi. Oh, and I love Harry Styles."

"Not Zayn?" Dua says, teasing.

Fatima frowns. "Zayn needs to get his act *together.*"

"And I'm Dua. Obviously."

Heads swivel to me.

"Um, I'm a sophomore at Providence with Dua." *Steady hands, Allie! You're introducing yourself to a group of peers, not giving a TED talk.* "I was born in Texas, but we moved here over the summer from outside Chicago. And I'm Circassian—well, half-Circassian. My dad is from Jordan, and my mom is American." I look at Fatima and smile. "I like Harry Styles, too."

She beams back at me.

"Allie, why don't you tell us more about Circassians?" Samira says. She must have noticed the confusion on Leila's face. "I'm sure we could use a little primer."

I twist my hands. The first few lines of "I Have Confidence" play through my head again.

"So Circassians are from southwestern Russia, in the Caucasus Mountains near Turkey," I say. "You know when the Olympics were in Sochi? That's basically my ethnic backyard. Most people don't know who Circassians are, but they used to be famous in the 1800s, mostly because the women were totally beautiful, and P. T. Barnum would exhibit them as the famous 'Circassian Beauties'—supposedly the most beautiful women in the entire world. Except, he was too lazy to get real Circassian women and would just find random girls from New York City to pass."

Shamsah shakes her head and rolls her eyes.

"I know," I say. "Oh! And the women in the harems of the sultans of the Ottoman Empire were usually Circassian, because they were prized as concubines for their beauty and smarts and, um, mannerisms, I guess. Although if you think about it, how they're light-skinned, it's kinda problematic, actually. I mean, more problematic than it already is."

Fatima nods at me. "Colorism."

"Exactly. Oh! And they made wine!"

"Did they *drink* it?" Leila asks, frowning.

"Uh, I'm not sure? But my parents drink," I confess.

Leila cringes.

"Everyone's on their own journey, at their own pace," Samira says.

"Nobody ever thinks Circassians are Muslim because of their skin color, and you know how people are with assumptions," I say, "but, yeah, we're Muslim." I stop, realizing I've become animated and feeling silly. "So, that's Circassians in a nutshell."

"We're happy you're here, Allie." Samira gives me a warm smile. "How far along are you in your studies?"

I blush red from the roots of my head to my toes. *Uh, by how far along, do you mean . . . nowhere?*

"I'm new at this," I say.

"No problem," Samira says, nodding. "We're each at different phases in our studies, too. *Hamdulilah* you're here now. That's enough."

It's that word: *enough.*

I am enough.

Tears well in my eyes. I swipe them off my face furiously, horrified. "Oh my God. Sorry. I don't know why I'm crying."

"It's okay," Samira says.

This is *not* how I imagined this going.

"Can I take a guess?" she says. "Your parents aren't religious."

"Yeah. I mean, no. Definitely not." The more I cry, the sillier I feel. The sillier I feel, the more I cry.

Fatima reaches into her sparkly purse and pulls out a packet of Kleenex tissue. As I blow my nose and rub away the tears, I stare at the purse. It's cat-shaped, with a cute felt nose emblazoned on the front. For some reason, this undoes me.

"Sometimes I don't feel Muslim enough," I blurt out.

What are you doing? Are you serious? Stop.

First impressions are everything, and here I am, ruining it.

"Please. You're Muslim," Shamsah says firmly. "You have as much right to be here as anybody else."

"I don't know why I'm emotional. You're not my therapy session. It's not all about me. I'm sorry."

Fatima reaches over and gives my hand a single gentle squeeze.

It's so quiet in the room I can hear the *tick-tick* of the clock on the fireplace mantel. I want to sink into the couch and disappear, but Samira says, "Okay, y'all. I've seen a phrase making the rounds on Twitter: 'Islam is not a monolith.'" She lets it sink in.

Tick-tick-tick.

"Islam is *not* a monolith," she says. "It's time we stopped feeling guilty about not being Muslim enough. Or being too Muslim. Or not being the 'right kind' of Muslim. Whatever that means."

"I can relate," Fatima says, clearing her throat. Her voice is soft but steady. "As a Black Muslim, as a convert, I feel like an outsider, too, you know? Sometimes."

Leila nods at her sympathetically.

"Uh, cosign," Shamsah says. "I bet most of us do, Allie. You just don't realize it."

And I feel *slightly* less like the most embarrassing person to have ever lived.

The meeting is divided up into sections: First, we read from the Qur'an and work on memorization, then we discuss passages, and, finally, we ask questions.

I keep my head down, listen, and barely speak.

Shamsah talks about going back to India every summer to see her extended family, mentioning that they occasionally tease her she's become too American—which is frustrating, because she doesn't fully fit in with her American friends, either. Leila, who's half-Egyptian and half-Palestinian, was born in America. Both of her parents have been citizens for over a decade. She's never been to the Middle East and wants to see where her parents came from, but they think it's not worth the money. Like my dad, they say there's nowhere better than America, so why leave? Meanwhile, Fatima says she converted to Islam when her mother remarried. Her Baptist dad blames her Muslim stepdad for "making" Fatima wear a headscarf, even though Fatima keeps explaining it's her own choice.

Everybody has a backstory. Nobody's is simple.

Maybe I'm not as alone as I thought.

After class is over, we text our parents to come and get us.

Dua's mom pops into the living room with a fresh plate of cookies and a hug for me.

"Hey. We're gonna go to Avalon. Wanna come?" Leila asks. "My mom can drive."

Wait, is she talking to me*?* My heart skips once I realize she's inviting me to the outdoor mall with them.

"Oh! Yeah, that sounds awesome," I say. "Except, ugh, I can't today. I promised my dad I'd go to Home Depot with him." His limited free time is devoted to sprucing up the house. Normally, I like our outings, but I suddenly feel resentful.

"Okay, maybe next week," she says. "What's your phone number?"

"We have a group WhatsApp going," Dua explains as everybody takes my number. "I'll add you. Next week is at Fatima's."

Immediately, my phone pings with a notification.

Welcome to the group!

I blush, feeling excited.

The text finally comes that night while I'm in my room doing homework.

WELLS: Do you hate me?

ME: No

WELLS: I was kind of a jerk

WELLS: I'm sorry

ME: Me too.

ME: He's still your dad. I shouldn't have said anything.

WELLS: It's hard to talk about.

I don't know how to respond. Luckily, I see ellipses as he keeps typing.

WELLS: To answer your question, yes, he knows Zadie is Mexican, and he's fine with Joey.

I have to keep myself from responding sarcastically. *He's fine.* How noble. Here's a cookie for managing your racism.

ME: Cool

Now might be a good time to tell Wells. I almost chicken out, but something in me presses forward.

ME: Can you talk on the phone for a few minutes?

WELLS: The phone? What's that?

ME: Haha

My phone rings.

"Hey," he says. His voice sounds nervous. "How are you?"

"I'm good. Finishing up homework. You back from soccer?"

"Yeah. Everything okay? Why are you calling me on my texting machine?"

I laugh. "Yeah, everything's okay." I pause. *Maybe I should tell him in person so I can read his reaction.* "Hey, would you mind picking me up for school tomorrow?"

"That's it? The reason for the phone call?"

"Yeah. Well, also, I need you to know the Foo Fighters are extremely overrated."

"Nope. We're broken up."

I know he can't see the huge smile spreading across my face, but I still put my hand over my mouth to hide it.

Instead, I adopt a world-weary tone that doesn't betray how I feel. "See you tomorrow morning."

We hang up, and I feel conflicting emotions: elation mixed with fear.

Tomorrow's the day.

CHAPTER FOURTEEN

Wells picks me up for school the next morning. He's running ten minutes late, kicking my anxiety into overdrive.

"Sorry, sorry, sorry," he says when I get into the truck. "It's been a morning."

"Why? What's up?"

He frowns. "Stuff with my dad."

I nod, not knowing what to say.

He leans over, and we bump into each other for an awkward hug. I can feel his heart beating through the thin fabric of his shirt. Despite myself, my lips gravitate toward his like magnets. His lips are warm and soft, his arms tightening around my back.

Can't we stay like this forever?

Making out . . . no messy parental issues to deal with . . . no religious guilt over being in a relationship . . .

That'd be great, thanks.

He pulls away, looking meaningfully into my eyes as if they hold the long-sought answer to a fervent question. We smile at each other, and then he puts the car into reverse and backs onto my street. "What's—"

"I have to tell you something." My father's admonition that people will treat me differently if they know I'm Muslim rings in my ears. I'm past the point of no return. I can't stop hiding anymore. I need Wells to know me.

All of me.

"Okay?" he says.

"My family's Muslim."

We come to a red light, and he stops, looking confused.

"*I'm* a Muslim."

It takes a second for him to react. His face is blank, his eyes darting this way and that, as if he's processing.

The light turns green.

"It's something you've been hiding from people," he says as he drives. It's less of a question, more of a statement.

"Yeah."

He nods.

"No," I say, contradicting myself. "I just don't tell everybody."

"You don't tell everybody, or you don't tell anybody?"

My silence is the answer.

I can read his mind: *Sounds like hiding to me.*

"So what happened?" he says. "Why are you telling me now?"

I catch him up on the past couple of months, starting with the airplane incident.

"They treated my dad like a terrorist."

"Thank God you were there."

"You mean, thank God his white daughter was there to save him?"

Wells reaches out and gently takes my hand as he drives, entwining his fingers in mine. The gesture sends an energizing jolt through me. He's never held my hand before.

"Is your mom Muslim, too?"

"She converted."

"Are they religious?"

"The only thing my dad believes in is the American dream." I laugh bitterly.

"That's not a bad thing," he says. "Right?"

"I don't think he gets that the American dream is only for white people—the *right* kind of white people. Muslims need not apply."

I almost say: *Your father knows a little something about that.*

I change the subject. "Allie's not my real name."

"It's not?"

"It's Alia."

He smiles. "That's beautiful."

"I like it, too," I say, smiling back.

"Why don't you use it? Which do you prefer?"

"Allie's who I am now." I shrug. "Want me to blow your mind again? My real last name isn't even Abraham."

"Next you're going to tell me you're not a real redhead," he jokes.

I laugh, despite myself. "My dad changed the name when

he moved to America. It was Ibrahimi. And *that* wasn't my great-grandfather's last name: It was something impossible and Russian. My family keeps reinventing and reinventing and reinventing. Never comfortable in our own skin, I guess."

"They're Russian Muslims?"

"Not exactly. Russian is the easiest shorthand. We're Circassian." I see the confusion on his face. "Nobody's ever heard of Circassians. Even a lot of Muslims don't know who they are."

I stuff as much family history into the ten-minute drive as possible: how the tribal Circassians, known for horses, sword fighting, and dancing, lived in their small mountainous communities at the crossroads of Asia and Europe, in a dangerous tinderbox of ethnicities and cultures, thriving by adapting and soaking up the dominant culture, language, or religion—whatever happened to be necessary for survival at the moment.

How the region was considered one of the world's jewels, with jutting mountain peaks, green rolling hills, deep, quenching rivers, and one of the world's oldest wine regions—so beautiful the czars of Russia wanted the area for themselves and launched a series of wars in the 1700s and 1800s that would result in a Circassian genocide in the 1860s.

How my ancestors were expelled from their homeland and forced into displacement in Turkey, Jordan, and Syria: Jordan for my grandfather's family, Syria for my grandmother's.

How my dad moved to America in the late nineties to go to Columbia University, not realizing the dream he'd always prized was heaving its last dying, sputtering gasps—if it ever existed at all.

To Wells's credit, though I'm giving him a history lecture as we drive through the winding backwoods of Providence, his eyes never glaze over. Instead, as he drives toward school, he asks more rapid-fire questions, wanting to know why the Russians prized the land; how the families could live with themselves selling their daughters into Ottoman harems; if the girls tried to escape bondage; if they had their own language.

"My family speaks both," I say. "Circassian and Arabic. My dad is fluent in Circassian—all my aunts and uncles are. I guess my family is more intense about keeping it alive than most. They consider themselves Circassian first, Jordanian second. My cousins take dance lessons at Circassian community centers in Dallas and New Jersey, they dress up in Circassian outfits at weddings, and they still make a few Circassian recipes. But what's weird is none of my family has visited the area, and I don't think any of them taught the language to their kids. It'll probably be extinct in a few more generations—it's a dying language."

"What does it sound like?"

"*Daghwas*," I say, slaughtering the word for "good." "It's the only word I know. I wish I could say more, but nobody taught me."

"I'm asking too many questions."

"It's okay. I love that you're interested. You can ask more. I don't mind."

"Are you allowed to date? As a Muslim."

I flush. "My family is liberal, but if I'm going by the book . . . technically . . . not really."

He looks nervous. "Do we have to stop hanging out?"

"I mean, no, but . . . okay, I read about something called 'halal dating.' You don't do anything you wouldn't do in front of your parents." I squirm in the seat, feeling embarrassed on multiple levels. "I don't know. I'm figuring it all out."

"Last one. Do you practice?"

I look down at my hands. "I want to. I went to my first Qur'an study group."

"You did?" Surprise colors his face.

We pull into the parking lot, and he takes his usual spot, in the back where there are fewer cars. He's constantly nervous about his truck getting scratched.

"Yeah," I say. "Is that weird?"

"No. I don't know." He pauses. "It's kind of weird. But *you're* not weird. Neither is Islam. It's a different situation." He clears his throat.

I press ahead, feeling like we're discussing something deeply uncool, deeply shocking—like religion is taboo somehow. "It's hard to explain, but . . . it's like there's something missing."

He nods. "My mom is Episcopalian. She says going to church makes her feel better about life. Helps her through stuff. I get it. I mean, I don't *get* it, but . . ."

"You sure you don't think Islam is weird?" I ask quietly.

He takes the keys out of the ignition, unclicking his belt and leaning back in his seat. He doesn't look at me. "Because of my dad?"

"Yeah."

He turns to me, his cheeks red. "I'm sorry I didn't say this before, Allie. I'm *not* my dad. I don't believe what he believes."

In the past, this might have been enough for me. But now, I need to hear him spell it out. The stakes are too high for a misunderstanding.

"So, you don't support your dad's stance on Muslims? To be clear."

"No. None of it. We don't share the same views. Period."

Relief floods my body.

We get out of the car and walk into the school building, heading for the library: our recent preclass hangout.

"He wasn't always like that," he says as we settle in at a table by the new releases.

"What was he like?"

Wells bites his lip. "Less intense. Less angry. My mom says he was a different guy in college."

"I'd bet my entire vintage dress collection that your dad was president of his fraternity and still talks about the good old days."

Wells laughs deeply. "Okay. Maybe. They met in the Young Republicans club. My mom says he was a 'pure Republican,' whatever that means. Smaller government, fiscal conservatism, personal responsibility, I guess."

"He doesn't believe in that stuff anymore?"

"I don't know. Maybe. But now he's all about getting America back to 'how things used to be.'" He uses air quotes. "What did the girls in your study group say?"

"About what?"

"About my dad."

I burst out laughing. "Wells, you are straight-up high if you think I told my friends about your dad. Or my parents, for that matter."

"I can't picture your dad being thrilled with it."

It takes me a second to remember that Wells has met my dad. "Yeah. No."

He leans back in the chair, stretching out his body. My eyes run the length of him, and I have to turn my head away so he can't see my burning cheeks. I'm in deep with this guy.

"If your dad isn't religious," he says, "what does he think about you practicing?"

"That would be a negative on the informing of the parentals," I joke in a robot voice. "My mom knows. But my dad . . . religion . . . it's complicated."

"Try me."

I snort. "Where to start? My dad drinks wine—"

"But that's cool 'cause he's Circassian?"

"Ha! Doesn't quite work like that. And nice pronunciation."

He grins. "I try."

"He doesn't pray. He barely taught me Arabic. My *teta*—" I stop, to correct myself. "My grandma hardly understands me when we try to communicate. When I was little, I looked way more like my mom than my dad and his side of the family, because my hair was light. Imagine my family reunions: a bunch of brunettes, and then me, sticking out like a sore thumb."

"What about the other side of your family?"

"What about them? My mom grew up in a mansion in Key Biscayne and went to prep school. My grandfather was a cardiologist who played golf at the club. They couldn't be more of a cliché if they tried. My grandmother is on boards in Miami and Palm Beach. She likes Wheat Thins. *Her name is Genevieve.* She is the living embodiment of beige."

"Obviously, they were thrilled when your mom married a Muslim."

"Obviously."

"Do you care?"

"They're my family, too," I say quietly. "Of course I care."

He reaches out, grabbing my hand again. I close my eyes for a second, reveling in the feeling of his skin on mine.

"Sorry. You're not my therapist," I mumble, ducking my head.

"Don't be. Thanks for telling me."

I feel safe with Wells.

That's a new one.

A flood of gratitude overwhelms me. He sees my tears welling up and averts his eyes, which gives me a chance to wipe them away.

We both pretend it didn't happen.

The first bell rings, and we start gathering our stuff.

In the hallway, Wells clears his throat. "So. Now I know. And the other Muslim kids know. Who else?"

I shake my head. "Nobody. I got into a fight with Emilia and Mikey recently. They were going off about Muslims."

"I'm sorry."

"Why? It's not your fault."

"Mikey and I have history. But sometimes, I wish he'd just . . . go away."

I nod.

"I'm surprised Emilia pushed back, though," he says. "That's gotta be frustrating. Especially since she's all 'woke.'"

"That's the thing. You'd be surprised who says the stuff that sticks. It's not always the bigots. Sometimes it's the good guys."

"Why now?" he says. "What changed?"

"I'm sick of feeling like I'm rejecting my family. That's what it's about, right? Finding yourself. Learning. All that nonsense."

"It's not nonsense," he says, and smiles.

"Besides," I say, feeling emboldened, "somebody's got to combat your dad."

Cue awkward silence.

Crap.

"I'm just kidding," I say quickly.

Wells flushes, looking guilty. "No, you're not. And you're right."

Bigotry has been gold for Jack Henderson's ratings, with half of the audience hate-watching him and the other half eagerly turning the dial to hear him preach their gospel. I Googled him last night and watched a video of him on TV passionately extolling the forgotten virtues of white America and arguing in favor of a complete Muslim ban.

That was a fun five minutes.

"What would your dad say?" I ask.

"About you?"

"Yeah."

Wells looks queasy, as if he's been stuck on a small boat for too long. "In public, he'd be nice. In private, he'd lose his mind."

“Ouch.”

“I don’t care what my dad thinks.”

I’m not sure if I believe him.

We kiss each other goodbye in the hallway by my locker. I enter my combination, swing open my locker door, and stare at my face in the tiny mirror I’ve put up. In the reflection, I see Wells’s back as he walks away.

Please, please, please let him be for real, I say to myself.

I’m surrounded by well-meaning people who don’t want to hurt me with their ignorance—but still do.

I couldn’t take it if Wells was just another one of them.

CHAPTER FIFTEEN

With a little help from my friends in study group and Professor Google, I've been tiptoeing further into the religious waters these past couple weeks.

I still haven't said anything to Dad. Scratch that—I'm actively hiding it from him.

Part of me wonders if he suspects something. I feel like I have a giant blinking neon sign over my head saying I'M KEEPING THINGS FROM YOU.

But he hasn't said anything to me, and, in fact, is acting normal. I don't think he suspects a thing.

I get my chance to talk to Dad the next weekend when he suggests we go for one of our drives.

Driving around and gawking at big houses followed by lunch—that's kind of our thing, no matter the city.

We know all the good spots. In Texas, it's Meadowood

Road in Dallas, and Armstrong Parkway in Highland Park. In Miami, near where Grandmother lives, it's Indian Creek, hands down. (Although, good luck getting in.) And in Atlanta, there's nowhere better for mansion-lusting than Tuxedo Park and the winding stretch of West Paces Ferry Road in Buckhead.

The mansions there put even Wells's house to shame.

Dad changes stations on the satellite radio, looking for the Beatles channel. We both sing along as he pulls onto GA-400, zooming toward Buckhead. He's adorably off-key.

He turns onto West Paces Ferry. There's a Sotheby's real-estate sign in one of the front yards, in front of wrought-iron gates. "Check that one out—your kind of place," Dad says. "Place your Zillow bets?"

"Fifteen million," I guess.

"I'd say thirteen," he says. "The hedges need work. Not enough privacy."

He doesn't say anything else as we drive farther down the road, winding around a bend. I realize he's waiting for me to look up the price, so I do.

"Twenty-two," I say.

"Oh!" he groans. "Nowhere close."

We continue this familiar game for a while. Despite my anxiety, I manage to lose myself in the pleasures of house-gawking. But eventually, I get bored and I have to fake it so I don't hurt Dad's feelings.

"You sure you're okay, pumpkin?" he asks, looking at me sidelong. We're at a light, about to turn onto Peachtree Road for lunch at Phipps Plaza—our usual postgawk destination.

I put on a bright smile. "I'm great, Dad. Everything's perfect."

Once we're inside Phipps Plaza, we head to our regular lunch spot: The Tavern.

These just-the-two-of-us trips have been rarer since we moved to Atlanta. Neither he nor Mom have said it, but I can tell Dad's much more stressed here, even though it's a better job, better pay, and more prestige.

Now that I'm seeing everything through a new lens, I realize it's never occurred to me to ask if his colleagues know he's Muslim.

So I do.

"Weird question," I say, as our burgers come. "Do the other professors know you're Muslim?"

He frowns. "What prompted that?"

"Just curious."

A scowl takes up residence on his face. "My colleagues and I don't talk about those sort of things."

"But, I mean, *Abraham*. They must suspect."

"If anything, Abraham makes people think we're Jewish," he says.

Mind. Blown.

"Is that why you changed the name when you moved to America?" I ask. "Because you were trying to distance yourself from seeming Muslim?"

"What's bringing up all these questions, Allie?"

I sense we're skirting the edge of danger.

I let it go, moving on to more acceptable topics as we tackle our burgers: the school musical, my World History grades, a highly sanitized retelling of my first date with Wells.

What I really want to ask is something I can barely bring myself to articulate:

Why are you self-loathing?

But I can't. It would crush him.

And I couldn't live with myself if I hurt him.

What's funny is, even though Dad is an outsider now, in Jordan he was the ultimate insider.

I've heard the stories so many times, not just from Dad but from Aunt Bila—about how they grew up with drivers and staff in walled compounds, bodyguards accompanying the kids to school because *Jido* was so high up in the government. How my aunt was best friends with the current king of Jordan's sister when they were kids—back when they were forgotten heirs of a displaced wife. Even now, one of my distant cousins is married to another sister of the king, a daughter of the beloved previous king.

That's Jordan: everybody's a cousin of a cousin.

I wonder how that affects you. Being part of the inner circle, keys to the kingdom in hand. You give up your comfortable life, moving to America to pursue the next phase of the dream you've been promised.

And suddenly, you're nobody.

Your new country doesn't care that you went to a prestigious military college, that you graduated from an Ivy League university, that the king of Jordan was the guest of honor at your parents' wedding, that your grandfather received the pope on his first official visit to the Holy Land, that you're a good conversationalist, a kind and funny person, fluent in five languages, a wine connoisseur, a Beach Boys fan, a complicated human.

All they see is your face.

All they hear is an accent.

The home that was advertised has locked its doors—shut for reasons too painful to believe.

So you burn down your past, desperate to be accepted.

Which leaves me sifting through the ashes.

CHAPTER SIXTEEN

I've started smuggling my Qur'an out of the house for study group, living in fear of being caught by Dad. Other kids hide drugs and alcohol from their parents; I hide a translation of the miraculous word of God.

After a study session at Fatima's house the following week, Dua invites me back to her place to hang out. I text Mom from the back seat of Dua's mother's car, updating her.

At Dua's, I spot an open notebook on her bed. "What are you drawing?"

She picks up the notebook and hands it to me. "Feel free."

It's a rough sketch of an elderly man sitting at a table, with a cane resting by his knee. The pencil strokes are bold and assured. "This is incredible!" I say.

"Thanks."

I flip through the book, looking at Dua's sketches: Each one is better than the last.

"You're beyond talented," I say. "These are great."

"I know," she says, grinning. "Thank you. I'm proud of them."

"Have you sold any?" I ask.

"A few. Etsy, ArtFire, the usual. I made decent money, too. I don't have time to focus on it, though."

"Because of school?"

"Yeah. I'm in five honors classes."

"*Five?* Yikes, I thought four was pushing it."

"World History, Mandarin, English, Visual Arts Two, and Algebra Two," she says, ticking them off on her fingers. "Plus AP Chem. You?"

"World History, English, French, and Algebra Two. Then regular ol' chemistry, and AP Comp Sci."

"Whoa, comp sci. My dad would be impressed."

"They're not impressed with your five honors classes? With AP Chemistry? With *Mandarin*? Let a girl live."

She laughs. "If I came home with a C, believe me, they'd notice."

"My parents don't even bother checking to make sure I've done my homework," I say. "They have it easy with me."

"You know parents. They take the good ones for granted."

We both laugh.

After snacks and small talk with her mom downstairs, we go back to her bedroom, where the conversation turns to today's meeting. The group focuses on a different topic each week;

today's discussion was on the importance of *zakat*, or charity. It's the third pillar of Islam, with every Muslim of a certain age and means required to give 2.5 percent of their income yearly to the poor and those in need. I love the idea behind it: not only to remind you to be free of greed and selfishness, but also to emphasize that everything comes from God and we're merely trustees.

"Do you volunteer?" Dua asks.

"Sort of. I found a senior center in Johns Creek after we moved here and was going a couple times a month. But my homework spiraled out of control before finals, and I haven't been since the holidays. Both of my parents' families are really into charity work, so I grew up with it as something you just automatically did."

"Same. But I get it—it's impossible finding the time."

"Where do you volunteer?"

"This domestic violence shelter," she says. "I go once a week, help support the counselors, provide a little cheer."

"Sounds intense."

"These women think they're doing their religious duty by staying in bad relationships. It's beyond. I have to keep quoting the Qur'an to prove that their men are being selfish and completely *un*-Islamic by treating them like garbage."

"It's an Islamic shelter?" I say.

"Yeah."

"Here? In Providence?"

"No, downtown, near that mosque on Fourteenth Street."

Dua's phone rings: At first, I think it's somebody calling her, but then I realize it's melodious Arabic singing—the type of music I've heard in Dallas or New Jersey with my family.

"What's that?" I ask.

"Come on, really?" she says, laughing. "It's an app that tells you when to pray. It also tells you which direction the *Qibla* is in and gives daily supplications." She holds up the phone, flashing the screen in my direction, but the only thing I see is Arabic writing. "It's time for *Asr*."

"You're going to pray now?"

"Yeah, it only takes five minutes. I could make it up later, but I've been trying to do it right. You keep delaying and putting other things first, and then where do you end up, you know?"

"In the fiery bowels of hell," I say, and Dua laughs.

"Do you want to pray with me?" she says.

"I mean . . . uh, is that okay?"

"Of course."

Together, we go to the adjoining bathroom and make *wudu* in the two sinks, purifying ourselves before prayer.

I haven't made *wudu* since I was a kid, when my *teta* taught me how to pray. I didn't even do it for *Jido*'s funeral. So I follow Dua's lead, watching her and imitating her movements: rinsing each hand and arm multiple times, washing my face and behind my ears, taking a sip of water and gargling with it before spitting it out, and awkwardly washing my feet in the sink, trying to keep from splashing water on the counter, down my pant leg, and on the floor.

Back in her bedroom, Dua finds a prayer dress in a drawer and hands it to me.

"Ready?" she asks.

I look at myself in the mirror, wearing a long white *abaya*, which hides every part of my body except my face and hands. Even my feet are hidden.

"I feel weird," I say.

"Not weird. Beautiful. Humble."

"Humbly, I feel weird." I follow her back into the bedroom.

Dua lays out the prayer rugs and stands in front of one, raising her hands to her ears.

"Allahu akbar."

She crosses her arms, folding her hands together over her heart, gazing with humility at the floor. It's powerful hearing her say those familiar words. Something stirs inside me.

"Subhanaka allahumma wa bi hamdika wa tabara kasmuka wa ta'ala jadduka wa la ilaha ghairuka."

She cycles through the motions of prostration and standing, slowly, softly reciting rhythmic Arabic phrases. I try to repeat the words, but it's difficult to follow, because I don't understand Arabic.

Still, I find comfort in the rhythm of it, the repetition, the ceremony. It's meditative and feels yogic. She's right: It *is* beautiful.

We fold up the prayer mats and take off our *abayas*. I place mine neatly on Dua's bed.

"Nice!" she says.

"That was humiliating," I moan. "I need to memorize the prayers."

"It's easier once you do."

"How long did it take you?"

Her eyes narrow as she tries to remember. "I was pretty young. Seven or eight?"

"I'm screwed."

"Ha! Look, it's not only about memorizing them. You've gotta feel them. Plenty of people recite the words, but what good is a prayer if it's meaningless to you?"

"Better than not praying at all."

"Yeah, but plenty of Muslims rush through the motions without thinking." She shrugs. "I don't know. You should at least *get* what you're saying. Plus, it's more likely they'll be accepted." She grins. "So *Allah* tells me."

"I wish I spoke Arabic," I say.

"Do you know any?"

"*Shwaya shwaya.*" A little. "I understand more than I speak. But I can barely communicate with my *teta*."

"Does she speak English?"

"As much English as I speak Arabic. Although she's fluent in Circassian, too."

"Did your dad teach you?"

"Circassian?" I snort. "My dad wouldn't even teach me Arabic. I begged him when I was a kid. My mom wanted to learn, too."

She frowns. "Bizarre."

I backtrack, feeling disloyal to my father. "I mean, I get it. He moved to the States, he went to an American university, he married an American girl. He's obsessed with American traditions and American customs. He always says when he was growing up in Jordan, he saw America as this beautiful place where everybody was equal and nobody was better than anybody else, and if people worked hard, anything was possible. That's how he raised me."

"Still true," Dua says. "Work hard, good things will happen. Dreams can come true. Mostly."

If Dua believes it, I don't want to be a downer. "It's a nice thought," I say diplomatically. "What about you? What are your dreams?"

"Go to Georgia Tech, become a doctor, marry a nice Muslim boy and move out of the house, pop out a soccer team," she says, and laughs.

"Not your parents' dreams! Yours."

"*Ya'ani* they're not the same thing? My parents would be shocked." She glances over at her desk, and I follow her line of sight. There's a brochure for online art classes.

I pick it up, thumbing through the offerings.

"Yours is way better. Would your parents be cool if you pursued art instead?"

"Nope. Zero chance. Not going to be living some after-school special where I teach Mom and Dad a poignant lesson about following your dreams. My parents are . . . how do I say this?" She purses her lips. "*Intense.*"

"What parents aren't?"

"Yeah, but mine are ridiculous. They logged into the student portal two hundred times last semester to check my grades. The vice principal had to call them in for a meeting. As if they're not embarrassing enough."

"Whoa," I say. "That *is* intense."

"They're such a walking cliché," she says, shaking her head and switching to a high-pitched voice. "Oh, the immigrant parents who are all up their daughter's backside to make sure she gets into a good university."

"I don't know who you're imitating, but it needs work," I say.

"I'll do art in my spare time," Dua says. "I don't want to be one of those kids forced to live at home until I'm thirty."

I laugh. "Can you imagine?"

"The sooner I can save up my own money and have a safety net, the better—and art school sure won't get me there. I'm going to Georgia Tech, I'm becoming an ob-gyn, I'm not getting married and moving out until I'm at least twenty-seven—"

"Why twenty-seven?"

"Twenty-five is too young. Thirty is way too old. Twenty-seven is Goldilocks. I'm *not* getting married until I have my own money. Plus, I'll be done with school and won't have some farting loser distracting me from my studies."

That cracks me up. "You wait until graduation to marry the farting loser?"

"Exactly. And when I'm thirty, I'll start having kids—hopefully three, maybe four. The whole biological clock thing is a patriarchal myth to entrap women, you know."

"You've got everything figured out."

She shrugs. "It takes hard work. A little bit of luck."

"And a lot of realism," I point out.

"School, homework, family, sleep. Lather, rinse, repeat."

"Yup."

After Dua pulls out her computer, we plop onto her bed and watch funny YouTube videos. She shows me clips of a famous Muslim YouTuber, and we cry from laughter watching him prank his parents into believing he's drunk.

An hour later, my mom calls me to say she's outside. I load one last video for Dua to watch after I leave—a Kacey Musgraves song—and stop by the living room to thank Dua's mom for having me over. She's in the center of the room, white *abaya* flowing over her hair and body, hands up to the side of her face and facing the brick fireplace. The mantel is covered with family photos and a bevy of candles and fresh flowers. It looks similar to our own spring-friendly decorations at home, but our flowers are fake and our house has a tiny bar cart in front of the fireplace, not a basket for prayer rugs. Otherwise: same, same.

I decide to leave unannounced, to give Dua's mom privacy.

As I shut the door behind me, she kneels on her mat, prostrating herself, her lips moving in a prayer echoing with silence.

CHAPTER SEVENTEEN

"Okay, so, I've got a new one for you," Shamsah says to the girls.

The group is at Leila's house the following Sunday, meeting for another study session. While we wait for Samira to arrive, everybody's chatting in the living room and mainlining the cookies that Fatima baked for us.

Shamsah continues. "Would you rather never see another human being, or be surrounded by annoying people twenty-four seven?" Seems like a game they play frequently.

"Never?" Leila asks.

"Never."

"Annoying people for the win," Fatima says. "I'd get too lonely."

"I mean, I'm already surrounded by annoying people twenty-four seven," Dua cracks. "So solitude sounds pretty fantastic."

"That's sad." Leila frowns. "Like—never seeing another person? Think about that. *Never.*"

"You don't have to keep repeating it, Lei," Dua says.

I nod. "Leila's right. I couldn't do it. You need people."

"Maybe *you* need people. I need more alone time in the bathroom." Dua pops another cookie into her mouth.

"Same, same," Shamsah says.

The doorbell rings, and Leila gets up to let Samira in. After a few more minutes of small talk, we begin the readings.

Following my prayer session at Dua's house, I've decided I need to properly memorize the prayers. I also ordered a long white *abaya* and a prayer rug, using the credit card number Mom gave me for emergencies.

I mean, this obviously qualifies.

Mom is being supersupportive, as per usual. When the prayer items arrived, she sent me a text saying, I received your things. They're in your closet xoxo.

Toward the end of class, during questions, Leila tentatively raises her hand.

"I'm having an inner struggle," she confesses, tucking her feet underneath herself on the chair. "I've been constantly missing prayers. I don't know why it's so hard for me to pray, even though it takes five seconds."

Samira nods. "Can you think of any explanation?"

Leila shakes her head, wrinkling her nose. "I know every time you don't pray it counts as a sin. But I don't know why. I'm just not doing them."

"But you are still praying a little," Fatima says, looking worried. "Right?"

"I pray at sunset usually every day, and when I wake up, I'll pray, but I'm missing those other two or three—sometimes I'm just like, ugh, I'll do it later."

Fatima furrows her brow. "Maybe you don't want to make *wudu*. It could be that," she says helpfully.

Leila nods. "Yeah, maybe. Sometimes I won't make *wudu* and I'll think: 'God, please forgive me.'"

Everybody nods. "Been there," Shamsah says, laughing.

"I worry I'm lazy," Leila whispers.

I expect Samira to provide an explanation, but she simply nods. "It's good for you to be asking yourself these questions." She says this warmly, without judgment. "Keep at it. Check in with yourself every day. It's more important for you to do the prayers and mean them than say them with no intention or connection. With no faith."

Dua and I exchange a look, and I'm reminded of what she said about the importance of intention.

"And you, Allie? How has your week gone?" Samira asks.

"I prayed for the first time! Well, not the *first* time, but the first time in a long time. Like, in almost a decade. Dua helped."

Dua nods. "She rocked it."

"Honestly, I didn't expect to like praying so much. When I'm done, my head feels clear and my anxiety is just, like, gone," I say. "And I prayed at home a few times and started reading more of the Qur'an, too. I've got a ton of homework, so it's kind of hard to keep up, but I'm doing my best."

"That's all *Allah, subhanahu wa ta'ala*, can ask of you. To do your best," Samira says, smiling warmly. She picks up her notes, about to launch into this week's lecture.

I clear my throat, gathering courage. "Actually, *I've* been struggling with something, too," I say. "Can I ask a question?"

"Go for it," Samira says. "We're all ears."

My hands go clammy. "Okay," I say. "So I was researching the *hajj* pilgrimage, and I went down the rabbit hole about going to Mecca, getting the visas, things like that. And I came across the official Ministry of *Hajj* page, and it talks about how women can't go on the pilgrimage without a man. I think it was called a *marhaba*."

"A *mahram*," Samira says, smiling. "*Marhaba* means hello."

"Oops. Right, a *mahram*. And if you're older than forty—"

"Forty-five."

I cringe at my mistakes. "Sorry. Um, if you're older than forty-five, then you can come without a man, but you still have to be with an organized group and have a notarized letter from your husband, son, or brother giving you permission to travel?"

I pause, looking around the room, gauging their reactions. Everybody's face is open and encouraging. I tuck my hands under my thighs, as much to warm them as to steady them, forcing myself to plow forward.

"And I read this, and I'm like . . . is this for real? A grown woman might need to get permission from her *son*? And it's confusing, because Islam is so feminist—I know it is, and it's irritating when people say it isn't. But then things like that . . . it's hard to stand behind that and say it's okay. You know?" I hold my breath, terrified about how my question will be received. Maybe I shouldn't have brought it up.

Samira pauses, weighing her words.

"Great question. That particular tradition is established by *hadith*. I'd be lying if I said it's not frustrating. Although, side note: The Ministry of *Hajj* is run by the government of Saudi Arabia. Salafis are not exactly the world's foremost experts on women's rights—at least, not to Western eyes."

"Okay, right," I say.

"Look, you can still be a faithful, devoted Muslim and acknowledge that we live in a patriarchy," Samira says. "According to the Qur'an, men and women are equal. And, of course, the women in the Prophet's life had extraordinary rights. The equality of women is not up for debate where the Qur'an itself is concerned. It's the way traditions have evolved and been interpreted that's the problem."

"It's like what we studied recently," Dua says. "'You have rights over your women, and your women have rights over you.'" She's quoting the Qur'an. "Right?"

"Right," Samira says.

Dua relaxes against a couch cushion, smiling. "I freaking love that quote."

"Okay," I say. "Thanks."

Samira picks up her notes, as if we're about to move on, but then sets them down again. "You know, before the Prophet, daughters were killed at birth—all the time. Can you imagine? His teachings were the dawn of equality and respect for women around the world—absolutely *revolutionary* at the time. Way more than any woman in Europe had back then. People don't know the history, so they laugh when you say Islam is feminist, but women keep their own last names; they were the first in the world to have property rights, the first to initiate divorce. His blessed wife Khadijah was the first convert. Think about that. The first Muslim after Prophet Muhammad, peace be upon him, was a *woman*."

"Peace be upon him," everybody says.

"Our world is patriarchal—across cultures, across religions. We live in a patriarchy *right here in the US*." Samira raps her notes with a manicured fingernail. "Sexism in Muslim-majority countries resembles sexism here, too. So that frustrates me."

Shamsah raises a hand. "Hi. Me too."

Samira nods. "We're blessed to practice this beautiful religion. Then again, many of our sisters have suffered under men in power for centuries. They reject any deviation from their own position, they bar women from interpreting religious texts, they inject their own traditions into the religion and call it dogma." The passion in Samira's voice excites me. It's inspiring.

"Plenty of traditions that aren't even in the Qur'an, you know?" Shamsah blurts. "Besides, how do we know every single *hadith* is real?"

"Are you on this again?" Leila says, looking irritated. "Come on."

"You see it in Christianity occasionally," Samira says. "It's a religion of love, tolerance, and humility, right? But we've all met people who say they love Jesus in one breath and then are completely hateful to their neighbors in the next. We have a similar problem in Islam: interpreting religious texts in a manipulative way to suppress women."

"And then," Fatima says, "it's those traditions everybody else jumps on and says, 'Oh, Islam! It's horrible! Why did your family choose *that* religion'?" She smooths down her hijab, as if unconsciously. She sighs. "Nobody wants to hear it's not real Islam. It's bad men in power."

"Okay, everybody, hold up," Leila says. "You're doing that thing again. Can I say—it's, like, critical not to paint all conservative men as bad?" She sounds frustrated. "Just because you're a fundamentalist doesn't mean you're a terrorist. And individual men don't equal government policies. Like, c'mon, not every man from Saudi Arabia is a misogynist monster. I feel like that gets ignored."

Shamsah nods and looks at me. "This is something we debate a *lot*."

Leila shakes her head. "And some debates go over more smoothly than others."

I wonder what that means.

"No matter what any Muslim believes, no matter how loudly they proclaim it, they cannot definitively speak for *Allah, subhanahu wa ta'ala*," Samira says.

"*Tafsir* versus *ta'wil*," Shamsah says. "Right? The literal meaning versus the mystical."

"*Sharia*—the unchangeable principles—versus *fiqh*—the interpretation," Fatima says.

I don't know if they're right or wrong, but I'm ridiculously impressed.

"Look, if our faith is to grow and thrive," Samira says, "I don't think you can ignore the outside world. And I don't believe one type of Muslim is better than another. Are Sunnis better than Shias? Should we completely dismiss Sufism? We're pilgrims on the same journey, with the same destination—it's only the route that differs. Saudi Arabia and Iran don't hold the monopoly on Islam. We're two billion strong. But we've got to be allowed room to breathe in the West, too—not only by Westerners, but by Muslims ourselves."

I've found myself in the middle of Muslim revolutionaries.

"But isn't that . . . apostasy?" I ask tentatively.

SAT word. Ten points.

"I struggle with some of it," Fatima confesses. "It's lonely being a revert, and I didn't come to Islam until later . . . but I still want to do it right. My mom doesn't pray anymore, so this is the only place I can talk about most of this stuff. Some of it makes sense, but if I disagree with the rest . . . I just go back to the Qur'an and the *hadith*. No offense, girls."

I look around the room, feeling emboldened. "You're on the same page?"

Shamsah nods enthusiastically.

Leila shrugs.

Samira takes a deep breath. "It's safe to say our conservative brothers and sisters would not appreciate us discussing Islam and reform in the same sentence. There are many in the *ummah* who would consider it the height of apostasy, yes. *Shirk*."

"You can't pick and choose which parts to follow," Leila argues. "To say Islam needs reform is *literally* missing the entire point. The beauty of the religion is that it transcends time: It's the same, always, forever, perfect, done, *khalas*. You can't reform Allah himself. It's not possible."

"There's Reform Judaism. The Catholics have Vatican Two. Why can't I want that as a Muslim? I'm a *kafir* just because I don't want to pray in a separate room from my dad at the mosque? Just because I think women should be allowed to lead prayers, too? No way," Shamsah says passionately. "That's not Allah. That's men being men." I've never heard her speak so much as in the past twenty minutes.

"My mom and I told my stepdad about the women's prayer room at the *masjid*," Fatima says. "He couldn't believe we have to watch it on this tiny little TV while they get to be in the room and see it up close. He's never been in there, right? So he had no idea. He thought we were watching it live, like him. Lots of guys think there's room for improvement."

Dua sighs. "You don't want to talk about stuff too much in public, because everybody is always so down on Islam. You've gotta put on a united front. If we're not perfect, then people jump down our throats. Backwards! Regressive! That BS."

"Total BS," Shamsah says. "Other people get space to be complex and question and screw up and grow. Why not Muslims, too? Why is it all or nothing? It's like, devout or terrorist, no in-between. It's not fair."

"All religions suffer from the same issue," Samira says. "The message is divine, but the interpretation, practice, and enforcement is too human. *We* are too human. And we are flawed."

She looks frustrated, and for a moment, I see her not as an older group leader but an irritated girl, just like us.

"You study history, you talk to our parents and grandparents, they'll tell you the Middle East was a very different place before the Iranian Revolution," she says. "Personally, I don't believe the word of God or an error-free Qur'an has anything to do with men and their politics. But, of course, I don't know. It is the height of arrogance to claim you know *Allah*'s mysterious heart or his plan."

"*Ameen* to that," Shamsah says. Sadness falls across her face.

I look at Leila, who still seems irritated. "What do you think?" I say.

She shifts uncomfortably. "Honestly, I get that y'all have issues, but I don't have a problem with it. 'Islam' *literally* means 'submission to God.' I love my faith, and I'm proud of it."

"So do we, *obviously*," Shamsah says.

"I know, but who are we to say it needs changing?" Leila says. "Like, being a secular Muslim—it's an oxymoron. You always say plenty of Muslims don't understand the Qur'an and are misinterpreting it, but they'd say the same thing about you. And we haven't studied it the way the real scholars have. No offense, Samira—"

"None taken."

"And I feel the way it's written, men and women *are* equal," Leila says. "You know it says men and women each have their place. We each have important responsibilities. Do I think it's silly we're separated by a rope or in different rooms at the *masjid*?

Sure. But sometimes my dad will ask me to lead the prayer for the family at home, and he'll pray behind me."

"That's cool," I say.

"It is! And that's why the whole reform thing bums me out. I mean, Saudi, Iran, Sudan, yeah, maybe they have some issues. But for the most part, I feel like it's Islamophobia, like it's, you know, centering the Western gaze. In the Qur'an, it says men, women, dogs, cats—they're *all* equal in the eyes of God. We only have different duties, different things that have to get done. My dad doesn't have power over my mom any more than she does over him. It's about cooperation: *shura*," Leila says. "Maybe I'm lucky because I come from a family where they're equals. But at the end of the day, I think it's about respecting each other. And I *am* a feminist. The Qur'an allows me room for that already."

Samira smiles. "Well reasoned."

My heart is bursting.

"I think it's incredible this is a safe space," I say shyly. "The fact you can be respectful to each other, even though you disagree on, like, sort of fundamental issues . . . it's awesome."

Fatima beams. "Agreed."

"Like the Supreme Court," Shamsah cracks. "We've got the textualists and the intentionalists. What it said at the time versus what it means now."

"Ugh. Does that mean I'm Gorsuch?" Leila says.

Dua groans. "Y'all are serious nerds."

I recite the *Isha* prayer that night for the first time at home, feeling grateful for the day. I face the *Qibla*, taking a few deep breaths and stilling my mind as I set my intention. I raise my hands to my ears, my gaze soft, my heart light. As I say *Allahu akbar*, I feel a whoosh of energy and love and peace. *Hamdullah*, I'm not alone.

I repeat the motions: putting my hands on my knees, bending down, curling myself into a ball, resting my forehead on the ground. I try to be present in the moment, doing more than simply saying the mindful words of devotion and appreciation.

I feel them.

Generations of my family have done this before me: my father and my grandmother and my great-grandmother; relatives in Jordan, relatives in the Caucasus. I picture them on their knees, uttering the same words I'm saying now, whispering up their dreams and desires for the same God. Maybe their intentions are different. Maybe their interpretation is not the same. But right now, at this very moment, Muslims across the East Coast are doing the exact same thing. Today, hundreds of millions of Muslims—maybe more—have gone about these five prayers, showing God the strength of their intentions and humbly submitting, quietly asking for recognition. Countless millions more will tomorrow, and the day after.

I am finally part of something bigger than myself, part of the *ummah*, and it is beautiful.

CHAPTER EIGHTEEN

I don't know much about dating, but I'm pretty sure it's twice as hard when your boyfriend's father is a famous jerk.

And ten times as hard when the famous jerk invites you to dinner.

And fifty times as hard when the same famous jerk absolutely, positively cannot find out you're Muslim.

As Wells drives us through the back streets of Providence, lush with trees recalling the sleepy one-horse town it used to be, I ask myself for the fifteenth time what I'm doing.

"Do you think it's a good idea?" I say.

He turns down the long road leading to his property. We both know what I mean.

"It's probably an awful idea," he says.

"I can't promise I'm not gonna go off on him."

"I hope you will."

I shoot him a look. "We both know you don't mean that."

We hold each other's gaze, but he looks away first. "It's better if he doesn't find out. I don't want him to . . ."

"Hate me?"

He chews on his lower lip.

When Wells told me his father had invited me over for dinner, I nearly vomited. How could I break bread with this man?

But I'll admit it. Curiosity got the best of me.

So here I am on a Saturday night, hair perfectly done, wearing the preppiest dress I own, sitting across the table from Jack Henderson for my *Guess Who's Coming to Dinner* moment.

"Allie," Mr. Henderson says. My name is loose in his mouth, his drawl an untraceable jumble of accents. "Thanks for coming! Wells is very taken with you."

Wells's mom smiles at me while Wells's ten-year-old brother, Sawyer, plays with an iPhone under the table. Wells and I exchange looks.

"Are you from Providence?" his dad says.

"I'm originally from Texas. We moved here last year." I leave out the details. Details are for people I feel safe with.

"Texas! What a state. I spent some time in Dallas myself. Decent barbecue. Gorgeous houses. And good shopping! You wouldn't think I'd care about that, but . . ." Mr. Henderson grins at me, a dimple popping on his right cheek. "You like Georgia?"

"It's great," I say. "I love so much about the South. The trees, the food, the people." He doesn't seem to notice what I've left unsaid.

"So do I! It's much more authentic than the North, don't you think?"

I take a bite of my salad, wishing I were anywhere else but here. Wells's dad is nothing but charming and polite. I guess *I'm* the small-minded jerk, because I can't get past our political differences.

"And what brought your family to Atlanta?" He looks at me expectantly, a pleasant smile on his face. It irritates me that he's handsome. His outside should match his inside.

"We moved for my father's job. He's a professor at Emory." Without meaning to, I've slipped into my best For the Adults voice.

Not coincidentally, it's also my I Might Be Muslim, But Don't Worry—I Am Not a Threat to You voice.

"Emory's wonderful," he says. "I gave a talk there years ago. I had a good friend on the board."

"That's nice," I say. "Uh, you went to Yale?"

"Wells told you?"

I nod.

His eyes sweep over me, as if he's sizing me up. He pauses before smiling. I wonder how often he whitens those teeth.

"I can tell you're smart, Allie. Just the kind of person I'd like to see Wells with. He's a lucky guy."

"Wells is smart," I say, "so I'm lucky, too."

"Of course," Mr. Henderson says, looking over at him. "But that's only because he's like his mom." He puts his hand on his wife's, and she faintly lifts the corners of her mouth before pulling her hand away and taking a sip of wine.

I notice the gold bracelet on her wrist—one of those expensive lock bracelets that have to be removed with a screwdriver. They're supposed to symbolize love. Clamped around Serena's dainty wrist, it looks more like a handcuff.

"Did you know Serena and I met in college?" Mr. Henderson says.

"Oh?" I move my food around my plate, trying to look interested. I was worried tonight might devolve into a shouting match as incendiary political ideas were hurled. Instead, it's a snoozefest.

And as an only child—I don't get bored easily. Conversing with adults has been drilled into me since birth. It's the reason I'm able to spend so much time with my parents.

"Young Republicans mixer," he says. "She was a big-city gal from Vancouver, too good for the slowpoke likes of me."

"Oh, please!" Wells's mom laughs, coming alive. "I lived in Victoria, and I barely left the island! I had to make myself seem sophisticated to keep up with you." She turns to me. "He was full of ideas, full of enthusiasm," she says. "It was the end of the nineties, there was this fervor in America, and I wanted to be a part of it. I joined Young Republicans but didn't tell Jack for several months that I couldn't vote." She laughs again, caught in a reverie. "He assumed I was a dual citizen—impossible for him to *fathom* anybody who wasn't American!"

"I had to ask her to marry me immediately," he says, stabbing his filet. "Couldn't let her get away."

"There was no saying no," Mrs. Henderson says, a faraway look in her eye. She takes another sip of wine.

Wells makes a discreet vomiting motion, forcing me to swallow a giggle. As much as I can't stand Jack Henderson, even I think it's cute watching him and Wells's mom reminisce.

Then I remember Jack makes money by exploiting fear. He denies millions of Americans their humanity. He's not cute. He's dangerous.

Don't forget it, Allie.

"You're Canadian?" I ask Wells's mom.

"I'm afraid so," she says, smiling, her tone playfully apologetic. It's a tone I recognize. It's the same tone I employ whenever my family's background comes up, or somebody says, "Abraham? What kind of last name is that?"

"Um. Where did you go after college?" I say.

"We made our way down to DC, where I took a job with the government," he says. "Nothing but bloat and bureaucracy. Total indifference to human suffering. Heartbreaking."

It's funny hearing somebody like him talking about human suffering when he's directly responsible for so much of it. I'm pretty sure I know what he's talking about. *White* suffering.

The right kind of humans.

"Wells was born in DC," his dad says. "Best day of my life. Nothing prepares you for becoming a father for the first time. Being responsible for another human." His voice is tender. He smiles. "Of course, when Sawyer was born, it was equally spectacular."

His younger son yawns.

Mrs. Henderson suddenly looks sad. "Wells was such a cute baby."

"Uh, I'm right here," Wells says. "I'm not dead."

His dad drinks wine. "We moved to Georgia after Sawyer was born. That's when I woke up," he says. "The poverty. The way the government plays politics with its own people. The cancer eating away at the heart of this country."

Mrs. Henderson clears her throat.

"I decided to use my voice. I got involved in local politics, started reporting for a small TV station . . . and the rest is history," he says.

I look at him, eyebrows raised: *Is this guy for real?*

Should I stand up, flip over the table, and shout, *We all know what you mean when you say "cancer." You're nothing but a bigot!*

I mean, really. That's not happening.

Do I break up with Wells because his father's a jerk?

Do I smile and nod and take another bite of steak?

Whatever I do, I lose. I'm either going to be patronized and ignored, or I'm complicit. I wonder again if it's possible for me to keep dating Wells when he's related to this man.

Mr. Henderson misunderstands my silence, taking a sip of his wine and chuckling in a self-deprecating way.

"Sorry. This isn't appropriate dinner-table conversation," he says. "What do you do in your spare time, Allie?"

I sneak a glance at my cell phone. It's 8:05 p.m. I've showed up. I've played nice. How much longer do I have to sit through this before I can go home?

"I don't have much spare time with my studies, sir," I say, "but I'm doing the school musical. Last semester, I joined the

Quiz Bowl team and cheerleading and was volunteering at a senior center."

"That's great. Giving back is essential. And how did you two meet?"

"Dad, you're grilling her," Wells says, jumping in. "It's not a work interview."

Mr. Henderson smiles again, although his expression is tighter this time. Across the table, Wells's mom pours herself more wine.

"I wanted to make our guest feel welcome," he says.

"It's fine," I say politely. "Wells and I met at school. In Algebra Two. We do chorus together, too."

"Hey, by the way, I forgot to tell you," Wells says. "I uploaded a new video to YouTube, and it's had over five thousand views in ten days."

I smile at him gratefully.

"That's great, son," Mr. Henderson says. "But please don't interrupt our guest while she's speaking, okay? We can talk about your little videos later."

"She wasn't speaking," Wells says.

"That's enough," his dad says with a frown. "We don't want to give the wrong impression."

"She's not a guest. She's just Allie."

"That's enough," Mr. Henderson snaps. He turns to me with a smile. "And your mother? What does she do?"

I look back and forth between Wells and his dad, not sure what's happening.

"Um, she's a psychologist specializing in child development."

"That's must have been a pain in the butt growing up—pardon my French! I bet she was always torturing you with the latest child development theories." He chuckles.

I laugh, despite myself. "Yep. It was pretty annoying."

"Brussels sprouts, Allie? I made these specially for you—without bacon," Wells's mom says, pushing a platter my way and giving me a conspiratorial look. "I hope you like them."

Wait. Does she know?

"Uh, thanks, Mrs. Henderson."

"Call me Serena."

"And you can call me Jack," Wells's dad says.

"Um, okay. Thanks, Mrs.—Serena." What is up with parents wanting to be called by their first name?

"You don't eat pork?" Jack asks, looking at me with interest as he tucks into his bacon-laden brussels sprouts.

You can't tell him. You promised Wells.

I rack my brain, searching for an excuse. "I had a bad incident last year. I haven't been able to stomach it since."

Why not tell him?

I could just say it:

Actually, Mr. Henderson, there's another reason I don't eat pork. I'm Muslim. You know, like those people you give speeches against and write books about.

But I don't.

And I sort of hate myself for chickening out.

"Have you gone to any of Wells's shows?" Jack asks. "He's very talented." His tone is odd, especially after condescendingly calling Wells's YouTube uploads his "little" videos.

"Not yet," I say. "I can't wait to see one."

Wells groans. "Don't get your hopes up. I've been trying to lock down a gig for months. Why aren't clubs dying to book a kid with more than *twelve hundred whole subscribers* on You-Tube?" He looks at me and makes a silly face.

"You know, when I was a kid, my favorite band was Talking Heads," Jack says. "I'd blast it in my room and drive my father up the wall. He'd call it noise and tell me real music wasn't the garbage I listened to but stuff like jazz and blues—Buddy Guy, B. B. King, Robert Johnson." Mr. Henderson shakes his head, and his eyes go fuzzy as if lost in a memory. "I didn't get it until I became a dad. That stuff *you* listen to." He rolls his eyes at Wells. "That's not music."

"Thanks, Dad." Wells's face goes slightly pink.

"But you're talented—at least there's that."

"I can't wait to hear him play live." I look over at Wells and smile. "Don't always listen to a ton of jazz or blues, but I do love country."

"American music, like jazz," Jack says, turning toward Ser-ena. "Serena hates country music, don't you, honey?"

She flushes, smiling at me apologetically. "I don't have an ear for it. We didn't get much country music in Victoria when I was a kid."

As Serena serves the dessert and Jack continues talking, Sawyer plays a noisy iPhone game under the table. Jack is quick to disci-pline Wells but doesn't pay much attention to his younger son.

"I made strawberry shortcake for you, Allie," Serena says,

presenting the whipped-cream-covered dessert—my favorite—with a flourish. "Wells said—"

"Speaking of your music, Wells," Jack says, interrupting his wife, "why aren't you playing Danny? The school's doing *Grease*, right? You should be Danny." He's gone through a bottle of red wine, his tone getting progressively louder as he drinks. Now he's on to the bourbon.

Wells and his mom exchange a look. Volumes pass between them, but I don't speak their language enough to decode it.

"He's a sophomore, Jack," Serena says in a soothing tone. "The best roles go to seniors."

"If he's good enough, he should get it. Right, Allie?"

I stare back at him, wide-eyed.

Wells clears his throat. "I'm playing Kenickie. It's a good role."

"Not good enough. Who's playing Danny?"

"This kid Billy Jackson."

"What year is he?"

Wells's jaw tightens. "A junior."

Jack turns to Serena. "So much for that excuse. He must be better than you. Why did I spend all that money on your drum kit and your guitars and your lessons if you can't even get the lead in a high school musical?"

My heart pounds as I clear my throat, wanting to defend Wells. "Actually, Mr. Henderson, it's kind of political. The chorus teacher loves Billy Jackson. And I guess he made him Scarecrow last year in *The Wizard of Oz*."

Jack startles, as if he'd forgotten I was there. "I'm sorry, Allie. You must think I'm a buffoon. I'm hard because I love him. I want Wells to succeed."

"Of course," I say tentatively.

"He's talented," he says. "Sure, he's my kid, but I can be objective. He's got 'it.' When you're a parent, you want everybody to see your kid through your eyes."

Although Jack is technically complimenting his son, Wells scowls at him.

Serena clears the dishes while Jack holds court at the head of the table, oblivious to the emotional disruption he's caused. "Let's play a board game. Something competitive," he says. "I know! Risk!"

I look at Wells, alarmed.

"Dad, it's late. Allie needs to get home," he says. "She's working on a huge comp sci project."

"Computer science?" Jack says. "That's unexpected."

"Why?" I ask.

Jack pauses. "What am I saying? Of course you're right. Girls can do anything boys can do."

This time, I don't fake a smile.

I clear my throat. "I do need to be getting home. My curfew is nine thirty. Thank you both for your hospitality."

Serena is now in the corner, sipping a cup of tea with her feet tucked under her, looking emotionally drained.

If Jack is annoyed, he doesn't show it.

"Of course. It was an absolute pleasure meeting you, young

lady," Jack says. "Thanks for putting up with us. We're a madhouse, huh?"

I give him a tight-lipped smile in return, running through all the things I wish I had the courage to say.

I say nothing.

Wells is quiet as he drives me home, his posture hunched and self-protective. I address it as we round the bend and turn onto Holcomb Bridge Road.

"Whew," I say. "That was intense."

"I know."

"It's strange. He wasn't what I expected. Kinda . . . charming? Although the musical stuff was weird."

"He knows how to turn it on. When he wants to." The bitterness in Wells's voice is tangible, shimmering. I could reach out and touch it, and it would burn me. "Plus, he probably assumes you're like him."

"Safe."

"Right."

I laugh harshly. "Been on *that* receiving end before."

"I bet. Thanks for keeping everything on the DL. I know it's a lot to ask. It's just . . . easier."

"What would do if he knew I'm Muslim?"

He thinks about it. "Nothing. He'd be nice to your face. He'd keep inviting you to dinner. He'd wait it out."

"Until we broke up?"

A smile slides across Wells's face. "Are we together?"

I blush, embarrassment searing my insides. "That's not what I mean."

He waits until we're at a light, reaching over and taking my hand in his. When the light turns green, he drives on, our fingers still locked together.

"You think he'd be nice to me?" I say.

Wells squeezes my hand before taking it away and putting it back on the steering wheel. "Yup."

I shake my head, irritated.

"You know the worst part?" he says. "My dad is smart. I don't know how he believes that stuff. How he sleeps at night."

"So, what *is* his deal?" I ask. "What *does* he believe in?"

He groans. "You really want to hear?"

"Yes. No. Yes."

"I mean, it's not original. Immigration is horrible, political correctness is stupid, everybody's a snowflake."

"What about your mom? She believes all that, too?"

He shakes his head. "She doesn't. No way."

"You sure? They're still married."

"There's stuff you don't know," he says, his voice quieter. "Mom is tough. She's a good person. She practices what she preaches."

He turns the corner toward my house, sinking into loud silence.

I want to make Wells feel better, especially after what a jerk his dad was to him—but something inside me is bubbling up.

"I hate to say it, Wells, but . . . you know . . . you're condoning his behavior, too."

"What am I supposed to do?" he explodes. "Leave? Sleep on the street? It's easy for you to condemn. You don't live in that house."

"I'm sorry. It's gotta be hard," I say, backpedaling.

"It *is* hard."

"Okay. I get it."

"You *don't* get it. Do you know what it's like having a dad people hate? He's an embarrassment, but he's still my father."

I don't know what to say.

He exhales in a puff of frustration. "Sorry. It's not your problem."

"Don't be sorry. We don't pick our parents."

He pulls up to a light, his hands clenching the steering wheel. "You don't have to be nice about him."

"I know."

"He's a jerk."

I nod.

"It's everybody who's not white." His voice has dropped to a whisper. Sunny Wells has been replaced by something darker, deeper. "I'm ashamed of him."

"You're not your father."

"My mom says he wasn't always like this."

"You've mentioned."

"You're not a monster just because you believe in states' rights and small government," Wells says. "And she says plenty of people don't like what's been happening—not just progressives.

But *he* genuinely believes we'd be better if America went back to the old days."

"The days when life sucked for everybody who *wasn't* a straight, white middle-class able-bodied cis dude?"

"Basically."

I look down at my hands, thinking, *How did I end up here?*

He shakes his head. "Let's change the subject. Please."

"Okay."

But we drive in silence.

As we pull up to my house and Wells puts the car in park, I start talking about my *teta*'s upcoming visit. After a few seconds, I realize he's not listening to me. His hands are on the steering wheel, and he's breathing heavily, loudly.

"Are you okay?" I ask.

He doesn't respond.

"Wells?"

"Allie," he whispers.

His hands grip the steering wheel, trembling.

"Are you okay?" I ask again.

He bends over, putting his head on the wheel. "Gimme a sec." I strain to hear him over the music.

I don't know what to do. I think he's having an anxiety attack.

"Can I help?"

He clutches the steering wheel so tightly his knuckles turn white.

I go into protective mode, turning the radio off. "Come here. Lie down." I stroke his back, trying to soothe him. It's wet—he's sweating through his shirt.

Eventually, after several tense, quiet minutes, Wells's hands relax. The blood comes back to his knuckles. He sits up, and his posture returns to normal.

When he looks at me, there are tears in his eyes. There's something else, too. Fear.

And shame.

"It's okay," I whisper. "I'm here."

"I'm sorry."

"Don't be sorry. It's okay," I repeat. "I'm here."

I think about how Muslims aren't supposed to date or have physical contact with the opposite sex. But hugging and comforting him in this situation is okay.

It has to be.

And if it's not, I don't care. I'm doing it anyway.

CHAPTER NINETEEN

Wells doesn't want to talk about it on Monday morning.

"It happens," he says. "It's not a big deal."

We're outside by the school's log cabin, sitting at a picnic bench waiting for the warning bell to ring for first period. It's a game day, so he's wearing khakis with a collared shirt and tie.

"Have you seen a doctor?" I say.

"It's fine, okay? I can take care of it."

"But it might be an anxiety attack. There's stuff you can do. You could go on medicine, you could do therapy—a whole bunch of stuff. It's no wonder you're so stressed-out, with your dad . . ."

And now because of me.

He frowns, his face tight. "No offense, Allie, but I don't wanna talk about it—and I don't need you to fix me."

"Okay." I put my palms up in surrender. "I'm sorry. You got this."

We sit in awkward silence for a moment or two. Wells brightens up. "Hey, so my dad's paying for studio time now."

"Oh, that's great." I feign enthusiasm.

"He felt guilty about what happened over dinner. He didn't say, but I know. I know him."

"Cool. That's great." In all honesty, it feels icky—like Jack is trying to buy Wells. But I can't tell him that, especially not now. It worries me. If Jack has leverage over Wells because he's the key to something Wells wants, will there come a moment when Jack makes him choose?

I shove the worries out of my head. "We've got five more minutes before the bell rings. Show me one of your videos again."

In March, there's a giant spring festival not far from Providence. Dua and I make plans to meet up there one Saturday night.

"Hi!" she says when I walk up from the drop-off point. "New boots?"

"Yeah," I answer, looking down at them self-consciously. "You like them?" I was going for a country vibe by pairing them with a gingham dress.

"You look honky-tonk," she says. "I mean it in a good way."

"Am I getting you closer to a country concert?"

She scrunches her nose. "Who are we talking here?"

"Pick your poison. Miranda Lambert, Garth Brooks, Brad

Paisley. Ooh, Kacey Musgraves! She sings that song I played you a couple weeks ago, remember?"

"Oh, the song about following arrows? Yeah, that was pretty good."

"'Follow Your Arrow,'" I say. "Obsessed."

"Actually," Dua says, "I watched some of her videos recently. While doing homework—while avoiding homework, more like it."

"By yourself? Which ones?"

"Something about a merry-go-round, and then another one about biscuits."

"Ahh! So good! She's the best, right?"

"Yeah, she's all right." Dua laughs when she sees my annoyed face. "Okay, she's incredible. I'll make you a deal. I'll see Kacey Musgraves with you if you see Haim with me." Dua has two main Spotify playlists she curates obsessively: modern Arab music, and dreamy rock with female singers.

"Double deal." I point to the Tilt-A-Whirl. "Do you get dizzy? Wanna go on that?"

After the Tilt-A-Whirl, we wander through the carnival, figuring out which rides we want to do next. We ride the Ferris wheel and the Flaming Dragon roller coaster before hunger hits.

"I love this carnival," I say, chomping down on a charred corn on the cob. "All the best parts of the South rolled into one."

"They've been doing it for years!" Dua says. "My siblings and I used to go together."

"Why don't they come anymore?"

"Oh, they do. They're around here somewhere. I just don't hang out with them voluntarily."

"You never talk about your siblings," I say.

"What's to talk about? They take pleasure in torturing me. They take up my parents' extra time. End of story," she says. "You must *not* have siblings. Otherwise, you'd get it."

"No. Only me."

"Didn't your parents want another?"

"They tried. A few times. It . . . didn't work out."

"Ah. Sucks. I bet you'd be a good big sister. Way less annoying than mine."

"Famous last words," I say. "How many siblings do you have again? Four?"

"Three." She ticks her fingers. "My older sister, Amina. My older brother, Zaki. And my younger sister, Tahirah."

Not long after, a guy with intelligent eyes, a brilliant smile, and dimples approaches us.

"Can I borrow your phone, please?" he asks Dua.

"Why? Is yours dead?"

"Yeah. Please? I'll be five seconds."

"Fine." She sighs, handing it over.

I look back and forth between them, noticing their similar features. "Your brother?"

"Hey, I'm Zak," he says, turning on his megawatt smile. "You must be Allie. I've heard a lot about you."

"Off-limits," Dua snaps.

"Whoa, chill. I was being polite. Be right back." And he wanders off with her phone.

"You don't get along?" I ask.

She laughs. "He's my favorite sibling."

"Why?"

"He minds his own business."

We play Skee-Ball, and between a run of good luck, Zak returns with a giant bag of candy. He offers it to us, along with Dua's phone and coins for the arcade. "I traded in cash for you. Thought you girls might like these."

Dua pockets the coins and pokes through the bag, taking out her favorite candies. "Thanks, Zaki!"

Her brother hangs out with us for a few minutes as we all play water-pistol derby. Dua's phone pings with a text, and before I know it, a giant group of Zak's friends has joined us, turning two into what feels like twenty.

"Allie, Dua, this is Fareed, Abdullah, Isham, Eisa . . ." Zak goes down the list as we each say "hey." The guys are around Zak's age, about seventeen or eighteen, but they seem more interested in laughing at something on Isham's phone than paying attention to us.

After a few seconds of pleasantries, they head en masse toward the old-school arcade—a herd of jeans, Adidas sneakers, and soccer jerseys—Abdullah waving goodbye to us and flashing Dua a grin as they walk away.

"Um, your brother's friends are male models," I say.

She looks incredulous. "You think they're cute?"

"You *don't*?"

"I've known them since I was, like, five. Ew."

"No crushes? Ever?"

She struggles to hide a smile. "Okay, I have eyes. Abdullah isn't bad looking."

"Understatement of the year. Abdullah is like if Zayn and Omar Borkan had a love child. Is he nice?"

"How do *you* know about Omar Borkan?" she says.

"Please. Kicked out of a country for being too gorgeous? I know how to use the Google. You're avoiding the question."

"Sure. He's nice."

"Have you two ever . . . flirted?"

Dua looks alarmed. "No way."

"What's the issue? He's cute, he's nice, he's religious—isn't he?"

"All of Zaki's friends are. But I told you: No guys. Not until I'm ready to get married, in a billion years."

"You can still *look*," I tease.

She doesn't seem amused.

Dua and I are walking back toward the Flaming Dragon when we cross paths with Emilia and Sarah.

"Allie!" Emilia says, looking guilty. "Hey!"

"Hi! What's up?"

"How are you?" Sarah asks, in an overly polite tone normally reserved for people you've observed from a distance—not people who've been to your house for a sleepover and have seen your parents fighting.

"Good," I say. "You?"

"We're good!" Emilia does this thing when she's nervous, where she twirls her hair. She's twirling up a storm right now. It makes me feel a little protective toward her. She's not a bad egg.

She's just not *my* egg.

"Oh, hey, this is my friend Dua," I say. "Dua, this is Emilia and Sarah."

"Hi!" Dua raises a hand in greeting. Emilia and Sarah say "hey" back.

"Where's Wells?" Sarah asks me.

"Home, I guess?"

"Oh. Right. Ha ha," she says weakly. "We would have invited you, but we assumed you'd be with him."

"No worries, honestly."

"You go to Providence, right?" Emilia asks Dua.

"Yep."

"Cool. Thought I recognized you."

"We're about to go on the Flaming Dragon again, if you want to come," Dua says.

"Ooh, thanks, but I don't do roller coasters," Emilia says. "Rain check?"

For when? Never?

"Totally," I say. "We'll see you around."

"They seem nice," Dua says as we stand in line.

I shrug. "Nice enough."

On Monday, Wells makes it to chorus before the bell rings.

"How'd you do it?" I say.

"Do what?" he asks.

"Get to class on time for once. Do you go home between

Spanish and chorus every morning for a quick *Game of Thrones* binge-watch?"

He laughs.

"You never get in trouble." I sigh. "You're one of *those* people."

"Why do you sound disappointed?" he asks, poking me in the side.

Emilia walks into the room and sits on the other side of me.

"Hi!" she says brightly. "I *love* that dress, Allie. You look gorge."

I'm surprised she's making an effort after our semiawkward carnival encounter. She and Sarah were obviously excluding me, which would have upset me over winter break. But now, she can probably sense I've pulled away, too. And she doesn't like it when people don't like *her*.

A fellow people pleaser, I suppose.

"Hi," I say. "What's up?"

"Drowning in algebra homework. Martinez has been going hard recently. You?"

"Yup," I say, nodding. "Same. Did you have fun at the carnival?"

"Definitely. You?"

"Yep."

"Your friend seemed nice. What's her name?"

"Dua."

"Dua. That's . . . unique."

"Yep."

We sit next to each other silently, our conversational limits reached. It would be so much easier if Wells were involved.

But he's playing on his cell phone, reading comments on his latest YouTube video.

Finally, I decide now's as good a time as any. Honestly, I want to see what she'll say.

"Hey, Emilia."

"Yeah?"

"Did you know I'm Muslim?"

She blinks. She blinks again.

After the third round, I have to stop myself from asking her if she has something in her eye.

"You're being serious, right?" she says.

"Yep."

"Wow," she finally says. "I had no idea!"

"Most people don't. I keep it quiet."

"*Oh,*" she says, realization dawning on her face. "So *that's* what that thing was all about."

"What thing?"

"I'm not trying to start something," she says. "Seriously. I just mean it makes more sense now. When you went ballistic in the cafeteria with Mikey a while back."

I squint, looking at her.

"You mean, me calling him out?" I say. "And you, too?"

She pauses, her expression wary. "Right."

"Okay."

"Allie?"

"Yeah?"

"I won't judge you for being Muslim, if that's what you're

worried about. I think it's cool." She smiles expectantly at me, like she's waiting for praise and undying gratitude.

Breathe deeply, Allie. Just breathe.

A verse I read recently comes to mind: *And him who seeks thy help, chide not.*

Be cool, Allie.

"I'm not worried," I say. "But thank you."

"I know you were sticking up for your people," she says. "And I know you're a good person."

Literally everything about the conversation is rubbing me the wrong way.

"You mean a good Muslim?"

"Well, yeah, of course."

"As opposed to a bad one?"

She looks wary again, as if I'm leading her into a trap. In a way, I am. But I'm sick of this good Muslim/bad Muslim crap. "Um," she says. "I guess?"

"A nice Muslim? A Muslim who does 'normal' American things, like drinking or eating bacon? A Muslim who doesn't cover their hair and who doesn't pray and who doesn't make people uncomfortable, right? That kind of Muslim?"

She puts her hands up. "Look, Allie, I don't want to fight. I'm sorry I didn't know, and I'm happy you told me, and can we leave it at that?"

I turn back to face the front of the classroom, seething inside, and I don't even know why. Is Emilia in the wrong, or am I?

"You okay?" Wells asks quietly, leaning over.

"Yep."

Am I overreacting to nothing?

I don't know anymore.

"Did you do something different to your hair?" Sarah asks me as we wait for the bus. Wells has soccer practice followed by an hour at a recording studio—paid for by Jack, of course—so I'm on my own for getting home.

"Not really. I haven't done much to it at all recently."

"That's what it is," Sarah says, snapping her fingers. "Your roots are kinda brownish. You stopped dying it red?"

My bus comes, and I stand. "Time for a change."

Sarah does debate, so she's good at controlling her emotions, but something fleeting passes across her face—a flicker of the brow, a widening of the eyes.

I'm dressing a little differently at school, too. While normally I'd wear a short, flouncy, flippy dress, recently I've been experimenting: Last Wednesday, I wore straight-leg jeans and a black-and-white polka-dot long-sleeved silk shirt. Truthfully, it's not like it's superconservative, but I can't remember the last time I wore pants. Dresses have been my thing here.

I guess other students have started noticing.

"Actually, Emilia told me you're Muslim. Is that true?" Sarah asks.

"Yep."

"Oh. Cool."

"Yep."

"Did your family convert? You don't look Muslim."

"What does that mean? Looking Muslim?"

"You know."

"I don't, actually. I'd love to hear you say what you mean. Do Muslims look a certain way?"

Am I being too aggressive, or do I have less tolerance for BS recently?

Is Sarah being rude, or am I?

She blanches. "I'm just trying to have a conversation, okay?"

"I'm Circassian."

"What's that?"

I long to say, *Google is your friend*, but I don't. Maybe she does want to learn.

I launch into an explanation of my background, only to realize her eyes are glazing over about five seconds into it. I cut myself off, feeling insulted, and say, "Anyhow, that's the deal."

The next day, it happens again. Wells and I are standing together at my locker, and he's showing me cell phone video from his recording session, when Mikey Murphy stops by. "Yo, Lincoln. There's a rumor going around you're Muslim. True?"

"True," I say flatly.

"That's crazy."

"Why?"

"Huh?"

"Why is the fact I'm Muslim 'crazy'? Which, by the way, is an offensive thing to say in itself."

"It's offensive to say you're Muslim?"

"No, it's offensive to say—never mind."

I'm not going to waste my breath on Mikey. He's a lost cause.

He looks at me like I'm weird and shrugs. "'Kay. Gotta get to class. Later."

Wells watches him walk away. "Why are we still friends with him again?" he says.

"Hey," I say, "that's on you, not me."

A couple days later, when the subject of terrorism comes up during World History, a few kids throw glances my way.

I know what people who've never experienced it would say:

It's not a big deal.

You're looking for a problem that doesn't exist.

Stop being so sensitive.

But I'm not imagining it.

I've gone from being just plain Allie to being Allie the Muslim. My identity boxed in, just like that.

CHAPTER TWENTY

This week's study group is at Shamsah's house. It's my second time here, and her place reminds me of mine—unlike Dua's and Fatima's houses, there are few visible signs of Islam.

"Did y'all have fun at the movies Friday night?" Fatima asks. "I saw your photos on Insta. Sorry I couldn't make it!"

"We did," I say, smiling. "What'd you do?"

I'm beginning to slide nicely into their routine. The text messages are coming on the regular, and the girls send me invites to things outside normal business hours: a Friday night dinner with family, an after-school meet-up at the bookstore. I have to decline most weekday invitations, because my course load is getting intense—but weekends are rife with hangout opportunities. When I'm not with Wells, obviously.

"My cousin got married out in Snellville," Fatima says. "And my mom took me to the *masjid*! She never goes anymore, so it was a pretty big deal."

I nod. "Nice!"

"It's gonna take work," Fatima says, "but I can get her back on track."

Leila starts giggling.

"What?" Fatima asks, peering at Leila's phone.

Leila swivels the screen to show us something on Tumblr. "It's a bunch of *fiqh* memes."

"What's a '*fiqh* meme'?" I ask.

"It's, like, poking fun at the way people interpret Islamic law," Dua explains.

Fatima nods. "It's a whole thing."

Leila laughs again, scrolling. "I'm obsessed with this account. It's hilarious."

"Yeah, but you're obsessed with Tumblr period." Dua turns to me. "Leila follows every Queen Rania account on Tumblr."

Leila's ears turn red. "So? She's gorge."

Once Samira arrives, we begin: first reading, and then discussing Qur'anic passages. At the end of class, I bring up the question I've been working up the courage to ask for weeks.

"Is there an updated stance on dating in Islam?" I ask Samira. "I know we're not *really* supposed to. But isn't that kind of outdated?"

Samira shakes her head. "It's not allowed. Dating is a Western concept."

"Oh."

Samira's cool and progressive, so I wait for her to say something like, *But don't worry, it's all good!*

She doesn't.

"So, it's like *haram* haram?" I ask. "Or a tiny bit *haram*? *Haram* lite."

This elicits a laugh. "I know you want me to say dating is fine," Samira says. "Perhaps I'm being a hypocrite: progressive on some issues, conservative on others. I'm sorry. The Qur'an is clear. Do I think you're going straight to hell if you kiss a boy once? No. But, yes, it's *haram*." Forbidden.

"Okay," I say glumly. "Thanks."

"I'm dating," Shamsah says loudly.

"You are?" I ask, feeling relieved.

Panic flashes in her eyes, replaced by something stronger, more defiant. "Yeah." An upturn of the chin, a setting of the jaw. *And what of it?*

"Cool," I say.

She relaxes visibly.

I want to know everything. *Haram* loves company.

"What's his deal?" I say.

"Um, not much to say," she responds.

"Where does he go to school?"

She pauses for a second. "Chattahoochee."

"Where'd you meet?"

"At the homecoming game. In September."

"So mysterious." I laugh.

Shamsah smiles, shrugging.

"Name?"

She pauses again. "Jamil."

Dua frowns. "Shamsaaaah." She wraps the name in disappointment and disapproval.

I look at Dua, surprised.

Like I had with Samira, I'd assumed she would be cool with it.

Dating as an American Muslim can be a bizarre through-the-looking-glass experience. None of my cousins raised in the US were set up through arranged marriage like their Jordanian parents—they met people on their own, like everybody else here. Some met on Islamic dating sites, others were set up through friends, and a few—like Houri and Rashid, my cousin Amal, and even my parents—dated American-style.

The difference is in the timing: My family moves *quick*. From first date to engagement took my parents three months. For Houri and Rashid, it was six, and for most of my various other Americanized cousins, it happened in a matter of weeks. But it's also more organic than it was back in the day, like for *Teta* and *Jido*, whose marriage was arranged between close family friends when she was seventeen and he was twenty. (I can't.)

"You're big girls, and you're going to do what you're going to do. You know I support you and don't judge—that's not my place," Samira says, looking around at the group. "But I'd be failing you if I didn't emphasize that the Qur'an is quite clear on the subject of dating before marriage."

"The Qur'an is clear about other things you disagree with," Shamsah says, looking irritated.

"I never disagree with the Qur'an—only skewed interpretations. But this is different," Samira says. "Physical contact before marriage is *haram*. And that's not a sexist thing—when the Qur'an is applied properly, it applies to men and women equally."

"Men don't get a pass," Dua says.

"Different only because you say so," Shamsah mutters, ignoring Dua.

Shamsah and I exchange glances.

"What if there's no physical contact?" I ask. "What if you're not kissing and holding hands, and definitely not having sex—is that okay?"

Samira frowns. "According to the Qur'an," she begins, launching into a series of translations explaining why not, before getting into various teachings about relations between the sexes.

"Thanks. Cool," I say, trying to keep the disappointment off my face.

Shamsah sighs and folds her arms over her chest. "Not cool."

After study group, Dua and I wait outside for our moms to pick us up.

"There's so much I don't know," I say. "I might as well be a convert. Converts know *more*. They try harder."

She gives me a serious look. "How's it going?"

"Good, I guess. I love the group, and I love the girls . . ."

"But?"

I swallow. "Sometimes I feel really alone. You know?"

She nods, though I'm not sure she gets it. "Have you told your dad?" she asks me. "You mentioned last week you were keeping it from him."

I bite my cuticle. "No. He's going to be weird about it. I told Wells, though. He took it fine."

Oh no.

"Who is Wells?" Dua asks.

No, no, no.

"Um. He's . . . well . . ." I should have brought it up in study group, but with Samira being down on dating, I didn't have the guts. I'm already breaking tradition by doing one of the things you're *not* supposed to do as a Muslim—I was hoping I could ease into those confessional waters. Dua seems liberal, so I hadn't been superworried about telling her, but considering how weird she was with Shamsah, now I'm concerned. "He's . . . um . . . We . . ."

"Your boyfriend."

"Yeah."

Dua looks disapproving. "Oh."

"It's new," I tell her in a rush. "We've only been . . . whatever . . . this semester."

"Okay." She licks her lips, nodding. "Is he a Muslim?"

"No."

"Ah."

A wellspring of anxiety bubbles up in my chest. I know this feeling. If I don't let it out gently, it'll explode, making a bad situation way, way worse.

"You think it's a bad idea?"

She sighs. "What do you want me to say, Allie? Do you want the honest response or the encouraging response? I'll give you whichever one you can handle right now."

"Honest." I don't mean it.

"Dating is *haram*. And dating outside the faith is even worse."

"I thought marrying outside the faith was the problem."

She looks alarmed. "You want to marry him?"

"No! I don't know! We've been dating for like eight seconds. I just mean"—I exhale my frustration—"I'm trying to do it properly. I want to get it right. But it seems kind of arbitrary: Men can marry 'People of the Book,' but women can only marry Muslims? I get why that was the case in the six hundreds. But it's like fourteen hundred years later. It doesn't make sense anymore."

Dua seems offended. "Look. I understand you're new to this. But there are people who've been studying this way longer than you. It's *literally* the exact opposite of arbitrary. It's *literally* the word of *Allah*."

"Or maybe it's a giant game of Telephone."

She gives me a look saying, *You have got to be kidding me.*

Oh, Allie. You're on thin ice here.

I clear my throat. "I'm just saying, the Qur'an wasn't written down for like seventy years after the Prophet, peace be upon him, died. Maybe the guys who wrote it down got some of it . . . wrong?"

"Allie." Dua looks disappointed.

"The Qur'an is divine, I get that. But how do we know the

hadiths are really true?" I say. "Okay, the Authentic Six . . . al-Bukhari . . . Sahih Muslim, fine. But *all* of them? They're memories of what the Prophet said and did, but some of them weren't compiled for generations after his death. Like, if Leila and I wrote down everything we remember you saying and doing last month, we'd have two different memories. Two different insights. Two different interpretations. Right?"

"You can't remake the religion in your own image. Sorry. That's not how it works. And besides, the *hadiths* have been examined and authenticated and ranked. By *experts*."

"Ok*aaay*. Sorry."

I have no idea how the conversation ended up like this—and with Dua, of all people.

We both pick up our phones, fiddling with them as we wait for our moms. And as we stand there, I keep swiping away the tears pooling in the corners of my eyes.

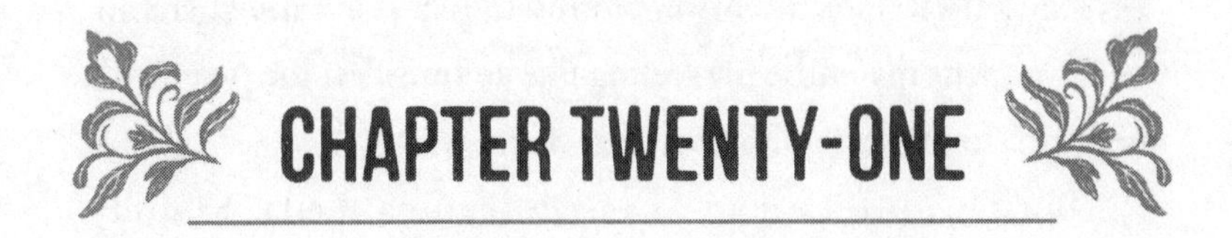

CHAPTER TWENTY-ONE

Most days, I love French class—an excuse to pretend I'm Amélie—but today, I'm distracted, thinking about how Dua reacted yesterday to the news that Wells and I are dating.

After searching for so long, I'd started to feel like I'd finally found my group. Like I was safe.

But maybe they're not my group at all.

Maybe I'm just as alone as I've always been.

Ms. Carter stands at the head of the classroom, a gold fleur-de-lis pinned to her navy blazer. She's born and raised in Georgia, and speaks both English and French with a heavy Southern accent.

"*Très bien*, y'all. Let's move on to *croire*, *le subjonctif*." Behind her, the chalkboard is marked in her distinctive cursive.

Je croie. Tu croies. Il croie. Nous croyions. Vous croyiez. Ils croient.

From time to time, I glance up at Ms. Carter as I repeat conjugations aloud with the rest of the class. I scribble in my notebook and try to look attentive, but my thoughts are elsewhere.

I've spent my entire life feeling like an outsider: the perennial new girl, forever the tiniest bit out of sync.

But Dua is different. Shamsah, Fatima, Leila, Samira: They're different.

It's hard to explain, but these past couple of months, it's felt like they could be family.

I think back to praying with Dua at her house and how alienating it is being unable to speak Arabic. Language is more than words. It's a story, a history, a shared experience. From the time I was young, I understood there was a chasm between me and my dad's family—an impenetrable wall because of the failure of my ears, the failure of my tongue.

"What does this mean, Daddy?" I'd ask, repeating a phrase I'd heard Aunt Bila or Houri say.

My father's answers were short, terse. Replies designed to shut the conversation down.

"English is so much more beautiful than Arabic," he said once at the dinner table, after I questioned a phrase I'd heard him utter. "You're lucky you grew up speaking it. It took me years to master."

"I think Arabic sounds pretty cool."

"Eh."

Maybe if I'd grown up speaking Arabic like the rest of my family, I'd feel more in touch with my heritage. Less tentative about taking control of my religion and saying, *I have as much right to this as any other Muslim*. More willing to challenge and question and push back when things don't make sense to me.

Maybe I wouldn't have spent my life feeling like the outsider who didn't fit.

"*D'accord*, y'all. *Très bien*."

Ms. Carter erases *croire* and moves on to the verb *vouloir*, conjugating it in her loopy handwriting as the class dutifully chants, "*Je veuillle. Tu veuilles. Il veuille. Nous voulions. Vous vouliez. Ils veuillent*," sounding like the world's least inspiring mob.

I pull my phone out of my purse and discreetly scroll through the app store until I find the prayer app both *Teta* and Dua use: Muslim Pro.

I am becoming a professional Muslim.

I stifle a giggle.

"Allie? *Ça va?*"

"*Oui*, Mademoiselle Carter. *Ça va*." She looks at me suspiciously. I smile back sweetly.

After downloading the app, I play with it under my desk. It has *hadiths*, so you can read prophetic conversations and lessons on the go, plus it gives you *duas* for the day. (I can't believe it's taken me this long to realize Dua's name has a meaning: supplication.) Most people use the app to face the right way while praying—the *Ka'baa* in Mecca—and to know the five daily prayer times: *Fajr*, *Dhuhr*, *Asr*, *Maghrib*, and *Isha*.

When the bell rings, I've been poking through the app for a good twenty minutes. I realize I have no idea what the homework is, so I lean over to the girl next to me, whispering, "What did she say the assignment was again?"

She looks surprised, her eyes widening behind her glasses. "*You* weren't paying attention? It's the subjunctive worksheet at the end of chapter three."

"Cool, thanks." I gather my bags quickly, stuffing my phone into the unzipped side of my purse and rushing off to chorus.

We're in the middle of practicing "Summer Nights" when it happens: a plaintive call in Arabic, melodic and mellifluous, the *adhan* of the Qur'an.

"Allahu akbar. Ashhadu an la ilaha illa Allah . . ."

It's my prayer app.

I fumble in my purse, reaching for my phone to turn it off, stabbing at the button to silence the call to prayer piercing through the now-blazing silence of the chorus room.

Every face in the room is trained on mine, eyes wide, jaws slack.

Wells, Emilia, Mikey, Mr. Tucker . . . they all look incredulous.

The blood rushes to my ears, and my face grows warm, but I force myself to hold my head high. Why should I feel embarrassed? Why should I apologize?

"It tells me when to pray," I say, gripping my phone as I hold it aloft, as much to show them as to keep my shaky hand steady. "Right now is *Dhuhr*. It goes off five times a day."

My heart jackhammers against my chest.

The bell rings, and Mr. Tucker dismisses us.

I avoid making eye contact with anybody as I put my sheet music into my bag, purposely taking my time so I'll be the last to leave the room.

Wells waits next to me, looking awkward.

I wave him off.

"It's okay," I say. "I'll meet you later."

"You sure?"

"Yeah, yeah. I need to stop by my locker."

"I don't mind . . ."

"Wells, it's fine! I'm okay!" I fumble with the music, trying to jam it into my backpack. The sheets scatter around me.

He backs away—message received.

"See you soon," he says tentatively, looking back at me before exiting the room.

What's wrong with me that I feel so humiliated? I wonder. *What's the big deal?*

I have no idea. But I feel embarrassed down to the core of my soul.

The embarrassment sticks until I'm out in the hallway, when I hear a student make a high-pitched *la-la-la-la* noise. Maybe it's Mikey. Maybe it's another loser.

There's more laughter, then the smack of hands slapping together in high fives.

I think about how beautiful and pure and hopeful praying makes me feel, and my embarrassment is gone—replaced with anger. How dare they?

Later that night, in a fit of pique, I use the credit card my mother gave me for emergencies to order a pretty blue iridescent hijab from Amazon.

I'm done hiding.

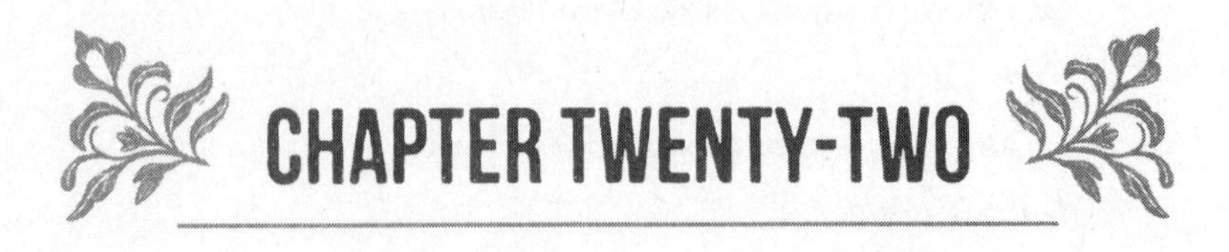

CHAPTER TWENTY-TWO

The next morning, Dua sends me a text.

Wanna go to the mall after school? We can talk shop

When I tell Wells after algebra that he doesn't need to drive me home because I'm going out with Dua, he seems apprehensive. He knows about our tiff.

"Is that a good idea?" he asks as we stop by my locker.

"We have to clear the air sooner or later. It's been awkward."

"I'm not surprised," he says, frowning.

"Hey," I say, setting my backpack down and reaching over to grab his hand. "She's not talking me out of dating you. Not happening."

He looks like a vulnerable little boy. "My dad, your friends," he says. "We're like Romeo and Juliet."

I burst out laughing. "Minus the poison, okay?"

I stuff my books into my backpack and then sling it over my shoulders, smoothing down my tunic—it's similar to something

I saw one of my favorite Muslim fashion Instagrammers wearing. I know it's silly to be concerned about whether I look Muslim enough, but the truth is, I *want* to show the world I'm changing. That I've changed.

I'm not wearing a hijab—not yet—but lengthening my skirts and choosing modest tops seems like an easy place to start.

It's shallow. I *know* it's shallow.

But I also find it empowering. No one gets to see my skin—not unless I choose.

I don't know. I'm still figuring the whole thing out.

"Has your dad said anything?" I ask Wells after we stop by his locker.

"About you?"

"Yeah."

"Nope. That would require talking about someone other than himself."

I think back to our dinner with Jack. There *was* something off about the entire situation—something I couldn't put my finger on. (I mean, something *other* than the lingering stench of bigotry.)

"You and your dad don't get along, do you?"

Wells face tightens. "Nope."

"What about your mom?"

We exit the school doors, where I see Dua waiting across the street. I wave at her, pantomiming that I'll be there in a minute.

He shuffles back and forth in his sneakers, looking antsy. Suddenly, I realize the question might be too intrusive. "I'm sorry. Not my business."

"Have fun with Dua. Just be careful."

He leans down, gives me a fit-for-public-view kiss on the cheek, and then lopes across the street toward the parking lot.

"Listen," Dua says by her car. "I want to apologize."

"You do?" I say.

"Yeah. It came out wrong. It's not okay for me to judge you."

"Thanks, Dua."

"I mean, I wish you *wouldn't* date. I really don't think it's Islamic, and if I'm being honest, it irritates me . . . but it's not my business," she says. "I kinda like ya, Allie," she cracks, trying to lighten the mood. "And I know you're going to mess up and it'll take time to find your way, because I've messed up and it's taken time to find mine. I'm still finding it, I guess. But I'm here for you while you get there, however long it takes. And if you never get there . . . that would be the worst, but it's between you and *Allah*, *subhanahu wa ta'ala*, and He knows best."

I can't help it. I reach over and give her a hug. She immediately hugs me back.

"Thank you," I whisper. "It means a lot to me."

"You dork," she says, and she smiles as we get into her car.

Dua tells me on the ride that she's invited Fatima, Leila, and Shamsah to meet up, to get their take on the best fund-raising strategies. We meet up with the girls half an hour later by the food court, standing in line for chicken sandwiches.

"Ugh. I always feel guilty coming here," Leila says.

"Why?" I ask.

"I mean, it's hardly halal."

"But it's so good," Dua says.

We're camped out at a table when a group of guys walks by. I'm so engrossed in Fatima's suggestions that I barely notice them at first.

I hear them before I see them.

"Go back where you came from."

I look around in alarm, trying to figure out who said it.

Was it directed at us?

Yes.

A white boy in a baseball cap emblazoned with red fraternity letters is looking at us. His face is laughing, his teeth bared, but his eyes are unsmiling. He means it.

"Stupid ninjas," says another boy. His pale biceps flex, and his right fist clenches against the waist of his khaki pants. On his wrist, an expensive watch gleams. I stare at him, deconstructing him to a series of details I could provide the police if I needed to: red polo shirt, ruddy cheeks, ruffled blond hair, watery blue eyes.

Leila stares down at the table, her eyes on her sandwich. She picks up a French fry and puts it in her mouth, chewing it slowly. She catches my gaze and shakes her head imperceptibly, hijab gently rippling from side to side.

The girls maintain their focus, suddenly extremely interested in their meals. Nobody talks. I keep the guy in my sight line as he walks around the corner with his friends, laughing.

Finally safe, we unpause ourselves.

"What was that?" I say.

Leila shrugs wearily. "Losers." She sips her Coke.

"Does that happen a lot?"

Fatima nods. "Recently? Yeah. All the time."

"What about at school?"

"All. The. Time," Leila says.

Dua, Shamsah, and I exchange glances. The three of us don't wear headscarves, and there are no visible markers of Islam. To most of the world, I'm simply a basic white girl with red hair. Until recently, the type of Islamophobia I've experienced has been secondhand—directed at others by people who don't know they're insulting me, too. But Fatima and Leila, by making the choice to veil, are inviting ignorance and unwanted comments every single day. More than ever, I understand their decision to wear the hijab as brave and beautiful.

Dua speaks up.

"You know, when I'm in Jordan, I feel safer there than when I'm in America. When I visited my family in Amman, I felt I could walk on the streets by myself and nothing would happen to me, nobody would touch me. I don't feel that here, even though I don't wear a headscarf. It's easy to get scared. And it's gotten worse recently. But"—she lifts her chin defiantly—"we can't let fear rule our lives. *They're* the monsters, not us."

So I guess I was wrong about it happening only to Fatima and Leila.

"That's the first time anything like that's happened to me," I confess. "I mean, my family has had incidents, but it's been different." I explain how I helped defuse the situation on the airplane with my father over Christmas break. "It's like, hello, white privilege," I say.

Fatima nods. "I get it from both sides. Ignorant people saying stuff about my hijab—it never gets easier, but at least I'm used to it by now. But I don't always feel one hundred percent in the *ummah*, either. The Black Muslim experience is erased so often—you have no idea. I feel like a second-class citizen in two spaces."

"Love you, Fati," Leila says, looking doleful.

Fatima reaches over to squeeze her hand. "Love you, too, Lei."

Leila sighs and then leans back in her seat. "I wish I could get it through people's thick skulls that I love wearing hijab. It reminds me of what's important. Nobody is forcing me. It's an honor."

"Yes!" Fatima says. "It's not an act. It's a choice."

"It's you existing," Dua says quietly. They nod in return.

As we finish our sandwiches, the guys long gone by now, an older white man comes over to us. His face is kindly, etched with concern.

"I saw what happened, girls. I'm sorry. Are you all right?"

Dua nods. I recognize the polite look taking over her face. And when she speaks, I know the Don't Worry About It voice coming out of her mouth. "We're okay. Thank you."

"You girls don't know them, do you?"

As he talks, I realize he's primarily addressing me.

It reminds me of going out to eat with my parents, when the

waiters always address my father and never present the check to my mother.

Even when my father was finishing his degree, and my mother was the breadwinner.

Maybe I'm wrong. Maybe I'm reading into it.

But it certainly feels like the überwhite dude is talking to *me*, over my friends, because he identifies *me* as überwhite, too.

Dua and I exchange a glance. She reads it.

"We don't know them," she says. "But we're safe. Thank you for asking."

"I'm so glad," he says. He's still looking at me.

This entire exchange is miles over his head.

For multiple reasons, I'll never forget it.

"But what did they say *exactly*?" Wells asks.

I repeat the story over the phone word for word, lying back on my bed and staring at the ceiling.

I can hear him frowning through the phone. I wait for him to diminish what happened. Instead, he says, "It's horrible. I can't believe it."

"You can't? I can."

"Our country is better than this."

"But we're not."

"You think it'll be like this forever?" he asks.

"Like what? Racist?"

"Divided."

"It's always been divided."

"Yeah, but it's different now. It's worse."

I consider the question. "I don't know if things are worse. It's just—people who aren't marginalized are finally paying attention. Maybe that's insulting, but it's still a good thing. Maybe it has to get worse before it gets better."

"So wise, young Jedi," Wells says.

I laugh, pleased. "On to something more fun, okay?" We talk about the end of the soccer season and his latest studio session before moving on to the MSA fund-raiser. "We're trying to get to five thousand dollars," I say.

"How much have you got so far?"

"Just past six hundred."

"Ouch."

"Believe me. It's not like Providence is *the* national poster child for woke schools, but I thought we would have raised more."

"Can I help?" he says.

"Sure you're up for it?"

"Yeah, as long as we don't tell my dad." He laughs.

I don't.

He clears his throat.

"Has anything else happened to you?" he says. "At school, I mean."

"After my prayer app blared in class? Nah, that was enough. Although I do wonder what would happen if I . . . say . . . came to school wearing hijab."

Silence.

Finally, he says, "You think that's a good idea?"

"I'm not doing it. Just wondering."

There's something unspoken in the air between Dad and me.

I try to make up for it that weekend, canceling Saturday night plans with Wells to watch a movie with my parents. My dad's face looks so happy when he hears I'm staying in that it makes me feel like the worst daughter on the planet.

"Should we watch *Singin' in the Rain*?" I scroll through options on the Apple TV without waiting for his response.

"Ice cream?" he says.

"Obviously."

He practically bounds to the kitchen. "I'm getting us all some ice cream," he sings slightly off-key, to the tune of "Good Vibrations." "Our Allie is craving ice cream . . . Al, Al, Al, she wants ice cream . . . bop bop."

He does this when he's happy. Makes up songs about real life.

Mom looks at me, grinning. "You did good, kid," she whispers.

When Dad comes back, he's carrying a tray laden with three different kinds of ice cream and a host of toppings, including cherries, strawberries, hot fudge, and whipped cream.

"Sundae bar!" He places the tray on the table next to his stack of paperwork and turns to me. "One Allie Abraham special?"

"Sure, Dad."

"Coming right up!"

He places two scoops of chocolate ice cream in a bowl, topped with a dash of vanilla, sliced bananas and almonds, a mountain of chocolate syrup, and fruit garnishes.

We settle in at our usual spots on the couch, the old, familiar routine. Life is good.

But as I watch my parents giggling at Cosmo Brown's pratfalls during "Make 'Em Laugh," I've never felt sadder.

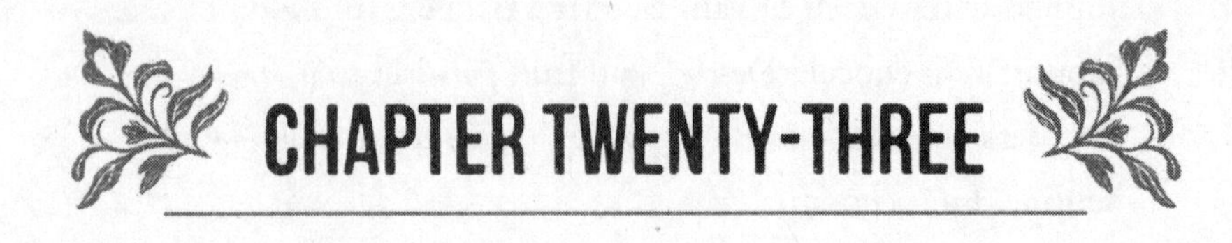

CHAPTER TWENTY-THREE

"We're home!" Dad says, ushering *Teta* through the front door. I mute the TV and rush into the foyer to greet her.

Whenever *Teta* arrives for a visit, gravity bends to her will. Gone are the Netflix dramas, the droning of cable news, the radio tuned to NPR over dinner. Instead, the satellite TV shows an endless parade of Arabic news, soccer games, music videos, and Turkish soap operas. Tea is brought. Pillows are fluffed.

Dad takes her bags, and Mom and I give her double-cheek kisses and hugs. Mom ushers her into the living room so she can put her feet up and we can serve her tea. Behind them, the colder-than-usual March air floods the house.

After dinner, the family gathers in the living room to begin a subtitled repeat viewing of *Teta*'s favorite old series, *Aşk-i Memnu.* (Dad always complains about it, but he knows the characters' names and clucks disapproval over Behlül and Bihter's forbidden romance, so he's obviously been paying attention.) I'm zoned out, working on homework, when I realize *Teta*'s gravelly voice has become raised. She's gesticulating wildly and seems to be talking about me. Despite our fawning and my facade, she must have realized something's up. Dad frowns and shrugs. Then he sighs, leaving the room looking defeated.

"*Ta'ali*," *Teta* says, waving me over to her.

I obey.

She pulls me in close, plopping me onto her lap and patting my back as if I'm a toddler. At times, I find this annoying—and always embarrassing—but it's also weirdly comforting. I am loved.

"*Baba*," she says, referring to my father. She makes an exasperated shaking gesture with her head, clicking her tongue, before launching into an Arabic sentence I can't quite grasp.

Although I want to ask what's wrong, want to have a meaty conversation with her, I respond the only way I know how: by politely smiling, laughing, and nodding.

My dad likes to tell a famous family story about when the king of Jordan came by the Ibrahimi compound in Nablus before he was born, back when my grandfather was governor of the area. The king said something *Teta* didn't like—whatever it was, lost to the ages—and Teta responded by telling him off. The household staff froze, unable to believe anybody was speaking to the king this way.

The king simply laughed, saying he'd heard of Nabila Ibrahimi's infamously sharp tongue. Nobody intimidated her.

I could take a page or two from her book.

Whether king or commoner, it didn't matter. She bowed to nobody.

Every night after dinner, *Teta* goes into the living room while Mom and Dad clean up. After decades of cleaning up after other people, she's earned the right to put her feet up. Our culture is nothing if not hierarchical.

Her routine is the same. While she relaxes, she flips through the Arabic gossip magazines she's brought with her—what has Assala Nasri done this time?—as YouTube videos of *Arab Idol* stream through the Apple TV onto our flat-screen. Mom brings her coffee, Dad brings her dessert (either fried dough balls with honey, a Circassian specialty, or a rice pudding covered in pistachios), and after making her way through both, she calls back home to Dallas to video-chat with the family, who are always awake into the wee hours.

I come downstairs with a stack of homework, hearing Dad on speaker in the kitchen with Aunt Bila. From the tone of it, he's giving her advice. I settle next to *Teta* on the couch, and she leans over to give me a big wet kiss on the cheek. "*Ya rouhi*," she says.

Dad sounds exasperated, his voice carrying. "You can't expect them to listen to you all the time, *habibti*." Knowing Aunt Bila, this conversation has gone on for some time.

"*Wallahi*, I know, Muhammad," my aunt says, and she switches into Arabic. They do this, switch indiscriminately between Arabic, Circassian, and English, even when there are no English speakers nearby.

I always assumed they spoke Arabic because they knew it better.

Maybe they speak it because they'll lose it if they don't.

I hear my cousin Asad's name and realize my aunt is complaining about Houri's younger brother. He's seventeen years old and a bit of a troublemaker in the family: sneaking out, drinking, making bawdy comments at inappropriate times, and generally getting in trouble. His behavior is even more noticeable because he's a fraternal twin, and his brother Amir is a perfect Muslim gentleman: has a kind word for everybody, helpful to Aunt Bila and *Teta*, thoughtful, dependable, and devout.

My dad says something else in Arabic, then he switches into English. "You can't be so hard on him—you know how it is with children. And in any case, you have to let them grow. They need to make their own mistakes."

It's funny hearing my dad be levelheaded with other people. I'm still afraid to tell him I'm becoming religious, because I know he won't extend the same courtesy to me. Maybe I'm being dramatic, but I think he'll be furious when he finds out.

Dad comes back into the room, handing the phone to *Teta*.

"*Ya habibti*, Mama!" Aunt Bila says in her distinctive high-pitched voice.

The two of them go back and forth, switching from Arabic to Circassian. The language started dying out after the Circassians were forced from their homeland. Even my cousins who are fluent in Arabic don't speak much Circassian—it's only the older generation in our family who still does.

Yet another example of assimilation erasing little bits of home.

My great-grandparents learned Arabic.

My dad learned English.

And I've learned nothing.

"Is that Alia?" Aunt Bila says, switching into English as she sees me next to *Teta*. "How are you, *ya rouhi*?"

"Hi, *Amto*! I'm good. How are you?"

"*Wallahi*, missing you, *ya rouhi*. I wish I were there with you!"

We chat about the weather in Dallas, her bad hip, and my upcoming midterm exams. By the time Mom and Dad have finished cleaning the kitchen, we're on to my university hopes, with Aunt Bila encouraging me to keep studying "computers." Suddenly, she switches gears.

"Houri told me you've been praying, *mashallah*."

I freeze, feeling under the microscope. My father is sitting across the room, head down and pen to paper as he tweaks upcoming lectures. Whenever possible, he's analog.

"Mmm?" I say quietly, noncommittal.

"*Wallahi*, God will provide good things, *ya Alia*. I'm so proud of you. You know I didn't even start praying until I was forty!" She laughs.

"Oh?" I wish my dad would leave the room so I could have a real conversation with my aunt.

"Does your school have any Muslims?" she asks.

"A few."

"Are they your friends?"

"Sure." I don't want to get into it in front of my dad.

"I'm proud of you, *ya rouhi*," she repeats. "You got there on your own. God will provide for you *twice* as much."

"Thanks, *Amto*."

"People have these ideas about Muslims," she says, oblivious to the fact I don't want to continue this conversation with my father around. Her normally sunny face looks downcast, her voice dejected.

My father puts down his stack of papers and walks into the kitchen with his coffee cup. Alone at last.

"What do you mean, *Amto*?" I ask. "What ideas?"

"The women are oppressed, the men are monsters. I am not a second-class citizen! The Qur'an uplifts women, not oppresses them!"

I've heard my aunt go off on this line of reasoning before, but I give her the space and respect, nodding as if to say, *Go on*.

"Before Islam, women were treated horribly. The Qur'an allowed women property, the Qur'an provided for inheritances, it gave women legal status, it allowed them the right to vote, and it encouraged their education. Here in the US, women couldn't vote until last century. Muslim women have had that right for centuries! *Wallahi*, if people just *knew* Muslims are like them. We are the same. Maybe there wouldn't be so much fear and hatred."

I want to reach through the phone screen and hug her. "I love you, *Amto*," I say.

My dad walks back into the room with a fresh cup of coffee, and I feel self-conscious again. I change the subject, asking how Houri is doing and complimenting my aunt on her new haircut.

When we hang up the phone, Dad looks over at me, curious. "What was all that?"

"All what?"

"Aunt Bila, talking about praying and that nonsense."

"Uh, she's confused," I lie. "*Teta* asked me to pray with her, that's all."

My dad nods, mollified.

Later that night, after I give my parents and *Teta* hugs and kisses, I retreat upstairs to my room. I shoot Wells a good-night text, even though I don't plan to go to sleep for ages, and I reach into my closet, pulling out my copy of the Qur'an.

Despite going to study group and meeting with the MSA, I'm still not serious enough about my studies. I'm not praying five times a day, and definitely not at the prescribed times. I'm dating Wells, which is obviously *haram*. And I'm lying to my dad on the regular.

Things need to change.

Allie 2.0.

I open the Qur'an, running my hand over the pages. It's such a beautiful, miraculous book. I'm realizing it doesn't matter to me if it's the perfect, unchanging word of *Allah* or a giant game of Telephone or pieced together by men with political agendas or nuanced, gray, and somewhere in between.

When I read it, I feel connected. I feel calm. I'm part of something bigger than myself.

I flip open the cover and lose myself into the wee hours.

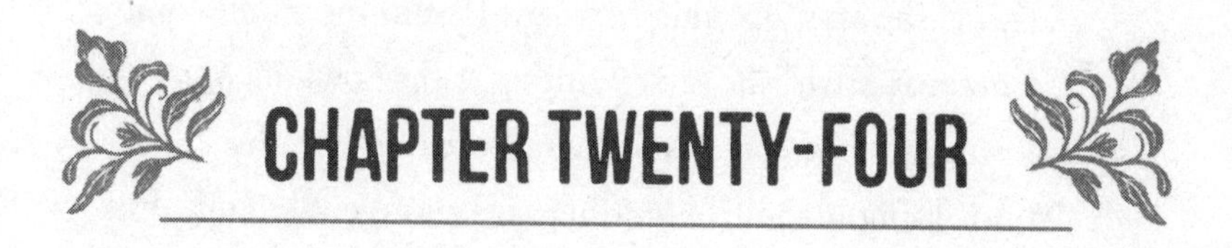

CHAPTER TWENTY-FOUR

It's the smell that makes it feel like home.

The sizzling onions, the pungent garlic, the spices—the sumac and allspice and cumin and turmeric—all of it brings the comfort and safety of my childhood rushing back.

Of all the members of my family, *Teta* is unquestionably the cooking master. Her specialty is spiced meats: rolled in flour and fried, sautéed with umpteen different herbs, baked in a colorful vegetable and blanketed in oil and salt.

It would be tragic to be a Middle Eastern vegetarian. I don't know how Houri does it.

On the days *Teta* is visiting, I come straight home from school—no lingering in the parking lot with Wells, no trips to the mall with Dua and the girls. I find myself wanting to spend time with her.

And despite the fact we can barely talk to each other, somehow, we understand.

"*Ta'ali,*" she says, opening her arms toward me, and I come.

"*A'ateeny hadtha,*" she says, pointing at the bowl full of green squash waiting to be cored, and I hand them to her.

"Am I doing it right?" I ask her, as I plunge the long, thin corer into the squash, scraping out the insides and dumping them into a bowl, the vegetables expelling their guts as if they're secrets waiting to be spilled. She glances at my squash and shakes her head.

"*Laa. A'afeel hadtha,*" she says, grabbing the squash and the corer from me and showing me how to slice it—thin, thinner, thinnest.

For the most part, cooking doesn't require talking, which is why I think we love doing it together. It's rhythmic and productive, our assembly line of food.

I mix the rice and the spices and the beef together, while *Teta* expertly cores the squash one by one, a flick of her wrist and a tug of her arm and, voilà, they're ready. (As opposed to my sad version of stuffed squash, where I end up stabbing the squash and cutting holes into them, though I try so very hard to do it right.)

The ritual takes about half an hour, and once the squash are cored and the rice-meat mixture is ready, it's time to stuff them.

Wordlessly, the two of us sit at the table, filling the squash halfway with the rice mixture. Only once does *Teta* talk to me during the procedure, when she sees me overfill a squash.

"*Laa,*" she says, shaking her head in disapproval. She's adamant the squash should be loosely stuffed.

I tip over the squash, allowing a little of the rice to fall back into the bowl, and she nods in assent, smiling. "*Aiwa*," she says.

As we work together, there are so many questions I want to ask:

Why didn't you learn English? Why didn't you teach me *your language?*

How long did it take you to fall in love with Jido*?*

Did you feel pressured to get married so young? Did you have a say?

Teta was seventeen when she married my grandfather. They were third cousins once removed, an arrangement that might seem weird by American standards, but wasn't bizarre by Circassian ones. (Hey, Queen Victoria and Prince Albert were first cousins, and theirs was one of the greatest love stories of all times, if Netflix is to be believed.)

There are so many questions I want to ask her, but I don't.

Because I can't.

The call to *Dhuhr* starts, a plaintive wailing from *Teta*'s phone on the coffee table. Dad's face tightens at the sound, but he doesn't say anything.

Teta is sitting next to my dad, her fingers clutching her prayer beads. She threads them mindlessly all day long—except I'm realizing it's probably not mindless.

After the call to prayer rings, *Teta* motions to me. "*Ta'ali.*"

She takes me by the hand, leading me out of the room and up the stairs toward the guest bedroom she's turned into a temporary home with silk flowers and a framed photo of *Jido*. I sense my father's eyes heavy on my back as we walk away.

In the room, she pulls out a prayer rug, an intricate black-and-gold woven mat with the *Ka'baa* embroidered in the center. She gestures at it, saying something in Arabic. When I don't respond, she repeats herself, pointing at my bedroom. *Ah, I get it*: She wants me to grab my own rug.

I return with my mat and my abaya, leaving them on the bed and following *Teta* into the guest bathroom, where we splash water on our hands, faces, and feet.

"*Ta'ali*," she says again. I move closer to her, and she washes my feet, her hands vigorously rubbing soap and water over my heels and toes. The gesture is slightly awkward, more physically intimate than I'm used to being with my sixty-year-old grandmother, but it's also sweet.

After she performs her own ablutions, we return to the bedroom, where *Teta* leads the prayers.

While we pray, I focus my intentions on gratitude.

Gratitude for my life. Gratitude for my *teta*. And, yes, gratitude for my dad—even though he's being exceptionally frustrating.

I sneak glances at my *teta*, feeling connected to her as we pray. It's a special feeling—as though we are one.

4:28 a.m.

My alarm goes off.

For once, I don't hit SNOOZE.

I crawl out of bed well before sunrise. The house is silent; even my mother won't be waking up for at least another hour.

She always gets up early, to hit the pool at the gym and swim thirty laps. When I was young, my father would rise in solidarity, though he didn't have classes until ten most days, and the two of them would pad around the kitchen together. Every once in a while, I'd wake to their voices wafting up the stairs, the sound of laughter making me feel cozy in bed.

Today, it's quiet. *Teta* flew back to Dallas last night, and her departure left a void. No hum of cable news or satellite TV in the background. No grinding of coffee. No chatter and laughter between my parents as the two of them talk about what they're expecting from the day and teasingly push each other's buttons.

I peek out of my window into the darkness. Our house is at the end of a cul-de-sac, nestled in the middle of Cape Cods and brick Colonials, rife with picket fences, Uga bulldogs, and American flags—Dad's dream street made real.

I turn on the lamp next to my bed and pull open my drawer, pulling out my copy of the Qur'an. I'm rereading it more slowly in the hopes of absorbing it—of truly understanding what it's saying.

I'm on the thirty-second surah, known as *Surah as-Sajdah*. I learned at study group that the Prophet Muhammad, peace be upon him, reportedly recited it every night before bed. It's an intense one, full of fire and brimstone, like the Old Testament of the Bible. I've been rereading the *surahs* several times, trying to soak them up, to understand them, to feel them in my soul.

And what a soulful time it is. It clicks: That's the advantage of getting up early to pray. No background noise, none of my friends posting on social media—just me and my thoughts.

It's been a rough year, with so much uncertainty. But despite the bumps—with Wells, with my dad, with everything—things are changing for the better.

I can feel it.

PART THREE

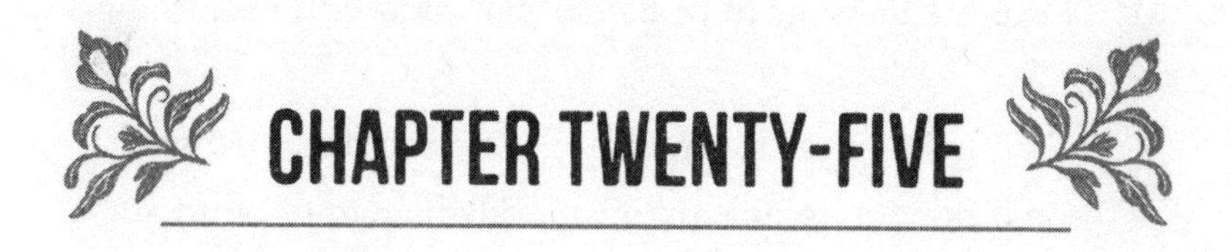

CHAPTER TWENTY-FIVE

"Salaam a'alaykum," Samira says to me as I walk into my living room. In the kitchen, I hear Mom puttering around, making a snack platter.

This part is easy.

"Wa a'alaykum as-salaam," I respond.

"Kefic, ya Alia?"

"Hamdullah."

I'm a few weeks into my Arabic lessons with Samira. So far, spring has been all about new beginnings: starting Arabic, helping the MSA raise more money, learning my lines for the school musical, memorizing prayers and studying the history of Islam, trying to match my words to my deeds.

We've been doing Arabic lessons once a week, on Saturdays at my house. Dad knows about it—I lied and said Teta begged me to—but I've been trying to minimize exposure by scheduling the lessons in the early afternoon, while he's sequestered upstairs slogging through research or grant applications.

I expected lessons to be harder, but shocker: I'm learning easily.

"You have an ear for it, Alia," Samira told me last week. "You're picking it up much more quickly than most of my students."

"Really?"

"It's clear you grew up hearing it. Your accent is strong. Not perfect, mind you, but strong."

"That's awesome!"

"No pressure, but you might consider studying without transliteration."

"What's that?"

"Instead of studying with an English alphabet, which isn't precise, we could essentially start from scratch with the Arabic characters. I think you'd learn it quickly."

"You think?"

"Sure. You're a fast study. You're good with languages. Most importantly, you have the motivation. Wanting to learn is nearly as important as doing the work. Motivation is key."

I loved the idea of being able to not just speak with my teta but to read the Qur'an in the original language, of being able to connect with my ancestors through the written word.

"Let's do it," I said, internally squashing worries about juggling Arabic lessons with my course load. I ordered all the textbooks that night, including a giant one called Al-Kitaab, written almost entirely in Arabic. There's something so satisfying about crisp, new pages. And reading from right to left is even cooler.

"How did you find the homework?" Samira asks me now.

I pull the Al-Kitaab book and some loose-leaf papers out of my backpack. "It was harder than I expected," I admit. I was awake until three in the morning doing homework.

"Which languages do you study at school?"

"French."

She nods. "How long did it take to learn?"

I think back on the years I've spent studying French. "I started in sixth grade, so . . . four and a half."

"And are you fluent yet?"

"Ha! No way. My French is okay. Decent," I say, making a *so-so* hand gesture.

"Look at your French as a guide. It's taken you years of diligent study, and you're still not fluent. I bet you'll pick up Arabic much faster."

"You think I'll be able to speak to my teta the next time I see her?"

"When?"

"At the end of the year, at the family reunion in Dallas."

"If you stick with it, by the end of the year you and your teta will be speaking Arabic to each other over the dining table. No doubt."

I would *die*.

I can't wait to surprise her.

After group one Sunday at Shamsah's house, I'm texting with Wells when Shamsah pops her head outside the front door.

"You still here?"

"Yeah, sorry, my mom's late. Dua just left."

"No use hanging out on my porch like a fugitive. Come back inside while you wait. Have more besan ladoo."

I follow her through the foyer into the kitchen, where she pulls out a Tupperware container filled with the same sweet, nutty little balls we ate during group. I hop onto a kitchen stool next to her and we sit, side by side, popping the balls into our mouths.

"This is so good," I moan.

"I gotta get rid of it," Shamsah says. "Otherwise, I'm gonna eat the whole batch. I was obsessed with it as a kid." She eats another one. "Some things never change."

"Love those." I gently kick her sparkly Converse under the counter. "I wish I could wear them."

"Why can't you?"

"My arches. I get cramps without proper support—it's this whole annoying thing. My feet are basically eighty." I point down to my flats resting on the stool. "I can't do heels, either."

"I loathe heels. You know men used to wear them, right?" she says. "They were for nobles."

"Really?"

"Yeah. For horseback riding. And to look bigger and more intimidating. Persians actually wore them first, but then eventually, the European nobles started wearing them, and then the middle and lower classes started wearing them, and suddenly—boom—the snobby upper-class white dudes didn't want anything to do with them anymore. They became a thing solely for the womenfolk."

"Is that true?"

"I mean, don't go quoting me in the school newspaper, but yeah. Basically."

"Typical. Once the foreigners and the poor people like something, it's not good enough—oh, but the *women* can have it."

"Yup."

Shamsah stands up and grabs a bottle of sparkling water from the fridge. Without asking, she pours a glass for each of us, leaning across the counter and handing me one. "How's it all going?"

"What do you mean?"

"School, study group, the haram dude. Life," she says, making a dramatic sweeping gesture before laughing. She seems more relaxed than I've seen her with the rest of the group—it's like she's always putting on a facade with them, but alone in her kitchen, she's accidentally forgotten to keep it up.

"I mean—fine. Good. Great."

"A resounding endorsement," she says, and laughs again.

My phone pings with another text from Wells. I glance at it:

Big news: my dad's paying for a music video!

I roll my eyes. Wells was telling me yesterday about having to intervene when his parents got into a fight. Jack must feel guilty again.

"Everything okay?" Shamsah says.

I'd forgotten she could see my reaction. "Yeah, it's . . ." I pause. What to say?

"You can tell me."

"The dude. The one I'm hanging out with? He's kind of . . . problematic."

"You mean, more problematic than hanging out with a dude in the first place?"

I laugh. "Believe it or not."

She starts chewing on a nail.

"It's just like . . . why is it such a big deal if we date? We're not living in the seventh century anymore. I mean, you have Jamil, I have Wells—that's his name, by the way. And before you ask, yeah, he's a generic white boy," I say. "Actually, he's worse than a generic white boy. His dad basically hates Muslims. And *my* dad doesn't even know about that. And, obviously, we're not having sex—like not even a little bit—but part of me thinks I'm the worst Muslim ever for dating in the first place."

I blurt it out, without thinking of the consequences. I have to get it off my chest, and for some reason, in this moment, Shamsah feels like a safe space.

She stares at me, and I wonder if I made a mistake.

"Please don't judge me," I say.

"I don't judge you."

"I know I should tell my dad. I'm just . . . scared."

"I get it."

"You do?"

"Yeah."

She chews on another nail. I take a giant gulp of water.

"I wanna tell you something," she says. "You have to swear you won't tell."

"Okay."

"Not good enough. *Swear it.*"

"I swear," I say, putting my hand up solemnly.

"I . . . look, I know it's weird. We barely know each other. But I'm sick of carrying it around. And I'm good at reading people. I know I can trust you."

"Okay, now you *have* to tell me."

"It's about Jamil."

"Right . . ."

"Swear it!"

"Shamsah, good Lord, yes, I swear it! I double swear it. My lips are zipped forever, and I mean it. I'm a vault."

"Jamil's a girl. Her name is Jamila."

It takes me a second to realize what she's saying.

"You're dating a girl?" I ask.

She nods.

No wonder she was so irritated with Samira when she said dating was haram. If dating a boy is haram, dating a girl is next-level bad.

Obviously, I don't share that viewpoint.

Shamsah chews on her lip. "So," she says. "Are you going to say something?"

I feel that whatever I say right now is of critical importance. "To be honest, I don't know what to say. I've never had anybody come out to me before. I support you one hundred percent. And I'm here for you, if you need me."

"Do you judge me?"

"Absolutely not," I say quietly. "And I get why you haven't told the girls."

She twists the rubber band around her wrist anxiously.

"Is Jamila Muslim, too?" I ask.

"Yeah. But her family is cool with it."

"And yours wouldn't be?"

She looks at me blankly. "My parents would die, and I mean it would literally kill my mother. Being gay is one hundred percent not okay with them. They think it goes against the religion, the culture, everything."

"Are you sure the girls wouldn't support you?" I ask. "Everybody loves you. I know I'm still learning, but . . . didn't Allah make you this way?"

"That's not how they'll look at it," she says. "A lot of Muslims see it as a choice. And not only choosing to be a lesbian, but choosing to be in a relationship with another woman?" She shakes her head. "Nope."

"Dua said she didn't like me dating, but she'd still support me," I say. "They're more open-minded than you realize. If you tell them, they might surprise you."

She grimaces.

"You're sweet, Allie. I appreciate it. But you're new to this. You don't get how it works."

My mom's car pulls up. I wave at her through the kitchen window, indicating I'll be outside in a minute.

I try not to feel wounded by what Shamsah says. It's not about me.

I lean forward, giving her a hug. "Your secret is safe. I'm honored you shared."

She wipes away a single tear with a clenched fist. "Whatever. Don't get mushy about it."

"Text me if you want to talk."

"'Kay."

"You're not a bad Muslim," I say firmly.

Her eyes well up again.

After I get in the car with my mom, I quickly lapse into silence, staring out the window.

I've been thinking about it a lot, this good Muslim/bad Muslim thing.

What makes you bad?

Is Samira a bad Muslim because she thinks the scholarly positions could be reformed? Is Shamsah a bad Muslim because she was born liking girls? Is Leila a bad Muslim because she doesn't want a rope separating her from the guys while she prays?

Am I a bad Muslim because I want to kiss Wells?

Is there *any* wiggle room?

Does it have to be all or nothing?

There's a war on Muslims, but I'm starting to realize it's not just from everybody else. It comes from within us, too.

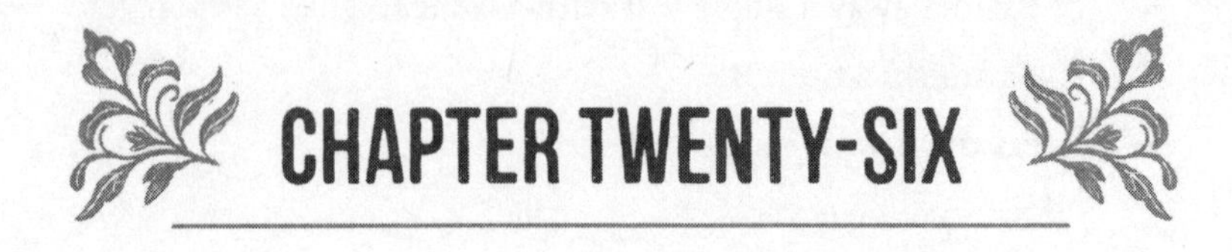

CHAPTER TWENTY-SIX

"Hey. So I've got a master plan," Dua says, calling me one night after school.

"Sounds dastardly."

"I keep thinking about what happened at the mall. I've wanted to wear a hijab for like ever—see if it's for me. So tomorrow's the day. Wanna do it together?"

My breath catches in my chest.

The truth is: I've been thinking about it, too.

Nothing visibly identifies me as Muslim. And whereas I used to feel weird about it, now I want people to know. I'm proud.

But I don't have the guts to do it alone.

"Yes," I say. "Let's do it."

I spend the next half hour in front of my vanity, watching a series of YouTube videos while trying to find a flattering style.

Dua calls back on FaceTime as I'm struggling to properly arrange a random scarf around my face.

She bursts out laughing. "Wooow. That's a look."

"Not. Helpful."

I stare at myself. My face looks like a pumpkin.

"Hijabs are like hairstyles—one size doesn't fit all. You need a different style." She's wearing a hijab, too, but whereas my thick beige scarf looks dumpy, hers is thin black silk: elegant perfection setting off her heart-shaped face. "An al-Amira might work, since you don't have to fiddle with pins."

"Amira? How do I do that one?"

"It's not one you do; it's one you buy. It's a piece of fabric you slip over your head. Easy-peasy."

"Well, that doesn't help me now, does it?" I say, feeling panicked.

"It's going to be okay," she says soothingly. "I'll send you this tutorial I found. Watch it and call me back."

I hang up, then watch the video and try to replicate the style. It requires hijab pins, something I don't have.

She answers on the first ring. "Yeeees?"

"I don't have hijab pins. I'm screwed."

"You can use a safety pin. Or borrow one of your mom's brooches. Or use an earring."

"Call you back."

I grab a tiny safety pin from my desk drawer.

After ten minutes of arranging the fabric and pins . . . just . . . so . . . I finally have a style I'm pleased with. I snap a few selfies, pick the best one, and then text it to Dua.

Thoughts?

She texts back immediately.

You look AMAZE!!!

Let's do this thing.

The stares and whispers begin from the minute I step onto the school bus.

I stare straight ahead, my heart walloping the inside of my chest.

How's it going? Dua texts me.

ME: Heart attack. I snuck out so my dad wouldn't see, and now everybody's staring at me.

DUA: Let them stare.

ME: You?

DUA: Soooo many stares 😜

I avoid Wells before school, hiding out in a corner of the cafeteria and ducking into French just before the bell. Normally, I would have told him last night, but something stopped me. *He* might have stopped me.

So now, here I am in first period—which I don't share with Dua.

And, in fact, we don't have any classes together.

Which means until lunchtime, I'm basically on my own.

In French class, this random guy stares at me before turning to the kid next to him and whispering. He's not subtle. I smile brightly at him. I'm not going to be angry. I'm not going to be a stereotype.

I'm not going to let him make me feel less than, either.

My hands feel clammy with each step I take. Still, I force myself to plunge forward.

In chorus, Mr. Tucker raises an eyebrow when he sees my headscarf.

"Hi!" Emilia says. "So, what's with the . . . uh . . ." She points to her head in a circular motion as she sits down.

"It's a hijab."

"I know, but isn't that only for, like, devout Muslims? I thought your family wasn't that religious? Is your dad making you?"

"I am a devout Muslim," I say sweetly. "And it has nothing to do with my family or my dad. It's my choice."

That shuts her up, to my face at least.

Just before the bell rings, Wells strolls into class.

He sees me, stopping so abruptly in the doorway that another student runs into him.

"Mr. Henderson. Today, please," Mr. Tucker says, his voice full of irritation.

Wells comes over and sits next to me, eyes wide. I've saved him a seat with my purse.

"Hi," he whispers.

"Hi," I say back. "How do I look?"

"Are you . . . Is this . . . Wow." His eyes sweep my face, as if he's trying to piece together familiar details to reassure himself I'm the same person. "You didn't tell me." He sounds hurt.

I lick my lips. "It was a spur-of-the-moment thing."

The truth is, I knew Wells would be weird about it, and I knew he would have the power to talk me out of it.

And it's not about him.

Later in the day, I'm walking down the hallway before comp sci when somebody yells, "Allahu akbar!" It echoes all the way from the lunchroom to the library.

A hush descends.

I turn around, trying to figure out where the voice came from.

"Who said that?" I say.

A few people giggle nervously. As I look from face to face, I notice Mikey laughing. He's with a few of his football teammates. Guys I know casually. Guys who have always been nice to my face.

They glance at him, confirming my suspicions.

I mean. What a cliché.

I walk up to him. With each step I take, his smile grows smaller.

"Not cool, man," a guy's voice mutters quietly.

"Douchebag," somebody else says under their breath.

The support surprises me—but maybe it shouldn't. Maybe I'm not giving my classmates enough credit.

"Hi, Mikey," I say.

"Hey, Lincoln."

"You're so clever, right? Do you even know what it means?"

"Yeah," he says, and laughs. "That's what terrorists say before they blow everybody up."

"No, Mikey. It means, 'God is great.' It means you love God."

He looks at me and shrugs. "Okay. So?"

"Are you making a public declaration that you love Allah? I can take you by the mosque with me if you want to convert."

He snorts. "Naw. I'm good."

"Except you're not. A good person doesn't insult somebody because of their religion—especially a religion they don't understand. And that's what you just did: insult me, and my friends and my family. Oh, and Muhammad Ali, who I know you're obsessed with," I say. "You can't just go around bashing somebody's religion because you think it's funny."

"Lighten up, Lincoln. I was playing."

"Say it *one* more time to my face. Say it." I take a step closer to him. "I dare you."

He looks at me, eyes widening.

"That's what I thought."

"Good for you," a girl's voice says behind me.

Some mysterious girl I don't even know has my back.

The crowd of students gathered around us parts as I walk down the hall to my next class, my head held high, even as I have to hold my breath and clench my fists to keep it together.

At the end of the school day, I approach the bus line to find Wells waiting for me. Any lingering hurt seems to be gone, replaced by calm. Whatever mental processing he did, it worked.

"You look cool, you know," he says.

"Hijab Barbie?"

He laughs, leaning down to kiss me. But then he stops.

"Wait, *can* I kiss you?"

"Kiss me, dummy," I say, reaching up and grabbing him behind the head.

This moment sponsored by wildly confused all-American Muslim girls.

"Can I drive you home?" he asks me.

"Only if I control the radio."

And together, we turn and walk toward the parking lot, hand in hand, pretending to ignore the stares.

CHAPTER TWENTY-SEVEN

Despite Dua's best fund-raising efforts, the needle has barely moved, so we make plans to brainstorm at my house over snacks. Incredibly, Dua suggests I invite Wells, in the hopes that they'll get to know each other. He gives us both a ride home after school.

Worlds colliding: Obviously, I'm petrified.

We're in my living room, the coffee table covered in snacks and laptops. I'm in the process of setting up a fund-raising page online, Dua next to me on the couch. Wells sits as far away from Dua as possible—whether out of politeness or fear, I'm not sure.

"Dua? Allie?" he says. "Can I get you more Sprite?"

"That would be great, Wells," Dua says. "Thanks!"

"I'll get more napkins, too. Hmm. And maybe carrots." He hops up, loping into my kitchen. I don't know what he's doing in there, but the sounds of various things opening and closing echo: *thud, whoosh, slam.*

"Why are boys so *loud*?" I ask. "Can't they shut a drawer like civilized human beings?"

Dua laughs. "What are you complaining about? You've got that boy trained."

"He's trying to impress you. He's still terrified you're going to talk me into breaking up with him."

"Ooh, I didn't realize I was so powerful," she cracks. "Do my powers of persuasion extend into rides home from school every day?"

"So *that's* why you invited him. You needed a chauffeur."

"Busted." She laughs, dipping a carrot stick into my dad's homemade hummus. "Oh my God, this is so good."

"It's my dad's secret recipe."

"What's in here—unicorn tears? I mean, good *Christmas*. This is freaking delicious."

"Garlic," I say. "So . . . much . . . garlic." I tear off a pita square and scoop up a giant bite. "Boyfriend kryptonite."

She smiles faintly, and I suddenly realize maybe a kissing joke wasn't the best call.

"Uh, what do you think of him?" I say. "He's cool, right?"

"He's okay."

It takes me a second to realize she's kidding. I crumple up a sheet of paper and lob it across the room at her.

"He's friends with that Mikey Murphy guy?" Dua says.

"Unfortunately. They grew up together. They were closer as kids."

"I heard about him telling Mikey off," she says. "In the hallway on hijab day."

"He did?"

"You didn't know? Yeah, I guess he cornered Mikey after last period and told him he was being an ignorant loser—or something like that. It made the rounds. Good for him."

"Wow. Go, Wells." I pause. "But does he really get credit for basic human decency?"

"C'mon, calling out your friends isn't easy. Wells gets points in my book."

I lean back on the couch, chewing over her words.

Wells comes back into the living room, with my mother following behind him. She's carrying a giant snack tray: a bowl of air-popped popcorn, more carrot sticks, a bowl of fruit, and three cans of lime LaCroix.

"I got help." Wells laughs, gesturing toward my mom. She must be taking a break from work upstairs.

"Hi, Dua! How's it going?" Mom says, putting the food on the table and leaning down to give her a hug.

"Hi, Mrs. Abraham."

Mom sits down on the couch, looking around at the computers and my Bullet Journal—I've been taking notes and writing ideas in it. "This is quite the battle station," she says. "Any good ideas yet?"

"We're a little stuck," I say. "Everything we've tried so far has resulted in, like, two hundred extra bucks, tops."

"And most of that was from your allowance, and from checks everybody's parents cut," Dua says, leaning across the table and grabbing a LaCroix.

"So now we're setting up a fund-raising page online," I say.

"People don't want to donate?" Mom asks. "That's disappointing."

"Are you really surprised?" I say.

"Well . . ." She makes a noncommittal face. "Anyhow, I don't want to blow up your spot. I know you're itching for the parental unit to get out of Dodge."

I laugh. "That is such a dorky-mom thing to say."

"I aim to please, buttercup," Mom says. "Later, kids. Have fun, and call me if you need me. I'll be upstairs working."

"What's your mom do?" Dua asks once she's gone.

"She's a psychologist. Which you wouldn't necessarily know by the pleasure she takes in negging me."

"You seem pretty close," Wells says.

"We are." I shrug. "My mom's awesome. Plus, we move a lot. There were some cities where I wasn't there long enough to make good friends, so my mom and dad were all I had. I don't have brothers or sisters. Your relationship with your parents is probably different when you're an only." I think about how close I used to be with my father, and my stomach tightens.

"Only child." Dua sighs. "Dare to dream."

"Seriously," Wells says.

She looks at him. "Siblings?"

"Younger brother. With a mission in life to annoy me."

"He's always buried in a video game when I see him," I comment. "I've barely heard him speak."

"Believe me, he speaks. But only to beg for money for snacks and video games and new baseball caps and God knows what else."

“He doesn’t get an allowance?” Dua asks.

“He does, but . . .” Wells’s face tightens. “My dad’s kind of weird about money.”

Dua doesn’t know Jack Henderson is Wells’s dad. I mean, I know I should tell her. But she’s already being supercool by accepting Wells, period. Would that tolerance extend to finding out how intolerant his dad is? Doubtful.

Baby steps, right?

After dinner, I’m in my room doing homework when a notification pops up on my phone. It’s an Instagram message from a random girl at school. Her name is Mikayla, and we’ve interacted precisely zero times.

Hi Allie! I saw you at school recently and I hope you don’t mind me reaching out. Have you ever been exposed to Jesus? You always seemed like such a nice girl and it would genuinely make me so sad if you weren’t able to experience salvation. Can I send you some information about the Good News? Hugs!

There’s so much here I don’t know where to begin.

Let’s unpack.

I draft a reply:

Hi Mikayla! Thanks so much for reaching out! I DO mind the insinuation I’m going to hell, actually . . . but you always seemed like such a nice person, too, so I’m going to forgive you this one time. (Like Jesus!) 😊 My mother was born a Christian, so I am already aware of the Good News, but thank you. I’m a Muslim,

I'm happy, and I don't need to be saved. If you ever want to hear about Islam and the divine revelation of the Qur'an, I'm here for you. If not, no worries and see you around school. Xo, Allie. PS: Jesus is a messenger in Islam, too.

This is the kind of reply I've always wanted to send but never would. I should delete it and write something generic.

Or take a selfie of myself making a grinning thumbs-up, and Photoshop flames around my face with arrows pointing to the words *me* and *in hell.* (That probably wouldn't go over well.)

Or ignore her altogether.

Mikayla's trying to be nice—even though she slid into my DMs like a literal gift from God—and I'm sure her intention is good.

Intention is really important in Islam.

But I'm done. I've had it up to here with people's thoughtless, offensive, and harmful good intentions.

I press SEND.

A couple days later, Dua cracks up when I mention the exchange with Mikayla.

"Did she reply?" Dua asks.

"Nope. Although, she looked freaked out when I saw her at school yesterday, like maybe I had some secret Muslim superpower and was going to zap her with it."

I pretend to shoot spiderwebs from my hands, and Dua mockingly puts her hands up to her face. "Noooo!" she says.

I reach into the bowl of veggie chips and munch on a stack. "These are way too good."

"Mom insists they're healthy," Dua says. "She's obviously deluding herself. But they're delicious, so I'm not complaining."

She pulls up another YouTube video, crunching on a chip as she continues my musical education. (Which, I think we both know, is more for her enjoyment than mine.) "Okay. Elissa—have you heard of her? She's superfierce and kind of controversial. This song was popular back in the day, and the guy in this video is soooo cute."

This is something funny about a lot of Arabic music videos. The women look like Kardashians, the guys look like movie stars, and there's always more skin than you'd expect—but even conservative Muslims eat it up.

The door flies open.

"Did you take my hair dryer?"

It's a tall, beautiful girl with long, glossy black hair almost to her waist. She has soulful eyes, like Dua's father, and dimples, like Zak.

"I already told you no," Dua says.

"I doubt Mom took it," the girl says, "so you must have it."

"Are you serious, Amina? It's probably lost in your room."

Amina stands in the doorway, looking irritated. Her glance lands on me, but she doesn't say anything else.

"This is my friend Allie."

"Hi!" I say, and smile.

"Hey, Allie." She raises a hand in greeting, quickly smiling at me before looking at Dua again. "If you find it, let me know, okay?"

"Okaaaay," Dua says. "For the fifth time. Byeee."

Amina starts to shut the door behind her, but then her gaze moves to something on the bed. It's the Qur'an we were flipping through earlier.

"Are you teaching your friend Islam? Dua, c'mon. Don't bore her."

"I'm Muslim," I say.

"You?" Amina gives me the once-over. "Really?"

"Yes."

She looks skeptical. "Are you in that band of revolutionaries together?"

"Yes, now please go away," Dua says. "You're annoying me."

"What do you think, Allie? About that nonsense your leader spews." She leans against the doorframe.

"Um, what nonsense?" I say.

"You can't remake a religion in your own image. It doesn't work like that. Either you're Muslim or you're not. I don't want to hurt your feelings, but what that Samira chick is teaching you isn't reform: It's Islamophobia. Junk-food spirituality. I went to one of the meetings with Dua last year. Haram. Total garbage."

I look back and forth between Dua and her sister, unsure what to say. What's ironic is that she seems to think Dua is some wild liberal, when I find Dua kind of conservative.

"Amina thinks just because she's one year older, she's smarter," Dua says.

"Never said I was smarter," she says. "But it's not smart

deluding yourself that your misinformed study group is bringing you closer to Allah. You should spend less time worrying about changing Islam and more time worrying about changing yourself."

It's interesting watching the two of them square off: Dua, who's continued wearing a hijab, getting accused of being a raging liberal, against clearly more conservative Amina, who looks like she's about to go model for Pantene.

Amina laughs. "Cognitive dissonance?"

"Huh?" I say.

"You're sizing me up. Looking at my hair. Don't judge a book by its cover, okay? Or by whether it covers, period."

Dua rolls her eyes at Amina's religious pun, pantomiming vomiting.

"You judged *me*," I say quietly.

"Sorry?"

"You assumed I couldn't be Muslim because of the way *I* look."

Dua looks over at me, grinning. "Yesss," she whispers.

I expect Amina to clap back, but instead she says, "Ouch. Not cool of me. Sorry, Allie."

"I'm sorry, too." I say.

"Anyhow, gotta run. Don't fall for their propaganda," she says to me, pointing her finger in my direction. "There's a Sunday study group at the masjid over by Georgia Four Hundred if you want to do it properly. Later."

As Amina closes the door behind her, Dua groans. "She's so annoying."

"She didn't seem bad."

"Wrong. She's such a know-it-all. She started going to these classes over the summer, and now she won't shut up about it. What's hilarious is *her* friends are on her case for not wearing a scarf, and then they get into these arguments about scholarly positions on hijab."

"Maybe I should start studying with her instead of you."

Dua throws a chip at my head.

But as the two of us go back to watching YouTube videos, I fret. *Am* I being Islamophobic? Is that why I want to keep dating, and why I think Islam has room to be modernized?

Instead of nourishing my soul, am I feeding it junk?

On Fridays, the holy day in Islam, Muslims gather at mosques after noon for the Jum'ah prayer. The Prophet reportedly once said that those who pray on Friday will have their wishes granted.

This is one of the most rewarding aspects: learning all these new traditions, hadiths, and guidelines.

The thing I'm struggling with is trying to keep my Islam from being like a buffet: cherry-picking the cool parts I like, ignoring the inconvenient parts I don't.

I like the emphasis on family.

I don't like the exclusion of LGBTQ people from the narrative.

I like the Qur'an's support for women's rights.

I don't like the men who alienate women in the name of Islam.

I like the framework for how to be a compassionate, kind, charitable person.

I don't like that every single guideline from the seventh century must hold true in the twenty-first.

Maybe if I'd been a practicing Muslim from the beginning, I wouldn't feel as tentative questioning parts I'm not enthusiastic about. Houri was raised in a much more by-the-book family than mine and is married to a wonderfully devout man in Rashid, yet she's unapologetic about being lapsed. But for me, who came to the party late—I feel like if I don't do it perfectly, I'm not allowed to do it at all.

It's spring break, so Samira is taking us on a field trip to the mosque in downtown Atlanta. Mom knows the truth, but Dad thinks I'm going to a museum with friends.

"Baking is so annoying," Shamsah says after Fatima tells us she's gotten into a new course at the cooking institute. "But congrats, obviously."

"Baking isn't annoying," Fatima says, looking over at her. "Baking is amazing. It's like a series of tiny, precise math problems where you get to eat the results. It's edible perfection."

"Except it's never perfection," Shamsah says. "It's always too soggy, or too flat, or too dry, or too whatever. Baking is totally setting you up to fail. If you make a tiny mistake, screw you, thanks for playing."

Next to me, Dua laughs. "So is the problem with baking, or is the problem you're the worst at it?"

Shamsah frowns at her. "Thanks."

"That cake you made for my birthday was pretty good," Leila tells Shamsah, looking at her kindly. "I really liked it. I had two pieces."

"What, you mean the Betty Crocker cake? The box I bought at Publix and mixed together with eggs, water, and Crisco? Ugh," Shamsah says, sinking down in her seat.

"I agree, baking is impossible." I smile supportively at Shamsah. "Cooking is way better. You can make it up as you go along. If you have the magic mix—this spice, that seasoning, a lot of love—it can still taste good. It doesn't have to be perfect."

Shamsah nods. "Allie gets it."

"No metaphors here," Dua quips.

"Speaking of food, Ramadan is coming up next month," Samira says, looking at me in the van's rearview mirror. "Of course, you'll have your family for support, but we'll all be here, too. The first one is always the hardest."

"Um . . ." I clear my throat. "Actually, my dad doesn't know I've been practicing. So . . ."

Dua makes a frustrated noise. "Seriously, Allie? Tell him already."

"I can't. I've been lying to him for months. He's going to be upset."

Samira looks at us in the rearview mirror, eyebrows raised. "Your father doesn't know you're practicing?"

"Erm. No."

"He converted when he married your mother?" she says.

"No, the other way around. My mom is the revert. My dad was born Muslim."

"Ahh," Samira says, nodding. "I understand."

"You do?"

"It's not unheard of. Many people raised in religious households rebel by rejecting their faith as adults."

"Plus, Allie's dad is a professor," Shamsah says. "He's allll about science."

"Were your teta and jido strict?" Samira asks.

I snort. "What grandparents aren't?"

Leila laughs.

It's not a divine revelation. It's pretty freaking obvious, in fact. But I feel silly for not understanding until now: As much as I'm reacting against my parents, Dad's reacting against his. "You think this is because my teta and jido were too hard on him growing up?"

"I'm not a therapist," Samira says. "I have no idea." She smiles gently at me through the reflection. "But parents are people, too, you know."

I lapse into silence as the van navigates through the traffic on I-75. I'm clutching the amethyst headscarf I've brought to wear. I haven't worn a hijab since trying it at school last week. I'm happy I did, but it's not for me—at least, not right now.

As Dua and Shamsah start talking about a new cruelty-free halal makeup line they're both obsessed with, I think about Dad.

I need to tell him.

He deserves that much.

"I had no idea this existed in Atlanta," I say as we get out of the van. We've reached the masjid, a beautiful, majestic domed structure. "Have you been here before?"

Everybody but Fatima and Samira shakes their heads no.

There are mosques closer to home in Providence—more than you'd expect, considering how pervasive Christianity is around here. Although Providence is full of transplants from the North and the Midwest, this is still a town where a third of the cars flash bumpers with John 3:16 stickers and Jesus fish. I pulled up one of the local Islamic center websites a few nights ago, after Amina called me out, and I was scared off after only a few minutes of clicking around.

The website was clean and cheerful, advertising a youth halaqa and clearly trying to draw in more young people and women. But in the community forum, somebody wrote: *Masjid is for praying, not for socializing. Women should not be sitting here every afternoon talking instead of praying.*

So, yeah. Yet another reason why I'm scared of going to the mosque. I get enough of feeling unwelcome in my daily life.

We wrap our scarves around our heads before entering and make our way to the women's prayer section, putting our shoes in the cubbies and performing wudu in the footbaths. I follow Fatima's lead.

"When was the last time you went to a mosque?" I ask Dua. She runs her hand back and forth across her soles, letting the water wash over them.

She grimaces. "It's been a loooong time. Don't worry, Amina makes sure to guilt me about it daily. It's not always the most welcoming place, despite what my parents say. I prefer praying at home."

To hear that Dua feels that way is both surprising and comforting. I'm not alone.

"It's called being 'unmosqued,'" Samira explains quietly as we dry our feet. "A lot of young women feel out of place at the masjid."

"Some guys, too," Dua says. "My brother, Zaki, feels the same, and he's good about sticking to his prayers. Sometimes it feels like the mosque is only for old men."

"The masjid is for everybody," Leila says. "Besides, women aren't separated from men in Mecca or Medina."

"But that's exactly it! It's like, do I want to hang out in the basement like a second-class citizen when I don't have to?" Dua says. "It feels like a club and you don't belong. Like, everybody's upset about building walls, but we have our own walls between the men and the women. Plus, *our* area is so much smaller. I'd rather pray privately with y'all . . . with people who understand me and share my views and don't stuff me away as an afterthought."

Leila sighs as we walk into the women's area. "C'mon. Do you really want the men staring at us? I *prefer* being separated. It's more private, anyway."

"There are women's mosques popping up around the country now," Samira says. "One in the Bay Area, another in Los Angeles. Change is slow, but it's coming."

I'm mildly irritated we're separated from the men, but as the imam begins the khutbah, I'll admit there's also something nice about being free from prying male eyes. I've been lucky to have wonderful men in my life, but I know that's not true for everybody. I understand the appeal of wanting a safe space, a respite, a male-free sanctuary—if only for forty-five minutes.

However, as the prayers start and I raise my hands to my ears, setting my intentions, I think, *I'd rather* we *had the cavernous room and the men were somewhere else, a location of our choosing.*

That night, I FaceTime with Houri looking for guidance. I've been feeling guilty about Shamsah—we haven't had an in-depth conversation since she came out to me. I wanted to talk to her today in the van, to show more support, but there was never an opportunity.

Houri answers on the first ring.

"That was quick," I say.

"I'm waiting for the doctor to call me back. Lulu has this weird rash."

"Blech."

"You're not the one looking at it. What's up?"

I push away from my desk, moving over to the bed and plopping down among my pillows. "Can I ask your advice?"

"Yeah, shoot."

"So, you know I've been doing the study-group thing, learning about Islam, praying, et cetera, et cetera."

"Right," she says, setting the phone down on the table and pulling out her laptop. "Don't mind me. I'm multitasking. It might be hand, foot, and mouth."

"There's a rash called 'hand, foot, and mouth'?"

"Whatever you do, *don't* Google it," she says, picking up the phone and swiveling it around to face her computer screen. I'm confronted with a series of horrifying images.

"Houri, I can't unsee that."

She puts the phone back on the table. "Sorry, continue. You're religious now, yay! Go, Islam! What's the problem?" She frowns at her laptop screen, tapping on her keyboard.

"Okay," I say. "For the most part, my study group is pretty progressive—"

She stops me. "*Progressive* progressive, or Muslim progressive?"

"I don't know. Is there a difference?"

"Your friends are still doing a Qur'an halaqa. I doubt they're *that* off-the-leash."

I feel mildly offended. "Can we not with the judgments?"

"Gross."

"Huh?"

"These images. They're horrifying. Sorry, sorry. Continue."

"*As I was saying.* One of the girls came out to me. Like, she's a lesbian."

Houri laughs. "I *do* know what coming out means, Allie."

"Well, I don't know what to do."

She pauses her typing, looking at me through the screen. "Why do you need to do anything?"

"Because I want to help her. And I want to help the other girls accept her. And she feels alone. And she wants to tell the other girls, but she's worried they'll judge her."

Houri sighs. "Look, I know your heart is in the right place. You don't need to be her savior. Just be her friend. Be there if she needs an ear. Have her back if you need to. But don't feel like you need to 'help' her or bring the other girls around to your viewpoint. She's not a project needing fixing."

I'm reminded of what Wells said last month after his anxiety attack.

"She'll come out if she wants to come out," Houri says. "When she's ready. On her own terms."

I mull it over.

"Good advice. Thanks."

"Any time."

"Kinda ironic," I say, "you giving me advice about how to be a good Muslim."

"Why? Because I'm not?"

"Uh . . . yeah."

She laughs. "News flash: You don't have to be religious to be a good person."

"I know."

"Do you?" she asks, arching an eyebrow at me through the phone.

"Houri, let's not. I enjoy praying, okay? I like reading the Qur'an. It doesn't make me some brainwashed dummy just because I like the teachings about how to be a good person and I believe the Prophet was the messenger of God. I still believe in science and marriage equality and intersectional feminism and the Fourth of July and Santa Claus. I find the idea that you can't simultaneously be intelligent and religious and American and Muslim offensive."

We stare at each other through the screen. Obviously, that outburst was not entirely directed at Houri.

"You still believe in Santa Claus?"

I roll my eyes. "You know what I mean. Christmas trees and eggnog. *Love Actually*. American culture."

"I *don't* know what you mean, but I'm all ears. You're sixteen, Allie. We might need to have a serious conversation about it," she says. "*Love Actually* is British, by the way. And a terrible movie."

"Goodbyeee. Hanging up now."

"Oh, the doctor is calling! Gotta go!"

"You can't hang up on me. I'm hanging up on you!"

We rush to be first, laughing.

CHAPTER TWENTY-EIGHT

Wells's mom stables horses in a two-story barn out by the edge of the fields surrounding their house. After school one day, Wells and I park in his driveway and take a walk down to see them. Before moving to Georgia, I never knew anybody who owned horses as actual pets. But in this corner of suburban Atlanta, they're as common as dogs.

Hugely expensive, ridiculously high-maintenance dogs.

I expect to step over manure and hay as we enter, but the cavernous barn is pristine. "Wells. Come on," I say. "This is nicer than my house." It's paved in brick, and wood-paneled, with gleaming chrome gates for the horse stalls, a vaulted wood ceiling, and air-conditioning. "Your horses have it better than I do."

Wells leads me to the last stall and reaches his hand over the gate, patting the glossy mane of a spotted black-and-white horse. "This is Sprite." He laughs as the horse nuzzles the side of his face.

"Sprite?"

"She's my favorite. She's down-to-earth, not a stuck-up show pony like the rest. If you bribe her, she's yours."

"Bribery? That's your thing?"

He laughs again, reaching into a bag and pulling out a horse treat. He seems at ease. "Here you go, Sprite. Sweet girl."

As he talks to her, his voice is gentle. It makes me feel like he could horse-whisper me, too.

"Do you ride?" I ask.

"Not much—at least, not anymore. It's my mom's thing. She spent summers on a horse farm in Canada. These horses aren't all hers, though—she rents out stalls. She always talks about how horses are great therapy . . ." He clears his throat.

I change the subject, hoping to make him feel comfortable. "I wish I could ride. The closest I've come has been pony rides at state fairs."

That seems to brighten him up. "Hey, I can teach you!"

"Deal. Just not today, please." I gesture down at my outfit. "I had to save three weeks' allowance to buy this dress."

"Worth it," he says.

He reaches for my hand, threading his fingers through mine. Never gets old.

"Uh, I wanted to ask you something," he says. "My parents were wondering if you wanted to come to church with us for Easter." His cheeks are pink. "I don't care. It's not a big deal to me. But it's kind of a thing for my parents—especially my mom. They rarely invite people to church. They like you."

"Kind of ironic."

He looks apprehensive. "You mean because . . . ?"

"You don't think?"

He sighs. "If you don't want to come, I get it."

Sprite whinnies, nodding her head up and down vigorously.

"Why wouldn't I want to come?"

"Are you even allowed?"

"Wells, it's not like Muslims are vampires and Easter is garlic. I won't burst into flames if I see a cross—or a chocolate bunny, for that matter. It's all good. Jesus is a major prophet in Islam. Mary is all over the Qur'an—more than in the New Testament. Muslims even believe in the Psalms and the Gospels. The Torah, too."

"Seriously?"

"Yeah, Muslims believe they're books of God—although they've probably changed over the years. Unlike the Qur'an."

He looks surprised. I'm tempted to blow his mind with more facts about how Islam is mischaracterized, but I don't.

"Plus, my mom grew up Catholic, you know."

"Right. I forgot."

"I've even . . . been inside a church! *Ooooh*," I say in a spooky voice, waving my hands in the air.

His laugh doesn't have its usual tenor, and his eyes are quiet. He runs his hand down Sprite's mane over and over.

"You're nervous," I say.

He nods.

"It's not like I want your dad to know, either. I've got enough to worry about without 'Jack Henderson' up in my business." I say his dad's name in air quotes, and he winces. "It'll be fine."

The anxiety radiates off him. Sprite takes a step back and walks to the other side of the stall, poking her nose in a bucket of hay. "He'll know something's up when you don't take Communion," Wells says.

I'm reminded of my mother taking me to church with my grandmother on Easter when I was younger—how my grandmother scowled when my mom stayed seated with me as everybody else made their way toward the altar.

I shrug. "I could take Communion. Throw him off the scent."

He cocks his head to the side, considering. "Are you sure?"

"I mean . . . you're not supposed to lie in Islam. But maybe it would be okay, because I'm trying to help you and keep the peace? You're really only allowed to lie in life-or-death situations . . ."

He exhales. "Okay. If you're cool with it."

I didn't necessarily expect him to take me up on it.

"Life-and-death it is," I joke, feeling uneasy as we exit the barn and make our way back up to the main house.

On a scale of one to the fiery bowels of hell, how big of a sin *is* it to lie in a church? Even if you're not Christian? Because that's what I'd be doing.

But now that I've given Wells my word, I feel like I can't back out.

Way to pull a fast one on God, Allie.

Despite Wells's worries, I'm not concerned about it being Easter.

I *am* concerned about it being an entire day spent with Jack Henderson.

As Mom drives up the hill to Wells's house, we see the mansion festooned with lights and Easter decorations. It looks like a southern White House.

"I'm never going to get over this place," Mom says.

"Me neither."

"What do his parents do?"

I haven't told Mom about Jack—for obvious reasons.

"Family money, I think," I lie.

The car pulls up in front of a valet station. A man in a suit, white bow tie, and white gloves opens my door.

"Don't tell Dad, okay?"

"About you going to church?"

"Yeah."

She opens her mouth and shuts it. Her eyes search mine. My mother's understanding look transports me back to childhood—back to that warm place where I knew I was safe, as long as I was with her.

She sighs. Nods. "Okay, Al."

"I'll call you when I'm done, Mom."

"Have fun," she says, blowing me a kiss and putting the car in drive.

I walk up the remainder of the driveway. It's lined with tall white candles blazing in glass lanterns, each adorned with robin's-egg-blue and cotton-candy-pink bows: There must be a hundred of them on either side of the stone tiles. As I approach the house, I see through the tall windows into the living room beyond, where caterers are bustling around, getting the party ready for later. I want to text Dua a photo, but then I remember I lied to her about my plans today.

I've been doing that a lot recently. Lying.

To my dad. To Dua. To strangers. To friends.

It's exhausting.

What would happen if I just . . . told the truth?

I'm about to knock on the front door when it swings open and Wells is standing in front of me. He's wearing a white suit.

I start giggling.

"What?"

"Nice outfit."

He grimaces. "My dad made me."

"Very Gatsby."

"Or Colonel Sanders. I'm glad you're here," he says. "This is going to be so boring."

"Gee," I say. "Just what everybody wants to hear when they're walking into a party: It's boring!" I'm happy to see him, though. He leans down and gives me a sweet kiss on the cheek, like we're five.

"So, hi," I say, grinning at him. I twirl in a circle, letting him admire my dress. It's a knee-length canary-yellow frock, which I found online for twenty dollars. Score. "For once, I'm not going to be the most dressed-up person at the party."

"You look incredible," he says, his face relaxing into a wide smile. "Come on. We leave in five. My dad's driving."

Despite my joke about not bursting into flames, I do feel weird half an hour later stepping into the Hendersons' huge Episcopalian cathedral in Midtown Atlanta. I look around the church, taking it in: the altar, the vaulted stone ceiling, the blue-and-purple stained-glass window, the smiling congregation in their beautiful pastel-colored Easter finest. I have to keep myself from flinching as people glance my way, instead pasting on a fit-for-public-consumption smile. I feel vulnerable. Major imposter vibes.

"You okay?" Wells whispers, looking at me with concern as we follow his parents down the aisle, Sawyer trailing behind us. It takes a while to reach the front of the church; people stop Jack every few feet to greet him and shake his hand.

"Am I that transparent?" I whisper back as Jack bursts into laughter, vigorously pumping the arm of a short white man in a cream-colored suit.

"This would suck without you," Wells says as music plays. "Thank you, for the thousandth time."

"For the thousandth time, you don't have to thank me. I'm glad to be here." I mostly mean it. That's what being in a relationship is about—showing up, even if it's not your thing—right?

I smooth down the front of my dress and sit next to him, trying to avoid picking at my cuticles as the ceremony gets underway.

It's a lot of standing and off-key singing, following by sitting and listening, before doing it again. Eventually, a woman in white robes stands in front of the congregation and reads from Psalm 118. I follow along, enjoying the meta message and poetry of the words, and I attempt the right notes when it's our turn to warble again.

At one point, Wells looks over at me. He smiles. He's pleased. I'm happy to make him happy.

But the awareness dawns that we're approaching Communion, and everything is happening so fast.

"We offer our sacrifice in praise and thanksgiving to you today," the priest says as he blesses the bread. He calls for Eucharistic Prayer B, and the congregation turns their pages, reading and singing, "Holy, Holy, Holy Lord, God of power and might, heaven and earth are full of your glory . . ."

"In him," the priest says, "you have delivered us from evil . . . 'Take, eat: This is my Body, which is given for you. Do this for the remembrance of me.'"

Everyone kneels.

It's funny how people mock Muslims for the intricacies of our prayer, but I'm struck by how the mass shares similarities with Islam: the repetition, the group reciting familiar words in unison, the kneeling and genuflecting, the sincerity and seeking.

"'Drink this, all of you: This is my Blood of the new Covenant,'" the priest says, proffering a cup of wine.

Now it's a detailed analysis of how Jesus was crucified, and what Christians believe, and something about the Holy Ghost, and baptism, and the resurrection of the dead, and it's overwhelming, and—

Oh no. I don't believe this. I don't want to do it, this is a horrible idea. I'm being a total hypocrite by pretending I do to make my boyfriend's father happy.

This is going completely off the rails.

Before I know it, everybody is reciting something I recognize through cultural osmosis and childhood memories as the Lord's Prayer. I struggle through it, feeling like a bad person, when I notice Jack's eyes on me.

He smiles.

What would happen if I just told the truth?

Everybody gets up, and Wells reaches over, squeezing my hand. I squeeze back and mouth, *I'm sorry* before sitting down. He looks back at me, alarmed, but it's a wave of people propelling him forward, and he can't do anything without calling more attention to the thing he wants to hide. He follows his family up the aisle to receive Communion, kneeling as the bread wafers are placed into their mouths.

As they're making their way around the front of the altar and back toward our row, people politely stepping past me to get back to their seats, Jack and I lock eyes again. His brow furrows.

And as Wells comes back to sit next to me, his cheeks pink, his lips set, this time he doesn't reach for my hand.

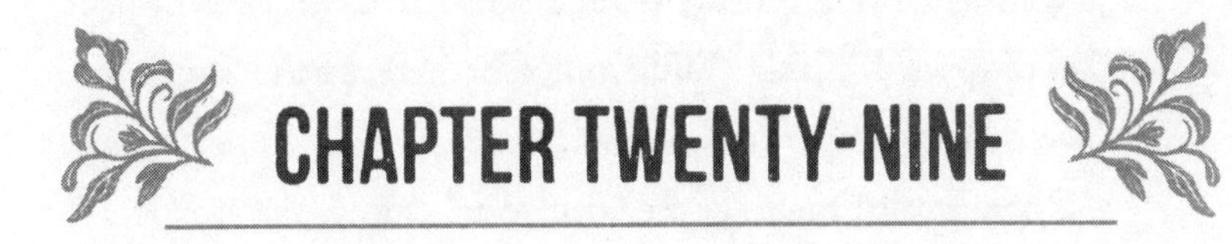

CHAPTER TWENTY-NINE

Back at Wells's house, the caterers are done setting up the party, and Serena and Jack immediately swing into host mode.

Wells and I are left alone in the kitchen, among a bunch of waiters in white tuxedos.

"What happened?" he asks. "I thought we, uh, had a plan."

I stare through the windows, where the vast backyard has been turned into a garden extravaganza. Guests are piling in to find an Easter egg roll, candy-colored lanterns, balloons, and floral bouquets, and somebody in a bunny costume waiting to take photos with kids.

"Let's go outside." Clearly, I'm stalling.

We walk outside, where a photographer descends on us.

"Let me take your picture!" she chirps.

We put our heads together, smiling obediently, before continuing down the lawn in silence. We've mostly hung out in the basement, so I didn't realize Wells's backyard is the size of Central Park.

"Wells!" a voice bellows from across the lawn, over near a thicket of roses. It's Jack. "Will you come here, please, son?"

Wells's face drops.

"Do you want me to come with you?" I say.

He grimaces. "Do you mind?"

I sigh.

Jack is holding court with a gaggle of old white men, all wearing sunglasses, and linen or seersucker suits. He's clutching a tumbler of something brown.

"Here he is," Jack says. "You know my son, Wells."

Wells smiles, tight-lipped.

"And this is his darling girlfriend, Allie. She came with us to church today."

I look at the men, blinking, unsmiling. I wish I had a pair of sunglasses to demonstrate I'm not messing around. Instead, I have to stand there, hand over my eyes, squinting uncomfortably as I probably sprout five freckles per second.

The men talk over one another greeting Wells, who politely accepts the hellos. This is something Wells and I have in common: We both know how to treat people to avoid "poking the bear," as my dad calls it.

One of the men clapping Wells on the back and nudging Jack with his elbow as he tells his own story is Bill McGuinley—a famous bow-tied conservative talking head. He catches me looking at him and flashes me a thousand-watt smile. I smile back politely before looking down, suddenly exceedingly interested in how my silver flats look against the blades of grass.

"Sorry, Allie," Jack says, looking at me. "This must be boring for you. I'll send Wells back your way soon. Why don't you go find Serena inside?"

I've been dismissed. I spin on my heel, hightailing it back toward the house. The less I can say to this guy, the better.

I wish I could say more.

I want to tell Jack Henderson what I think of him. To get in his face and say, *The way you treat people isn't okay. The way you marginalize people is horrible. The stereotypes you float are dangerous.*

But what good would come? I'd have five seconds of euphoria, it would go in one ear and out the other—there's no way it would resonate with Jack—and then what?

I'd be mocked. Wells would be humiliated, furious, maybe even forbidden from seeing me. Who knows what Jack is capable of?

So I smile and nod, like I always do.

But, oh. How I want to.

Inside the house, Serena beckons me to the corner by the fireplace.

As I'm walking over, however, my phone vibrates. I take it out of my clutch purse and realize it's the Muslim Pro app signaling the call to prayer. Hastily, I turn off the notification and stuff my phone in the bottom of my bag.

"Are you having fun, dear?" Serena asks me. She seems distracted and slightly tired, as if she's spent too much time in the sun and needs a nap. She wears a small but glittery diamond cross around her neck, dangling from a dainty gold chain.

"Yes, ma'am."

She leans in. "You don't have to lie. These parties are excruciating." I'm surprised by her honesty.

"The gaggle of old white guys is kind of brutal," I say. "But I appreciate you letting me come."

"Poor Wells," she says, looking through the window at her son. He looks miserable surrounded by Jack and his friends. "He hates these things. Jack's little trophy on display."

I've misjudged Serena. She seemed like a fragile flower the first time I met her, but she's steelier than I realized.

"I'm sorry," she says.

The apology catches me off guard. "For what?"

"Wells likes you a lot. Thanks for taking a chance. I'm sure it hasn't been easy on you because of Jack. I appreciate you coming today."

She *does* know.

"Thanks, Mrs.—er, Serena."

She sighs, watching the crowd and looking defeated.

I decide to go upstairs to pray, sneaking into Wells's room and quickly making wudu in his en suite bathroom. After I finish praying, I rejoin the party. Wells has come back inside with

Jack and his father's friends, and they're now in the living room. Wells shakes his head discreetly, eyes wide, but I'm sick of skulking around. I'm here to hang out with Wells. The crusty old dudes can shove it.

Once I hear the discussion, I discover why Wells warned me off.

"Muslims love crowing about women's rights and how feminist the religion is," Jack says, "but let's be real—Islam is completely sexist."

My heart starts pounding. Anger simmers inside me.

"Beyond that, many Muslims are trying to push forward their radical agenda and codify Sharia law in the United States," Bill McGuinley says authoritatively in his lofty, patrician voice, punctuating the air with his tumbler of whiskey. Droplets splash on the expensive-looking carpet.

The men nod and murmur, a Greek chorus of disapproving assent.

It's your boyfriend's father, Allie. You're a guest in his house. No good will come of it.

"Everybody knows it," Jack says. "Although, of course, the social-justice warriors won't admit the truth. I swear, they'd throw their own in front of a bus to defend a Muslim."

I can't take much more of this.

"You know the worst part?" he says. "These bleeding hearts pretend they care about women's rights, but they cry and evaporate like snowflakes when you remind them Islam is the most oppressive religion on planet Earth."

Don't say a word, Allie. Don't do it.

"Wherever Islam goes, Sharia follows," Bill McGuinley says. "It's a moral threat."

"Absolutely." Jack, leaning against the edge of a leather-upholstered armchair, takes another sip of whiskey. "We've got to stop letting those people in. Too dangerous. I don't care if you're six or sixty—if you're from a Muslim-majority country, you have no business entering the US, period."

No more.

"Are you for real?" I say.

The words explode from my mouth, heat-seeking missiles aiming for Jack's chortling bubble of ignorance.

Wells cringes.

"What part do you take issue with, honey?" Jack asks.

"Where to start?" I tick my pointer finger as Wells shifts uncomfortably. "You call Islam sexist. Women in Islam were some of the first in the world to own property. They keep their last names instead of taking their husband's names. More women than men get degrees. Men are *not* superior."

I'm not going to get into my own issues regarding the finer points of the patriarchy in certain countries and regions. Nuance is for those in my inner circle, not these blowhards.

I expect him to respond with condescension. Instead, his face registers something closer to—could it be called concern? "Ah," he says. "I've heard these lines before. You're a kind girl with a good heart, Allie. But a religion that forces its women to veil can never be called feminist. No amount of liberal apologia will change that."

I bristle. "Why is everybody so obsessed with whether

Muslim women cover their hair or not? Women in Islam aren't forced to cover. They *choose* whether to cover. What could be more feminist than having a choice?"

He nods. "Mmm. I'm sure those women in full ninja cowering behind their husbands in flip-flops and shorts are thrilled with their 'choices.' You and I both know they'd throw off the hijab in a heartbeat for a bikini."

Serious question: Is it wrong to punch a bigot in the face?

"You're dead wrong," I say. "And you have zero right speaking for any woman. Are there some women who are forced to do things they don't want to? Obviously. That's not a Muslim issue, that's a *patriarchy* issue. It happens in every country where horrible men—of every religion, by the way—are in charge of women's bodies and women's lives, and use the government to enact their stupid misogyny. Um, hi: It happens here."

He's struggling not to laugh.

I'm just getting started. "Besides, nobody is trying to 'codify' Sharia law in the US. Most people don't even know what 'Sharia' means—the word means 'path,'" I say, trying to distill an hour-long study group into ten seconds. "It's principles *by* Muslims *for* Muslims—like canon law for Catholics, or Halacha for Jewish people. If you're not a Muslim, it doesn't apply to you. The way people discuss Sharia is complete fearmongering. More than that: It's plain old Islamophobia."

Ah, there's the hint of condescension creeping into his face.

I'm not done.

"And another thing. Everybody yells about Islam, but nobody takes the time to educate themselves and read the Qur'an. But

I bet you've read the Bible. No issues with the ban on women priests in Catholicism? The way the church has rushed to cover up pedophilia? With Saint Paul saying women should be silent and can't have authority over men? With Peter commanding slaves to submit to their cruel masters?" I count the issues on my fingers. "There is some great stuff in the Bible, and there is some screwed-up stuff in the Bible, but everybody shrugs and ignores the bad and says, 'Oh well. John 3:16, Psalm 23:4. It's all good!' And then they refuse to do the same for Islam. You want to talk about threats to women's rights and human rights *right now*, in America, you can focus on people twisting Christianity's message for their purposes in your own backyard. Pay attention to *that*. Worry about *that*. Leave Islam out of it."

There's pity in Jack's face. "Allie, Allie, Allie." He shakes his head, sighing heavily as if to say, *What am I going to do with you?* "You're clearly well-meaning. Your heart is in the right place." He smiles sadly at me before continuing. "But it pains me to say you simply don't understand what you're clunkily defending."

"I do understand what I'm defending," I say, angrily.

It's now or never.

Do it, Allie.

Claim it.

You're ready.

I stand up straight, pulling myself to my full height. My voice carries, crisp and clear. "I know it better than anybody in this room. I'm a Muslim. My grandmother is a Syrian immigrant. *I* am what I'm defending."

Game, set, match.

For a fleeting second, his face contorts into a mask of shock, only to quickly morph into a smile.

There's a new look in his eye, but I can't quite place it. "I apologize for speaking dismissively of your religion, Allie. I wasn't aware you were a Muslim."

"You admit you were wrong?"

"Wrong? No, I'm not wrong, sweet girl. Islam is a regressive, backward religion. Its mission is fundamentally different from what we, as Americans, are about. You cannot be a Muslim and be a true American; they're mutually exclusive."

Breathe, Allie.

"So why did you apologize?" I say.

"It was rude of me to denigrate your religion in front of you." There it is again—that weirdly kind look. Like he's doing me a favor.

"You'd have preferred to do it behind my back."

"Sometimes it's kinder to spare people from the truth."

"Sometimes kindness is overrated."

"Muhammad was illiterate, you know," Bill McGuinley says, butting in. "The idea that he spoke directly for God is a joke."

"So? Jesus was a carpenter," I say. "Who preached love, tolerance, and inclusion, by the way. I don't see any of that on your horrible TV show."

"Oh, a viewer!" Bill says in his distinctive voice. He smirks, fiddling with his bow tie. "Lucky me."

"Bill. Please," Jack says, shooting him a disappointed look. "I know you must think I'm evil," he says to me. "Believe it or not, that bothers me. I can tell you're an idealist. Good people are often misguided. I was once, too. You mean well, Allie, but you'll understand when you're older."

"I'll never understand thinking you're better than somebody else because of the religion they practice or what country they were born in," I spit. "And the only thing I understand is, you're a condescending old bigot." I spin on my heel, storming for the door.

Everything about this situation feels wrong. I should feel triumphant, but instead I feel ashamed that I diminished my religion, using it as a weapon in an argument.

"Sorry," I say to Wells as I leave, "but just because he's *your* dad doesn't mean *I* have to listen to his crap anymore."

"Spirited young thing," I hear Mr. Henderson say, chuckling behind me.

As I hurry down the driveway, Wells chases after me.

"Allie! Wait!"

I turn around, putting my hand up. He stops right in front of me, and my hand lightly brushes his chest. His hand engulfs mine, pulling it flat against his heart.

"I can't do this," I say.

He reels as if I've slapped him. "What? Why?"

"You know why."

"Because of him? C'mon, Allie. I'm not my dad."

"You keep saying, 'I'm not my dad,' but his oppression

literally pays for your life. Every time your father says something disgusting on TV and you keep your mouth shut because you know he'll eventually feel guilty and pay for a music video or buy you a new car, you're complicit."

He looks stung. "You think I'm as bad as him?"

"Are people who stand by and give the racists and the bigots free rein blameless?"

"Yeah, but—"

"Ignorance doesn't exist in a bubble. We have to give it air to allow it to breathe."

"I know, but—"

"If we sit by silently, because we don't want to make people uncomfortable, because we don't want to rock the boat, *because they're our family*, we're part of the problem. I don't want to be part of this problem anymore. I can't, Wells. I literally can't."

"Please don't do this, Allie," he whispers.

"I don't want to," I whisper back. I want to grab him and escape together, away from our parents, away from expectations, away from everybody who wants us to fit the mold of what they need us to be. I just want to be with him—no shame, no fear.

"So don't."

"We all have choices." I throw my shoulders back, to display a bravery I don't entirely feel. "It's time for you to make yours."

I turn and walk farther down the driveway, pulling out my phone to call my mom.

"Allie? What's wrong?" she says. "Why are you crying?"

"Mom. Come get me. Please."

The second Mom puts the car in park, I race into our house.

"Allie?" Dad says, calling after me as I clomp up the stairs, my flats slapping against the wood.

I close the door without answering. I can't face Dad right now. Everything is falling apart, and the ground feels shaky underneath me.

I take a deep breath, and I do the one thing I know will calm my racing heart, slow my jagged breath, quiet my troubled mind:

I pray.

I've been so afraid to be me. To show myself. To show all the parts of me: happy, sad, complex, fearful, angry, hopeful, wrong.

I don't want to be the bright and shiny Allie who puts on a happy face and tells everybody else it's okay, who implores them to accept her as a good Muslim.

What if it's not always okay?

What if I'm not always a good Muslim?

I'm still a Muslim.

And I'm still good.

I've always worried they won't love me anymore if I'm not perfect. They: my parents, my classmates, my boyfriend, now my Muslim friends, too.

I want approval—but I'm sick of the contortionist act: hiding myself away, jumping through hoops, whispering half-truths to please everybody else.

Yes, I want to be loved. But for me.

Not for the ideal of what I could be.

CHAPTER THIRTY

It's been three days since the Easter party, and Wells and I have been completely avoiding each other, which makes for awkwardness at school. At least we have different lunch periods.

"Trouble in paradise?" Mikey asks, jamming a sandwich into his mouth.

Mikey's been nicer to me since the hallway incident. He saves me a seat at lunch and sometimes offers me extra Hershey's Kisses that his mom packs. I appreciate that he's trying to be a better person, but I'd rather he was never a jerk to begin with.

I shrug. "I dunno."

"C'mon, Mikey, leave her alone," Sarah says.

He rolls his eyes. "What, I can't *ask*? You girls are so touchy."

"It's not touchy. It's rude. And it has nothing to do with

being a girl. Allie will talk about it when she's ready," Emilia says, giving me a little smile.

I guess Emilia's nicer now, too.

"Wells doesn't tell me anything. You don't tell me anything. Nobody tells me anything," Mikey grumbles, and just like that, I picture him as an old bald guy with high school trophies on the shelf and his best days far behind him. Suddenly, I feel a little sorry for him.

My World History class is across the hall from Wells's chemistry class. I try my usual trick of showing up just after the bell rings so I can avoid the slightest chance of conversation with Wells. But after several minutes in the girls' bathroom fluffing up my hair and reapplying makeup, I exit to see him practically inching down the hallway, buried in his phone. Looks like he had the same plan.

"Oh. Hey," he says, looking pained.

"Uh, hey."

"Is . . . Did . . . How was . . . How's it going?"

"Good, good. You?"

"Fine." He swallows. "I've been better."

I press my fingers together behind my back, quelling my impulse to reach out and touch his face. His skin is so clear and soft. His eyes are the perfect shade of brown. His curly hair was made for fingers to run through it.

Focus, Allie. Principles.

The bell rings.

We walk inside our classrooms, spell broken.

After World History, I walk into the hallway tentatively. He's bolted, which makes me feel both disappointed and relieved.

I'm propped up against pillows on my bed after dinner, diligently working my way through math homework, when my phone pings with a text.

I grab it hopefully. *Wells?*

Just thinking his name makes my heart hurt.

Nope. A puzzlingly terse text from Dad:

Come downstairs, please.

In the living room, Dad is surrounded by paperwork, bags dragging down his eyes from the longer hours he's been working ever since moving to Atlanta. He doesn't look happy. *West Side Story* plays on the TV.

Mom pats me on the shoulder and says she'll be upstairs taking a bath. She licks her lips, looking apprehensively back and forth between the two of us. Dad nods her off.

He pats the seat next to him. "Come. Sit."

I sit next to him on the couch, feeling nervous.

"Homework going well?" His voice is controlled, steady. I can tell it's killing him—he wants to get to whatever it is he's about to say—and yet he's still managing to keep it together. My dad: cool under pressure as always.

"Yep." It's as if I'm discussing the weather with a stranger, not talking to the person who I'm closest to in the entire world.

Scratch that: who I *used* to be closest to.

He sighs. "Look, Allie. I found something in your room, and I want to talk about it."

I breathe deeply, trying to quell my rising anxiety. *Here we go.*

"I found a prayer cover and rug," my father says. My heart starts beating double-time.

"Dad, I swear—you're being dramatic."

That phrase—*I swear*—reminds me of a memory I'd buried.

We were sitting on the couch together, laughing at a YouTube video. He expressed disbelief at something I said—about YouTubers making more than a million dollars a year? who knows?—and I replied, "I swear to God!" I laughed as I exaggeratedly made the sign of the cross.

I don't know why. I probably thought it looked cool.

My father stopped laughing. His face went slack, his warm eyes turned concerned. He looked at me, his happy face suddenly deflated.

"Don't do that," he said.

"Don't do what?"

"The cross," he said. "We're Muslims. You're a Muslim."

"Okay, jeez, sorry." I said it standoffishly, but I was burning with humiliation and hurt. I changed the subject. The two of us sat there a few more minutes watching videos, but all the joy had gone out of it.

Later, I remember thinking: *How can I be a Muslim if I don't know what being a Muslim* means?

It was wildly out of character for my dad. I'd seen him suddenly get weird when the subject of his religion came up. But it was the first time he got weird about it with *me.*

As I look at my dad on the couch now, watching me with confused eyes, I know I'm in for another uncomfortable situation.

It's been a long time in the making.

"I found your Twitter," he says.

"Okay." The unsaid hangs in the air: *So what*?

"I didn't know you had a Twitter."

"Well, you don't know everything. And it's called a Twitter *account*. Not 'a Twitter.'"

"Pumpkin, this isn't you. You don't talk to me like this."

"Dad." I sigh. "What's the big deal? So I have a Twitter account. I barely use it."

"Yes, but it's what you've Twittered about." He clicks around on his phone.

Has he downloaded the app? I think. My dad doesn't even have Facebook.

"You posted a photo of yourself wearing a hijab."

I need a defibrillator, because I just had a heart attack.

I lick my lips, buying time, gathering courage.

"Yeah. And?"

"And this. This is from last month." He reads something I retweeted from a firebrand Muslim who breezily takes on trolls.

"I retweeted somebody," I say, somewhat sullenly. "So?"

"Retweeting implies an endorsement. It takes something you didn't say yourself, and uses your force to put it out there in the world. It implies you believe it."

"It's not a big deal. People retweet stuff all the time," I say. I pause, my heart pounding, before saying, "But I do believe it.

Muslims *are* treated like garbage. Look at Teta and Fairouza and Aunt Bila."

"That's why you need to be careful," my dad says. "Things are not normal right now. You've gone shouting about Islam to the rooftops, and now you've made yourself a target."

"Shouting to the rooftops? I've tweeted like five times!" I cross my arms. "What you're really saying is, you want me to hide who I am."

"I don't want you to hide. I want you to be smart!" His frustration is palpable. He opens something on his laptop screen. "I take it you haven't seen this."

"Seen what?"

He moves the computer in front of me. It's a clip one of his work colleagues emailed to him. The subject reads Allie?

On the screen is a freeze-frame image of Jack Henderson on his show *The Jack Attack*.

"Jack Henderson," he says. "From his show earlier tonight."

"I know who it is."

"Wells's dad." It's both a challenge and a statement.

We stare at each other.

"Yeah," I finally say. "Wells's dad."

"How could you keep something this important from me?"

"It's not a big deal," I mutter.

My dad presses PLAY on the clip.

"And that brings us to the subject of Muslims," Jack says in his monologue, a giant red graphic with the word *Muslims* taking up the screen next to his face. "You and I both know there's a serious Muslim problem in this country. We have refugees pouring in from countries like Syria. We have those who seek to wage jihad and impose Sharia law. And, of course, we have the moral imperative of needing to help these poor women who are being forced to veil against their will.

"Well, what would you say if I told you I'd met a Muslim who changed my mind? I know, I know. Hear me out. She goes to high school with my son, and she's a Muslim, but she's just like you and me. And this Muslim girl, well, she defies your expectations. She's this sweet little pale redhead named Allie, and she looks like she could be the girl next door. Now, Allie and my son have been spending quite a bit of time together—you know how teenagers are—and so I've gotten to know this lovely little lady, and I'll tell you—she's a delight. Such a surprise. And I mean it when I say: You'd never know she's Muslim! She wears normal clothes, and she doesn't have anything covering her pretty hair, and she's articulate and she wears makeup, and she's very, very normal. She's not radical.

"And as I've gotten to know this little lady, I've realized: You know, for the most part some Muslims really are just the same as you and me. They don't want their husbands telling them what to do any more than you or I do! Take Allie's parents: They drink, they don't pray, they're almost as normal as can be. And so I say, if a Muslim family is here legally through the proper channels, if they're hardworking, if they're willing to put their culture aside and embrace America, well, then they're welcome, too.

"This is your food for thought. Muslims are people, same as you and me. Good night, everybody, and thanks for watching."

Dad clicks the laptop shut.

"We're not— That's not— He's using me!" I say.

"I know he's using you," Dad says quietly.

"He's trying to act like he's being tolerant and inclusive, but he's furthering harmful stereotypes. He's saying the only Muslims worth anything are the ones who don't seem Muslim, period."

Dad nods.

"So why are you mad at *me*? That's not my fault!"

"This isn't a game, Allie. I've spent your life trying to teach you, but I clearly didn't do well enough. Our country isn't safe—it never has been."

Safe. He doesn't think it will ever be safe. I guess I can't blame him, given the history. I don't remember a time when we weren't outsiders.

I've heard the stories about what happened when the twin towers fell. My family lived outside Dallas, our town a Muslim island in the sprawling seas of Bible Belt Texas. Safety in numbers both comforted my newly converted mother and worried her; crowds of Muslims drew crowds of protesters. The first time the house was egged, the police didn't show up for hours.

My father assured her it would be fine—he'd weathered worse; people were grieving; they needed to vent their fear and anger somewhere. People like us were the recipients of that anger as they tried to make sense of a scary new reality, he said. History was cyclical, and progress always won in the end. It would pass. Goodness would prevail. We simply needed to have faith.

Dad was right, as always: The taunts and graffiti and slurs against anybody who even remotely looked Muslim eventually died down. Slowly, people tolerated our family's presence:

first in Richardson, and then in Wayne, in El Segundo, in Evanston.

But no matter where we lived, the anxiety we provoked—the fear and anger—never went away.

Even among so-called good liberals.

Not really.

Dad continues. "You don't know what it's like to cover. You don't know what it's like to have people hate you because you look Muslim. You have no idea what it means to identify as a Muslim and live in this world. You risk letting a monster like Jack Henderson in? Why? And why would you post things publicly? You're lucky. You pass as American, like everybody else, and you want to throw it all away? Most Muslims would be grateful to be in your position."

"Lucky enough to pass? I'm *ashamed* of myself for passing!" I shout. "I've spent my entire life rejecting who I am so people won't judge me. My friends don't have that luxury. Leila doesn't have that privilege. Fatima gets discriminated against on *multiple* fronts. How I can live with myself if I call myself a Muslim, but only when it's convenient and doesn't get me into trouble?"

"Allie. Pumpkin. I know you mean well." He's launched into his professor voice. "But this is—I cannot abide this."

"I can't help who Wells's father is!"

"You didn't have to spend months lying to me about it."

"I didn't lie. I just didn't . . . share."

"The abaya is especially puzzling to me. Are you honestly telling me you're praying now?"

The fight seeps out of me like a deflated balloon. "Yes."

"This is your grandmother's fault."

"It's not Teta's fault. I started praying *before* she visited."

He looks baffled. "We didn't raise you like this. Our family is not about apocryphal stories and emotional appeals. We're about reason and facts," he says. "Does your mother know?"

Now I'm on thin ice. I don't want to lie to my dad, but I don't want to get my mom in trouble, either.

I take so long debating whether to tell him that my silence accidentally serves as the answer. His face falls.

"What is going *on* in this family? Religion is a means to control people—a political tool. Your mother knows that. We're on the same page. Team Abraham believes in *science*."

He's playing the Team Abraham card.

"Okay, you're being beyond hypocritical," I say. "My entire life, I've been told I'm a Muslim. The family are Muslims. You're a Muslim. Mom converted when you got married. We went to the mosque when Jido died. Teta taught me how to pray. And now that I want to know what it all means for myself, I'm supposed to back off? That's not how it works. It's not fair."

"Your mother converted as a formality," he says gruffly.

"She meant it in her heart. I know she did."

"I know that's hard for you to hear, Pumpkin."

"It's not hard to hear, because it's a lie. A convert is a real Muslim, and *she's* a real Muslim, and *I'm* a real Muslim. I'm sorry I didn't tell you about Wells's crappy dad, and I'm sorry I hid things from you, but whatever. You don't have the right to take my religion away from me."

He sighs, clearly frustrated. "Look. I'm glad you're passionate.

But it's not a good idea to be putting yourself out there so publicly with this Muslim thing. Just . . . cool it, okay?"

I shift on the couch, feeling antsy. "Dad, it's not a 'thing.' It's not a phase. This is forever."

He frowns again, looking disappointed, as if he expected that his speech would change my mind. On the TV screen, Tony is singing "Maria." We watch the song without talking, the flickering TV still on mute.

Finally he says, voice low, "You're growing up. I understand I can't tell you what to do. But I'm flabbergasted you wouldn't have felt safe confiding in me. I'm extremely disappointed."

"Dad, will you please stop with the disappointment? It makes me feel horrible," I say. "I get it. I'm such a disappointment to you. A disappointment because I'm praying. A disappointment because I'm dating. Get *over* it. Maybe I didn't tell you because I knew you'd be annoying about it—and it's *my* business, not yours. When are you going to get the message? I don't need your advice. Just *stop*."

My father looks as if I've slapped him across the face.

I know what's coming next: He's going to explode.

Instead, he gets quiet. A look of sadness crosses his face—worse than sadness.

Hurt.

He scratches his cheek awkwardly. He stands up without looking at me. "Good night," he says in a small voice.

I exhale. I've never spoken to my father like that in my life. My head is pounding.

Behind me, steps.

I turn to find my mom. Of course she's been listening. She'll say something diplomatic. She'll make me feel better.

Instead she shakes her head.

"That was out of line," she says. "Nobody's perfect, but we don't have room in this family for cruelty."

She turns and follows my father upstairs, leaving me alone in the middle of the living room, "America" flickering on the screen.

It's past midnight. I should be sleeping, but I have too much work to do. Between Arabic lessons and my comp sci project and Algebra II worksheets and history papers and my English books, it's a miracle I'm still standing. I'm working my way through algebra when I hear them.

Mom and Dad.

Fighting.

My parents never fight.

They bicker. They get annoyed with each other. They raise their voices a tad if one of them is frustrated—usually my mom, losing her therapist cool and allowing my dad under her skin.

But they never fight.

I move closer to the door, opening it quietly and sticking my head into the hallway.

It sounds like they're downstairs, maybe in the kitchen.

"You can't treat her like a child!"

Mom. She sounds pissed. I'm surprised she's standing up for me after everything that went down tonight.

"She *is* a child!"

Dad. Equally pissed.

"She's sixteen."

"A child."

Now I hear cabinets opening and closing, slamming. They're worked up.

"What do you want me to do, Elizabeth? Should I shut my mouth? Close my eyes? Let my daughter go down the wrong path?"

"She's not going down the wrong path. She's exploring her faith. She's exploring *your* faith!"

"It has nothing to do with me."

"It has everything to do with you! She's trying to figure out where she came from. It's healthy, Mo. Why can't you see that?"

My dad mumbles something unintelligible.

"You can't pick other people's parents," Mom says. "Don't you remember what it was like with *your* parents? Remember the guff they gave you about moving to America and marrying somebody who wasn't Circassian? A *Catholic*?"

"It wasn't like that."

"It was exactly like that. You can't tell your children how to live their lives. You raise them, and you do your best, and you put them on the right path, but eventually you have to take a step back and let them be themselves. We raised a good kid."

"She's still a kid. She doesn't know what she's getting herself into. Look what's happened already."

Loud sigh from Mom. "I know I'm not as qualified as you to talk about this. Far be it from me to erase any experiences you've had over the years. And I know there are bigots out there—I deal with them myself."

More mumbling from Dad.

"I do!" Mom says. "Believe me, I get it. I know you're trying to protect her, but you can't coddle her forever. And your religion is something you should be proud of, not ashamed of."

"I'm not ashamed of it," Dad says forcefully.

Mom says something I can't hear.

"I'm *not*. I'm concerned," he says. "There's a difference. Her name is out there now. She could be assaulted. She could be targeted. I don't want her putting herself in harm's way unnecessarily. If she wants to practice, practice. I accept it, but I don't get it. That's not how we raised her. How's she going to go believing that mumbo jumbo suddenly? And does she have to advertise it? Make herself a target? Open herself up to a snake like Jack Henderson? She's being naive!"

My feelings are crushed. I've never heard my father talk about me that way: He's always telling me how smart I am, how capable I am, how mature I am. To hear he thinks I'm being naive hurts my soul.

"Can't you talk to her?" Mom says.

"I tried. What else is there to say?"

"I don't understand how it escalated. She's a good kid. She's not doing drugs. She's not out drinking. She's *praying*, Mo. Big whoop. You need to cut her some slack."

"She's been changing for months now," Dad says. "I don't

appreciate her moping around the house, throwing me these looks, acting as if I've wounded her."

"She's a teenager! Welcome to parenthood!"

"We didn't raise her like this."

"We raised her to think for herself—and that's what she's doing."

"By thinking like everybody else? By subscribing to a religious cult?"

Silence.

Finally, Mom's voice again. It's icy.

"You didn't seem to have an issue with me joining the 'religious cult' when it suited you."

More silence.

Dad: "That's not fair."

"Maybe not. But when you insult the religion I joined you in, it insults me, too. It makes a mockery of my decision."

"We're not religious! Saying a few words in front of an imam to please my mother isn't the same thing as praying five times a day and doing all that bloody nonsense!"

"How many times are we going to go through this?" she says. "It wasn't to please your mother. It was for *me*! You don't have the right to look into somebody else's soul and make moral judgments about intent!"

"You don't pray, Elizabeth."

"How do you know?"

"Come on. You don't fast. You're a Muslim in name only, like me," he says. "Unless you're doing things behind my back, like your daughter."

A gasp.

It's silent for a long time.

"We need to take this down a notch," Mom says. "*Now.*"

Finally, my father's voice, small and regretful: "I'm sorry. You're right."

"Okay. Thank you. I'm sorry, too."

"I shouldn't make your issues mine."

"No, Mo. You shouldn't." She sighs. Cabinets open and shut forcefully, and then I hear the flicker of the stove. She's probably making tea. "I know I shouldn't have kept things from you. I didn't want to betray Allie's confidence—and furthermore, I think it's important to keep this whole thing in perspective. You're sorely lacking it."

He grunts.

Hearing my parents go at it because of me makes my cheeks burn in shame.

I close the door, not wanting to disturb them and upset them further—they'd be mortified if they knew I'd been listening.

My father calling me naive rings in my ears.

Muslims are targets. I get it. And I didn't handle everything properly.

But I can't erase who I am. And I shouldn't have to. And I don't want to.

Leila and Fatima and Dua and my grandmother and my cousins and every Muslim woman who wears hijab or publicly identifies as a Muslim—they're not naive. And it's unfair of my dad to imply they are.

I might never wear hijab again, but it's bigger than that.

Why should Muslims be the ones who have to change? Why shouldn't it be everybody else?

I'm tired of people pleasing. I'm tired of hiding.

I'm proud of being a Muslim. I want to show it to the world.

And if that makes somebody uncomfortable—even if that somebody is my dad—maybe they're the problem, not me.

CHAPTER THIRTY-ONE

Samira was right: I'm picking up Arabic at light speed.

It's not like I'm going to be fluent anytime soon. It's going to take years. But with every lesson, every chapter of Al-Kitaab, every Amr Diab or Nancy Ajram song on I play on repeat until I can sing along with comprehension, I'm assembling puzzle pieces. It doesn't feel like I'm learning Arabic for the first time. It's like I knew the language all along, and long-buried words are simply being excavated, dusted off, and carefully brought into the light.

Dua continues taking charge of my musical education, curating Spotify playlists and forcing me to listen to them with her after school.

Soon after Easter, the two of us sit in front of her computer, listening to the newest playlist she's made.

"We could have done this over FaceTime," I say.

"Where's the fun in that? I wanted you with me while you listen." She puts on a Nancy Ajram song. "She's amazing, isn't she?"

"Better than Beyoncé," I say teasingly.

"Okay, let's not go *there*."

Together, we sit and listen. Dua sways a little in the chair, feeling the music and waving her hands in the same distinctive, undulating way my cousins do, while I look on awkwardly. I wish I were the kind of girl who looked cool dancing. Instead, it's like somebody's stabbing me with a hot poker.

"This one. This line"—she sings along, off-key—"I freaking love it." She looks at me, a mischievous look on her face. "Pop quiz. What's she's saying?"

"Play it again?"

Dua drags the song back a few seconds with her finger on the iPhone screen, and plays it again.

"She's saying, 'I'm in love with you,'" I say. "And something about your eyes?"

"Awesome!" Dua cheers.

"I mean, that's hardly advanced Arabic. I've known 'I love you' since I was like four."

"Whatevs. You've gotta celebrate the victories where you can find them. Where's your Arabic textbook?"

I pull out Al-Kitaab from my backpack. She flips through it, whistling.

"This is no joke," she says.

"What do you mean?"

"They jump right into it. And it's written in Arabic!"

I nod.

"You know *I* can't read and write Arabic, right?" she says.

"You can't?"

"My parents never taught me. I can barely write my own name. You're supposed to learn Arabic to read the Qur'an, but most of my cousins born in the US are the same. My parents were born in America—we all learned English first and Arabic second."

"Same with my family. My cousins are fluent, but English is their first language, not Arabic."

"Kind of ironic," she says. "Considering everybody thinks we're so foreign, but we were born here, English is our native language, and we can't read a lick of Arabic."

"Caught between two worlds."

She shrugs. "Us and half the country, right? We're all immigrants." She clicks around, pulling up another playlist. "Hey, what's up with Wells?" Her tone is nonchalant.

"What do you mean?" I ask dully.

"I've seen you ice each other in the hallways. You don't sit together in the library before school. You're taking the bus again. What happened? Did you break up?"

"Are you sure you want to know?"

"Yes, silly."

I raise my eyebrows.

"I told you I'm here for you, and I mean it," she says. "Bad things happen when people feel alone."

"I've felt alone a lot recently," I admit. Then I give in and spill the whole story about the Easter party.

"Wait, step back," Dua says. "Jack Henderson? From TV?"

"That's the one."

"*That's* Wells's dad? Whoa. Intense. And you went off on him? In his own house? On Easter?"

"Not my finest hour," I say, and grimace.

She laughs, leaning back in the chair as if she's personally reliving the moment. "I wish I was there to see it. My parents *loathe* that guy."

"He and Wells don't have the best relationship."

"Okay," Dua says, "but why are you punishing Wells for his dad?"

I explain what Jack did on TV.

"I mean, if I'm with Wells, I'm condoning his dad, don't you think?" I say. "I'm saying what he does is okay."

She shrugs. "If you say so. I barely know Wells, but he doesn't seem like the poster child for toxic masculinity. He seems like a pretty good guy."

"He *is* a good guy," I whisper. "I miss him."

She scratches her chin. "Is he supportive of the religion?"

"Yes. Definitely."

"Look, maybe you're catching me in a good mood, but Allah, subhanahu wa ta'ala, works in mysterious ways. You're not marrying him. If he's supportive of you practicing, and if you're not—you know—going buck wild—"

I start giggling. "Buck wild?"

"*You know what I mean*," she says. "Halal dating. Maybe you guys can do that—if you're so despondent without him. You think he'd be cool with it?"

"I don't know. We left things pretty messy. We haven't spoken since his dad's . . . performance."

"Oh, please. I've seen how that boy looks at you in the hallway. He'll forgive you. Maybe you'll get lucky and he'll convert—and then you *can* marry him."

"Wells? As a revert? That's the funniest thing I've ever heard."

She shrugs. "Your mom did it. Every convert starts somewhere."

I laugh. "Hey, weird thought. Maybe I can make it to the end of sophomore year still in a functional relationship before I start trying to get my brand-new sixteen-year-old boyfriend to *change his religion to marry me.*"

Her cheeks redden. "It sounds silly when you say it like *that.*" She clicks around on the computer. "Wait, it's May first. Astrology Universe is up."

"It's not up. She's always late. I checked this morning."

Dua spins the computer screen to face me. "Boom. It's up now."

"Ooh!" The two of us crowd in front of the screen. "Do mine first."

"Too late." She's already clicked to hers. "Okay. Leo, Leo. Whadda we got . . . ?" She skims, calling out key phrases. "'Mercury ends retrograde'—that explains my iPhone falling in the toilet last week . . . 'Your social life is going to be on fire'—what's new?" she says, and grins at me. "'Primed for success'—going to rock my final exams . . . Blah-di-blah, same old. Okay, let's do yours." She clicks on Aquarius.

I read it out loud. "'Family and friends will play a huge role this month'—that's not a surprise. 'Secrets are in your chart'—whoa, that's kind of freaky."

"She's always right." Dua nods solemnly.

"'Stuff that happened in April, around the middle of the month, is going to come to the fore in May'—oh my God. Wells? My dad? Both?"

"There's no fighting your horoscope," she says.

"Oh, good, you're reading your horoscopes," Amina says sarcastically from the hallway.

"Amina!" Dua shrieks. "Privacy!"

"Not my fault your door is open. It's haram, you know," Amina says, waggling a carrot stick before taking a bite. "Mom wouldn't be happy."

"Well, so is your flirtation with Fareed," Dua snaps. "Should we tell her both and see which one pisses her off more?"

Amina's cheeks go pink. "I'm not doing anything. We're talking."

"You sure? You two looked supercute in the backyard yesterday as he was leaving. Does Zaki know you're dating his best friend?"

"Wallahi, Dua, if you say one single word, I will end you. We're just talking," she says between clenched teeth.

"You owe me one," Dua says, blowing her sister a kiss. "Close the door, please."

Amina slams the door in a huff as Dua turns back to the computer. "You're so lucky you're an only," she says. "Okay, what's Wells's sign? Let's do him next."

"Leo, just like you."

"All the best people are," she says. "One point for Wells."

As I'm doing homework upstairs before dinner, I get a text from Wells.

WELLS: Hi, it's me

WELLS: Can we talk?

ME: Sure

ME: Like, on the texting machine?

WELLS: I'm nearby. Could be at yours in five?

Soon after, we sit on the screened-in porch overlooking my backyard, drinking from a freshly made pitcher of sweet tea my mom put out for us. She closes the porch door behind her, peeking through the screen at me quizzically.

Okay? she mouths.

I nod at her discreetly. She nods back and then leaves.

"I wanted to show you something," Wells says.

"Yeah?"

He reaches into his messenger bag, covered with patches of his favorite bands, and pulls out a black-and-yellow book. It's one of those Dummies guides, about Islam.

I burst out laughing. His cheeks redden.

"It's funny?" he mutters.

"It's sweet."

"I wanna learn. I'm trying to understand it better, so I can understand *you* better. I've"—his voice cracks, and he clears his throat—"uh, I've missed you."

I reach out and take the book, flipping through it while I try to calm my racing mind.

"I'm sorry about my dad," he says. "My mom told me what he said on TV."

"What'd she tell you?"

"They got into a big fight about it. She wasn't happy."

I nod.

"We got into a fight, too," he says.

"Yeah?"

"Yeah. I told him he needed to back off. He said . . ." Wells pauses, shakes his head. "Anyhow, he tried to get me to break up with you. I didn't explain that we already kind of . . ."

I reach over and touch his hand. I can't help it. I have to.

"Sorry I made a scene at your house," I say.

The touch seems to relax him. He threads his fingers through mine, and we look at each other.

Just like that, I know we're gonna be okay.

"The thing is," Wells says, "you were right. He threatened to stop paying for stuff. Never heard *that* one before."

"Did he?"

"He tried. My mom got in the way."

"She stopped him?"

"I guess she's been putting money away—a lot of money—for a while. Turned into a fight, it got ugly, and . . ." He clears his throat. "Anyhow, Dad's back now. He does that when they fight. Disappears for a few hours, goes to the club for cigars or whatever. Then he gets over it and pretends it never happened."

We fall into silence.

"So I have this theory," I say eventually. "Not really a theory, but more of a realization. Your parents are human."

He laughs. "Breakthrough."

"No, hear me out. Everybody is like, 'Oh, you need to obey your parents. You need to respect your parents.' It's a major point in the Qur'an. And in a lot of cases, it's true. But think about the most ridiculous person you know. Like Mikey Murphy. He's probably going to be a dad someday. And suddenly, because he had sex, a tiny human who shares his DNA has to respect him? Even if he spouts nonsense? Even if he's a bad person? Just because somebody is a parent doesn't mean they transform into a saint. It doesn't automatically mean they're worthy of respect."

He nods. "Yeah. Makes sense."

"What if your parents aren't worth obeying? What if they're wrong?"

He laughs. "We're screwed."

"Or maybe," I say, "we're free."

"You're lucky," he says. "You've got good parents."

"Yeah. I do. Except . . ."

"Except what?"

And I catch him up on my fight with my father.

"We've barely spoken since. Mostly silent dinners. No more movie night. Just awkwardness," I say. "He gets that I'm growing up, but it still bugs him that I'm not his little girl anymore and he can't make me listen. He's annoyed I didn't tell him about your dad. And he's hurt that I hid the praying thing from him."

"How long will it take him to get over it?"

"I don't know if he'll ever get over it. I mean, the thing with your dad—yeah, whatever. But the religious thing . . . that's a pretty fundamental disconnect. He thinks I'm stupid for being religious, which means he doesn't respect me anymore, and I'm so hurt for knowing he looks down on me I can't bring myself to talk to him. It's a big mess."

"I wish there was something I could do."

Okay, time to kick this awkwardness into high gear.

"There is. But you're going to hate it."

"Maybe. Tell me anyway."

"It's silly."

"Allie. C'mon. Tell me."

I take a deep breath, suddenly feeling freezing. "I want to try halal dating."

"Sounds like something you eat on a high holiday. What is it again?"

"It's like . . . we date, we're in a relationship, but no sex," I say, blushing. "Like, ever. I mean, yes, *someday*, but only if we're married. Not that I want to marry you . . . Not that I *don't* want to marry you." *Oh God. This conversation is a disaster.* "Anyhow, it's kind of like PG dating, and I'm going to go hide in my room for a hundred years now."

Despite himself, he laughs.

"PG dating?" His face looks like he's smelled something weird.

Then he chews on a thumbnail.

"Can we make out? Can we be alone? Are you going to be grounded forever if I put my arm around you?"

"I hope you're joking. First of all, I'm not doing this for my parents. And, secondly, hour-long make-out sessions lying down in a dark bedroom obviously aren't okay, but—"

"Can I bargain you down to twenty-second make-out sessions sitting on a lit porch? In a row?"

I giggle. "More like two seconds. And once."

"No sex. Yeesh. That kind of sucks."

He starts chewing on the thumbnail again.

"But who am I kidding?" he says. "I mean . . . I've made it sixteen years."

I push through my embarrassment. "The idea is that you take away the physical temptation, so you build a real connection instead."

He nods. "I get it. When Mikey had his first girlfriend last year, all they did was make out—like, seriously, *get a room*—and he barely knew her favorite color. He didn't know her favorite band, and he never went to her softball games. He didn't even know that she hated *The Empire Strikes Back*."

"Sacrilege."

"Why are you even dating, you know? I mean, hooking up is one thing, but if you're gonna be in a relationship—" He stops, looking panicked. "Don't tell him I said that. He'd never stop busting my balls."

I laugh. "I'll try to restrain myself."

We stare at each other, and I feel that familiar nervous thumping against my chest.

To calm myself down, I start playing with my hair, twirling it into a corkscrew and then pulling the ends through my fingers over and over. "I'm not against getting physical," I say, "if that's what people wanna do—get on with your bad self—but I like this way more. The closer I get to Islam, the more I study, the stronger I feel. I want to keep it up and see where it goes."

He's quiet, staring at his hands. Finally, he looks at me, resolved.

"Whatever I have to do to be with you, Allie, I'm in."

As relief courses through my body, warmth returns to my fingers. "I was scared."

He reaches over to grab my hand and, just as quickly, drops it.

"Sorry, is that okay?" he asks.

"Yes," I laugh, grabbing his hand again. "The kissing thing . . . so I've seen a couple people online say you can kiss as long as it doesn't lead to anything else, but then others say . . . well, you can imagine. I feel like we're making it up as we go along."

We lean into each other, kissing—but instead of a passionate take-the-chrome-off kiss, it's sweet and tentative.

And short! Superquick. *I see you, God.*

We pull away, looking into each other's eyes.

"Does this mean we're still on for prom?" he asks.

A frisson of excitement shoots through me. "Uh, were we ever on for prom? We're sophomores."

He gives me a confused look before laughing. "Right, I

forgot you're new. Our school lets everybody go to prom. It's an inclusion thing." He makes air quotes around the word *inclusion*. "*Purely* coincidental it helps them raise more money."

"At least they're inclusive on one count."

"Unless you'd rather go with somebody else?" he says.

"Who, Mikey?" I laugh.

"Is that a yes?" he says teasingly.

"I don't know. Aren't you supposed to do some big promposal? Where are my balloons? Where is my helicopter? I don't see a marching band." I lean forward and give him another short kiss. "But I suppose it'll do."

CHAPTER THIRTY-TWO

The doorbell rings. Wells must be here.

I give myself a look in the mirror. I've decided to mix up my formal wear this year. Instead of the sleeveless V-neck dress I wore to homecoming, I've chosen a sparkly champagne-colored floor-length gown with long sleeves. I picked it up at the mall a couple of weeks ago with Dua, and we agreed it was gorgeous and set off my red hair: elegant, regal, and very prom-appropriate. She's wearing an iridescent navy-blue gown to match her favorite new hijab, and she promised we'll meet up once she arrives at the hotel.

I tiptoe down the stairs. I've been imagining this moment for ages. Prom.

But what actually happens when I walk down the stairs—really, I glide, I'm freaking gliding—is that nobody is looking up to see me come down.

My mother and father are fumbling over the camera while Wells looks on in amusement.

"It's *this* button," my mom says.

"No, Elizabeth. For the love of God, let me do it."

"I've got it!" My mom holds the camera away from him, as if they're playing a game of Keep-Away. Dad sighs heavily.

Next to them, Wells is trying to keep from laughing.

That gives me a chance to feast my eyes on him as I descend. He's wearing a black tuxedo with a quirky blue bow tie, and a little white handkerchief poking out of his breast pocket, like men have in old black-and-white movies. His shoes are shiny and brand-new: he must have bought them specifically for the dance. He looks confident. Reliable, strong, steady ol' Wells.

Finally, I make it to the bottom of the steps. "Do you need help?" I say.

Everybody jumps.

"Allie! Wait!" Mom fumbles with the camera. "We didn't record you coming down the stairs!"

"I've been in the foyer for a full minute. I was practically crawling down the steps."

"Go back up, go back up!" she says. "I've fixed the camera."

"I wouldn't call taking off the lens cap fixing it, per se," Dad says.

"I'm not doing it again," I say. "That's silly."

"Please! We've been dreaming about this for years!" Mom has on her earnest pleading face, which she knows gets me every time. Parental guilt *works*.

"Fine," I sigh. "Let me just—" I approach Wells to give him a hug.

"Not yet!" My mom shoos me back with her hand. "We'll get it on video."

"Sorry," I say to Wells from over my shoulder as I walk back up the steps. "Parents' orders."

He laughs.

"All the way to the end of the hallway—out of sight!" Mom commands. "We want to get your grand entrance!"

"Is this better?" I bellow from down the hallway.

A photo of Dad and me from my sixth birthday catches my attention. I'm on his shoulders at Disneyland, beaming at the camera while he looks up at me proudly.

"Okay . . . ready, set, go!" Mom calls.

I walk down the hallway and descend the steps. I could pantomime silly, exaggerated moves, but I know this is important to them. They'll probably rewatch it over and over, like they do with home movies from when I was a kid. It's only fair I try to get it right for them.

Mom smiles up at me, her face bright and shining, as she trains the camera on my entrance.

Dad stands next to her in the foyer, his brow knitted. He seems wistful. We still haven't officially made up. He clears his throat, swiping at something in his eye.

And then there's Wells, standing at the bottom of the steps with his hands in his pockets, grinning up at me.

"You look nice," I say politely to Wells.

"Thank you," he says. "So do you." We pat each other on

the back like we're two grandmothers saying hello. "I have this for you." He unearths a corsage, which he offers to me. I put my wrist out, and he slides it over my skin, his fingers warm.

"Mom, where's the boutonniere?" I say.

"On it!" she says.

She triumphantly produces it from a hallway console, handing me the plastic carton. I take out the white flower, pinning it to Wells's tux but careful to leave room between the two of us.

"Okay, photo time!" Mom says, brandishing the camera. "Allie, come stand over here. Wells . . . right there . . . That's right."

The two of us stand side by side, barely touching. We've been through this with my birthday. He's an Awkward Photos at Allie's House veteran. Although, after my showdown with Dad, the awkwardness has been kicked up to a whole new level.

Hey, at least Dad gets major brownie points for trying.

"Oh, for goodness' sake, son," Dad says. "You can put your arm around her for the photo. You look like you're in a military lineup."

Mom giggles.

Wells and I look at each other, our stiff smiles relaxing, as he loosely puts his arm around my waist. I lean into him, wanting to remember this moment for the rest of my life.

After we've gone through solo photos at my place, we have to meet up with our friends to repeat the entire process. Joey's house is the designated photo spot, Mr. and Mrs. Bishop corralling us outside for pictures. Mrs. Bishop holds a DSLR camera, snapping pictures like a paparazzo, while Mr. Bishop wields a GoPro mounted on a tripod, providing a running murmured commentary like a sportscaster as he darts around the gardens.

"And here's Mikey Murphy, with his date Claire Sanchez. An unusual choice—some might say out of his league—but they do make a fine-looking couple. Behind them, on the landing, we have Emilia Graham and Brian Davis. Brian's had a perfect GPA three years running, so he's a lock for valedictorian next year. Word on the street is he's a shoo-in for either Howard or Georgetown, his parents' alma maters, and Joey says he'll be president one day. Exiting the house, it's Zadie Rodriguez with her girlfriend Tessa Chu, a junior at North Springs. We all miss Tessa since she moved last year, but she made the trek out here just for prom. Braving Atlanta traffic, that's true love . . ."

"Sorry," Joey says, coming over to stand next to us as his dad backs up, panning across the group for a wide shot, still murmuring into the GoPro.

"Why?" I ask. "They're parents. That's what they do."

"Document crap?" Wells says.

"Embarrass us."

"It must be in the parenting manual they hand out when we're born," Joey says. "The chapter after stalking your social media accounts, but before the one about guilting you for not spending enough time with them."

I think about my dad valiantly putting aside the painfulness of the past month to make sure I had a good prom, and I feel a rush of gratitude.

I've been too hard on him recently.

After all, it's not like we can snap our fingers and have things go back to normal. I don't know what normal means anymore.

"Okay, Joey and Sarah, you stand on the first step—that's it, right there—and Wells, you stand behind Joey. Allie, not that step, one down. Perfect," Mrs. Bishop says, art-directing us so that the group forms an inverted V up the steps leading to the gardens.

Joey and Sarah are going to prom together, which is kind of adorable, since I've long suspected Sarah was harboring a secret crush on Joey. Meanwhile, I still don't know how Mikey managed to land Claire as his date—although they *have* been spending a lot of time together during rehearsals for *Grease*.

When I see the other girls' dresses, I have a moment of feeling out of place. With the exception of Tessa, they're wearing long gowns, too, but theirs are displaying mounds of cleavage—they're all arms and legs and skin and shimmer lotion. Then I catch a reflection of myself in the sliding glass doors on the Bishops' verandah, and I relax, thinking, *I look good.*

I don't need to fit in—I still belong.

Wells reaches out his hand, and I walk over to him, entwining my fingers in his. He twirls me, wraps his arm around me, and pulls my back to his chest.

"You look gorgeous," he whispers.

I lean against him as Joey's mom and dad take the group photos, feeling content.

At the dance, inside an expensive five-star hotel in Buckhead, Wells and I thread through the crowd of classmates in their formal dresses, tuxedos, and suits.

"Looks like the Men's Wearhouse exploded," Wells comments. "I include myself."

"Yeah, well, at least you're not wearing something that looks like your grandmother is about to serenade a nursing home in Las Vegas."

He laughs, a deep, throaty guffaw. "Come on, you look incredible. You look like a movie star."

I take the compliment to heart, squeezing his hand.

As Bruno Mars plays, people rush the dance floor, the ballroom a sea of arms undulating and booties popping.

But then I see somebody who makes my stomach lurch.

"Uh, Wells . . . what is your father doing here?"

He looks across the room, startled. "What?"

"He's right over there, by Mr. Tucker." We stop dancing, and I discreetly point. "Didn't you say your mom was going to be a chaperone?" I was hoping we could spend the duration of our relationship away from Wells's house. I wasn't mentally prepared to see Jack tonight—or ever.

He scowls. "Something's up."

We stare at Jack. He's standing near the center of the room, in a position where he can see and be seen. A blond woman with a sticker saying PARENT VOLUNTEER walks up to him, smiling.

They shake hands, Jack laughing as the woman says something animatedly. She must be a fan. Nearby, Brian Davis glares at him. Maybe I shouldn't be surprised, but Emilia and Sarah don't look too thrilled, either. I look around the ballroom and notice Jack is garnering wildly different reactions—about half the kids are shooting daggers at him while the other half look starstruck.

As the music comes to an end, I hear a snippet of Jack's conversation.

"I just think you're so strong for how you handled that Muslim girl dating your son," the woman says. "I know you didn't say as much, but we could read between the lines. I don't know what I would do! But you took it like a champ!"

"You know, you'd be surprised. She's quite a nice girl, actually," Jack says.

The woman nods. "Of course, of course."

The knowledge that the two of them are talking about me makes my skin crawl.

"God, he doesn't let up," Wells says. "I'm sorry."

"You don't pick your parents," I say shrugging. "Don't let him ruin our night."

"Okay," he says, in a voice heavy with doubt.

When you tell somebody you want to try halal dating, you should expect about fifty feet in between the two of you on the dance floor.

"Am I contagious?" I say.

"Huh?"

I gesture toward the gaping, cavernous space between us. "This buffer zone you've got going on here."

I love how cute Wells looks when he's embarrassed.

"Halo" comes on, and the room goes into slow motion. He takes a step closer to me—about three steps—and holds out his hand. His fingers are warm as our palms press together.

"Is this better?" he murmurs, now close enough for me to see his eyelashes.

"Much." I lean up and give him a tiny kiss, relishing the softness of his lips before resting my head on his shoulder.

The two of us sway together in a private world of our own making.

Then I see Jack Henderson in the corner again. He's watching us.

His gaze yanks me back to the present moment. I take a step back.

"Everything okay?"

"Sorry, but your dad is creeping me out," I say honestly. "I wish he wasn't here. I just don't *like* him."

"Stop apologizing. I get it. I hate that he's here."

I know he does, but it still feels incomplete. Unresolved.

"I need a sec, okay? I'll be back."

As I'm leaving the ballroom on the way to the bathroom, I hear footsteps behind me, muffled on the carpet.

"Allie?" a male voice says in that distinctive drawl.

I turn, and it's Jack Henderson.

"Hi, darlin'," he says, taking a step toward me. I instinctively take a step back.

He puts his hands up, as if calming a horse. I'm reminded of Wells. It's unsettling. They are nothing alike, and yet my boyfriend is *of* this man.

"Didn't mean to startle you."

"I have nothing to say to you." The strength in my voice surprises me.

"Allie. Look, I know you probably think I'm a monster." He shakes his head, giving me a hangdog smile. "I'm not a bad person. Politics isn't personality."

I look past him, unwilling to engage further. I want to get out of here. I want to go back to the ballroom and slow dance with my boyfriend and be a normal teenager who doesn't have to fight so hard to exist.

"I know what you probably think, Allie," he says. "I don't hate Muslims."

"Congratulations."

"Wells has been distracted this year. You might not realize it, but he's not focusing on his studies, not pursuing his music, and his practice PSAT score was abysmal."

It was?

Jack smiles, catching my reaction. "You're a distraction," he says. "A lovely one, but a distraction nonetheless."

"Mmm."

"And, in any case, college is approaching. It's a high school fling, no? Besides, you're a Muslim—you're not supposed to date, are you?"

I stare at him.

He keeps going.

"You're an incredibly smart girl, Allie. You care about your religion, your family . . . Why don't you part ways with Wells now? Then you won't hold each other back."

I cross my arms.

"Surely, your parents can't be happy with the relationship. I'm not exactly popular with the Muslim community," he says with a self-deprecating smile.

My phone vibrates in my hand. I glance down at it.

WELLS: You outside? Can't find you

"I have to go," I say tonelessly.

Jack takes a step toward me. "It would help Wells. I know you care for him. We both want what's best for him."

"I have to go."

Jack clears his throat. "I get it. But I think it's important to clarify: There would be something in it for you, too."

I make a buffer between us, sweeping as close to the wall as possible as I walk back toward the ballroom.

"I'd make a donation to the Muslim Student Association," he calls after me. "Serena told me you're trying to fund-raise. You have such a kind heart."

I stop.

"A substantial donation."

I turn around. "Please. You going on TV and spouting some kumbaya crap about Muslims to make yourself feel like a good person is one thing. But actually supporting refugees? Like *that* would play with your base. Keep your money."

"Anonymous," he says, his gaze serious.

We lock eyes.

"Substantial," he repeats, all levity vanished.

And as I consider his proposal, my heart sinks.

I walk back into the ballroom, dazed.

I run into Dua near the DJ booth, dancing with her arms in the air. She looks happy and carefree, swaying joyfully. I don't want to ruin her night. I decide I'll figure it out on my own.

"Something's wrong," she asks, seeing my face.

I guess I'm not as good at hiding my emotions as I thought. I hesitate.

"Tell me," she says.

"Jack Henderson cornered me in the hallway."

She stops dancing. "He didn't. What is he doing here?"

"He's a chaperone, I guess? He gave me a sob story about how I'm distracting Wells, and how everything he's done is because he's a concerned parent, and how he's not a horrible person at all, just a poor, misunderstood nonmonster."

"He's the worst."

"There's more," I say. "He told me if I broke up with Wells, he'll give us a huge donation for the MSA. Like, huge. And anonymous."

She laughs. It's a loud, brusque "ha."

"Allie. You can't trust anything he says."

"I don't know. He seemed pretty serious. That's how badly he doesn't want me dating his son."

"Are you considering it?"

"I don't know. Maybe."

"Allie."

"Are Wells and I going to be together in a year? Two years? Five years?" I say. "Maybe Jack is right. Maybe the smartest thing to do is cut our losses now—and we raise a ton of money, too."

She closes her eyes and lets out a puff of frustration. "*Look.* I want to raise money for the cause—but you can't trust a single word out of that man's mouth. He's trying to manipulate you."

"Obviously. But what if he's right?"

"He's a big ol' liar."

"Probably."

"And besides, we don't want any of his tainted bribe money."

"I know."

"Like, not a dime."

"You're right," I say, hanging my head.

"Here's what I find more curious . . . Why are you willing to throw Wells under the bus?"

"I don't want to stand in his way," I whisper. "I want him to be happy. I don't want to be the thing standing between him and his family."

"He's a big boy," Dua says. "There's something else you're not saying."

I pause. Finally I say it: "I feel guilty for dating him. I can call it whatever I want—but he's still my boyfriend. You and I both know what the Qur'an says. He kisses me, and I kiss him back. When he looks at me, it's . . . it's . . . indescribable. It's like the literal reason clichés exist. And I want to be a good Muslim, but I want him, too. And I don't know how to have both at the same time."

"Allie. Habibti. Stop feeling guilty for being *normal.* We're not robots." She reaches over and gives me a hug. "Our culture tries to erase Muslim sexuality, but it still exists. Like, sorry, Mom and Dad: You don't stop *wanting* the second the hijab is on. It's another form of erasure—Muslim erasure *and* female erasure."

"We talked about doing halal dating," I say hopefully.

"Look," Dua says. "A lot of people will judge you for trying to have it both ways. I did for a hot minute. But the fact is, your parents allow you to date, so you're not sneaking around. Your boyfriend respects your limits, so you're not being pressured to do something you're not comfortable with. You want to marry him down the line? Let's circle back and chat about the shahada. Until then, the busybodies can keep it to themselves. We don't have to be perfect twenty-four seven."

"Don't worry, nobody thinks you're perfect," I crack, smiling weakly as I try to lighten the mood.

She playfully brushes something imaginary off her shoulder.

"We spend so much time worrying what our fellow Muslims will think of us," Dua says, "if they will judge us for our behavior. The only judgment we should be worried about is Allah, subhanahu wa ta'ala. And right now, the only person we know still judging you is *you.*"

Her words are a balm. "I need to talk to Wells," I say. "I need to tell him what his dad said."

"As if he doesn't already know what a snake his dad is."

I think back to Wells's panic attack. "I don't want to hurt him. But he has to know."

CHAPTER THIRTY-THREE

As Dua gives me another hug, I catch sight of Abdullah across the room.

"Hey, Abdullah's here," I say. "I wonder who his date is."

She squirms. "Um . . . I am. Sort of."

"Wait, what?"

"Zaki couldn't get out of something tonight—he made this commitment ages ago, and he's all about keeping his word—so Abdullah agreed to be my chaperone. My parents arranged it."

A grin spreads across my face. "You've got to be kidding me."

"Stop," she says, clutching my arm. "Abdullah is the most gentlemanly gentleman who ever existed. He wants to become a hafiz—he's already halfway through memorizing the entire Qur'an. His father is the imam at the mosque my dad goes to. There's nothing there. Less than nothing. Double zero."

"Okaaaay." I smile.

"He's here to make sure I'm okay."

"So it's not a *date* date?"

"It's *not* a *date* date."

"That's a shame," I tease.

I glance back across the room, to where Abdullah is filling up two glasses of punch. As we watch him, he makes his way over to us and then offers one to Dua. "I thought you might like some," he says. Then he turns to me. "Hi, Allie!"

"Hi, Abdullah! I'm about to take off. Later, Dua."

"Let's go find your friends," Abdullah says to Dua. "I'm sure you don't want to be stuck here with me."

She shoots me daggers, her cheeks pink. Abdullah looks innocently between the two of us as I wave goodbye and pick my way through crowds of dancing kids, looking for Wells.

I feel a tap on my shoulder and swing around to see him, looking concerned.

"I've been trying to find you," Wells says gently. "Everything okay?"

The conversation with Jack comes rushing back, full-force.

They say scent is connected to memory, and as I lean into Wells, breathing his crisp, clean scent, I know I'll remember him forever, no matter where tonight leads us.

"Let's talk a walk outside," I say, threading my fingers through his.

We walk down the steps toward the sunken garden, where an ornate fountain splashes iridescent droplets backlit by shimmering blue lights. We sit on the edge of the circular fountain, our backs to the ballroom above.

"What's going on, Allie?" he says.

I love that he can tell something's wrong. But I hate what I'm about to say.

"It's about your dad."

He stiffens.

I tell him everything: how Jack cornered me in the hallway, how I did my best not to engage with him, how Jack told me I'm standing in Wells's way, how I feel like a horrible Muslim for dating him, how Dua accepts us.

"He got in your head," Wells says. He looks hurt, and I wonder if it's because of me or because of his father. "That's what he does. He can make you think something was your idea, not his."

"Wells, maybe he's right," I say. "I don't want to be a burden to you. I'm not supposed to have a boyfriend, you're putting your music on the back burner, we keep butting heads over him . . . maybe we're fighting an uphill battle."

"Allie. Listen." Wells gently cups my face in his hand. "I want you. As long as you want to be with me, I choose you right back."

"That's sweet, but maybe—"

"You've gotta hear me out. There's always a catch with my dad. My dad told me if I broke up with you, he'd give me a full ride to *whatever* college I get into. He'll stop giving me crap about Yale. I can apply to Juilliard or Oberlin or Berklee or wherever. No student loans. Total support. Just as long as I dump you."

"And if you don't?"

"The rug sweeps out from under me, I guess. He can't stop

me from doing what I want, but he doesn't have to pay for it. That's his trump card. Money."

I wonder about the emotional toll it's taken on him, knowing that everything he wants is within his grasp, if only . . .

"What are you going to do?" I say.

He shakes his head. "Nothing. I don't want his stupid offer. He's trying to play me. It didn't work, and now he's trying to play you, too."

My hands ball into fists by my side. "What an absolute piece of—"

"He told me he'd let it go and that he respected my decision." He laughs, but there's no joy there. "I can't believe I fell for it. Again."

I look over my shoulder up at the ballroom, where the lights stream through the glass windows. "Who knew I was so powerful?" I say. "Jack Henderson terrified of little ol' me. I'm like a superhero, if my power is Existing While Muslim."

He laughs. "To be fair, you are pretty intimidating."

"Quiet, or I'll zap you."

He pulls me closer and looks down at me with those soulful eyes. "Promise?"

I tilt my head, and his lips gently meet mine.

Back inside, Wells is on a mission. Hand in hand, we sweep the room, looking for Jack.

We find him by the appetizers, popping pigs in a blanket into his mouth.

"Dad," Wells says.

He swallows. "There you two are!" Jack says, acting as if *he's* the one who's been looking for *us*.

"We need to talk."

Jack's eyes swivel back and forth between the two of us, and I see the mental calculations taking place. He knows.

"Okay, you gotta stop," Wells says. "This is *my* relationship. My business, not yours."

Jack doesn't say anything, merely folding his arms across his chest and staring his son down.

"What you pulled on TV was messed-up. And I don't care if you like Allie or not. She's not going anywhere."

Jack raises an eyebrow.

"If I need to apply for student loans and work a campus job and go into debt, fine," Wells says. "Then that's what I'm gonna do."

It's not a big thing, not like some climactic movie scene where the hero gets onstage with a microphone. It's quiet and private, Wells's voice low. People a few feet away probably don't notice it's going down.

But to me, it feels as if Wells rented a billboard in Times Square to stand up to his father.

Through it all, I don't say a word to Jack. No more trying to prove myself. No more caring if he likes me or accepts me or thinks I'm good enough.

Because he's not worth my time—and not so much as a single word.

I write my story, not him.

"Can we go somewhere?" Wells asks. "I don't want to be here with him." Jack is now on the other side of the ballroom, holding court among a group of starstruck teachers.

I look at my phone. It's 8:43 p.m. The prom isn't over until ten, and my parents extended my curfew tonight until eleven.

"What did you have in mind?"

Half an hour later, we're on the outskirts of Johns Creek, down by the Chattahoochee, where the town meets Suwanee. Wells texted Joey to tell him we're not taking the group's limo back to the house. Instead, he called a car, and Wells took me to his secret spot by the river.

"You sure you're okay in that?" Wells gestures to my dress. "Maybe this isn't a good idea."

"Please. Like my dress is stopping me from the awesomeness that is your secret hideaway."

"I think I oversold it."

"No way, Henderson. Uh-uh. I'm expecting a *lair*."

He laughs, hopping over a wooden KEEP OUT! sign and then holding out his hand to help me clear it. Hand in hand, we carefully navigate through a tangled outgrowth of trees and kudzu, stepping over rocks and branches as we make our way down to the river. Around us, fireflies spark.

A long wooden dock leads to the water. Near where the dock meets the riverbank, a gnarled tree holds a wooden swing, hanging from a thick branch. Gauzy moonlight streams through the tree, lighting Wells's face angelically.

"Be real," I say. "How many girls have you brought here?"

His cheeks go fire-engine red.

"Five? Ten? *More than ten?*" I ask.

"You're the first," he mutters.

"Why so embarrassed?" I tease, sitting down on the swing and reaching out for his hand. He sits next to me, and I lean my head on his shoulder, the deafening sound of cicadas rising up around us.

"I don't know why you think I'm some big player. I've never had a girlfriend before."

"Never?"

"Never."

"Allie Abraham, one. Girls of the world, zero."

He snorts.

"How are you feeling?" I ask.

His face falls. His fingers drum a staccato rhythm on the suit fabric stretched over his knees. "I hate him."

"You're allowed to hate him."

"You don't think it's messed-up?"

"Nope."

The swing creaks under our weight as we sway back and forth.

"I missed you," he says in a rush. He's stopped swinging and is looking down at his shiny shoes, the tips now flecked with mud, as if eye contact with me is too much. "Everything sucked without you."

He's opening up. I just need to listen. "Yeah?"

"When I was a kid, he was a good dad. He drove me to music camp. We played guitar together. He came to my soccer games. I remember him and my mom laughing a lot."

I find his hand again, taking it in mine. We swing again, our hands clasped as our bodies sway back and forth. The sides of the bench are a little out of sync, but soon, our swinging is in tune.

And we swing in silence.

My phone pings. *Please don't be my parents. Curfew's not for another hour.*

But it's just a Snapchat notification. Emilia's posted a new story.

Wells peers over with interest as I press PLAY, gently resting his chin on my shoulder.

Everybody's at Waffle House in their prom dresses, giggling and hopping around and looking about six instead of sixteen. Emilia shows a close-up of a plate of scattered, smothered, and covered hash browns before turning the camera on Joey and Sarah, laughing as they play Thumb War. The camera pans the group: Claire feeds Mikey waffles while Tessa and Zadie share a sweet kiss before Zadie notices Emilia is videotaping. "Girl, put your camera down and live a little!" she says. "You got this hottie Brian Davis on your arm and you're filming *us*?" Everybody laughs as the screen goes black.

I discreetly glance back and forth between Wells and the video. Instead of laughing, he seems lonely.

I think of the angry looks his friends were shooting Jack at prom. All those friends, but no real emotional support.

I put the phone back in my pocket.

He sighs, and I know he's still thinking about his dad.

"You can talk to me, Wells. Let me in."

Wells breaks down. He sobs, putting his head in his hands. I don't know what to do.

I jump off the swing, stand in front of Wells, and wrap my arms around him tightly.

I hold on to him as his shoulders shake, and I let him cry, let him pour it out onto me, let him empty his wounds for the first time, until there's nothing held back and he feels free.

A few days later, Providence High School's Muslim Student Association receives a donation.

Ten thousand dollars.

Anonymous.

PART FOUR

CHAPTER THIRTY-FOUR

"Allie! Dinner!"

I close my textbook, putting a bookmark on the page. Final exams start Monday, the musical is this weekend, and then it's the great summer beyond.

Downstairs, the dining room table is packed with steaming dishes. I'm barely hungry, however, because I'm hyperfocused on my goal.

I've decided to fast for Ramadan.

Every Muslim of a certain age is required to fast for the holy month. It's one of the five pillars, along with donating to charity, embarking on the hajj pilgrimage to Mecca, praying five times a day, and making the shahada profession of faith.

I still need to tell my parents—and I don't have to read my monthly horoscope to know Dad won't be thrilled.

He's talking to me again—but barely. As much as I've wanted

my dad to back off and give me space to breathe, it hurt when he took me up on it. I hadn't realized how much I needed his warmth until I was faced with a cold shadow.

"So, Ramadan starts next week." I spear a forkful of potatoes and bring them to my mouth, looking back and forth between my parents.

"Ah." Dad takes a large gulp of red wine, then reaches across the table to refill his glass. I frown at the wine.

"I'm going to fast."

"Must you?" Dad asks, looking weary.

"Yes. I must."

He picks up his cutlery, shoulders slumped.

"What can your father and I do to support you, honey?" Mom asks.

"Nothing. I'll wake up early to eat, and I'll eat again when the sun goes down. Don't worry, I don't expect you to fast with me or anything," I say, glancing at Dad. "I can do it myself."

"We'll keep dinner warm every night," Mom says. "And of course we won't eat in front of you."

Dad looks annoyed. "Fasting isn't good for your system, you know. When I was young, we had stomachaches all month long. And every Ramadan I gained weight, not lost it. The human body isn't meant to be eating heavy meals at nine p.m."

"Well, thank God I don't care whether or not I gain weight," I say defiantly, taking a large bite of chicken. "I'm not doing it to fit into a bathing suit."

"You've never fasted before," Dad says. "Your blood sugar will drop. It could be dangerous."

"Good thing I don't drive."

"It's difficult. You can't drink water. No gum. Not a single bite. Nothing."

"Dad, I get it. Ramadan is hard, and you think it's ridiculous—what's new? I want to do it, and I wish you believed in me. But I'm going to do it whether you support me or not. And I will succeed, inshallah." The idea of speaking to my dad like this would have been unfathomable to me a year ago.

He takes another swig of wine, putting the glass down before stabbing his food.

"It's your life."

The hardest thing about telling your parents you want them to back off and treat you like an adult is when they actually start doing it.

Ramadan terrifies me. It's become my white whale.

I confess to the girls a few days later at Fatima's house. She's testing new dessert recipes for her class, so we're her lucky beneficiaries, the coffee table covered in fresh pie, muffins, and cupcakes.

"I can't go two hours without food," I say. "I'm like a toddler. Or a linebacker."

"Don't worry," Samira says, smiling at me from the other couch. "Everybody is nervous for their first Ramadan."

"And you're lucky—it starts two days after school ends this year," Dua says. "*Literal* godsend."

"Hamdulilah," Fatima says.

"Are you still gonna do cooking classes over the summer, or are you pressing 'pause' until Ramadan's over?" Shamsah asks Fatima.

"I'm sticking with them this year," Fatima says. "I was on the wait list for this Classical European Cuisines course and I actually got in, so I'm putting on my big-girl shoes—or chef's hat, I guess. Plus, I figure, is it really that different than not eating while cooking iftar?"

Dua nods. "Good point. Although I stay away from the kitchen until the last possible second. Like, don't even let me *see* food until after eight p.m. this year."

"I barely remember my first Ramadan," Leila says.

"How old were you?" I ask.

She ponders the question. "I started half fasting when I was really young. Six or seven? The first time I fasted for real, I was in fifth grade, I think. I must have been ten."

"You fasted when you were *ten*?" I look at Leila in horror.

"You get used to it," she says, shrugging as she scoops another bite of peach pie into her mouth.

"The first two or three days are the hardest." Fatima nods in agreement. "But it gets easier somehow."

I chew on my cuticles dubiously. "I don't know."

"You can do it," Leila says. "You just need to think about *why*. Focus on Allah. Remember all the people around the world suffering."

"Or focus on your family and how ashamed they'll be if you break the fast, and how it's not worth the guilt and complaining." Shamsah laughs. "That totally works, too."

I must look aghast, because everybody bursts out laughing.

Fatima reaches over and pats my hand sympathetically. "We'll be here with you."

"You'll be fine," Dua says, handing me a cupcake. "Quick, eat this while you can."

I plaster a smile on my face as the girls giggle. But inside I'm thinking: *Crap, crap, crap. There's no way I'm making it through this.*

The headache starts in the middle of my skull, as if threatening to rip me in two.

I read that some countries, like the United Arab Emirates, consider eating in public during Ramadan a crime—even by Westerners. At the time, I thought it was excessive. Now, I understand. It's a necessary kindness for the greater good.

At least Ramadan started over the weekend, after the school year ended. The musical and final exams feel like a lifetime ago. The only thing that matters now: surviving Ramadan.

I've been fasting for hours now. *Hours*. It feels like I'm never going to eat again. But when I look at the clock, I see that it's only three. Not even time for Asr prayer yet, and hours until sunset.

I text Dua:

HELP. This is so hard.

She writes back:

Ha! Supposed to be hard. Makes it worth it. Think of God. Think of the less fortunate. Think of how good that food is going to taste later . . . wait, don't think about that. 😆

You can do it! One day (almost) done, only twenty-nine more to go . . . 😵

Houri texts me to check in, too. I respond:

I'm tired, thirsty, and hot. Go away.

She responds:

I'm going to chalk that up to Ramadan brain.

While lying in bed searching online, I find out there are places in the world where fasting lasts as long as twenty-one hours. I also find a verse saying God doesn't want you to suffer during Ramadan.

Well, if God didn't want you to suffer, he wouldn't ask you to fast.

Not being able to drink water is a special kind of torture: You can't take a sip if your lips are dry. You can't shotgun a LaCroix to put bubbles in your tum and fill you up. You can't even chew gum.

I want to take an Aleve to help with my headache, but then I remember that would require water, too, and I swear I almost burst into tears.

I pull my bullet journal out of my bedside drawer, but I can't motivate myself to write.

Finally, I turn a page and scrawl two words.

Fasting.

Help.

Day two.

They've lied.

They've all lied.

It doesn't get easier.

I miss food.

Getting through the day without snapping at everybody kind of sucks.

Doing my Arabic homework without thinking about food is the worst.

At least now that it's summer I don't have to worry about actual school, although computer camp has started, and I'm supposed to take my driving exam before school starts again.

And then I have to go home after camp and be a functional human with my parents, making an extra effort to be nice so I can repair our fractured relationship, while all I want to do is stuff my face and eat.

Instead, I think about God, reciting my favorite dhikr remembrance—a short little prayer—to snap me back into place, focus my intention, and remind me what I'm doing this for.

Subhanallah wal hamdulillah, wa la ilaha illa Allah wa Allahu Akbar.

I check in with myself. Did it work?

Nope.

This is torture.

Here's the truth. You *do* get used to being without food.

I'm a week into it, and I'm doing it.

I'm surviving.

I'm thriving!

Okay, let's not go that far.

One night, Shamsah texts me while I'm holed up in my room, sprawled across my bed reading, with the door closed. I think I hear my parents downstairs watching a movie, but I'm not sure.

SHAMSAH: How you holding up?

ME: Doing better. I barely notice anymore. Okay, that's an exaggeration, but I'm making it through.

SHAMSAH: Ha ha. It's hard in the beginning. You're rocking it.

SHAMSAH: So, listen, I just wanted to fill you in . . .

SHAMSAH: I told my mom

ME: !!!!

ME: OMG!

ME: How'd it go?

SHAMSAH: It was . . . dramatic.

SHAMSAH: Lots of tears. Hers and mine

ME: And? Was it as bad as you'd feared?

SHAMSAH: I mean, yeah. It was the scariest thing ever. But she's strong. She handled it. She told me she loves me. 😢

ME: That's amazing. I'm so, so, so happy for you

SHAMSAH: I made her promise not to tell my dad. We'll cross that bridge later.

SHAMSAH: Jamila is so excited 😀

ME: 🤗

SHAMSAH: I'm going to tell the girls soon. I think. Maybe. We'll see

ME: Thank you so much for sharing with me, Sham

SHAMSAH: How are things with you and Wells?

ME: Erm. Complicated. We're trying halal dating.

SHAMSAH: What on earth is halal dating?

ME: I don't even know

Mom and Dad have stayed true to their word. Mom orders take-out most nights, to keep the house from filling with the scent of chopped onions and sizzling garlic, and the two of them eat furtively—in their office, in the bedroom, outside on the patio. When I catch Mom eating a slice of pizza in the basement with a book on her lap and a rerun of her favorite show on the small TV, I tell her it's gone far enough.

"Mom, you can't live like a fugitive!"

"Sorry," she says, swallowing her pepperoni and wiping her mouth with a napkin. "I feel guilty."

"Well, you should," I tell her, laughing. "How *dare* you eat in your own home at the regular prescribed mealtimes?"

"How many days left?" she asks.

"Twenty."

She groans.

CHAPTER THIRTY-FIVE

Wells and I are at a morning Atlanta Braves game when I feel my phone buzzing in my pocket.

It's my dad.

"Hi," I say in a cool tone, putting a finger in my other ear so I can hear him above the din of the crowd. On the field, one of the players from the Cubs hits a home run, the stadium erupting into boos.

"You need to get home right now," Dad says.

"Wait, what? What's going on?" I huddle down into my seat, straining to hear.

Next to me, Wells pauses mid–hot dog bite, looking concerned. A dollop of mustard falls onto his jeans. I had to tell him three times it was okay for him to (1) eat a hot dog and (2) do it in front of me.

"Teta had a heart attack and went into cardiac arrest. We leave for Dallas ASAP."

"What?" I repeat, shocked.

"Can you meet us directly at the airport? There's not enough time for you to come home first. Your mom is packing your clothes now."

"Yeah . . ." I look over at Wells, wide-eyed.

"Okay, we'll meet you in an hour by the check-in counter. Make sure Wells stays with you. Love you." It's the first time he's told me he loves me in weeks.

The line goes dead.

I stare at the phone, in shock.

"Everything okay?" Wells asks, putting his hot dog on top of his messenger bag.

I look back and forth between him and the phone, trying to process what my father said. It takes me few seconds to gather my voice. I grab his Coke and take a sip without thinking, composing myself.

"My grandmother had a heart attack." The floodgates open. I collapse on his shoulder, sobbing.

Wells draws me into his arms. "What can I do?"

"Would you mind giving me a ride to the airport?" I sniffle. "We fly to Dallas this afternoon."

"Let's go."

"I hate making you miss the game. It's the second inning."

"It's nothing," he says. "It's just a stupid game."

Ten minutes later, we're in the car, Wells racing toward

Hartsfield-Jackson while I call Houri on my cell phone. She answers on the first ring.

"How is she?" I ask without bothering to say hi.

"Not good," Houri says. Her voice is low.

"Why are you whispering?"

"We're at the hospital. Baba is in with the doctors now."

"Who's there?"

Houri rattles off a list of names, including several aunts, uncles, and cousins who live in Dallas. "Aunt Samiha is on her way to the airport right now. She's meeting Uncle Omar and Khalila in London, and they're flying over together. They should be here tomorrow morning."

I frown. "They should?" Aunt Samiha lives in Jeddah, Saudi Arabia. If she's flying all the way from Saudi, it's not good news.

"Khalila said Amto was hysterical. She feels guilty enough living so far away. She's praying Teta will wake up."

"Khalila's coming from London, too?"

"They're all coming. Khalila and the kids. Uncle Sammy is flying in from New Jersey with the family. Aisha is already on the way from Cairo. Everybody."

The last time the *entire* family was together was for my jido's funeral. I'm elated by the prospect of seeing my whole family, but horrified by the circumstances.

By the time I hang up with Houri, we're halfway to the airport.

"Sorry. I know I've been on the phone the entire time."

"Don't apologize," Wells says. "It's your grandma. I get it."

"Are you close with yours?"

"I was with my dad's mom . . . but she passed away. My mom's mom still lives in Canada, so we never see her and my grandfather."

"You guys don't visit?"

"Not really. I guess it's too far. Gotta fly cross-country, take a ferry, and spend a weekend dealing with my grandparents' passive-aggressive nonsense. They're not close with my mom. You know how it is."

I nod but don't tell him about my family, where we gather together at least once a year—where even my cousins in Cairo and Jeddah and London are just a WhatsApp message away.

"Does she know you've been learning Arabic?" he asks me.

"I wanted to surprise her." My voice breaks again. I look down at my hands, concentrating on my nails as I try to steady myself. "I should have told her sooner."

"She'll be all right. I know she will. Don't worry."

I open and shut my mouth several times, self-censoring. Finally, I say quietly, "Thank you. I hope so."

I appreciate Wells's optimism, but I just don't feel the same.

"You're here!" Aunt Bila starts crying the second my father, mother, and I walk into the hospital waiting room, launching herself into my father's arms. She explodes into rapid-fire Arabic. It takes me a second to decipher any of it, because she's talking so quickly, but I recognize words and realize she's telling my father about Teta's condition.

"She's in a coma," I mutter to my mom, relaying the information in a low voice. "It happened in the car with Aunt Bila, thank God. So she was able to get her to the hospital in minutes."

"My God," Mom says, moving toward Aunt Bila and engulfing her in a hug. "How are you, Bila?"

My aunt sobs in response.

"You made it," says her grandson Zeid, coming over and giving us kisses on each cheek. He pats my father's shoulder dolefully. "Hamdullah, I hope the flight was good."

"As good as can be expected," my dad says, looking somber.

Mom sat in between us on the flight, with Dad by the window, staring out at the clouds below for most of the two-hour journey.

I desperately wanted to say something to Dad—anything to make him feel better—but I didn't know what. He hates platitudes, and the best words of comfort I have are from the Qur'an. Right now, I want to make him feel better, not worse.

Now, the rest of our family swarms around us, everybody hugging and double-cheek kissing and saying prayers of thanks we've arrived safely. In the corner, Rashid patiently gives Lulu a time-out while the toddler wails and smacks the air, saying, "No, Daddy! Away! Go away!" He sees me and attempts a smile, looking exhausted. Houri's brother Amir moves over to them, kneeling down and saying something to help calm the toddler, who magically stops crying and nods solemnly. Her uncle takes her tiny hand, and Rashid looks at his brother-in-law gratefully.

Dad leads Aunt Bila toward the hallway. "Can I see her?" he asks in Arabic.

"The nurses were in there changing her, but they should be done. Go."

"I will come with you," I say. My dad and aunt look at me, startled. It takes me a second to realize I've said it in Arabic. I switch to English. "I want to come see her. Please? If it's okay."

That was bizarre.

Dad nods briskly. "Okay," he says.

I catch my mom's eye, and she nods, as if to say, *Go*. She moves into the corner with the rest of the family, settling into a hospital chair for the long night ahead, as cousins chatter and swirl around her.

Teta lies in bed, fragile. Her pale skin is translucent, paper-thin, blue veins visible beneath the skin.

Fairouza sits next to her, eyes closed. With her right hand, she rubs Teta's arm; with the other hand, she holds the Qur'an. I've seen the same ritual before: in the hospital for Jido, on his deathbed.

She's reciting a dua seven times, over and over, praying for my teta to get better:

"I ask Almighty Allah, Lord of the Magnificent Throne, to make you well."

My dad clears his throat. Fairouza opens her eyes. She continues to quietly recite the prayer, her lips moving. Only after she's done does she squeeze my teta's hand before resting it gently back onto the mattress and placing the Qur'an under her pillow.

Fairouza and my father hug, exchanging words in Arabic. I can't tear my eyes away from my grandmother.

Gone is the fierce, proud Teta I've always known. She looks ancient, frail. She has a tube jammed down her throat, wires threading out from her arm, little rivulets of red running through the wires, a monitor next to the bed steadily *beep, beep, beep*-ing.

I turn to my dad to gauge his reaction. In that moment, my heart breaks.

His face is crumpled, tears streaming down his cheeks.

My father has never been good with death.

When Jido died, everybody said my dad took it the hardest. He withdrew into a deep depression, losing weight, sleeping when he wasn't at the university or writing.

Dad takes a step toward Teta, leaning over and kissing her on the forehead. "I'm here, Mama," he says in Arabic. "It's Muhammad." He sits down next to her, taking her hand and enclosing it between his. "I'm here," he repeats, his voice faltering.

"She's comfortable, Khaalo Muhammad." As she speaks in English, Fairouza bustles around Teta, fluffing her pillow and smoothing her blankets, though they look plenty fluffed and smoothed. "The nurses say she's resting comfortably. They induced the coma for her safety. She's not in pain right now."

"Let's hope, God willing." My dad clears his throat again several times.

"The doctors were in here earlier with Baba. You should probably go talk to them about the plan of care."

My dad juts his chin into the air, a single, dismissive thrust.

"They can discuss among themselves. I trust them. I'll stay here with her."

"When I was praying for her earlier, wallahi she squeezed my hand," Fairouza says. "I swear to you! On my life! She squeezed my hand, and I think she smiled. She's going to wake up, Khaalo, I know it."

I expect my dad to roll his eyes, or maybe say something kind, hiding his true feelings. Instead, he says, "What were you reciting?"

"I can repeat it, if you like." Sweet Fairouza, always trying to make everybody happy, putting her own needs last, never getting the credit she deserves.

Once again, I expect nothing from Dad, and once again, he surprises me.

"Yes. Please."

Fairouza gently reaches under the pillow, slides the Qur'an out from under Teta's head, and quietly recites.

Hospitals have a stench in the air:

Desperation. Avoidance. Resignation.

I think of what my mom says when she comes home after dealing with grieving families: we live in a death-denying society. Nobody wants to suffer through the inevitable down. We only want to enjoy the up, up, up.

Growing up with a mom like mine, who wanted me to face

the inevitable—because she believed it was necessary, because she believed I would be stronger for it—means I eventually developed a matter-of-fact attitude toward death, too. Healthy, Mom calls it.

Only weeks after we arrived in Providence, we lost our dog Kisser. She was part Great Pyrenees, part golden retriever, and part mutt: gigantic and human-sized, with the sweetest temperament imaginable. I'd come home from school, and she'd be waiting by the front door. She'd happily run in a circle around me, and we'd roll around on the floor in the foyer. After dinner, she'd jump on the couch next to me and snuggle into the curve of my hip, draping her fluffy body onto mine as if she were nine pounds instead of ninety.

She was seven years old, so the end was sudden and unexpected—like most endings are, I guess. Mom took her to the dog groomer before a visit from Teta, and they accidentally gave her a treat her system couldn't handle, though Mom specifically told them not to feed her.

We visited her at the dog hospital. I stroked her soft white fur and nuzzled her black nose, whispering into her ear, "It's going to be all right, Kisser. You're going to be okay. I'm here with you. Allie is here."

Kisser whimpered a little, and I was excited, because I knew that meant she'd understood me, but the vet told me not to get my hopes up. I longed to tell him to get out.

She died the next morning, and I cried for two weeks.

When Grandmother told Mom we should sue, because the groomer's negligence had killed Kisser, Mom told her it was unthinkable. Death was a fact of life, and whether it had been now or five years from now, there was nothing in heaven or on earth that would prevent the end.

Grandmother hated Mom's attitude toward death. I found it weirdly comforting.

If you know the worst thing in the world—the thing you fear more than anything else—is an inevitability, is *definitely going to happen*, doesn't that free you from worry? All the worrying is self-indulgence. It's going to happen. Focus on what you can control instead.

That's how I see it anyway.

Except, now that we're in the hospital and it's my grandmother on the bed and my father crying by her side, it's harder for me to be brave. I don't want my grandmother to die. I want her to get better, and I want my father to be happy, and I want my grandmother to hear me speak Arabic. I want her to tell me in Arabic that I made her proud.

I want her to live.

Fairouza and I leave the hospital room to give my dad privacy with Teta.

If I see him cry one more time, it'll break me.

The stench of cleaning products rises up as I walk down the hallway, and a wave of nausea passes over me.

My extended family packs the waiting room, subdividing into groups: The younger cousins are by the fridge and the stocked selection of Top Ramen. The older cousins are in a corner by the window, making a protective circle around the toddlers and children. Teta's children, my aunts and uncles, are in the middle of the room, alternatively pacing and laughing and yelling and weeping.

Every hour, another Ibrahimi family member arrives.

Two families wait alongside ours, one looking and sounding as white, Texan, and Christian as they come. They stare our way each time another family member arrives, everybody standing and crowding around them, waiting their turn for hugs and kisses. I squint, trying to see them through these strangers' eyes. Some of my relatives wear headscarves, and my Egyptian cousin Saif has a long, well-tended beard he's exceptionally proud of, and which occasionally alarms people. (Never mind he's a teddy bear, loves beer, and is covered in—haram!—tattoos.)

When my uncle Sammy arrives, it's with two dozen doughnuts in tow. Since he's traveling during Ramadan, clearly he's taking up the loophole of avoiding the fast. He puts them on a table by the coffee machine and, with a smile, waves the other families in the waiting room over. "Hey! You want some?"

The families look startled.

"Yeah, you!" Uncle Sammy says, pointing at them with stubby nicotine-stained fingers. "Come! Eat! I got extra."

They stand up, looking wary but creeping over to the table. Within five minutes, several of them are laughing at Uncle Sammy's jokes and trying to one-up one another with tales of oppressive traffic jams, debating whether New Jersey or Atlanta is worse.

I sit next to Houri in the corner with the kids.

"How are you doing?" I ask.

"Rough. You?"

"I'm okay. It's hard seeing my dad. His reaction is . . ."

Houri nods her chin in the direction of the aunts and uncles. My father is now sitting next to Aunt Bila, looking worn-out. "She's going to be okay. I know it."

"Inshallah," I say. "She seemed fine a few months ago. I don't understand it."

"Allah has a plan for us all."

"I didn't even have a chance to show her I've learned Arabic."

"It's not too late," Houri says. "Inshallah, you'll be able to speak to her."

"Inshallah."

We sit in silence.

"How much Arabic can you speak now?" Houri asks.

"A bit. It's been a couple months."

She laughs. "I took four years of high school Spanish, and the only words I remember are *hola* and *agua*."

"I can read and write it now," I say shyly.

"Arabic?" Her face is incredulous. "You can *read* it?"

Her reaction surprises me.

"Can't you?"

"No! Mama and Baba never taught me. They feel guilty about it. I think Fairouza might know, but that's 'cause she insisted on going to Sunday school."

"My teacher says I'm learning really fast."

"Do you understand me?" she asks in Arabic.

"Yes," I reply in Arabic. "Ask me again, more."

She quizzes me, rapid-fire.

"How old are you?"

"I am sixteen."

"Where do you live?"

"I live in Providence, Georgia. Near Atlanta."

"What are your mother's and father's names?"

"My mother is named Elizabeth, and my father is named Muhammad." I stumble over the words slightly.

"Are you still dating that boy? With the bad father?"

I blush. "Yes."

"You *do* understand me!" She's switched back to English. "Okay, now write my name." She rummages in her purse until she finds a pen. She grabs a magazine from the nearby table and flips it over until she finds a legible surface.

"Ha . . . waw . . . ra . . . ya . . . tā'marbūṭta . . ." I say each of the letters as I write down her name. "Houriya."

She squints at the page, looking doubtful. "That's it?"

I shrug. "It might be wrong. Sometimes the letters trip me up."

"Color me impressed. Hey, Yusuf, ta'al!" Houri calls over a nearby cousin. "Quiz Allie on her Arabic!"

Soon, a few different cousins are testing me.

"Say 'yellow' in Arabic!" Yusuf says.

"What's your favorite . . . ?" Amir says something I don't understand.

"My favorite what?" I ask in Arabic.

"Ice-cream flavor," he says in English.

I switch back to Arabic. "Chocolate."

And so on.

It gets stir-crazy in a hospital waiting room, so this game keeps my family going for way longer than it should.

My cousin Amal sits next to her husband, Sulaiman. "I need a drink," she mutters into his ear, probably thinking I can't hear her.

"Two more weeks," he mutters back.

Through it all, Dad says nothing. He's never heard me speak Arabic before. I want him to look impressed, to look disgusted, to look like *something*, but his face remains blank, impassive. Every so often, he returns to the coffee machine near the refrigerator for a refill.

"He's on his twentieth cup of coffee," I say to Rashid.

"Literally?"

"Not *literally*. He drinks coffee when he's stressed."

"He has a pretty good excuse," Rashid says, giving me a rueful smile.

"I guess so." I stare at my dad from across the room, watching as my mom walks up to him and puts her arms around him. He buries his head in her shoulder. They look like a young couple from the back.

When Dad raises his face, Mom cups it in her hands and murmurs something to him.

If I have a relationship half as good as theirs, I'll be the luckiest girl in the world.

CHAPTER THIRTY-SIX

After an endless, exhausting day at the hospital, it's time for everybody to pile in the available cars and take the ten-minute drive to Aunt Bila's house.

The family has decided to take turns sleeping by Teta's bedside. Tonight was supposed to be Fairouza's turn, but my dad volunteered.

He's been quiet all day. It's hard to believe it was only this morning I was with Wells at the baseball game.

I return to the hospital room before we leave, leaning over the bed to give Teta a kiss. Her skin is cold against my lips. I'm suddenly struck with the terrible knowledge that this might be the last time I see her.

"My heart, I love you, Teta," I say in Arabic.

"I didn't know you were learning."

I startle at Dad's quiet voice behind me.

"I started after she visited us."

"Your accent is good."

"Thanks. I'm trying."

He looks back over at Teta. It seems as if he's struggling to hold back tears. "She would be proud of you. She thought you should know Arabic. She was irritated with me. She said I was denying you your birthright."

I hold my breath, taking a chance. "Only the language? Or was she angry about the religion, too?"

His mouth tightens. "Your mother and I wanted you to make your own decisions. I didn't want you to be burdened by something that didn't make sense to you."

"The way you were burdened."

His silence is pained.

"I've made my decision, Dad. I like praying. I like being a Muslim. I *choose* Islam."

"She would be proud of you," he repeats, standing up to come over and give me a hug.

I wait, hoping he will say, "And so am I."

He doesn't.

Back at Aunt Bila's house, the family comes together over food for the iftar. Amir helps Aunt Bila serve everybody drinks, returning back and forth to the kitchen several times with Sprite, Coke, ice, and glasses, while Rashid plops Lulu onto his lap to share food off his plate.

All of the family living in Dallas stops by, most with their own platters of homemade Arabic and Circassian meats and breads and sweets.

After dinner, Fairouza stands up from the table and says, "Yalla. I'm going to pray." She looks right at me. "You wanna come?"

"Sure." I'm taken aback by the callout.

"You pray?" Amal asks, looking surprised.

"I started this year," I mumble.

"Nice."

Fairouza reaches out and grabs my hand. "Hamdullah. God will bless you a thousand times, Allie."

It's embarrassing but sweet to hear.

"Anybody else?" Fairouza looks around the room.

Amir, Yusuf, Rashid, Uncle Sammy, Reem, Aunt Ray, and Aunt Bila stand up, making noises of assent and following Fairouza. Everybody performs wudu quickly in the various bathrooms, and then the group goes into the formal living room near the front door, where Aunt Bila keeps the prayer rugs and flowing white abayas.

The Qibla is oriented toward the den, where the rest of my family sits sipping tea. I put my hands up near my ears, setting my intention.

Please, God, let Teta live.

And as I bend down, another prayer pops into my head:

Please, God, let Dad understand.

We stagger into the hospital waiting room the next morning in waves: one branch of the family after another. Mom and I drive in with Aunt Bila and Fairouza, who spent the night at her mother's house. Houri texts me to say she'll be there in the afternoon; Lulu didn't sleep well.

Once there, my mom beelines for the hospital room to see Dad. A few minutes later, he walks into the waiting area without her, looking exhausted. Bags weigh down his eyes, and his shirt is rumpled, a shadow creeping across his chin and cheeks. He excuses himself to go down to the gift shop and buy toothpaste.

A couple hours after we take up the day's vigil, Aunt Samiha, Uncle Omar, and Khalila finally arrive from London and from Jeddah. The family greets them as if they are returning from years away at war.

"Mashallah, Allie, you look beautiful, ya rouhi," Aunt Samiha says in her husky smoker's voice.

"Shukran, Amto. How was your flight?"

"Good, but, mashallah, your accent! Have you learned Arabic?"

Next, my cousin Ishan arrives with his wife, Leslie, and their four children in tow. Leslie is pregnant again, her belly ripe and swollen.

Sometime in the afternoon, when we've all been there for hours, the doctor enters the waiting room. My father immediately stands to attention. I exchange nervous glances with Mom.

"Mo, I'd like to talk to you," the doctor says, and my heart sinks.

Mom immediately walks over to Dad, entwining her fingers through his.

"Can I come . . . ?" I ask.

My dad nods.

I trail them down the hallway, looking behind me to see if any other family members are following. It's just us.

The doctor closes the door to his office.

"We have run a battery of tests," he says. "Because she was treated soon after the heart attack, and within minutes of cardiac arrest, it appears there was minimal damage. We feel likely we should be able to slowly bring her out of the coma today."

Mom and Dad clasp each other's hands.

"So . . . it's good news." Dad's face is hopeful but cautious.

"It's early," the doctor says, "and of course we will need to monitor her closely over the next several days, but all signs point to good news."

Why are doctors like this? Why can't they just say, *Yes, it's good news*, instead of a fifty-word don't-sue-me speech?

"Thank *God*," Mom says. "This is the best news."

"I'll go tell everybody." Dad stands up, and his cheeks are wet, but his face is happy. He puts his hand on Mom's shoulder, patting it, before leaning down to give me a kiss on the head.

The monitor beeps steadily. Teta lies in bed. She's been awake for a couple of hours, and the doctor is starting to permit visitors.

I enter the room tentatively, feeling out of place. *Am I allowed to be here?*

Teta hears my footsteps and turns her head a couple inches.

"Ya Alia." Her voice is raw and scratchy. No wonder: She's had a tube jammed down it.

"Ya Teta, ya habibti."

I sit next to her, taking her hand in mine. It's warmer than it was yesterday. Blood pumping. Good sign.

I take a deep breath, launching into my Arabic.

"How are you feeling?" I say.

"God knows, I'm tired. I'm alive, thank God."

"I'm happy you are healthy. We have been here two days."

Suddenly, Teta's face registers surprise. "You're speaking Arabic!"

"Yes! I am learning. A surprise."

"Thank God!"

"I am speaking good?" I'm aware my Arabic is incredibly stilted, and it's entirely possible what I mean to say isn't what I'm actually saying.

She laughs but then immediately launches into a coughing fit. Her face sobers, but she says, "Good. I'm proud."

My eyes fill with tears. This is the first time we've had a real conversation—ever.

"Are you praying?" she says.

I flush. "Sometimes. I try, but . . ." I clear my throat. "I am learning. I know I am not good yet. But I learn and I learn and I learn."

"Nobody's perfect, my love," she says, squeezing my hand. "Don't be too hard on yourself. I'm proud of you."

I burst into tears, wanting to launch myself at her for a hug but not wanting to hurt her. I settle for squeezing her hand back.

She lets go, putting her palm on my cheek and pressing gently, as if she's transmitting energy from her soul to mine. "Ya, Alia. I love you. You are my whole heart."

With Teta on the mend, the nightly gathering at Aunt Bila's house takes on a relaxed, festive atmosphere. Houri and Reem spent the morning rolling grape leaves and placing them in the pressure cooker, and Aunt Ray made her famous hummus and foul. I chip in by making a tabouleh salad before setting the table, Rashid and Amir helping.

"When do you fly back?" Aunt Bila asks us.

"Tomorrow night," my dad says. "We'll spend the day at the hospital with Mama, and then our flight is late. We'll get home after midnight."

"Yalla, stay one more week, ya habibti!" Aunt Ray says. "Why are you racing away so soon?"

"Elizabeth and I have work," Dad says.

"What? Why? C'mon, don't rush back!" Uncle Sammy says. "At least keep Allie here. She's done with school. Ya'ni, have her stay for a few weeks."

"A few weeks?" I say before I can stop myself. I exchange a panicked look with my mother. *Way too long.*

"Allie has summer school," my mother explains. "And she's finally beginning a driver's ed course next weekend."

I sigh.

"School in the summer? I thought you were doing well?" Aunt Ray asks.

"She is," Dad says. "She's taking advanced courses in computer science at the community college so she'll have even more of a leg up for next year and an advantage with her AP tests and college applications. When she eventually starts university, it will be as a sophomore, because of all the extra work she's doing." He looks over at me proudly.

"Mashallah," Aunt Bila says to me. "You're so smart, ya rouhi."

In the background, the phone rings as everybody passes around the dishes and tucks into the food. The adults sit at the main table, which seats twenty. Houri and I are the only two of the younger generation invited to sit with the adults. The rest of the kids wander in and out, eating in the kitchen, in the den in front of the TV, or waiting for people to clear from the table so they can take their turn.

A scream. Shattered glass. A moan.

"Ya Allah, ya Allah, please, God, no!" Aunt Bila wails.

Dad and I look at each other, and my breath catches in my throat.

It was a stroke, they tell us at the hospital.

The family mobilizes, rushing to hold vigil by Teta's bedside.

She went back into cardiac arrest—but this time, it doesn't look good. Now the doctors are trying to make her comfortable.

Normally, there's a limit on the number of people they'll allow in, but the nurse quietly waves us through, letting as many of us as possible squeeze into the room. Waiving the rules, ignoring visiting hours—these are bad signs.

We line her bed, Aunt Bila and Aunt Ray holding her hands, Amal holding up a cell phone so Teta's sister living in Syria, Great-Aunt Yara, can be with her at the end. Uncle Sammy and Uncle Omar place their hands on her arms, cousins clutch her feet, and Fairouza prays next to her head and wipes her forehead every few minutes, blowing gently on it as she says, "Rabbigh firlu, rabbigh firlu," praying for God to forgive and cleanse her sins.

She can't breathe without the help of the machine.

"Mama. Please don't die, Mama," Aunt Samiha wails, clutching her arms tighter and burying her head in Teta's torso.

"Let's go in the waiting room," Dad says, trying to lead her away. Aunt Samiha throws off his arm.

"Laa!" No. "I want to stay with Ummi! You go to the waiting room, if you want."

Dad backs off, retreating. Fairouza keeps stroking Teta's forehead over and over, murmuring prayers.

The room is controlled chaos, praying and crying and whispering. Doctors and nurses periodically stop by to check in, but for the most part, it feels as if she's been abandoned.

It's inevitable.

At some point, I need a break, so I retreat to the waiting room to stretch my legs and clear my head.

"I thought she'd live forever."

I turn around. It's Houri. We collapse into each other for a long hug.

"Where's Lulu?" I say.

"Home. Rashid's putting her to bed. I don't want to expose her to this."

"Maybe she'll still pull through," I say hopefully. "It's not always fatal, right?"

Houri shakes her head. "I heard Baba talking to the doctors. It's not if but when."

We sit in silence. Houri gets up to find the remote, changing the TV channel to *Judge Judy*. It's nice to simply be together.

Eventually, Houri stands up. "I'm going back in."

"I'm gonna stay here a few minutes," I say. "I want to be alone. Just for a sec."

She nods and pushes open the doors to the ICU.

I pull my bullet journal out of my bag, trying to find comfort in my favorite Qur'anic verses, hadiths, and poetry.

I've gone down the rabbit hole of Sufi poetry recently, and one verse I've inked into the journal stands out, by an Iraqi poet from the eighth century named Rabia Basri:

> *O God! If I worship You for fear of Hell,*
> *burn me in Hell*
> *and if I worship You in hope of Paradise,*
> *exclude me from Paradise.*
> *But if I worship You for Your Own sake,*
> *grudge me not Your everlasting Beauty.*

As I'm reading through the poems, my cousin Amir comes out, fatigued.

"It's time."

I've been gone less than an hour, but the room's atmosphere has changed. Nobody speaks. My father's face is tired and drawn. Teta lies on the bed, tubes gone. A decision has been made.

I hope Jido is there to meet her.

In the corner, my mother quietly weeps. She never cries.

Time bends as we wait for the inevitable. The room is silent except for the sound of Fairouza frantically praying over my grandmother's body, her lips and hands moving in desperation and love.

When it does happen, Teta's breath rasps and rattles. She never opens her eyes. She simply breathes, and then breathes less, and then she takes one last breath and breathes no more.

CHAPTER THIRTY-SEVEN

When I was six, my jido died. My mom tried to explain death to me, but everything about it was confusing. I failed to make sense of it, and I had so many questions: What happened after you died? What about before you were born? When people died, did they come back? Would it someday happen to *me*? It was all too scary and overwhelming. After the funeral, I slept in my parents' bed for weeks.

Now, thinking of Teta, wondering where she is, the old fear looms again.

So I do what billions of people have done before me.

I pray.

Dad comes into the room while I'm praying over Teta's body. My cousins Fairouza and Amal have left, giving me a rare moment of quiet with her. With so many people loving her, it's a special thing to be alone with her—an honor.

"Don't let me stop you," he says.

"Will you pray with me?" I ask.

We lock eyes. He doesn't say anything.

Wordlessly, he comes to stand next to me, clasping my hand. We stand over Teta's body together.

"I'm not going to make it to dinner with you and your mom this weekend," I say to Wells. Serena has offered to take the two of us out. I'm standing in the hallway outside the room where Teta still lies, whispering into the phone. We're waiting for the imam to arrive.

"Oh no. Is it your teta?"

"Yes. She . . ." I stop, unsure how to say it without it sounding too harsh. I can't stand the euphemisms for death: *passed away, moved on, departed, went to a better place.* "She died," I say.

"Are you okay?" Wells asks.

"I don't know."

"What can I do?"

"You're doing it right now."

"I'm here when you need me. On the phone, in person, whatever you need."

"Wells?"

"Yeah?"

"I miss you."

"I miss you, too." He pauses. "Hurry back, okay?"

"I'll try." The words tumble out of my mouth before I can stop them. "Love you."

A brief silence on the other end.

"Love you, too."

Home.

The Islamic custom of burying the body within twenty-four hours means the past day has been a flurry of activity, culminating in the family gathering by Teta's gravesite as her coffin was lowered into the ground at the Muslim cemetery outside Denton.

After the funeral, we delayed our flight for another few days, to grieve and mourn with the family—swapping stories, watching old videos of Teta, and passing around yellowing photo albums with snaps from her youth. I lingered so long over a photo of my dad as a baby, smiling on Teta's lap, that Aunt Bila offered it to me to keep.

The family gathering might have been suffused with quiet resignation, but there was also enough laughter and love and light to power the entire city of Dallas.

But now that we're home and I'm away from the helpful distractions of family, I don't know how to properly grieve.

I don't think Teta would want me to wallow.

I think she would want me to soar.

I tuck the photo of my father and Teta into my bullet journal, placing it next to my Qur'an on the bedside table before walking downstairs to help Dad set the table.

"How are you feeling?" I ask him.

"Sad," he says simply, setting napkins down. "She had years left in her."

I place the cutlery on the table, lining up the forks and knives at the proper angle. When Dad finishes putting his silverware down, I discreetly adjust it.

"You don't have to help," he says. "You're fasting."

"It's okay. The food smell doesn't bother me anymore."

"If you're sure."

I nod. "Thanks, Dad. For praying with me."

"How are *you* feeling, pumpkin?"

"I'm okay," I say bravely, wiping an invisible speck of dust off the table.

He nods. "It was a shock."

"I've been finding comfort where I can," I say. "I believe she's with God now. And I think she and Jido are together."

He swallows, clears his throat, reaching down to adjust a fork. He moves it around, this way and that, leaving it perpendicular to the plate. "I hope so," he says.

"What do you think? Do you think Teta is in heaven?"

"I don't know if I believe in heaven," he says honestly. "Part of me thinks we die, and that's it. Dust, cells, returned to earth. I'm willing to concede I could be wrong. It would be nice to be wrong. But . . ."

"But what?"

"You must not have come across this in your studies yet. Muslims don't believe we're sent directly to heaven or hell after death."

I flush, embarrassed to have gotten something so fundamental wrong. "We don't?"

He fiddles with a spoon.

"So . . . uh . . . what do we believe?" The word—*we*—feels tentative and precious in my mouth.

"It's been a long time . . ."

I nod, trying to encourage him.

"We stay in our graves until Judgment Day," he says, "punished or rewarded until then. Once Judgment comes, our deeds in life are weighed, and we'll be sent to heaven or hell. And even if you're sent to hell, God's mercy might still allow you into heaven eventually. Jannah, it's called. Paradise."

I don't know if it's my father teaching me about Islam for the first time, or my sadness over losing Teta, or my anxiety about the future, but I start crying.

Dad hugs me. I hug him back tightly.

"It doesn't scare you?" I eventually ask.

"What? Death?"

"Yeah."

He considers the question. "Sure," he says. "But the main thing that scares me is failing you and your mother. Living out of fear, and not being the man I know I'm supposed to be. That's what scares me the most."

I nod.

He sighs, sitting down in a dining room chair. He looks like he's aged five years in a week, some gray hair visible near his temple, his handsome face creased, his dark eyes tired.

"Hamdullah, she had a good death," he says. "Surrounded

by family. Our hands resting on her as she passed over. Warm. Loved." He's quiet for a second, contemplating. He looks at me and smiles. It's tentative, but hopeful, too. "Wonderful life, good death. Isn't that all you can ask for?"

That night, my parents come into the kitchen while I'm preparing my iftar. Five days left of Ramadan.

"How are you feeling, sweetheart?" Mom leans her forearms on the counter and cocks her head.

I pull a lone date out of a pouch, setting it on my plate. "I'm okay. Sad."

She nods sympathetically. "There's no right way to grieve. Allow yourself to cry, to be angry. Every feeling is valid."

"Thanks, Mom." I glance between my parents. "Thank you both."

Mom reaches over and takes Dad's hand. He accepts it gratefully.

"There's something we wanted to talk to you about," Mom says.

"Am I in trouble?"

"Not this time." Dad smiles.

Mom's voice is tentative. "We were talking, and we know it's late—"

"But better late than never," Dad says.

"And we thought it would be nice if we fasted together for the last few days of Ramadan," Mom says.

"But only if you want us to," Dad says.

I gasp. "Are you kidding? I'd love that!"

The two of them seem pleased.

I struggle to hide a smile while addressing Dad. "So, you're religious again, right?"

Panic flashes across his face.

"I mean, there are no atheists in a foxhole, you know . . ."

Mom laughs. "Mo, she's teasing you."

He chuckles, too, visibly relieved.

"When was the last time you fasted?" I say.

They look at each other, their brows furrowing.

"I did it in . . . was it 2000? Yeah, it must have been, because you weren't born yet," Mom says.

Dad makes a funny noise. "I was a teenager. Jido smacked me when he found out I'd been pretending. I was sneaking outside and eating when the staff wasn't around. Uncle Sammy got me in trouble."

"Sounds about right. Younger brothers." I turn to Mom. "So you fasted on your own, without Dad?"

She nods. "I was new. You know how converts are."

"Are you sure you're up for this?" I ask doubtfully. "It's really hard. And, no offense, but you're getting old."

"You're too kind to worry about us," Mom says drily. "We'll survive."

"Besides," Dad says. "It's only four days."

Mom laughs. "Famous last words."

Later that night, I get a series of messages on Instagram.

They're from Emilia.

Hi . . . sorry for the random msg. Been thinking about you recently, hoping you're OK.

I don't think I've been very supportive this year. I started googling stuff and went down the rabbit hole . . . anyhow, I'm kinda ashamed of myself, and I'm sorry.

I want to be an ally. If that's OK. No need to respond if you don't want. Hope your summer is going great. Xo E.

It would be easy to be dismissive of Emilia, to roll my eyes at her desire to "be an ally." But people have to start somewhere, and I'm impressed by her willingness to swallow her pride and reach out. Plus, forgiveness is a hallmark of Islam: People make mistakes. The key is owning up to them.

I write back:

Hi Emilia, it means a lot—thank you. The Muslim Student Association is planning events next year for interfaith outreach. Maybe we could put our heads together and plan something? Love, Allie

Mom, Dad, and I spend the entire Saturday together in solidarity, waking up together at 5:30 a.m. to eat suhoor and to pray Fajr before going back to bed.

Mom and Dad won't have the same luxury, of course. Dad comments on this at about five in the evening as our family huddles together on the couch, watching a movie marathon.

"I want to die," Dad moans.

"It's been half a day," Mom says. "Keep it together, dude."

"Why did we agree to this torture again?" he says.

"Because you love your daughter," I say cheerfully, "and you are wonderful parents who are trying to support her. Now please be quiet so I can hear Maria sing about lonely goatherds."

Around what would normally be dinnertime, Mom disappears to the store, returning an hour later with paper bags.

"Dinner?" I ask.

"Provisions," she says. "I couldn't bear the idea of cooking. I picked up everything premade from the Middle Eastern grocery store."

"I don't blame you," Dad says. "The idea of being around food without eating it is torturous."

"Hi," I say, waving a hand. "Welcome to my life the past twenty-six days."

Together, we lay out the spread on the table: dates, salad, hummus, pita bread, meatballs, rice with almonds, sticky desserts, Coke, tea, and rosewater.

My dad hands me a glass of water and a date.

"Here," he says. "You do the honors."

I take a sip of water, reveling in the feeling of doing this properly with my family. It's been lonely doing iftar each night by myself.

I bite into the date. It's dry, yet it still tastes like perfection.

I look at my father expectantly.

He looks back at me.

"Um," I say. "What comes next? I've never done this with anybody else."

"We say the supplication for breaking the fast," Dad says. "Do you know it yet?"

"Um. No . . ." Nobody had taught me.

He launches into it, seemingly from memory: "Allahumma inni laka sumtu wa bika aamantu wa alayka tawakkaltu wa ala rizq-ika aftarthu. Dhahabadh-dhama'u wab-tallatil 'urūūqi, wa thabatal arju inshallah." He smiles at my expression, continuing, "Translation: 'O Allah! I fasted for You and I believe in You and I break my fast with Your sustenance. Thirst is gone, the veins are moistened and the reward is certain if Allah wills it.'"

Wow.

"And now"—he smiles—"we eat."

After dinner, we stay up late, giving each other small gifts around the living room coffee table. Mom presents Dad with a box of his weakness—chocolate truffles—and then gives me a new bullet journal. I give my mom a handmade bracelet I found on Etsy, and my dad a hardcover political thriller.

"My turn," Dad says, offering a bag to Mom. "Sorry I didn't have time to wrap it, but you know how work has been. Tenure track waits for no one."

"A new Chanel purse?" Mom teases, looking inside the paper bag. She pulls out a white T-shirt. The front is emblazoned with a cheesy family photo of us at Disneyland, back from when we lived in Southern California and before my dad finished his PhD. On the back, it says:

Team Abraham
Ready for Adventure

My mother bursts out laughing. "This is literally the tackiest thing I've ever seen, Mo." She takes the shirt, sliding it over her Breton striped top and then kissing him. "I love it."

"Your turn," Dad says to me. "I know you've been learning . . ." He pauses. Clears his throat a couple times. Pulls out a book-sized present. "Teta gave this to me when I was young. I hope you like it."

It's a leather-bound Qur'an, in the original Arabic.

I walk over and give him a hug, holding back tears. "Dad. It's perfect."

We're back.

We might not be as fancy as the other families in our town, and we might always feel a little like outsiders—constantly pressing our noses against the glass, worried about leaving smudges when we pull away—but we're Team Abraham, ride or die.

Ready for adventure.

CHAPTER THIRTY-EIGHT

Eid dawns, and it feels like Christmas. After my early morning prayer, I go back to bed briefly, waking again to break the fast with my parents.

Soon after, they leave to run errands: There are decorations to buy, food to prepare, endless things to do before tonight. As a gesture, my dad has decided to host Eid at our house, inviting my friends from study group, as well as a few of his colleagues who are curious about it. Eid celebrations are supposed to be big and welcoming. Still, I find it incredible that he invites Wells.

I've never celebrated Eid before. In the past, Dad would make me call the family on Eid, saying "Ramadan Kareem" to my teta, aunts, and uncles, but that was the extent of it.

I hated making the series of phone calls. I felt awkward, out of my depth, unsure what to say. I always forgot: Was it

"Ramadan Kareem" or "Eid Mubarak"? Did you use those phrases at the beginning of Eid or at the end? Was I supposed to send them presents? Congratulate them on their fasts?

Eid was one more reminder that I didn't understand my own religion and didn't fit within my own family.

Now, everything has changed.

The WhatsApp messages ping all day long from my family in Saudi Arabia, Egypt, and London.

Amo Taareq: Eid Mubarak to everyone and praying to God next year will be a happy year

Amal: Eid Said to each and every one of you

Fairouza: Kol 3am wu entu b5eer InshAllah

Aunt Samiha, in Saudi Arabia, sends a GIF of Circassians in traditional dress dancing.

I send a text back in Arabic, using the keyboard shortcut I've downloaded to my iPhone, wishing them all an Eid Mubarak. This is the first year I don't need to ask my dad what to say.

After praying in my room, I go downstairs to find Mom and Dad in the kitchen.

The counter is laden with bags. The kitchen smells delicious and garlicky.

"What'd you get?" I ask.

"First, I stopped at the market and got a bunch of side dishes," Mom says. "Then I went to the bakery and picked up some baklava and some bread."

"Meanwhile, the mansaf is almost done," Dad says proudly from behind the stove, where a big bubbling pot of lamb, rice, and yogurt—the Jordanian national dish, and a *very* special delicacy—is curdling on the fire. I lean over the stove and peek into the pot, lifting the lid.

"Ooh, smells yummy." I take a spoon from the drawer and dip it into the pot, raising the tangy yogurt sauce to my lips. "Tastes yummy, too."

"Of course. Your father is the world's greatest mansaf chef," Dad says, grinning.

"You're in a good mood!"

"Am I? It's been a while since I cooked mansaf. It's a treat."

"I know it's annoying going through all this when you don't even believe in the reason for it," I say. "So thank you, Dad. It means a lot."

"But I *do* believe in the reason for it," he says, smiling. "The reason is you."

I give the place a final once-over as the doorbell rings. Mom calls, "They're here!" as Dad gives the mansef a final taste. He puts down the spoon and takes off his apron before joining us at the front door.

"Love you," I say to them before Dad swings the door open.

"Salaam a'alaykum!" he says.

"Wa a'alaykum as-salaam," Dua's mother says, with Dua, her father, and her siblings standing behind her.

"Please, please, come in. Welcome," Dad says, opening the door wide. "You're the first ones here. We expect the others soon." They enter with their own side dishes and desserts, placing them among the spread of foods on the dining table. Mom and Dad stuck to the Jordanian and Circassian classics—mansef, ships-wa-basta, maqluba, koosa, warak enab—but by the end of the night there will be food representing a slew of cultures: samosas, bean pie, and banana rice pudding, from Shamsah's, Fatima's, and Leila's families.

"I made mansaf," Dad says shyly to Dua's mom, handing her a glass of sparkling water. "Eid Mubarak."

"Eid Mubarak! It smells wonderful. Shukran!"

Dad looks pleased with the thanks.

As friends and colleagues stuff themselves inside, the house is filled with wonderful smells and the tinkling of laughter. Outside, Dua's sister Amina throws a short wave at me while talking on the phone, while her brother, Zaki, plays soccer with his friends, including Fareed. Amina and Fareed give each other shy looks. Abdullah smiles warmly at Dua and her parents through the window, waving hi. Dua's nose turns pink.

Dua, Shamsah, Fatima, Leila, and I retreat to a couch in the living room, the talk immediately turning to our summer plans.

"We're ignoring the elephant in the room," Shamsah says. "When is he getting here?"

She means Wells, obviously.

Soon enough, the doorbell rings.

"Hi," he says shyly, thrusting a bouquet of red roses into my hands. He's wearing a suit, with his curls combed and raked neatly across his head. I stop myself from giggling, because as much as he looks like he's heading to a funeral, I'm touched by the gesture.

"You look incredible." I smile, leaning up to give him a halal-for-the-peanut-gallery kiss on the cheek.

Wells's mother opens her arms, giving me a hug. "Allie. Thank you very much for the invitation—what an honor. Happy Eid."

"Thanks for coming!" I say. "Wells told me *you're* the one who made the huge MSA donation. So generous. Seriously, thank you."

"It was the least I could do." She squeezes my hand, lowering her voice. "And I was so sorry to hear about your grandmother."

"Thank you so much. It was . . ." I clear my throat. "Um, my parents are in the kitchen. Let me—"

But Mom and Dad are already warmly welcoming Serena, double-kissing and looking nervous but hopeful. My mom puts her hand on Serena's back, steering her into the kitchen as they chatter about life in Providence as transplants, and I'm grateful she's in good hands. My father claps his hand on Wells's back, thanking him for coming before retreating to check on the mansaf.

"Are you ready for this?" I ask Wells. "You have an audience."

"Girls," I say, leading Wells into the living room. From the fireplace mantel, a framed photo of Teta watches over us. "This is—"

"Wells!" Shamsah says, leaping off the couch. "We've heard so much about you!"

Shamsah and Dua give him a hug while Fatima and Leila

wave and nod in polite greeting, on their best behavior and at their most welcoming.

I wouldn't expect any less. My friends are awesome.

Wells and I sneak outside for a private moment before dinner, walking until we're obscured by trees. I reach for his hand, the noise of the house falling away until it's just the two of us.

"Is this still allowed?" he asks, squeezing my hand.

I smile. "I'll allow it."

"How are you feeling?"

"I'm okay. Sad. It's only been a couple of weeks."

"Some people say, 'Oh, it's just a grandparent, they're old,'" Wells says, "but it doesn't matter if you love somebody." He looks down at his hands.

"*You're* okay?" I ask him.

"Yeah. Mom and I talked about my anxiety. Started seeing a doctor, and they gave me a prescription for when I need it, plus therapy once a week. And Mom thinks I should start riding again. Got stuff to work through with my dad," he says. "Baby steps."

"I'm so glad. That you're doing therapy, I mean. Yay for doctors and medicine!"

"How are your parents?" he asks.

"They're hanging in. Them fasting means everything—especially my dad. I know he's not going to start praying five times a day, but at least he's supportive. I wish it were more, but that's all I can ask for right now."

"People can surprise you," Wells says. "Even parents."

"I've been thinking about it a lot."

"Parents?"

"People like my dad. Religion versus culture."

"Yeah?"

"People say being Jewish isn't just about religion—a lot of people are culturally or ethnically Jewish but not religious. Despite what people say, Islam might be like that, too. No matter what culture or country you're from or how diligent your practice is—or even if you're somebody raised in the faith who walked away from it—there's *still* something greater connecting you. You're part of an ummah. People think it's solely religion, but our shared experiences are impossible to escape. They've invisibly shaped us. They're everywhere."

He smiles, his eyes tender.

"You make me believe big things are possible," he says. "I love that about you."

I glance back at the house, to see if my father or my friends are watching. Coast clear. I lean in, giving Wells a sweet, tiny kiss.

I like certainties. I like order. I like precision. It's hard that I don't know if we'll last forever. We're sixteen. I doubt we'll go to the same college, even if we do last high school.

But just as I know my father will always be there for me even when the going gets rough, know there's something bigger than me out there in the universe, know as long as I keep learning and stick to my compass I won't get lost no matter how much well-meaning people tell me I'm straying from the perfect path, I know I'm in love with Wells.

That's the thing about love. It's not certain. It requires a leap. It means stepping into the unknown and surrendering to something bigger than yourself, against all obstacles.

Kind of like faith.

And it might be awkward and difficult at first, but if you're willing to take the risk, the rewards are beyond your wildest dreams.

The Eid iftar is a special time for reflection and taking stock.

I sit between my mom and dad at the far end of the table, next to Dua's family and across from Wells and his mom. Dua's parents smile at us, raising their glasses of iced tea to us and launching into a conversation with my parents.

Dad's eyes follow the mansaf platter, his chin raised like a proud father. Mansaf is traditionally eaten with your hands, but here guests use a large silver spoon to serve it onto their plates before digging in.

"So?" Dua says to me as we tuck into our food, dishes being passed up and down the table. "You made it! How do you feel?"

"Like there's something missing," I say. "A friend, or a limb. It's hard to explain. I thought I'd be thrilled once Ramadan was done, and instead I feel . . . sad. Like I wish it weren't over. It's weird."

Dua smiles. "That's not weird. People who don't know better think of Ramadan as this hardship, but it's a celebration. What could be better than getting closer to God, getting closer to yourself?"

"I would have found that cheesy a year ago."

"It's cheesy now," Dua says. "Doesn't mean it's not true."

As I look around the room, at Wells and his mom laughing at one of my dad's jokes, at Mom passing the koosa to Fatima, at Shamsah and Leila giggling over a picture of somebody on Shamsah's phone, I feel an immense wave of gratitude wash over me.

Life is not perfect, not by any stretch of the imagination. I miss Teta. I don't know where my meandering path with Wells will lead. My parents have a shaky relationship with their faith. And I have no idea where I'll go to college or if I'll even get into college or what on earth my future looks like.

And yet, I feel a sense of peace, hamdulilah.

Realistically, I don't think I'll ever have a triumphant movie-musical ending: a moment in my life when I say, *Yes! My imposter syndrome has disappeared. I've found the perfect balance. I have arrived!*

I will have to keep arriving, over and over.

I will have to reclaim my religion, repeatedly.

I will deny those who tell me I'm not Muslim enough.

I will defy those who think I'm not American enough.

I will anger people who dislike how I look and dress.

I will infuriate with my choice of boyfriend—or for choosing to have a boyfriend at all.

I will disappoint other Muslims for not doing it right.

And I will enrage bigots simply by existing.

Though I wish I could say I won't care what people will think, unfortunately, I will—because that's who I am. But I will stay strong, inshallah, and will continue questioning and learning and growing.

Hamdulilah, I am enough.

Just as I am.

ACKNOWLEDGMENTS

Thanks to:

Jess Regel, my fearless agent. You are wise, encouraging, and excellent at managing my neuroses. I'm lucky to have you!

Janine O'Malley, editor extraordinaire. You believed in Allie's story from the beginning and were endlessly patient as I brought her world to light. I am so thankful to have benefited from your grace, empathy, and vision.

The rockstar teams at Macmillan, FSG Books for Young Readers, and Foundry Literary, especially Melissa Warten and Hayley Jozwiak. Big thanks to my copy editor Elizabeth Johnson and my publicist Morgan Dubin!

My incredible sensitivity and early readers, who took such care in reading AAMG and were generous with your time, wisdom, and emotional labor: Fadwa Lhn, Adiba Jaigirdar, Silanur Inanoglu, Candice Montgomery, Hiba Tahir, Rania, Hafsah Faizal, S. K. Ali, Meg Eden, Kristie Frazier, Alexandra Ballard, Rebecca Denton, Kes Trester, Katherine Longhi, Christina June, Jerramy Fine, Felicia Sullivan, and Caroline Leech.

A very, very special thanks to London Shah, Fatin Marini, and Ausma Zehanat Khan: Your tireless championing, careful reading, and generous encouragement brought me to (dorky but grateful) tears on more than one occasion.

To my writing buddy Kristen Orlando: Thank you for all your excellent accountability mojo. Now get back to writing!

Thanks as well to friends that have been helpful and encouraging in ways big and small (and who might not even realize it!), both online and in real life, especially Patrice Yursik, Kayla Olson, Hebah Uddin, Celeste Pewter, Samira Ahmed, Farah Naz Rishi, Jamilah Thompkins-Bigelow, Hanna Alkaf, Jordan Reid, Meaghan MacMaster Kindregan, Saadia Faruqi, Shannon Chakraborty, Haneen Oriqat, Ardo Omer, Ashley Franklin, Sarah Klein, Christina Peng, Fitriyanti Tapri, and countless others I'm sure I'll kick myself for forgetting. As always, thanks and love to Amy Gibson-Grant, Katherine Harris, Jamie Pollaci, Kristin Forbes, Maggie Lee, Robin Phelps, and Allie Intondi. And, of course, Dara Smith, you are forever the best first reader (and friend) a girl could ask for.

To every librarian, YouTuber, Instagrammer, Tweeter, and blogger who recommended *All-American Muslim Girl,* thank you from the bottom of my heart for your support. Extra shoutout to my childhood friend Janet Geddis of the phenomenal Avid Bookshop in Athens, Georgia, and to the lovely people at DIESEL, A Bookstore in Brentwood, California, and Vroman's Bookstore in Pasadena, California. Support your local independent booksellers, please!

To my big, loud, loving, wonderful family, I love you all. Special thanks to my cousins Dua'a, Yasmine, and Leila, who I endlessly pestered while writing AAMG. Lots of love to my mom, Brigid Courtney, and a hug to the Sisters of St. Margaret in Duxbury, Massachusetts.

To my father, pretty much the greatest dad in the history of dads, I love you. I am so lucky to be your pumpkin.

Miss you, Mama, always.

Erik, it would be impossible to write a more supportive husband into existence. Thank you for believing in me, for giving me the space and support to write, and for being a full and equal partner. I am better in every way because of you. Every woman needs an Erik.

Aurelia, my bunny, my bug, my heart, my reason.

Jido, Allah yerhamak, I kiss your eye.

Finally, to my teta, Allah yerhamik: I love you and miss you. I hope, somewhere, you are proud.